FIRE

OF

THE

FOX

FIRE

OF

THE

FOX

The Broken Fae Trilogy

SYLVER MICHAELA

FIRE

OF

THE

FOX

Cover design: Emily Wittig Designs
Formatting: Enchanted Ink Publishing

ISBN: 978-0-578-38724-6

To my sister, **Lucy.**

Thank you for being my biggest cheerleader and for

believing in me and my stories, even when I didn't.

CHAPTER

ONE

My duffle bag hit the bed with a dull thud. Placing my hands on my hips, I surveyed the twin-sized bed and the mess that was my dorm room. It was going to take a lot of organizing and decorating make it feel like my new, temporary home.

"It's a pretty decent space for a college dorm."

Glancing over my shoulder at Greg, I nodded in agreement.

He flashed me a wide grin and patted my shoulder. "Are u excited, Kiddo?"

"Of course. The art professors here are supposed to really amazing."

"You and your art," Wendy laughed. Her dark rls bounced as she came in from the bustling llway. She carried the last of my boxes, drop- g them gently at the foot of my bed.

"That's an artist for you," Greg said, throwing his a
around her shoulder.

Staring at them now, standing side by side, it would be e
to tell they weren't actually my parents. Wendy was a rou
short woman with wild curls that framed her tanned face. H
small hazel eyes were warm, always crinkled at the sides i
smile. Greg stood at a good 6'2", and his physique greatly
sembled a bear. Dark head of hair, bushy beard, and big gr
eyes.

Then there was me. I was short with wide hips and la
thighs, and it was clear that I enjoyed one too many sw
snacks. My blonde hair stood out between the two of the
and my bright blue eyes were a complete giveaway that I di
belong with these two. I looked as different from Mr. and M
Ashmoore as one could get.

Taking one final look around the room, Greg's eyes fou
mine. "Well, I assume you want us gone so that you can unp
and get settled. We'll get out of your hair."

"You don't have to go yet," I said, trailing after them to
door. "We could grab a bite to eat before you leave."

"Oh, that's okay! We need to get home to the dogs anyw
Wendy grabbed my hand and gave it a good pat.

People rushed up and down the hallway with bags a
boxes. A girl and mom across the hall, already hugged in a ti
embrace, sobbed into each other's hair. Her dad gave her a g
squeeze, too, pulling back with tear-filled eyes.

"I love you, Pumpkinhead," her dad choked. "You hav
great semester. Work hard."

"Call us every day, okay?" Her mom's tears continued
streak down her cheeks, mascara following in their wake.

"I promise to call every day and come home as much
possible. I love you both so much!"

Turning back to my own parents, I waited with eager e
to see if this would finally be it. The moment when I got t

famous "I love you". They were great people with big, caring hearts, but there had always been this sort of invisible line none of us had ever crossed when it came to affection. We never exchanged "I love yous" or hugs or kisses. Patting was normal. A brief side squeeze was rare. A heartfelt goodbye was nonexistent.

I always wondered why they adopted a child if they didn't actually want one.

Waiting with bated breath, I prepared myself for what it would feel like. Would I cry when they said it? Maybe giggle and fall into their open arms? I swallowed hard, ready now more than ever.

"Well," Wendy said warmly, glancing up at Greg. Meeting my eyes again, she said, "Have a great school year. Do well in your classes."

"Make lots of memories, Kiddo." Greg's large hand patted my head and rumpled my hair.

Forcing a smile through the anticipation, I nodded. "I will. I promise."

"Take care, Bria! Talk soon."

They waved, then turned, walking hand in hand down the hallway. My eyes were glued to their backs as I watched them leave. A sharp pang flooded my gut, but I swallowed down those emotions. I never let it get to me that we didn't feel like a real family, but I thought this could have been the moment when the invisible wall came down between us.

As I stood there, watching their retreat from my doorway, a hard slap on my butt had me yelping and spinning around. Dallas stood right behind me, a smirk plastered on her mouth.

"Don't you dare get sad now! I know exactly what you're thinking. Don't! Who needs the Ashmoores when you have me?"

Laughing, I shut the door to our room and followed her to her bed. "I am *not* sad."

She waved dismissively before tossing her red curls over her shoulder. "Bullshit. I can see it all on your face. How many times do I have to tell you? Why cry over a plain baked potato when you could have a *loaded* baked potato?"

"You're a potato now?"

She paused, and after thinking it over a minute, she waved her hand and turned back around. "This is why I don't give pep talks."

I rolled my eyes and grabbed at the first of the boxes, which was labeled *clothes* in Greg's nearly illegible handwriting. Pulling them out, I started sorting them into the closet and drawers built into the frame of my bed.

Dallas and I were beyond excited when we got accepted to the private university across the state in Tennessee. We were even more elated when we learned that they approved us to room together. We spent the entirety of our last semester in high school planning everything we'd do once we got here. It was hard to believe the time had actually come.

"These white tiles are so ugly," Dallas grumbled from her side of the room as she glared at the floor.

"Agreed. We should run to the store later to get the twinkle lights and fluffy area rugs we wanted."

She spun around, grabbing my shoulders and forcing me to look at her. She beamed at me as she said, "Let's scope out the town while we're out! I saw loads of boutiques and stores on the way up here. We should grab a bite to eat, too. Maybe stop and ask some cute upperclassmen to show us around."

A knock came at the door. Sauntering over to open it, I was greeted with a cheeky grin that sent my heart into a fit of somersaults.

"Well, hello there, cutie."

Blushing, I opened the door wider. "Hey, Dax. Did you get to your dorm okay?"

"Yup! I'm all settled in."

Dax. He had gone to high school with Dallas and me. We didn't have too many of the same classes, but I still somehow found myself crushing on him all four years. His deep brown locks paired with his bright green eyes made for a picture-perfect face. Then there were his dimples. Those small dents in his cheeks never failed to make my knees turn to rubber.

If someone had told me Dax would end up asking me to be his girlfriend at the end of senior year, I would've laughed and told them they got hit with the crazy stick. Yet here we were, dating after years of my stolen glances and shy smiles.

He brushed past me and into our room. I closed the door behind us, turning to find Dax standing in the middle of our room, surveying the space.

"Sure, Dax. Just come on in," Dallas huffed. She leaned against the window across the room, frowning at our guest.

Here came the cat fight.

"Don't mind if I do, Firecracker."

Dallas glared at him, her manicured fingers balling into fists. "Don't call me Firecracker!"

Ignoring her, Dax turned back to me. He grabbed the belt loops of my jeans and pulled me against his chest. My cheeks heated as he looked down at me, his warm body pressed to mine. "Are you ready for classes?"

I nodded as a fog wrapped my head in a sweet bliss. "Of course. Are you?"

"That depends. Did you read that book for me over the summer and write down all the important points and quotes?"

Blinking, I felt the pleasant fog dissipate. Clearing my throat, I crossed the room to my book bag, which was slung onto my pillow. "Yeah. Here you go."

He skimmed over the paper. Giving it an approving nod, he beamed at me. "Sweet! I was sweating bullets when I got the email saying I needed to read this book before classes started. You're a real lifesaver. Keep up the good work, and I'll have all the time in the world to take you out on that date."

His phone rang, and he dug it out of his jeans. With a quick glance at the screen, he said, "Well, I've gotta dip. I'll text you later."

He gave me a peck on the lips before racing from the room. There was no denying the icy sting of disappointment. Being with Dax was something I had fantasized about for so long, but the reality was nothing like those dreams. He was a free spirit, always looking for the next fun and exciting thrill, without any pressures or obstacles.

I never wanted to admit it out loud, but I did sometimes wonder if I was holding out hope for something that would never be real.

"Well," Dallas began.

Slowly turning, I prepared myself for the speech she'd already given me a thousand times.

"You really know how to pick 'em."

Rolling my eyes, I gave her a gentle shove. "Hush. You know he's not the brightest. He just needed some help."

"Why are you still doing his school-work? You promised you'd stop that when we got to uni."

Here came another lecture, one I was determined to nip in the bud before it got started. "I'm sure it was just a one-time thing. He said he was gonna be too busy on vacations all summer to do the reading, and he didn't want to be stressed his first week of school by not having it done. He asked if I could read it and take notes for him so he could start off freshman year on good terms."

Dallas flung herself onto my bed, facing me with her all-knowing gaze. Crossing her arms, she pursed her lips. "Right. What was that about having time to take you on a date?"

I shrugged, pretending to be really interested in sorting my clothes. "If he has loads of assignments, he won't have time to see me. Since I'm faster with school-work, he thinks it might be better for me to occasionally help out with his so that he has time for me."

She blinked her big green eyes at me. "Do you hear yourself right now?"

Groaning, I collapsed facedown next to her. "I know. Pathetic. Even I can tell that he's using me. I just don't want to believe it, I guess."

The bed creaked as she lay down next to me. I turned my head to look at her from beneath my hair as she raised a brow at me.

"This is exactly why we're going out. You need to see that there are other people out there who aren't complete asswipes."

We spent the rest of the evening unpacking our stuff and organizing our desks and personal areas. Our mini fridge was in desperate need of drinks and food, and our snack rack was lacking in midnight munchies. Gathering our bathroom bags, we headed off to the dorm showers to rinse off all the sweat from the day of moving. After throwing on some clean leggings and a pink sweater, I pulled my long blonde hair into a high ponytail and waited on Dallas to finish getting ready.

"I'm starving," Dallas pouted as we walked to her silver Honda Pilot. "Let's find somewhere to eat first."

"Sounds good to me. I could use some food."

It was a short drive from campus to the main area in town. The streets were lined with stores, cafes, and restaurants. Since we wanted to walk the streets to sightsee, Dallas parked along the sidewalk. The setting sun painted the sky in strokes of orange and pink. Cool wind blew through the lingering warm air, making it the perfect weather for a stroll.

"Look at all these boutiques," I started. "A lot of them are hiring."

"Well, yeah. With the start of the new school year, these places are sure to be packed and ready for some new faces. Maybe we should think about applying to one."

I was so busy peering into one of the shops, I didn't notice the man standing outside a store until I knocked into him. Gasping, I grabbed onto Dallas to keep from falling backward. The stranger whipped around from where he'd been staring into a tattoo parlor window, and I was hit with a heavy wave of disdain. The dark-headed man narrowed his eyes at me, and his lip curled as he snarled at me.

Caught off guard, I stammered, "I-I'm sorry. I didn't—"

He shoved past me, and a chill rolled down my spine as he did. The man stormed down the sidewalk, and I stared after him in complete shock.

Dallas held me close to her side, staring after the guy. "What an asshole," she huffed.

I tried shaking off the collision, but something about him didn't sit well with me. My stomach was curled tight, and the heavy hand of dread settled on my shoulders. It was such a startling encounter, it took a while of walking with Dallas to finally feel grounded again.

We were able to put some pep back into our step as we talked in excited circles about plans for the semesters, goals we wanted to reach, and memories we wanted to make this year. As we planned our ideas for the school year, Dallas suddenly inhaled sharply, gripping my arm tight.

Alarmed, I snapped my head in her direction. "What's wrong?"

"Pizza. A big, cheesy, greasy slice of pizza. Straight ahead."

I froze. Immediately, I knew she wasn't talking about the food. Pizza was her code word for a ten-out-of-ten guy. Back in high school, Dallas and I had come up with a code for rating cute boys. We somehow decided that rating them via food was a good idea. Dallas's scale was based on unhealthy foods.

The healthier the food, the less attractive she found them. The unhealthier the food, the better the taste, she would say. Pizza was her max.

My scale was done by sweets. I had a huge sweet tooth, so the sweeter the treat, the cuter the boy. My max was my favorite treat, cinnamon rolls.

Composing myself, I tried to play it cool as I looked for this mystery person. Up ahead was a group of guys standing outside of a bar and grill. I scanned their faces and saw Mr. Pizza. He stood facing us, laughing at something one of the other guys had said. He was tall, dark, and handsome. What girl wouldn't like him?

He had large brown eyes set against rich, dark brown skin. His hair was thinly cropped, exposing a piercing in his right ear. I knew Dallas would eat that up. Even from this distance, I could tell he was built. His shirt pulled tightly over his muscles, and he could probably bench press Dallas from the size of them—also something she'd definitely be into.

Smiling sideways at her, I pulled her along. "We're gonna be walking past them in a minute. What's your plan?"

She scoffed at me and gave me that all-too-familiar smirk. "I don't have one. I don't need a plan."

We were close enough to have drawn their attention, and their attention we *did* draw. The conversation slowed as we sauntered past. As we stepped around them, Dallas grabbed my arm and pulled me toward the grill's storefront, where they had a chalkboard of specials.

"Oh, Bria, look! They're having a deal on burgers tonight. I wonder if they're any good here." She glanced over to the four boys who were watching, and the corners of her lips lifted just a fraction. "Have you guys eaten here before?"

Mr. Pizza smiled. "We have. It's really good. Best burgers in town for sure."

Dallas pondered it. "Best burgers, hmm? That's a pretty

bold statement. I wouldn't know any different of course. We just moved into town today for school."

"Oh, you girls are freshmen over at Brinkley?" asked a dusty blond who sat on the bench against the grill's front wall.

I nodded. "We are."

"Nice," Pizza man said. "We all go to school there too. We're juniors."

"Juniors. That's exciting. Is it pretty hard there? I heard that the professors are super strict." Dallas batted her lashes at Mr. Cheesy Pizza, who was already under her spell.

"Not too bad. For certain professors, there are tips and tricks to getting through their classes."

"Sounds interesting. Maybe you could teach me those tricks?"

His big brown eyes stared straight into hers, and a deep smile formed on his lips. A small laugh escaped him, and he held out his hand to her, tilting his head up. "I'm Rance."

Her small hand fit inside his easily. "Dallas."

"Dallas. Nice to meet you. Why don't you give me your number, and maybe we can arrange a time to go over those tips."

After they exchanged numbers, his group of friends wanted to talk about our majors and what to expect about college life. It felt like hours when we finally pulled ourselves away from the group and proceeded onward, our bellies even more demanding of food. While we could've joined the boys for burgers, Dallas had this idea of keeping Rance on his toes by not looking too eager. So we parted ways, leaving the boys to stare after us.

"Well, that was a success, I think," Dallas laughed.

I looped my arm in hers. "You are a mess! I can't believe you actually got his number and arranged a date."

She shot me a pout. "You doubted me?"

I laughed. "Never."

CHAPTER

TWO

The restaurant we settled on for dinner was a small Italian place. We sat in a booth at the far end of the restaurant, and the smell from the toasted garlic bread and seasoned tomato sauces made my mouth water. My stomach growled.

"Man, I need food now," Dallas groaned, flipping through the menu.

"Same. But first, I need to use the restroom."

She waved without looking up. "Have fun."

Getting up, I quickly turned to go down the back hall to the bathrooms when I smacked right into a wall. Or so I thought. What felt like a wall was actually a person. I gasped, stumbling backward, but the person's arm reached out to catch me. "I'm so sorry," I mumbled through my embarrassment.

Running into someone two times in one night, Bria. Nice one.

Looking up, I came face-to-face with a pair of startling amber eyes, their hue like that of liquid gold. The color was so startlingly vivid. I immediately took a mental snapshot to try to recreate that color in a future painting. My breath caught as he smiled down at me.

"No worries. Are you okay?"

My mouth opened, but no words came out. It was like I choked on them. His hair was so blond that I swear it was white. It was longer, barely reaching his shoulders, and it paired perfectly with those golden eyes of his. His full lips were turned up at the corners. He was almost too beautiful to look at.

Clearing my throat, I nodded. "I'm fine. You?"

"Totally fine."

I smiled up at him as he gave me one final nod before walking on toward a table with a few other guys at it. He sat down with them, leaning in close to say something. I swallowed hard and quickly dashed to the restroom before racing back to the booth.

I was out of breath by the time I collapsed onto the leather seat, and Dallas watched me with bread paused halfway to her mouth.

"Cinnamon roll."

She quirked her eyebrow at me. "Oh God, is Dax here? Please tell me—"

I frantically shook my head. "Cinnamon roll. Table up front, near the windows. White hair."

She slowly peeked out from the booth. Her bread slipped from her fingers. "Hot damn. That is definitely a cinnamon roll."

The waiter came up to the table to take our orders. Dallas went first, ordering something overly complicated as always. Daring to take a chance, I glanced up past the waiter at the front table. My heart leapt into my throat when I found his golden eyes staring back at me. His chin rested in his hand, which was propped on the table, and even from behind his fingers, I could see the smirk on his face.

I sucked in a quick breath and mumbled, "A steamy, fresh cinnamon roll with extra icing."

"I'm sorry, ma'am, but we don't have cinnamon rolls."

"Huh?" I looked at the waiter, who watched me with a look that questioned my sanity. Dallas bit back a laugh, and I cleared my throat as I hid behind the menu. "Uh, right, sorry. I'll have the cheese ravioli."

"Great choice!" He took our menus, sparing one more concerned look at me before leaving to put in our orders.

"I'm an idiot." My head collapsed in my hands, and I wished I could shrink away behind them.

Dallas spent the rest of dinner laughing and reminding me of how embarrassing I was. I spent it trying to distract her with other topics, while also sparing glances at Cinnamon Roll. It was as if he could sense when I looked at him because when I looked up, so did he. Our eyes would connect for a fraction of a second before I glanced back down at my lap, flaring red.

This was the longest dinner of my life.

Despite getting to the restaurant after those guys, Dallas and I managed to finish before them. We would have to walk right past their table on the way out, and I thought my heart was going to jump out of my chest. Was I supposed to say something? Was he supposed to say something? My feet felt heavy as I followed behind her, and to distract myself, I was making a point to count each breath I took as we drew closer.

Right as we neared their table, Dallas glanced over her shoulder at me, and said in a much too loud, giggly voice, "Hey, Bria. Wanna go get a big cinnamon roll with extra icing now?"

My face heated to a steaming temperature, and I glanced sideways at him. His eyes lit up with amusement, and he tilted his head at me. Thank God no one else knew what she was actually suggesting, but because *I* knew, I ducked out of there, too embarrassed to be near him.

When Dallas came out the door, she was clutching her belly, laughing so hard that I thought she might pee herself.

I smacked her hard on the arm. "That was so not funny!"

She grabbed onto my shoulder for support as I rushed along the sidewalk for her car. I couldn't get her to stop laughing about the whole thing as we got groceries and drove back to the dorm. It wasn't until we changed into our pajamas and crawled into our twin beds that she finally calmed down.

"Man, what a day. Who knew I'd find me a pizza named Rance, and you'd find yourself a cinnamon roll."

I pulled my pillow over my head, groaning. "Good night, Dallas."

She gave one more hearty laugh before slowly dying down to silence. "Night, Bria."

CHAPTER

THREE

"**A**ll right, everyone, class dismissed. Have a great Friday," Professor Lichen said as she shut down her powerpoint presentation.

The loud buzzing of chatter immediately filled the room as students started talking about their Friday night plans, and I took my time to gather my things. The first two weeks of the semester had flown by. I already adored my art professor, Lichen, but my English teacher was questionable. She thought way too highly of poetry and smelled too much like baby wipes. The assignments were plentiful, but it was nice to stay busy. It made free time all the more interesting.

Dallas often threw highlighters across the room while groaning about the workload, and oftentimes, I would end up tossing aside my textbook as she read me a sweet text Rance had sent. The two of them had been texting every day and had even met up on campus multiple times. She and I had designated girls' nights when we ignored all homework and boys to binge on junk food, watch rom-coms, and talk about everything.

Life couldn't get any better.

"Bria."

Looking up from where I'd been loading my sketchbook and pencils back in my bag, I found Professor Lichen beaming down at me.

"Oh, hi, Professor!"

"Hi, dear. Do you have another class after this?"

"No, ma'am."

"Wonderful! I was hoping I could have a word with you then."

My stomach dropped, but I kept my polite face in place. I followed behind her towards her office, but the entire walk, I was frantic on the inside. My nerves bounced around my gut as all the possible reasons for why she needed me floated around my head. We were only two weeks in. Had I already done something wrong? I made a mental list of all the homework and reading assignments we'd done. Could I have missed one? I didn't remember not doing an assignment, but maybe *that* was the problem.

Once in her office, she shut the door behind us. "Go ahead and take a seat, Bria."

I swallowed hard as I sank down in one of the brown leather chairs across from her desk. I decided to focus on the details of her space to keep my mind busy with anything except my mounting worries.

It was then I noticed all of the stunning paintings hanging around her room. The majority of them were landscapes, and each was beautifully detailed. The artist had a clear and steady hand with a unique vision of the forest, ocean, and meadows.

The attention to detail, along with the vibrant color scheme, was a dead giveaway as to who painted them.

"These are paintings by Luca Romano," I said with awe flooding my voice on his name. I tried not to focus on how embarrassingly that had come out as Professor Lichen rounded her desk.

Luca Romano was an Italian painter, and he was someone I had admired for as long as I could remember. He was a prodigy, a truly gifted artist who transported his viewers into every painting he did. If he painted a mountain range in winter, you could practically smell the fresh scent of newly fallen snow. If he painted the forest in fall, you could hear the chime of the wind blowing through the autumn leaves. If he painted an ocean, you could almost feel the sand beneath your feet and in between your toes. He was who I aspired to be as a painter.

Painting was my entire world, which was why I was majoring in art. Well, sort of. My major was technically art education. My dream was obviously to be a painter, capturing the beauty of the world within my brushstrokes. The thought of painting the things I loved always made my heart swell with an undeniable passion.

But it wasn't realistic.

There was no guarantee that my paintings would make me money, so my Plan B was to be an art teacher. Close enough, right? Yeah, not really, but it was a bitter truth I'd had shoved in my face my entire life.

Some dreams just couldn't happen the way you wanted them to.

Professor Lichen sank down in her desk chair. A light filled her eyes as she addressed me. "That's right. You know of Luca Romano?"

"Of course," I said, eyes wide and excitement bleeding into my words. My previous worries of why she'd called me in here were momentarily forgotten and replaced with my need to gush with a fellow fan. "He's my favorite painter. I have photobooks of his paintings and prints of his work in my room back home."

Her expression turned warm then. She settled her hands over a folder on her desk and leaned forward. "Well then, that's going to make this conversation even more exciting. I'm actually good friends with Luca Romano."

My composure broke, and my mouth fell open. I nearly slipped out of my chair in my effort to lean in closer.

"What? You are?"

"I am. I'm also involved in the study abroad program here. Have you ever thought about studying abroad?"

"I mean, I haven't *actively* thought about it, but of course it's something I'd love to do if given the chance."

"I'm glad, because I think I have a great opportunity for you." She grabbed the folder and held it out for me. "We have a program for art majors where you can study abroad in Italy. One of the most exciting parts about this program is that you get to study under Luca Romano himself."

My brain stalled, and it took a moment for me to recover from my shock. "L-Luca? *The* Luca Romano?"

She laughed. "Yes, *the* Luca Romano. There are, of course, other great classes and experiences that come with studying abroad there, but that's definitely a big one."

I flipped through the papers in the folder as I tried to process what Professor Lichen was telling me. There were pamphlets of a few different types of lodgings, a mock-up itinerary of the different museums and trips students would take, and all the amazing courses that would be offered. There, among the course work, was a photo of Luca Romano on a stool as he focused on the canvas before him. The breath in my lungs got stuck as I studied the image of the man.

Never did I think I'd meet Luca Romano. He was like a god in the art community, and I was a mere peasant among the thousands. Who was I to even dream of meeting him, let alone be given the chance to study under him? It felt like my heart was going to explode thinking about it.

"After looking over your high school portfolio and seeing the final product of your first piece for class, I really think you'd be perfect for this program."

I swallowed hard and tried to calm my racing heart. "Me? Really?"

"Really. It's a once in a lifetime chance, and I know with the skills you already have, Luca can help you hone that talent even further. You could go far in this industry."

"I-I—" I gave a small laugh and shook my head.

This day had started like any other, yet now I was faced with the greatest news I could ever have been given. I was at a loss for words as excitement stole them right from my lips. My dreams, my future, my hopes suddenly seemed possible. It was as if they were being handed to me on a silver platter.

No more pointless wishing.

No more being told it couldn't be done.

No more drowning in anguish every time I saw a painting hanging proudly and being told that couldn't be me.

This was it. This was my chance to prove everyone wrong and to show them my dreams weren't irrational.

I was going to be a painter!

"I know it's a lot to think about," Professor Lichen said, pulling me back to the here and now. "You don't have to make your decision now. Go through the papers, read up on the program and course work, and talk about it with your parents. There's also a page in there about the cost breakdown and where all that money goes. This program is one of the more expensive ones because of Luca Romano, so it's roughly five thousand dollars."

The light raining down on me suddenly sputtered and went dark. All the hope I'd previously felt was sucked right out of me like a wet rag being wrung dry.

"Five thousand dollars?" I croaked.

Professor Lichen nodded. "It's a lot. I know. We wouldn't need the money right now. You can talk it over with your parents. We'd just need the money and your answer by the first of November so that we can get everything ready since you'd be going in the spring semester."

I looked back down at the cream colored folder, one that held promises of my longed-for future. I clutched the papers to my chest and faced her again.

"Okay. I'll talk to them. Thank you so much for this opportunity, Professor. Really. You have no idea how much this means to me."

The corners of her mouth lifted as she nodded. "Of course, Bria. You deserve it. I hope it works out and you get to go."

I made my way out of her office. My mind was still in a daze as I shuffled through the halls of the art building. I was dumbfounded that Professor Lichen actually believed in me like that. When her class first started, she'd given all of us a simple enough assignment.

Create *anything*.

Students were allowed to draw, sculpt, paint, whatever they wanted. And the subject? That was up to us too. We'd spent the first week working on our pieces, both in and out of class, and I'd put my heart and soul into my painting.

It was of a lake's edge in autumn, and I'd slaved over the colors and details in an effort to make it perfect. I'd had no idea that the completed piece had left such a profound impression on Professor Lichen.

Not only that, but I couldn't believe that I was now faced with a chance to study under the great Luca Romano. With his aid and wisdom, I'd no doubt get even better at painting, something that could open doors which had previously been closed to me. I could create connections in the art community, establish myself as a gifted artist, and finally make real progress in achieving my dream. The idea alone was enough to make my feet lighter and my determination stronger.

The only problem was the money.

Five thousand dollars was a lot. Greg and Wendy lived paycheck to paycheck. I'd been incredibly fortunate, getting a full ride to Brinkley due to my academics and art achievements. To ask them to fork over five thousand dollars, all so I could go to Italy, made my stomach sour. Was it selfish of me to want something so expensive?

I couldn't help but think it was. To ask the people who had already done so much to raise a person that wasn't even their flesh and blood, to provide that kind of money for a dream they didn't support, wasn't an option. Which left me to sort it out myself. But how could I? There was no way I could save up that kind of money in three months.

My eyes slipped closed as I finally stepped out into the sunlight. I raised my face up toward its warm rays, and for a moment, I let myself wonder. *Would my real parents have given me the money? Would they support my dreams?*

My chest squeezed tightly as the questions plagued me. Would my mother have taken one look at the hope in my eyes, smiled, and told me my dreams were valid? Would my father have hugged me tight and told me he was proud of my talent? Would we have sat around the dinner table, the two of them joking and laughing over who I got my talent from between the two of them?

They were questions I often wondered, yet knew I'd never get answered. Because I didn't know them. Their scents, the feel of their hugs, the way they laughed or cried. I would never know those things, and while my dreams of becoming a painter suddenly seemed possible, knowing my parents was one dream that would always remain just that.

A dream.

CHAPTER

FOUR

Reaching behind me, I gripped my backpack and pulled it around so I could safely tuck away the folder holding my dreams. Once the papers were secured, I started my trek across campus for my dorm. It took a minute, but I shook off the somber mood brought on from thoughts of my parents and focused on how excited I was to tell Dallas about this chance to study abroad.

"Hey, Bria! Wait up!"

Speak of the devil.

Smiling, I turned around as Dallas ran smack into me. We tumbled down to the grass, laughing at our embarrassing collision. I sat up, wiping the dirt from my jeans as I looked at her. Her fiery red hair was piled on top of her head in a messy bun, and she wore a pair of jogging pants with a t-shirt.

She was in a rush to get to class earlier this morning after staying up way too late on the phone.

"Nice tackle," I said with another laugh.

We stood back up, and her giggles died down until she met me with a serious frown. "Well," she started, "I had to catch up with you fast. I saw Dax with that girl again."

My exciting news died on my lips. I looked down at my sneakers and toed a rock. Dax had been going around behind my back with a few other girls on campus. Dallas and I had caught him once or twice leaning up against them or holding their hands in a more-than-friendly way. Anytime we asked him about it, he'd blow it off as if we hadn't seen it with our own eyes. He'd say we were interpreting it wrong, insisting that he and the girls were just friends. He had a way of spinning the situations around to where *I* felt bad for accusing him of cheating on me when he was simply hanging out with friends.

I sighed and turned back in the direction of my dorm. I started walking, and Dallas jogged next to me. She threw her hands in the air and implored, "What are you doing? Aren't you going to confront him and say something?"

I shrugged and twirled a strand of my hair. "Why should I? I know very well that he's doing something, but confronting him won't change anything."

She was quiet for a moment. My eyes found hers as she asked, "Why do you stay with him?"

I didn't answer right away. It was hard to admit to her that I'd been trying to come up with a way to end things with him for the past week now. Dax was my first taste of being in a relationship, so I didn't know the best way to tell him I was done. Sure, he was a dick, but he had feelings, too. It wasn't in me to be rude or mean.

Dallas often made jokes that I was a soft soul, and she was right. I thought about others and their feelings over my own far too often. It was something Dallas was trying to help me get over, but it was hard to break that part of myself. So, even though Dax was clearly doing me wrong, I wanted to be as civil as possible about ending things, that way we could potentially stay cordial. I just hadn't figured out how to do that yet. In the meantime, I spent my time avoiding him and all discussions of him to try to lessen the pain of his betrayal.

As I was about to tell Dallas all this, Dax stepped into our path from the direction of the neighboring science building. His brown hair was styled as usual, and he wore his plaid button-up and khakis. Typical for Dax. He always had to look good.

He draped his arm around my shoulder and said, "Good afternoon, ladies."

We stopped walking, and Dallas stepped in front of him. Her glare could freeze over hell, and she put her hands on her hips. "Don't 'ladies' us. We know you were with another one of your side girls, Dax."

His arm fell from my shoulder as he shoved his hands into his pockets.

I stepped back from him to stand with Dallas.

He gave a noncommittal shrug. "I have no idea what you're talking about."

Dallas' laugh dripped with sarcasm. "Bullshit! You're always cheating on Bria!"

I looked back and forth between the two of them. Dallas always did this part. I was never confrontational. I'd always hated arguing and fighting. No good ever came out of it. All you got were hurt feelings on both sides. Dallas knew this about me, so she was always there to stand up for me when I wouldn't.

When I looked at Dax and saw the smugness on his face, I clenched my fists as my anger heightened. My passiveness aside, enough was enough. I was so tired of this.

I commanded his attention, stepping up to get in his face. "I'm tired of you cheating on me. Just because I won't give you any doesn't mean that you have to go get it from someone else."

Dax raised his eyebrows and gave me a condescending look. "Wow, Bria. Feeling brave today? Well, if I'm being honest, it doesn't suit you. Why don't you keep hiding behind your textbooks and let the adults do the talking?" He gestured between him and Dallas, his eyes turning wicked.

My jaw dropped, and I took a step back from him. Dallas shook with barely contained rage next to me. Before I could form a response, Dallas reared back her fist and smashed it into Dax's face. Her knuckles collided with his nose with a sickening crunch, and he let out a grunt as blood sprayed. He reached up to clutch the fluid now pouring from his nose.

Dax glared at Dallas from beyond his hand, then turned his venomous eyes on me. "We are done! I'm over this!" He stormed off, shaking the blood from his hand.

Frustration built up inside my chest in a rising scream, but I couldn't lose it here, especially since we now had onlookers whispering God-knows-what behind their hands. I held back the bitterness enough to look at Dallas and say in a hoarse voice, "I'm gonna go take a walk. Don't wait up for me."

I didn't give her time to respond. I turned and practically ran off for the trees near the school. My hair flew behind me as I raced through the woods, and bushes tugged at my cream sweater the deeper I went. I didn't care. I wanted to be alone where I could scream, and I knew exactly where that would be.

There was a creek beyond the trees, a distance away from campus property. I'd found it on the first day of classes. I'd been on a walk in the woods behind my dorm building, looking for a secluded spot to make my own where I could focus on schoolwork and art. As soon as I stumbled upon the creek with its soft trickling water and soothing natural melody, I knew this was it.

I fell to my knees by the water's edge and worked to catch my breath. The acidic mixture of anger, frustration, and disappointment burned as it settled deep in my stomach.

My feelings for Dax had been real, yet he hadn't felt a thing for me. What was wrong with me? How could I like someone so shallow? I'd been so blind liking him for so long.

I'd spent countless months conjuring up plans and ideas about what our relationship was supposed to be like. Coming to grips with the realization that my dreams with Dax were pointless was what made it hard to end things. I didn't want it to mean that *all* my dreams were futile, especially not my dream of being an artist.

Pushing past my heightened acrimony, I watched the clear water flow quietly through the trees. I wanted to feel the water's touch, so I slid off my sneakers and socks. Getting to my feet, I'd just stepped in the direction of the water when I heard a loud click and the cry of an animal.

I whipped my head around in the direction of the yelp. In the distance, I saw what appeared to be a smaller-sized black dog struggling against something. Desperate to see what was wrong, I raced toward him with my socks and shoes in hand, but when I got closer, I quickly came to a stop.

The creature looked at me, and I realized he wasn't a dog at all. He was a fox! He gazed at me with rich eyes, and the sight of the fox made me lose my breath for a moment.

I had never seen such a beautiful animal up close before.

When I remembered my reason for coming over here, my eyes traveled down to his front right paw, and it became clear that the noise I heard was a foothold trap going off. I looked around frantically and hoped whoever set the trap wasn't nearby watching.

Looking back at the fox, I gave him a reassuring smile and approached him slowly. "Don't be scared, little guy. I'm going to let you out."

The fox stared at me with those cautious eyes, and I waited with bated breath to see how he'd react to my creeping closer.

He didn't act aggressively, which took me by surprise. There was no snarling, no baring his teeth. He didn't even flinch. Meanwhile, my heart thundered against my chest as I waited for him to lose his cool and suddenly strike at me with his canines or claws.

Instead, he let me kneel down next to him, watching me the whole time. It was odd how placid he was, which made my heart trip over itself in worry. Could he be severely hurt, and that's why he wasn't reacting? Ignoring the oddity of his extremely calm demeanor, I assessed the trap. A small trail of blood dripped from his ankle where he was being held. I frowned at the sight of the red droplets and hoped it wasn't a sign that his foot was broken.

Looking into his eyes again, I put on the most soothing voice I could muster. "All right, this may hurt. Just trust me. I'm going to get you out."

I studied him for signs of attack as I pressed down on the levers of the trap to release their hold. When the fox felt the grip of the trap lessen, he quickly jumped out of it and backed away. I released the levers and let go of the breath I'd been holding as I sat all the way down.

"There you go. You're free now."

I waited for him to dart off in a panic, but instead of taking off running, the fox stayed rooted to the spot, watching me with his cut paw gingerly pressing against the ground. Mind reeling at how calm he was still being, I suddenly felt the first touch of real fear. This was a wild animal. What if he was calm and still right now because he was readying up for an attack? I mean, why else wouldn't he be fleeing?

With him so close, I also realized he wasn't all black. His coat was a deep onyx tipped in frosty white, and his bushy tail came to a snow-colored point. It dawned on me then that he was not just any fox. He was a silver fox.

I'd only ever seen the rare creature in reference books in art class. The odds of seeing such a fox were one in a thousand. Maybe this unlikely encounter was meant to serve as a sign that my dreams were still in my hands. If I could find a silver fox out in the woods, I could find a way to get to Italy.

The fox tilted his head to the side, reminding me of a dog studying a person. The longer he stood there unmoving, the more I wondered if he was tame. Some people had pet foxes, right? Perhaps he'd escaped from his owner's house and gotten lost, because a wild fox would've definitely lashed out at me by this point.

As soon as the thought crossed my mind, the fox slowly walked straight to my side, watching me with a steady gaze, and my eyes went wide. On one hand, his paw seemed relatively unharmed, other than the cut, since he was walking on it without issue. This news was good. On the other hand, seeing how unafraid the creature was rattled my rational mind. He shouldn't be *this* affable unless he really did belong to someone as a pet. I wasn't completely sure of his intentions as he closed in on me. The urge to run was at war with my desire to sit still and see how this played out.

Trying to keep myself calm, I said, "You're quite friendly, huh? I don't mind, though. I could use some company after the day I've had."

The gentle trickle of the creek drew my attention. Frowning, I could start to feel a hint of annoyance again. I sighed and glanced at the fox, who studied me once more.

Jokingly, I asked, "What? Would you like to hear about my stressful day?"

As if he knew what I was saying, the fox sat down next to me and stared up at me with an expectant gaze. My heart sped up. It was as if he could actually understand me and wanted to listen. Which was impossible. This was an *animal*. Animals couldn't understand people unless I was suddenly a princess in a Disney film and no one told me. It was most likely a coincidence that he sat down at that exact moment.

Nothing more.

I could roll with coincidences if it meant I got to vent to someone unable to judge me or talk back. I needed to release my pent-up emotions, and talking aloud would do that.

"All right then," I started, looking at the water. "You see, back when I was in high school, I had a crush on this guy for a long time. I never dreamed he would notice me, but at the end of senior year, he asked me out. I couldn't believe my luck, and I didn't ask any questions. He finally saw me the way I saw him."

My mood turned somber again, and I closed my eyes. With a sigh, I continued, "Although, I guess he didn't actually see me that way after all. To be honest, I knew the whole time that he was only using me. He didn't actually want to be with me. I didn't want things to end because I liked telling myself that Dax was mine. I was stupid, I guess. Today we finally broke up, but not before I got the best-yet-worst news of my life. That's why I came here."

I kicked at a rock and watched it roll into the water. After frowning at the stream for a while, my attention turned back to the silver fox. He sat there, still watching me.

I gave him a warm smile and added, "Well, I guess something good came out of it all. I got to save you."

He tilted his head at me again, and a laugh escaped me. Sitting here, talking to an animal as if it were human, probably seemed crazy. But it worked for me. Sometimes saying things out loud makes you realize how idiotic you sound. It makes you realize a change needs to happen.

"You know," I said, "You're a very good listener, and you cheered me up a lot. I hope we meet again someday."

The fox sat up straighter and seemed to peer deep into my eyes. Mine couldn't possibly hope to match the intensity of his. Where mine were like the deep depths of the ocean, his were like a blazing fire, promising to burn everything in its wake. They were a mesmerizing color, one that would be exciting to try to match in paints. I never wanted to forget those eyes.

Daring to take this chance, I slowly reached my hand out toward him. He went rigid at the sign of movement, and his amber eyes turned cautious. I stilled, afraid I'd startled him into fleeing. It didn't matter that I froze, because he pushed his head forward to nuzzle it against my hand. A mixture of awe and shock bubbled up in my throat, and I gently rubbed in between his ears.

This moment was one for the books. I didn't think I'd ever forget him, but just to be sure, I wanted to mark him somehow. That way I'd know it was the same fox if I found him again. It was a gut feeling, almost like a magnetic pull. It was like when you see a dog or cat for the first time, and when your eyes meet, your gut tells you that it's the one. It's your lifelong friend. I knew I couldn't keep him as a pet, but I could still leave a part of me with him, even if it was silly of me to do so. With that, I finally decided on the necklace that I wore.

It was a silver chain with a small, blue gem, and it reminded me of a clear stream. It was my favorite, despite coming from a cheap twenty-five cent gumball machine. Even though I knew I may never see it again, it felt right to give it to this animal.

I unclasped the necklace and held it up for the fox to see. "I want you to take this." The fox didn't move as I leaned forward to place the chain around his neck. It fit perfectly around his throat, which made me giddy.

"Thank you for listening to me. I know I'll never forget this."

I stood up, wiping the dirt from my jeans. The fox stood back up as well, and he watched me as I put on my socks and sneakers again. When I finished, I hauled my backpack onto my shoulders and looked back at the fox. I waved to him before turning and making my way back to campus.

My mind was in a daze the entire walk back.

Did that really happen? Did I actually pet and talk to a fox? What a day.

CHAPTER

FIVE

When I made it back to my dorm room, Dallas had changed into a tight black shirt that cut off above her belly button. She wore a red jacket over it, and her hair hung in loose curls down her back. She paired it with black leather leggings and red stilettos. As soon as I saw how she was dressed, I knew she had big plans for the night, and something in my gut said I was going to be dragged along.

She saw me come in and immediately dropped what she was doing to face me with worried eyes. "There you are. Are you okay?"

I gave her a reassuring smile. "I'm okay. My walk was … interesting."

Her face lit up at my reassurance, and she jumped up and down. Grabbing my hands, she squealed, "I'm glad you're feeling better, because we are going to have so much fun tonight. Now that you and that mega asshole are finally over, you can join me when I go out to clubs and parties to find you a new special someone."

I gave her a pointed look. "You know that's not really my thing."

She waved a dismissive hand and ran her free one through my long hair. She pursed her lips as she took me in from head to toe. "Let's figure out what to dress you in and how to do your hair. We want you to look your absolute hottest."

"Dallas," I groaned, already exasperated.

She ignored me and started digging things out of her closet. "You hush up. It's my job as your best friend to cheer you up by getting you all sexy so that when we go out, all the guys come crawling to you."

It was my turn to roll my eyes. "I don't want all the guys to come crawling to me."

She threw something black and red at me and turned to face me with her hands on her hips. "That's just the part of you that's still clinging to Dax talking. We *are* going out, and you *are* going to wear that."

I held up the clothes she had thrown at me. I looked back at her with a look that said, *Are you insane?*, but she crossed her arms and turned her head away from me. She snickered knowing I wouldn't argue with her, which I didn't. I sighed in defeat and changed into the clothes.

When I finished getting dressed, I turned to the full body mirror, and my jaw nearly hit the floor. Dallas had me in a black off-the-shoulder shirt that also failed to reach my leggings, exposing the lower part of my stomach. To go with it, she'd given me red silk leggings with black heels.

My wide eyes found hers. "I look ridiculous!"

She laughed and started curling my hair. "Yeah, ridiculously sexy! God, I'm a miracle worker. You look even hotter than me, which is a challenge in and of itself." She gave an appraising flip of her hair over her shoulder. It made me burst into a fit of laughter. Her confidence was enviable.

Talking about our upcoming evening, I couldn't help but get a little excited. It was during the height of my excitement that I finally told her about the study abroad offer. As expected, she couldn't have been happier or more supportive, which is why I didn't bring up the issue of the money. I didn't want to ruin the upbeat energy of the evening. Right now, I wanted to ride this lively mood with her. Tonight was about having fun. Worries could come tomorrow.

Watching Dallas curl my hair made her final vision all the more real. When she was done, she piled it on top of my head in a high ponytail, but my curls still managed to reach the top of my back. After checking our final looks in the mirror and locking our dorm room, we settled in her car, and she took off.

A smile was plastered on my face as we drove to the club. Despite how overwhelmed I'd felt earlier in the day, I was actually eager to get out and do something fun with Dallas. A lot of crazy things had transpired during the day. Even if this wasn't my typical idea of a Friday night, I wanted this tonight.

I'd been cooped up in our dorm room doing homework every day while Dallas often went out for a night of fun. It felt good to be going out for once, and now I could enjoy myself without having to worry about pleasing Dax by getting all his work done for him.

I was finally free.

It was evident when we neared the club, because I could hear the music above our own in the car. The place was a large brick building with its own street and fields for parking. It was at the head of the road, and the fields on either side of the place were filling up fast. We had to park a long way away from the club, so walking there in our heels sucked.

When we finally reached the line leading inside, the music was so loud, the beat pounded beneath my feet. Every change in the music was like a shock wave moving through my whole body.

Dallas' gaze took me in again to make sure all of her hard work still looked good. She fluffed my ponytail and tugged the v-neck of my shirt lower.

I smacked her hand away and pulled it back up.

She laughed and said, "Sweet pea, cleavage is good. If you have it, show it."

"I'd rather keep it to myself. Thank you for the advice, though." I looked at the large man who stood by the door to check IDs as people came in. My eyes turned into saucers, and I quickly grabbed onto Dallas and whispered, "Wait! We can't even get in. We aren't 21."

She rolled her eyes and patted my shoulder as though she were an adult talking to a child. "You don't have to be 21 to get in. You have to be 18, which you are. You have to be 21 to get alcohol from the bar, but that never stops anybody. If you pair up with someone who's at least 21, they can buy you drinks, which is what you'll do if you want something."

I faced forward again as we reached the bouncer. We each showed him our IDs, and after drawing an X on the back of our hands in black sharpie to signify that we were underage, he stepped aside to allow us in.

As soon as I walked through the door, a dark room greeted me. The only light source came from the flashing lights, and the smell of perfume and cologne overwhelmed me. People littered the space. Most of them occupied the dance floor, and those who weren't dancing were at the bar getting drinks. Seeing as it was my first time at a club, the loud music, strobing lights, and strong smells were a lot to process.

"This is crazy!" I yelled above the music.

Dallas laughed and nodded eagerly. She grabbed my hand and pulled me onto the dance floor near the side of the room that housed the bar. She started grinding and dancing to the electronic music, already seeming like she was on cloud nine. I stood near her, unsure of what to do with myself. I didn't know how to dance like that.

She noticed me just standing there and grabbed my hand again. Leaning in close, she yelled, "You'd better start dancing! There's a hottie at 9 o'clock who can't stop staring at you!" She paused, then said, "Wait a minute, is that—"

I spun around to look in that direction. I had to peer past people dancing around me, but when my eyes found his, my heart tripped over itself.

It was Cinnamon Roll.

His arms were crossed over his chest, and he watched me with those amazing amber eyes of his. He looked mouthwatering, standing there in a long-sleeved black shirt and jeans. His sleeves were pushed up to his elbows, and something akin to amusement played in his gaze. Warmth pulsed in my lower stomach at the sight of him.

It also seemed he wasn't alone. On one side of him stood a guy who had shortly cropped black hair. On the other side was a darker skinned guy with long black hair. They were the same ones he'd been with at the restaurant.

When they saw me looking at them, the one with short hair gave me a friendly wave. The one with longer hair looked at Cinnamon Roll and nudged him. Cinnamon Roll didn't move. His eyes stayed locked on me, turning my knees into mush.

I blushed and quickly looked back at Dallas.

She winked at me and yelled, "Why don't you go ask him to dance? Make sure you get his name this time. I'm tired of referring to him as food."

I rolled my eyes and shouted, "First of all, I can't dance. Second of all, I'm not good at flirting with strangers."

"Don't be afraid! Go for it! Have some fun for once!"

She gave me a gentle push in the direction of the guys, but I held my ground. I couldn't do it. I couldn't go talk to him, let alone ask him to dance.

"Dallas—" I started, but as soon as her name left my mouth, a guy came up behind Dallas and wrapped his arm around her shoulders.

She turned to him and squealed before throwing her arms around his neck. The lighting was so dim on the floor that it took me a minute to realize the stranger was actually Rance.

"I thought you'd be here," Rance said, meeting her grin with one of his own. "I've been looking all over for you."

He pecked her on the cheek before giving me a happy wave. I returned the gesture. It occurred to me then that the two of them planned to meet here, which meant I was totally a third wheel. Dallas was no doubt hoping I'd find someone to pair off with so that I wouldn't be alone. She was torn between wanting to have a fun Friday night with Rance while also wanting to cheer me up.

"You wanna go dance?" Rance asked her.

Dallas glanced at me, chewing on her lip as she struggled with what to do.

Laughing, I yelled, "Go! Dance! I want to go get some water anyway." I didn't want to hold her back from having fun.

After a few more reluctant moments, she finally blew me a kiss. They grabbed at each other's hands and disappeared into the sea of people.

I frowned, suddenly feeling alone. I glanced at Cinnamon Roll against the far wall. He was still watching me, but now the corners of his mouth were turned down at the edges. I quickly looked away and turned around, determined to get a drink. As soon as I spun on my heel, I came face-to-face with the person I least expected.

Dax stood there, looking astonished and abashed at first. He gave me a once over, and his expression quickly changed. He smiled.

CHAPTER

SIX

"Well, well, well," Dax said as he walked in a circle around me. "Don't you look sexy as hell." He stood in front of me, and after staring at my chest for longer than necessary, he finally met my eyes again. "Wanna go dance with me?"

He grabbed for my hand, but I quickly pulled it back and stepped away from him. Narrowing my eyes, I snapped, "Don't touch me! Why would I want to go anywhere with you?"

He threw back his head in a burst of laughter and yelled above the music, "I know you're still in love with me, Bria. You've had a thing for me forever now. This is your chance to make me happy and win me back. We both know that's what you want."

My stomach churned at his words. I was so sick of his toxic attitude. I noticed then that his nose was free of any bruising from earlier, and despite my good nature, I suddenly wished Dallas had hit him harder. He deserved some hurt for once—something I never would've wished on him before. That was before I snapped out of my delusion. Which was exactly what our relationship had been. My feelings for him had been fueled by hormones and unrealistic adolescent fantasies. In other words, he'd been a waste of time, and one I didn't want to repeat.

With a final icy look, I tried walking past him, but he grabbed my arm and pulled me back to him. He pinned me against his chest and leaned down to kiss my neck with aggressive lips. In the past, this would've thrilled me to my very core, but now it just sent a repulsed tremor through my body. I slammed my elbow into his rib cage, and he quickly let me go.

Slipping away from him, I turned back for only a second. "You disgust me, Dax! I'll never want you again. Do you understand?"

He recovered from my verbal blow and straightened. His hands balled into fists. "You're such a fucking loser! I hope you know that no one will ever want *you.*"

His words cut into me, and I couldn't help the build up of emotion that wanted to escape. His lips curled with a cruel tilt at the sight of my eyes watering, and he glanced around us until he spotted a girl with long brown hair nearby. She was drinking herself away when he grabbed her hand and pulled her face close to his, her eyes looking completely swept away and mesmerized by him.

Poor girl.

He glanced sideways at me with an evil glint in his gaze before looking back at her. "Do you wanna dance with me, beautiful?"

Her mouth dropped open, and she nodded in bobble head fashion. He turned up his charm before leading her away into the sea of bodies. Dax threw a look over his shoulder at me and laughed when he saw me staring after them.

Rage sunk its razor-sharp claws into me. He was toying with me, but I wouldn't let him. Not anymore. It was my turn to be the ringleader.

Glaring at the spot where he'd been standing, I adjusted my shirt a little, showing off more of my cleavage. Dallas would be so proud. I pulled my hair out of the ponytail, letting the curls cascade down my back. I received a few appraising looks from guys and girls around me, but it wasn't them I was going after.

I turned in the direction of Cinnamon Roll who still leaned against the wall. His eyes devoured me as I approached him with a confident walk. All the hesitation from earlier had been replaced by fiery determination. The guys on either side of him gave me impressed once-overs as I closed the distance, but Cinnamon Roll kept a straight face, communicating solely through the desire in his eyes.

When I reached him, I grabbed his hand and turned, pulling him toward the dance floor. He followed willingly as I navigated us to a spot in the center. Dallas was a few feet away, grinding on Rance. When she saw me, her mouth hung open. Her eyes darted between me and Cinnamon Roll.

She quickly nodded at something behind me. It was Dax dancing with the girl. Dallas gave me a look that practically said, *Does this have something to do with Dax being here?* She didn't miss a thing.

I flipped my hair over my shoulder and held my head higher to show her what I thought about him. *Screw Dax! Two can play his game.*

I glanced in his direction where he danced erotically with the drunk brunette. He noticed me looking, and smugness lit his eyes until he caught sight of me holding my new partner's hand. Confidence pulled my shoulders back, and I turned to look at Cinnamon Roll for the first time since leading him there.

Amusement glittered in his amber eyes, and something else danced there as well. Something smoky and alluring. Something that seemed to promise seductively wicked experiences should I add gasoline to that flame in his gaze.

Working to cool the heat from my cheeks, I forced myself to glance sideways at Dallas where she danced with Rance. I memorized her steps and the movements of her body. When the music built to a part with the same beat, I readied myself. I pulled his body nearly against mine and closed my eyes, mustering every ounce of courage I had. No backing out now.

Letting go of my hesitation, I lost myself in the music and the warmth radiating off my dance partner. I wrapped one arm around his neck, and my body moved against his to the beat. I spun around and rolled my hips, grinding close to him with my backside. Dallas cheered me on as I replicated her moves, trying hard not to encroach on his space too much. This guy didn't move with me, though. He stood there and let me dance on him.

My nerves were starting to get the better of me. Was he supposed to just stand there? Was I doing it wrong?

When the rhythm changed, I faced him again. I was out of breath, and I tried sneaking glances at Dallas for more moves as I swayed in sync to the music. Before I could, my partner crooked his finger under my chin and turned my head to look at him.

Color crept up my cheeks as he peered into my eyes and asked in a deep, velvety voice, "I'm going to assume you're trying to make that guy over there jealous?"

Dax was still in the same spot dancing with his new date, but he watched us with a grimace and furious eyes.

Looking back at Cinnamon Roll, I said, "I'm not trying to make him jealous. I just want him to see that I've moved on and don't want him."

He glanced at Dax, then turned his attention back to me. The music was beginning to climax again, and the sight of his growing smile made my heart pound against my chest. I swallowed hard as he said, "Well then, why don't we do a better job?"

He wrapped his arm around my waist to pull me flush against him, leaving no space between our bodies. He grabbed my arm and brought it up around his neck before his hand scorched a trail of fluttering heat back down my arm. His grip came to rest on my hip, but not before searing my bare skin where my shirt failed to cover my sides.

I was already breathless, and we hadn't even started dancing again.

His smile widened as the music crescendoed. Our bodies lined up in all the right places, and a sickly-sweet heat burned through my core with every push and pull of our bodies. We moved in sync, and there was no stopping the excitement spreading across my lips or the pink stain, no doubt, on my cheeks.

He spun me around so my back was to him and held my arms behind his neck before placing his own on my hips again. He moved our bodies together while trailing featherlight kisses along my neck.

Liquid fire flooded my veins, sending a buzz through my chest. I closed my eyes and held my breath at his touch. The roll of his hips and the press of his hands against my sides evoked brief flashes of wicked thoughts. Thoughts that involved him and me, far less clothing, and just as much breathless activity. I was prepared to pass out at any moment now from the dizzy euphoria he was eliciting within me.

When the song was over, I faced him again. We were out of breath and laughing. He was beaming at me, and I couldn't help but return the look, even when he leaned down to press our foreheads together. My eyes slipped closed, and I bit my lip as we started swaying to the new song, our breathing heavy and our skin sparking with excited shivers at the other's roaming hands. That exhilarating emotion was short lived, because a grip took hold of me by the shoulder and spun me around.

Dax stood there, looking like a kid who'd just had his favorite toy stolen. His wild eyes flicked from me to my dance partner then back. "What the hell do you think you're doing?"

I glared at him and placed my hands on my hips. "The same as everyone else here. I'm dancing."

The girl he was with tugged on his arm and complained, "Dax, come on. I wanna dance. Who cares what this girl does?"

Dax ignored her and narrowed his eyes at Cinnamon Roll. Balling his hands into fists, he yelled, "She was mine first, pal!"

Cinnamon Roll's arm draped over my shoulders as he stood proudly next to me. Smiling smugly, he said, "Well, she's not yours anymore."

Dax took a threatening step forward, and my dance partner met him with the same animosity. I could see a spark growing in their eyes, one that promised an ensuing fight.

Before anyone could make a move, a deep voice boomed, "Rune!"

We all turned. The guy with the long, black hair from Cinnamon Roll's group was looking at the scene before him with disgust. The guy with short hair stood behind him, biting his nails nervously. My dance partner, Rune, nodded to them.

Then, he looked at me and gave me a mouthwatering smile. "Thank you for the dance." He turned and disappeared into the swarm of people with his two friends.

That bitter taste of loneliness overtook me as I watched him recede through the crowd. My heart begged me to follow him. I didn't want a single night of dancing with him, only to part ways afterward. He was going to think I'd been using him, but that wasn't the case. The spark we'd had while dancing had been thrilling, and I wanted to stoke that flame to see what it would create. Now the chance to explore that potential chemistry was gone.

"Bria!" Dax yelled.

I looked back at him, and he grabbed my hand.

He turned and started to drag me toward the door. "We're leaving!"

I fought against his painfully strong grip and glared at the back of his head. "Let me go! I'm not going anywhere with you!"

"Dax, leave her alone!" Dallas shouted.

She grabbed where he held me and pried us apart. She quickly hugged me, and we both backed away from him. Dax fumed with slit eyes, and she matched his look.

"Dax!" I yelled. He finally met my eyes. "Just leave me the hell alone. I don't know how many times I have to say it to get it through your thick skull. I don't want to be with you! It's over. I'm done!"

He scoffed then turned in a furious retreat, shoving through the sea of people. Some had stopped dancing to watch our display, but most were still grinding, oblivious to what was happening.

I closed my eyes and sighed. The urge to scream out of frustration was hard to ignore.

Dax was an asshole, but the person I was the angriest with right now was myself. My ignorance. My blindness to his true colors. It infuriated me to the point my body shook from the mixture of embarrassment and resentment pounding in my chest. I hated that I let myself be sucked in and fooled by his charm for so long.

Dallas could sense my annoyance, so she and Rance walked with me to a table that was away from everyone. I collapsed into one of the chairs while Dallas got me a glass of water from the bar. When she came back, I took huge gulps. Water always had a way of easing me and making everything better.

"Are you okay?" Dallas asked, her forehead creased with worry.

Not wanting to dampen the mood any further, I gave her a reassuring smile and nodded.

She matched my expression and changed the subject. "You sure did some sexy moves out there, and when Mr. Rune joined in, boy was that something!"

I laughed, and heat spread across my cheeks and ears. It was like my entire being had come to life when we were dancing, and when he'd kissed my neck ….

I shook my head at the memory and released an embarrassed laugh. Those sorts of thoughts wouldn't do me any good now since he was gone.

Pushing past my salacious fantasies, I looked up at my friends. Dallas and Rance stood side by side, and I couldn't help but take them in. They really did look good together, and this was their time to strengthen their newfound relationship with memories.

Finding Dallas' eyes, I gave her an encouraging nod. "I'll be fine now. You two go dance and have fun."

Dallas looked hesitant, but I laughed and motioned for them to go on. Her reluctance slowly slipped away until she practically bounced with enthusiasm. "If you say so. But if you need me, I'll be right where I was before. We can ditch this place as soon as you want."

After making me promise I'd get her if I needed her, she took Rance's hand, and they ran back into the crowd. My heart was happy for them as I watched after the pair. When I could no longer see them, my eyes involuntarily drifted to the spot where Rune and his friends had stood before. No one was there now. They were really gone. A guilty sigh escaped me as I frowned and downed more of my water.

People of all shapes, sizes, colors, and walks of life filled the room. It was fun observing all the groups and seeing how they interacted. I wondered briefly what Rune and his friends were like. What space would they fit into among the crowds here?

As my gaze trailed the back wall, unease settled in my bones. Across the space was a dark-headed man who stood alone. An eerie energy filled the air around him, and the urge to shrink away hit me hard. His eyes unnerved me above all else. From this distance, they looked like narrowed onyx slits, and they seemed to be looking right at me.

When our eyes locked, he pushed away from the wall and stalked in my direction. He pulled out his phone from his pocket and, after tapping around the screen, held it up to his ear as he kept his stride toward my table. I glanced around to see if maybe his target was someone near me, but no one seemed to be paying him any mind. I wasn't sure if I was overreacting, but my gut told me he was bad news.

I was about to stand and look for Dallas when he drew close enough to really see him. Recognition flared in the back of my mind. It was the same guy I'd run into outside of the tattoo shop. Dread settled in my stomach, and I wondered if he recognized me too. Could that be why he was headed right for me? Was he really still pissed about my accidentally running into him?

He reached my table, but instead of stopping, he kept walking past me. I held my breath, waiting for him to continue on. When he was directly next to my seat, I heard him say into the phone, "Yeah. I see her."

Ice pricked at my insides. I whipped around to look after him as he vanished into the crowd. Surely to God he wasn't talking about me. If he were, wouldn't he have stopped and confronted me? I convinced myself I was being paranoid. He kept walking, so I figured he was referencing a girl who had been somewhere behind me in the sea of people.

"Bria, you clearly need to tone it down on the true crime shows," I mumbled to myself.

"Hey there."

I spun back around in my chair with alarm bells still ringing. Everything inside me wanted to jump around and scream, but it was no longer from apprehension. Rune stood across the table. He was back, and he stared down at me with a sexy glint in his eyes.

CHAPTER
SEVEN

Swallowing my shock, I met Rune's smile with my own.
"Hi again."

"Can I sit here?" he asked, pointing at the empty chair across from me.

"Yes, of course."

He sank down in the chair, and I watched his every movement with hungry eyes. Everything about him screamed seduction. His long, white hair, the embers burning in his golden eyes, the tilt of his lush lips, the fit of his black tee hugging his well-built frame. I subtly scratched at my mouth to make sure I wasn't drooling.

"Your name is Rune, right?" I asked, hoping my voice didn't give away the nerves he elicited.

"It is. I'm afraid I didn't catch yours."

"It's Bria."

"Bria," he repeated.

My toes curled inside my heels at the sound of my name on those lips. I bit the inside of my cheek to refrain from asking him to say it again in that deep, husky voice of his.

"I'm glad you're back. I wanted to say sorry about—" I looked sideways to where Dax had interrupted our dance. "You know, involving you in that drama."

He chuckled, the sound delicious and rich. "No need to apologize. I quite enjoyed myself, to be honest."

My cheeks heated at the memory his words called forth. His hard body pushing against my soft curves. Those decadent lips teasing the skin along my neck. The way his hips pressed into me, igniting wickedly delightful thoughts. I was going to make myself breathless just thinking about it.

Clearing my throat, I glanced around us. "Did your friends leave?"

"No, no. They're dancing out there somewhere. We stepped away for a minute when things were about to get out of hand, but they weren't done partying. I wasn't even close to being done here, either."

I didn't miss the way his eyes traced my body then, nor could I ignore the heat it sent spiraling through my core to settle between my thighs. It was starting to get hot, and I knew it had nothing to do with the actual temperature in the room and *everything* to do with the sexy stranger in front of me.

Biting my lip, I leaned forward to prop my chin in my hand on the table. "Well, I'm glad you came back."

"Not as much as I am." He tilted his head as he regarded me. "Do you go to school around here?"

"I do. I'm a freshman at Brinkley."

"Brinkley, huh? That's a good school. I know some people who went there. They said Brinkley was a top choice school for people in the fine arts."

"It is. That's actually my major, and I can attest that your friends are correct. They have some great programs for art majors."

"An artist. Very impressive. A friend of mine was into sculpting and got to go overseas to study in Greece. They said it was really awesome and urged anyone who got the chance to go abroad."

"Really? That's awesome, and honestly, something I needed to hear. There's a study abroad opportunity that one of my professors thinks I should get involved in, and I definitely want to."

"But?" he prodded.

"But it's five thousand dollars."

He paused before giving a low whistle. "Damn. That's pricey."

"Tell me about it. Unless I win the lottery, that trip is probably out the window."

He shrugged with something warm glittering in his eyes. "You never know. Maybe you'll get the money somehow. I've heard if you say something confidently and put it out into the universe, it's supposed to come true. It's called manifesting or something like that."

Laughing, I said, "Well then, universe, I am rich and have five thousand dollars on me right this second."

"There you go. Now you just sit back and wait."

"Your turn. What would you like to manifest into existence?"

He cocked a brow at me and leaned forward on the table. Those golden orbs held my gaze, and a heat smoldered in those depths as he watched me. His eyes traveled down from mine, over my throat, along the swells of my breasts, and back up. It was a slow prowl, one that almost felt like a physical touch. My heart pounded, and my core ached by the time he made it back to my gaze.

"I'm going to be back out there dancing with the beautiful girl in front of me."

My heart leapt into my throat, and I couldn't stop the smile that spread across my mouth. The universe didn't need to manifest his wish. I could do that all on my own.

Getting to my feet, I held out my hand for him. He took it, and I led us back onto the dance floor. We passed Dallas and Rance on the way, and she beamed at me when she noticed us. I winked at her before turning to Rune.

As soon as I faced him, he pulled me close, wrapped my arms around his neck, and we *danced*. Our bodies pushed and pulled each other's song after song after song. I was hot, breathless, and burning for the alluring man in front of me.

"You—" I panted. Our foreheads pressed together as we gyrated through another beat. "You're a good dancer."

He chuckled, and the deep sound vibrated against my body. The sensation didn't help the burning need that had settled in my core.

"So are you," he said, squeezing me tighter.

"I think I'm going to need a break after this one. My legs are going to give out."

"Sure. Want me to get us drinks?"

"I'd love some water."

"Water coming up."

The song finished, so we made our way off the dance floor. He kept his hand on the small of my back as we weaved through the crowd, and the touch made my heart thunder. It was a simple enough gesture, one that probably wasn't a big deal to a lot of people, but that small contact set off an explosion of fireworks in my stomach, lighting me up from the inside out.

"I'll be right back," I promised. "I'm gonna get some fresh air really fast."

"I'll be waiting," Rune said.

I made my way outside. The cold night air kissed my skin, but I welcomed it. I was burning up from all the dancing. A retouch of deodorant wouldn't hurt either, which was another reason I chose to make a quick trip outside. Having a few minutes to myself on my way to Dallas' car gave me plenty of time to reflect on what the hell was happening, too.

Rune.

My Cinnamon Roll.

He was incredible!

He was sexy as hell, and he seemed to be thoughtful and kind from the brief conversations we'd had both at the table and while dancing. I couldn't lie. I was having the time of my life dancing, flirting, and laughing with him. It made me wonder if this could be the start of something new in my life. Nothing serious, just something exciting that provided the mind-numbing bliss I needed sometimes.

As I neared Dallas' car with my head still in the clouds, a weight slammed hard into my back. I yelped and crashed into the grass. Pain shot down my knees and arms as I caught myself. Before I could process what had just happened, a hand came down on my shoulder and yanked me hard until I slammed into the tire now at my back.

"Give us the money," a deep voice spat.

A redheaded man glared down at me as he held a knife aimed at my chest. Moonlight glinted off the blade, and terror squeezed at my throat as realization hit me.

"Don't you dare scream, either, or I'll slice that pretty neck of yours."

I pressed further into the tire to get as far away from the sharp weapon as possible and held up my shaking hands in surrender. "Don't hurt me. Please. I don't have any money."

"Liar," the man spat, his rancid breath wafting into my face.

He shoved the knife at me, making me jump back, despite not being able to retreat any further. A sob choked me. The need to scream for help at the top of my lungs surged through me, but when I saw the way he shoved that sharp blade nearer my neck, panic made all my cries die out.

"We heard you," the man snapped. "You have five thousand dollars. Now give it here, or else!"

"Allen."

My attention shot over the redhead's shoulder to a second guy I was just now noticing. He was petite with messy dark hair. He fidgeted as his eyes flickered back and forth between Allen and me.

When he looked at his partner again, he stammered, "Allen, maybe we should—"

"Shut the fuck up, Blake. We've been over this. If you pussy out now, the guys aren't going to let you hang with us anymore. Do you want to be on the streets again?"

Blake paused, and his unsure eyes found mine again. If I had any chance of making it out of this unscathed, he was my key. Blake clearly wasn't resolved on this robbery like his partner. My desperate, tear-filled eyes silently pleaded with him to help me.

His face merely pinched tight with guilt as he turned away.

My heart sank with the break of his eyes.

"Fine. Let's hurry and get this over with."

"Please, no," I cried. My body shook from the tremors rolling through me.

Allen shoved the cold metal edge against my throat. All the air in my lungs froze as I fought to remain still. One wrong move, and he'd slice open my neck, leaving me to bleed out alone and in utter pain.

"The money," Allen bit out. "*Now.*"

"I don't have any money," I said slowly, trying hard to ignore the bite of the blade.

"We heard you inside. Don't fuck with us. Do you want to die?"

I realized then that they must've heard Rune and me talking inside about studying abroad. They clearly missed that it was a *joke*. I wanted so badly to cry out and slap myself for saying something like that in public. You never knew what kind of people were listening. You never knew what kind of demented criminals were nearby.

"That was a joke," I pleaded. "I don't have any money. Please. Let me go!"

"This bitch," Allen fumed. He leapt to his feet and grabbed me by the shirt. Yanking on me until I stood up, he shoved the knife into my face again. "Unlock your car."

I worked to take a steadying breath as I reached behind me and opened the driver side door of Dallas' car. I sent up a silent prayer of thanks that she'd left it unlocked because God only knows what they would've done to me if I couldn't get into the car.

Allen kept his hold on me with the knife pressed to my throat. "Blake, check the car for the money. It's in there somewhere."

Long, torturous seconds ticked by as Blake dug through the contents of Dallas' car. I knew all he'd find in there were discarded homework assignments, condoms, and a bag full of makeup and toiletries. But it was no use arguing and trying to convince him of that. They'd see it for themselves soon enough, and I hoped that they'd let me go when they did.

"You know," Allen said, his mouth curling upwards in a sinister sneer. "When we get that money, we can't let you go. You've seen our faces, heard our names." He leaned in close and whispered, "I'm still gonna slit your throat."

The heavy weight of panic settled over my shoulders and cries built up on my tongue. If I managed to scream, would people even hear me all the way out here above the music? I wasn't so sure, so I went to beg and plead for my life when Blake re-emerged from the car, empty handed and as pale as a ghost.

"Well?" Allen snapped at Blake. "Did you find it?"

"There's no money."

Allen's narrowed eyes zeroed in on me. "Why you little—"

"Hey!"

Allen and Blake whipped around as Rune came running down the aisle of cars. Hope surged inside my chest at the sight of him, because not only was I now not alone, he also provided the distraction I needed. I leaned my neck back just enough to be safe and smacked Allen's arm away. The sudden movement made him lose his grip on the knife, which disappeared somewhere in the grass around us.

"Shit!" Allen roared as he faced me again and grabbed me with both hands.

Rune was nearly to us now, and the two boys were weaponless. I was sure this fact wasn't lost on them, because with one final look at me, Allen shoved me backward. The force sent me reeling, and the back of my head slammed into the open doorframe of the car. Bright bursts of pain flared behind my eyes as I succumbed to the dark lullaby that quickly pulled me under.

CHAPTER

EIGHT

My entire body felt heavy, and I groaned at the skull-splitting ache that settled in my temples.

"Oh, thank God! She's awake. Bria, sweetie?"

Dallas?

Despite feeling like my eyes were full of sand, I forced them open and was met with golden eyes peering down into mine. Rune's face loomed above me, and I realized he was cradling me in his arms as we sat in the grass. We were still by Dallas' car, but now there was a group of people. Dallas was right by my side, holding my head in one hand and gripping my fingers in the other. Rune's two friends and Rance hovered at my feet. Everyone looked down at me with worry creasing their foreheads.

My eyes slipped closed, and I reached up to clutch my pounding skull. "My head hurts."

"Shit!" Dallas said, her words laced with concern. "Should we get her to the hospital?"

"I'm a nurse. Let me look at her," came an unfamiliar male voice. "Rune, you said she hit the back of her head, right?"

I opened my eyes as one of Rune's friends knelt next to Dallas. He offered me a warm smile.

"*Konnichiwa.*" His Japanese accent was thick as he continued. "I'm Akira, Rune's friend. I'm gonna check your head, okay?"

His small hands parted the hair on the back of my head as he, no doubt, searched for a wound. As soon as his fingers gently pressed the back of my skull, a burst of pain flared beneath his fingers, and I sucked in a sharp breath.

"There's no cut, thank goodness," Akira said. "But you have a decent knot back there."

"It feels more like a boulder," I groaned, reaching back to feel the sensitive bump.

Akira asked me a string of questions like my name, the date, and if I knew where I was. After having me track his fingers with my eyes as they moved back and forth and up and down in front of my face, he assured Dallas and me that I didn't have a concussion.

Dallas sighed, the relief on her face instant. She placed an appreciative hand on Akira's arm. "Thank you for making sure she's okay."

"Do you want to try and stand?" Rune asked me.

My eyes found his again. As soon as our gazes locked, warmth flooded my system. If he hadn't shown up when he did, I didn't think I'd be here right now. I'd probably be crumbled in the grass, blood pouring from a gash in my throat. Cold, alone, and dead.

Instead, I was warm from Rune's hold, surrounded by friendly faces, and still taking in air. Profound gratitude for him blossomed like a bud deep within me.

Finding my voice, I said, "Yes, please."

Rune guided me until I sat up straight. He and Dallas each held one of my hands, and with their help, I managed to get my legs underneath me, despite their current noodle consistency. As soon as I was upright, my knees buckled, and I nearly toppled back over.

"Easy there," Rune said.

He was quick to catch me around my waist, which sent excited jitters darting through my stomach. It was crazy how one person's touch could make me react so fully and quickly.

"Better?" Dallas asked after I'd regained my balance.

I took some tentative steps, and once I managed to get a feel of my legs, I nodded. "Better. My head still hurts though."

"Take some acetaminophen when you get home," Akira advised. "That knot will start to go down in the coming days. Put some ice on it. That will reduce some of the swelling. If your headache persists, make sure you go to the hospital or consult with a doctor."

"What happened to those guys?" I asked.

After getting a sense of my surroundings and feeling some of the earlier fog dissipate from my head, I remembered why I was here in the first place. I didn't see Allen or Blake anywhere nearby as I scanned the surrounding cars and shadows, but that did little to comfort me. They could be hiding anywhere, just waiting in the dark for a moment to strike. Fear clawed back into my mind at the memory of moonlight reflecting off the blade of the knife.

"They ran off," Rune said. I met his eyes as he finished. "We called the police, who should be here soon."

Our small group stayed tucked away by Dallas' car until the police arrived. Dallas kept her arm around my shoulder for support as I recounted to the officers what happened with Rune vouching for me. The two of us gave as good of a description as we could, given how dark it was, as well as their names. The officers recorded the information and promised to be in touch if they found anything.

"I think we should get you home now," Dallas said.

She gave me a squeeze as if to silently say that everything was okay now.

"That's a good idea," I said with a nod.

When Rune and I found each other's eyes, I hesitated. The night we'd shared before this insane robbery had been perfect. This wasn't the turn I expected the evening to take, but since it had, the question of *what now* lingered in the air. I didn't want this to be the end. There was an undeniable spark that had been between us when we talked and danced. The idea of leaving like this threatened to snuff the flame before it even got a chance to blaze to life.

I took a step toward him, fidgeting with my hands and searching for something, *anything*, to say. "Um—"

"Is it okay if I ask for your number?"

My heart leapt into my throat, and I bit my lip to keep from grinning like a mad fool. "Yes. Of course."

His two friends shared a surprised look as Rune pulled out his phone. I added my name and number as he leaned in close and whispered, "I'm glad you said yes. I was afraid that now wasn't the time, but I wasn't sure if I'd get—"

"Another chance?"

I glanced up, and our eyes collided. His face was angled toward mine and so close that our noses nearly grazed when I looked up at him. My breath hitched in my throat at the warmth his nearness induced within me, and I had to fight to keep my eyes trained on his instead of his lips, which seemed to beckon me.

Flashing him a brief smile, I finished, "Yeah. Me too."

His eyes softened, and he took his phone back. Dallas, Rance, and I waved to Rune's trio and wished them well. I sank down into the passenger seat while Dallas said goodbye to Rance outside the car. After minutes of their farewell, she finally got in, and we made our way back to the dorm.

The car ride was far from quiet. Dallas interrogated me the entire way about what happened. After I finished detailing the incident, she prodded at me to make sure I was actually okay, not only mentally but physically, too.

I wasn't going to lie. I was pretty rattled from the entire thing. I could've easily died tonight, all because two strangers decided they wanted to take my money. Money I didn't even have!

It was hard for me to look at someone and declare them as evil. I constantly looked for the good in people because I believed that everyone was capable of kindness. But I also knew there were people in the world with bad intentions, and I definitely felt that sinister hand on Allen. He was without remorse, and his eyes had lit up with each threat like he'd been enjoying the torment.

But Blake was more difficult to get a read on. The threat Allen made to him about being homeless should Blake not help made my heart settle with guilt, but I quickly set that emotion aside. My attackers didn't deserve pity. *They* chose to rob me, failed or not. Any consequence from that decision was theirs to carry, not mine.

"Promise me you're okay?" Dallas asked as we pulled into our dorm's parking lot.

I rolled my eyes and gave an incredulous laugh. "Dallas, for the hundredth time, I'm okay. It was scary, but I'm alive and relatively unhurt. I'm focusing on that right now, which is helping. What's *not* helping is the reminder of what happened."

"Okay, okay. You're right."

She shut off the engine, and we headed up to our room. Once inside, anymore lingering worry dissipated. I was safe here, and that fact was a comfort in and of itself.

"I'm exhausted," I told Dallas as I collapsed face-first on my bed.

"Just get some sleep. I know it's been a long day. We can hang out tomorrow, just you and me. We can watch movies and binge junk food, okay?"

I looked over my shoulder at her and felt the weight of the day lift from my shoulders. The promise of girl time, corny movies, and endless snacks was enough to almost make the drowsiness disappear from my system.

"That sounds perfect," I sighed.

"It's a date," she squealed and slapped my butt.

I laughed and shoved her gently in the hip with my foot. The two of us changed into our pajamas and crawled into our beds.

As I lay there waiting for sleep, my mind replayed everything that happened today, and I lingered on the trip to Italy in an effort to think positive thoughts. A well-worn apron covered in stains of white, emerald, Persian blue, and gold. The smell of acrylic paints greeting me every morning in my very own studio. Canvas after canvas depicting the beauty of the world around me. It was all seeming closer than it ever had before, and it started with Luca Romano and the trip to Italy.

I just needed the money.

Hope warred with doubt, making my chest constrict.

I started making a mental list of all the ways I could get the fee. I could apply for some jobs around campus tomorrow with Dallas' help. Hopefully, I could find one that worked around my school schedule. Even with the job, there was no way I'd be able to save up five thousand dollars before the first of November. It was already September 2. Maybe I could sell some of my stuff, or better yet, I could sell some of my paintings. It would take a lot, and I wasn't sure how I'd manage a part-time job, classes, homework, painting, and time for myself.

But I *had* to do it.

With a heavy sigh, I rolled onto my side and glanced out the half-closed blinds of my window. The stars twinkled in the black sky, and the moon bathed the sleeping world below in its silver light. I wondered if my parents were out there somewhere, lying awake and thinking of me. Were they staring at that same moon, seeing the same stars as me, and wishing upon them with all their might to find me? Or were they a part of those stars now? Were they looking down on me from their place in the sky?

I clutched my comforter tightly in my hands and pulled it up to my chin. "I miss you, Mom and Dad."

The words were barely a whisper. So much so, I wasn't sure if I'd actually said them. But my entire soul was tied to those six words.

I'd never met my real parents. I didn't know a single thing about them. That didn't stop the ache in my chest and burn in my eyes when I thought of them. I liked to pretend that if we were still together, my mother would hold me close and run her fingers through my hair after a long day. She'd tell me how much she loved my paintings and that she'd always be first in line to buy them. My father would twirl me around and laugh with pride before telling me that my happiness was all that mattered.

Not Greg and Wendy.

The Ashmoores were very kind people, but they were realists. When I first showed interest in painting as a little girl and told them I wanted to be a painter, they laughed and indulged the idea while exchanging a look that could only be interpreted as doubt. When I got older and still wanted to be a painter, there was no more pretending to support my "childish fantasies."

I still remembered the night they sat me down at family dinner. They had ordered Chinese takeout—my favorite—in an effort to lessen the blow they planned on delivering. During dinner, they told me it was time to grow up. They said I needed to think about my future realistically and to give up my dream because it wasn't reasonable. It was a *joke*. If I didn't think about getting a "real job," they'd stop buying me art supplies and letting me take art classes. I left that dinner table that night with tears streaming down my face, and my entire world shattered.

I locked away my hopes and dreams that night, hiding them in the deepest parts of myself. Who could've guessed that Professor Lichen would find that old key to hand back to me. All I had to do now was take it and unlock that door.

And I was going to.

I'd wipe away the dust, put the key in the lock, and swing the door open wide.

CHAPTER

NINE

"How many are you applying for?"

I glanced over at Dallas from where I'd been filling out my tenth application. She was curled up at the foot of my bed, and she crunched away on a potato chip. The two of us had been cooped up in our dorm all day. We'd started out with homework, and once we'd finished that, we got some snacks and movies to relax.

The Proposal was currently on, but I was too busy typing up and filling out applications to pay attention. After my resolve solidified last night, I knew I had a lot to do, which started with applying for as many jobs as I could. There had to be one that could fit into my schedule.

"It's just to be sure I get one," I told her.

"Well, at the rate you're going, you're bound to get a handful."

Her phone dinged, and she perked up. "Rance has our pizzas for us! He's on his way now."

"Why don't you invite him to stay and watch movies? I need to start working on some paintings anyway."

"Are you sure? I don't want to ruin our girl day."

I waved a dismissive hand. "It's fine, really. We've had all day together, and I'm sure you'd both like to see each other since it's Saturday night. And like I said, I'm gonna start working on a painting to sell."

Her face lit up, and she leaned over to kiss me on the cheek. "You're the best."

Smiling wryly, I went back to the application. "I know."

"Speaking of boys," she started, leaning in close. "Have you heard from Rune?"

I sighed as the first hint of disappointment brewed in my gut. He hadn't texted once since I gave him my number, and the question of why had secretly plagued me all day. I mean, *he* asked for *my* number. So why hadn't he contacted me? We'd clearly hit it off last night. The suspense of waiting for a text was driving me bonkers.

Picking up my phone from where I'd tossed it the last time I'd checked it for notifications, I said, "No. He still hasn't—"

My heart stopped, and my eyes went wide. There was one new text from an unknown number. I shot up straight from where I'd been lounging, and I thought my heart was going to break free from my chest as I opened the message.

> Hey Bria. It's Rune. How are you feeling today? Sorry for not texting sooner. I wanted to give you time to rest and recoup from last night. I was wondering if you were busy tomorrow?

Warmth flooded my veins. I reread his message a dozen times while Dallas fought to see what it said.

He texted. He wants to meet up!

My whole being sang with excitement at the thought of seeing him again. It felt so good to be, dare I say, *pursued* after being the pursuer with Dax.

> Hi! I'm doing better, thanks. :) It's good to hear from you. I'd love to hang out tomorrow. What did you have in mind?

"Holy crap on a cracker," I said, meeting Dallas' green eyes. "He wants to hang out."

Dallas and I squealed together and bounced on the bed as we waited to see what he replied. My insides bubbled with nervous sparks of anticipation. It was a new feeling for me, one that felt like golden rays of sunlight dancing around my insides.

> How about noon? We can meet at the mall downtown?

> Sounds great. See you then. :)

"Oh my God," I said, gripping Dallas' arm. "I can't believe it. I'm going out with Cinnamon Roll!"

"I'm so happy for you! You'd better give me every detail tomorrow!"

A knock came at the door, which paused our giggle fest. Dallas jumped up to get the door, and Rance came in with his ever-bright attitude and a stack of delicious-smelling pizzas. After much insisting from Dallas and me, he finally agreed to stay and hang with us.

We spent the remainder of the evening dining on cheesy, greasy goodness and binging movies. I took that time to also pull out my sketchbook and start planning different paintings I could sell. I easily got lost in the lines of my rough drafts, the planning of the colors, and the different images I wanted to create. Before I knew it, Rance and Dallas were asleep on her bed, and the clock read 11:30 p.m. I had three solid ideas for paintings, including one of a silver fox after my inspirational meeting with one, so with a big day ahead of me, I decided to call it a night.

Except I couldn't stop fidgeting and smiling to myself as I wondered what tomorrow held in store. What would Rune and I say? What would we do? The possibilities were endless, and I fell asleep in high spirits.

The next morning, I woke just as eager for the day. I hadn't been able to stop replaying the moments I'd shared with Rune at the club and the chemistry between us up until the moment I fell asleep. I hoped that same fire still lingered today.

I quietly climbed out of bed and found that Dallas and Rance were still asleep. She was lying in his arms with a look of contentment on her face. If our RA did a random room check, she'd flip out, but it wouldn't be the first time someone snuck a guy into the girls' dorm. I decided not to bother them and instead grabbed Dallas' phone to take a quick picture. She was the type to love stuff like that, and she'd most definitely thank me later.

After getting ready for the day, I barreled to my car. The drive to the mall seemed to take longer than normal, and the parking lot was more packed than I'd prefer. The amount of people already here on a Sunday forced me to park on the side, away from the entrance. It was bustling inside, and I realized I had no idea where I was supposed to meet Rune.

I pulled out my phone and dialed Rune's number. The ringing chimed in my ear as I reached the middle of the mall. The coffee shop was stationed in the center, and at one of the tables sat Rune. He was sipping a cup of coffee as he glanced at his phone.

I cut off the call as I approached his table with my heart in my throat. "Rune. Hey."

He looked up at the sound of my voice, and his golden eyes brightened a fraction when they met mine. "Bria. I'm glad you made it." He gestured to the beverage shop and asked, "Do you want a coffee or anything?"

I took the seat across from him with a warm smile plastered to my lips. It seemed to have gotten stuck there ever since I saw him sitting here. Shaking my head, I said, "I'm okay for right now."

"How are you feeling today? Is your head still sore?"

I felt the color rise to my cheeks. Glancing away, I gave a nervous laugh and ran a hand over the bump on the back of my skull. "I'm feeling good. The swelling has gone down some."

"Good. I'm glad to hear that."

He took another drink of his coffee before setting the cup aside. His eyes found mine again, and this time, the air suddenly changed. The spark that had been in his eye was gone and replaced by something colder. The atmosphere took on a note of seriousness, like that of a business meeting. I found myself suddenly on edge and confused by this swift change as Rune leaned forward in his chair with his hands folded on the table.

"I'm glad you agreed to meet me. There's something I wanted to talk to you about."

I hesitated as I tried to get a grasp on that look he was giving me. It was devoid of any warmth, comradery, or emotion. His gaze was … *empty.*

"O-okay. What is it?"

"I need you to pretend to be my girlfriend."

My mind stuttered in a futile attempt to process his words. "Excuse me?"

He gave a heavy sigh and explained, "It's a long story. I just need you to pretend to be my girlfriend for roughly two months. We'll spend the first few weeks letting you learn what you need to about me, and then we'll go to my hometown in Massachusetts to celebrate my birthday. It'll be a weeklong trip during the last week of October. My mother is expecting to play matchmaker, and I can't let that happen. I'll be forced to marry this person and start playing house with them. A wife and kids isn't in my life plan, so I need you to pretend to be my partner for the time being. If I already have someone, my mother can't set me up with anyone or force me to settle down."

I threw up my hands and shook my head. "Hold up! I'm not going to just go somewhere with you when I don't even know you!"

He chuckled. "Yes, yes. Stranger danger and all that. But again, we have roughly two months before then. We won't be strangers for long. Problem solved. You'll be my girlfriend for this trip, and after the two months, we can part ways, never to have anything to do with each other again."

This meeting was *not* going the way I had planned. The smile that had previously been plastered to my face was wiped completely clean as I stared dumbfounded at the man before me. This had to be a dream, or rather, a nightmare. Was this really the same guy I'd felt a spark with just 48 hours ago?

Narrowing my icy eyes on him, I asked, "Why don't you go get an actual girlfriend to take home?"

Irritation pricked the corners of his eyes. "As I've already explained, I don't want an actual girlfriend. I have my life—one I don't want to share with some girl just because my mother thinks I should. Thus, here you are. If I were to ask some other random girl, she could potentially get the wrong idea and think this arrangement is more than what it really is. You, however, have something to gain from this just as much as me, and because of that, I think you'll understand that this is strictly business. Nothing more."

"What could I possibly have to gain from this ridiculous idea?"

He smirked and dug out a small box from his bag. "I'm glad you asked."

He slid it across the table for me to grab. I narrowed my eyes at him then slowly opened the lid of the metal container. Inside were stacks of hundred-dollar bills. My eyes went wide as I snapped the lid closed and looked around us frantically.

"Are you out of your damn mind? Why would you have me open something with *that* inside? Are you not at all worried about prying eyes, especially after what happened before?"

He gave a small laugh and pulled the box back across the table. "I'm not worried about someone trying to steal it if that's what you mean. In fact, I'd love to see them try."

Arrogant asshole.

I glanced at the box then back up at him. "What is that even supposed to mean to me?"

"That," he said, pointing at the container. "Happens to be exactly five thousand dollars. In other words—"

The air in my lungs caught, and the world around me seemed to stop as I whispered, "Italy."

CHAPTER

TEN

I held Rune's gaze with wide eyes.

My trip.

My dream.

He had it right there.

I sat frozen in complete shock for so many reasons. First of all, how the hell did he have that much money to hand out to a stranger like me? That was a lot, and it brought up the question of why he was willing to spend that sum just to secure a fake girlfriend. Sure, an arranged marriage would have anyone dragging their feet, but to pay five grand to avoid it .... Maybe Rune had figured out how to grow money on trees, and therefore had an abundance. Not only was that puzzling, but I was still reeling from how drastically different he was now than how he'd seemed before. The

flirtatious gentleman had been replaced by an annoyed busi-
nessman. My head practically spun from the way the last five
minutes had played out.

I took a deep breath and said, "Let me get this straight. You
will give me five thousand dollars, all for pretending to be your
girlfriend?"

"Correct. Your trip will be paid in full, and I'll be happily
single with no restrictions on my life once this is said and done.
It's a win-win for us both."

Two months.

Two months of hanging out with this douche canoe and
pretending to be smitten with each other. That couldn't be too
hard, and it would be far easier than my plan to gather the
money via minimum wage jobs and selling paintings while trying to stay on top of school. But to go on a weeklong trip with
him? That's where I started to falter. There were way too many
unanswered questions and worries that came with something
like that.

I glanced back at the metal box, and I swallowed hard. My
worries were suddenly cracking.

I met his eyes again. "Well, I have school, so how am I supposed to leave for a week?"

"Are you doing poorly in school?"

Crossing my arms, I tilted my head up proudly. "No. I have
a perfect GPA and attendance."

"Then it won't hurt you to miss for a week. I'm sure you'll
be able to easily make up whatever you miss. You strike me as
the studious type. I bet you even do other people's work for
them."

Cocky bastard, thinking he knows everything. I bit the inside
of my cheek and ignored his spot-on comment.

"Anyway," he started, taking me in with those vivid eyes.
"We'll have a lot of work to do since we'll obviously need to

look like we've been together for a while. My plan is for us to spend every single day together from now through the trip, so let's try to get along. For now, we'll start with this."

He pulled out a folder with a packet of paper and handed it to me. Inside, I found a list of questions with answers beneath each of them.

He leaned forward as he explained, "That's a packet about me. It has everything you need to know from the smallest things like my favorite color to something like my greatest fear. I found the list of questions online and thought it was as good of a start as any."

I feigned shock, covering my gaping mouth with my hand. "Oh? Rune's actually afraid of something?"

He flashed me an unamused look. "Everyone is afraid of something. Fear is inescapable and can bring even the strongest of men and women crashing to their knees."

I nodded, mumbling my agreement, as I flipped through the packet. He really had included little things like his favorite color, food, music, and things to do. It got into deeper insights too, such as his biggest regret and his greatest wish.

I glanced at everything in the packet before setting it back down in front of me and studying him across the table while he sipped his coffee.

When he swallowed, he cleared his throat and said, "Well, I guess I'll go now. You can take the rest of the day to memorize everything on there."

"W-what? I did not drive all the way here just for you to disappoint me, hand me a packet, then send me on my way."

He cocked an eyebrow at me. "Well, what's the point in continuing if you aren't familiarized with me and vice versa? You can focus on memorizing that list and answering the same questions about yourself for me."

He started to stand, but I wasn't letting him leave.

Glaring at him, I shot to my feet. My palms slammed onto the table, and I leaned forward until I was in his face. "Your favorite color is blue. Food: fish. Music: classical. Thing to do: read. Worst fear: losing what you cherish most. Life's wish: to find something worth living for."

I spat every answer to every question at him without missing a single one.

His eyes widened as he took me in, and his mouth hung slightly open in shock.

When I finished, I added, "And other things that your little packet fails to mention are that you're an arrogant, condescending bastard who likes toying with people with no regard for their feelings."

With that, I sat back down proudly in my chair, fuming with quieted rage. As much as I wanted to storm off, the shock on his face was enough to make me want to see more. Plus, the money still called to me. A few people walking by shot us concerned looks, but I ignored their stares. I crossed my arms over my chest and narrowed my venomous eyes at Rune. My skin was practically on fire with anger simmering beneath the surface.

His eyes were still the size of saucers as he finally stuttered, "H-how did you memorize all of that when you barely even glanced at it?"

"This is why we should actually talk instead of reading stupid packets off the internet. Maybe you would've learned from normal conversation that I have a photographic memory. All I needed to do was glance at your ludicrous questionnaire to know everything it said."

The dumbfounded look left his face, quickly replaced by fascination. "Impressive. Well, I guess it won't take as long as I thought it would for you to learn stuff about me. I wish I had that handy-dandy skill."

I didn't even try to contain my eye roll. What a freaking jerk. I couldn't believe I'd thought he was a cinnamon roll.

If he was a cinnamon roll, he'd be one I let burn in the oven until it turned into black, crispy ash.

Dealing with him was turning into more and more of a pain with each passing moment, and I wasn't sure if upholding my end of the deal was worth putting up with him.

The metal box stared up at me.

Italy.

Luca Romano.

My dream.

I groaned inwardly. It was just two months, and really, what was two months in comparison to living the rest of my life as a painter. Anything would be worth living that dream. Even putting up with an asshole like Rune. I had to do this. I had to deal with him.

Rune plucked the box from the table and returned it to his bag as he got to his feet. "The next thing I had planned was bringing photos of my family for you to learn their faces and names, but I don't have them with me since I thought you'd need all day to study that packet. We can continue tomorrow."

I uncrossed my arms and quickly stood up, too. Even after all that, he was going to leave and waste my time? Frowning, I asked, "You're still leaving?"

He gave me a cocky grin. "Does that sadden you? Were you hoping to spend even more time with me? As I explained, we aren't actually a couple."

My fingers dug into my palms, and my teeth ached from how hard I clenched them. "I know that! I just—"

I took a deep breath as reality started to finally hit me. He only wanted to meet me for *this*. A business deal. My dream in exchange for his freedom. But I also knew it didn't start that way for him. It couldn't have.

Holding his eyes, I said, "When you sat down at my table at the club, you didn't know about Italy yet."

"I didn't, no."

"So what was that? What was all the dancing and flirting before that?"

Silence stretched between us for a long moment. He held my eyes, and I could see him weighing how to say his next words.

Finally, he answered, "I enjoy being single and having a good time. Infer that how you like and fill in the blanks."

My heart deflated. If my hopes for how this meeting would go hadn't been tarnished before, they were completely shattered now. He'd initially approached me to be a hook up. His plans only changed after he realized he could use me for his plan—a plan that would let him continue the lifestyle he had. No wonder his friends had seemed shocked when he'd asked for my number. That was obviously something he never did.

Because he just hooked up.

The reality of our initial meeting was a sucker punch to the gut. In an instant, my anger fizzled out until all I felt was embarrassment. I'd been excited for today. I'd been optimistic that this interaction would go somewhere, and while it definitely *was* going somewhere, it was nothing like what I'd expected. What I'd *wanted*. I'd never felt so stupid.

Shaking my head, I bit the inside of my cheek to focus on the physical pain instead of the piercing ache in my heart. "I get it. Okay. Go. I don't want to see your annoying face anyway."

"Tomorrow then. We can text about the details. See you around, Bria."

"Good riddance, Rune."

I listened to his fading footfalls as he walked away. I slumped down in my seat and picked at the corner of the packet in front of me. A twinge of disappointment tugged at me beneath the humiliation, and I didn't know why. What was I hoping for? A day with Rune? No, not anymore. He was a self-centered jerk. I was glad he was leaving after seeing what he was really like, so why was it that part of me wished he would turn around and come back?

It was probably the same part of me that thought there was some sort of decency in him, even after seeing his true colors today. I'd wanted to see *that* version of Rune. The one who smiled and apologized for bumping into a stranger. The one who liked dancing with me and holding me close. The one who came to my aid during the frightening robbery. But maybe that version had been a lie all along. Just a ruse to get me in his bed until he realized I could be used for something else.

It would be worth it though. It had to be. As soon as this was all over, I'd make my dream into a reality. There would be no more worrying about where I'd get the money for Italy because Rune was practically giving it to me on a silver platter. All I had to do was pretend. I could do this. I could push past the anger, disappointment, and my attraction to him for the sake of my future.

I tapped my finger on the table and decided to make the most of the day. I was at the mall after all, so I figured I could look around at the stores and perhaps gather some supplies to start on my fox painting. Maybe I'd even go to the creek to paint later, and hopefully, I'd find the fox there. It would be nice to see his face again and make sure he was still doing okay.

Preparing to stand, I looked across the mall, and instantly, the blood drained from my face. Up ahead, walking in my direction, was a group of four guys. Two of the men in the group made my blood run cold and my heart sink with a heavy dose of panic.

It was *them*.

Blake and Allen.

CHAPTER

ELEVEN

A s soon as I realized who they were, Blake seemed to look in my direction. He stopped laughing and nudged Allen, who followed Blake's gaze to me. When our eyes met, something dark and malicious overtook his expression. Allen patted the other two guys' shoulders and pointed at me. All four of them stared at me now, and bile rose up in my throat.

They started walking in my direction, making me snap out of my trance. I quickly grabbed the packet and my bag before jumping to my feet. I turned and walked as fast as my legs would carry me toward the exit. My heart begged me to run, but if I did that, it would draw unwanted attention. Attention that would spark questions with an explanation I wasn't sure how to give.

If I said these guys had tried robbing me, any passers-by would be too confused because they could clearly see that none of the boys were currently trying to rob me. I'd look crazy or paranoid to anyone here because they didn't know what occurred nights ago.

I closed my eyes as the fear inside of me grew to new heights. Were they close? Were they still following me? I glanced over my shoulder. They were still on my trail, laughing at the thrill of the chase. I faced forward again and somehow forced my legs to move faster. I had to get out of here. I had to get to my car.

When I made it outside, there was hardly anyone in sight. Just endless rows of cars. I clutched my bag as I took off in the direction of my Altima, and I dug my phone out of my pocket. After one of the officers took my statement at the club, he'd given me his business card with his number, should I remember anything else. I dialed that number now, preparing to give him this new information. I dared a peek over my shoulder, and an icy chill traveled down my spine when I didn't see the guys. Not knowing where they were was almost worse than knowing they were right behind me.

Reaching my car, I frantically dug around in my purse, looking for my keys. The first ring of the officer's number sounded in my ear as my hand clasped the cold metal at the bottom of my bag, and a relieved laugh escaped me until hands went around my arms. A scream instantly built on my lips, but a hand was quick to cover my mouth. Allen threw me on the ground by my car, hiding us from the view of anyone who might be passing by. His friends were laughing and helping to hold my hands down on the pavement while Allen picked up my phone and ended the call.

Allen yanked me to a sitting position by the neck of my shirt. The curl of his lips hinted at his wicked intentions as he said, "Fancy running into you here. I'm glad we did." He glanced at my phone again then met my gaze as his face fell into a serious scowl. "Snitch."

"Go to hell!" I spat.

My chest rose and fell in heavy gasps. Fear coursed through my veins as the gravity of my situation hit me. I was being restricted by two men and faced down by Allen, who no doubt planned on making good on his promise from Friday night. Tears pricked the corners of my eyes.

I wouldn't be leaving here alive.

One of the other guys started laughing when he saw how frightened I was. He nudged Blake and said, "Hey, look at that. I love it when they cry."

Blake went pale and swallowed hard as he met my pleading eyes. "Maybe we should go, guys."

Allen laughed and spat, "You're such a pussy, Blake. She may have tattled before, but she won't be doing that again."

Allen reached into his pants and flipped open a pocketknife. The loud snap of the blade opening made ice freeze my veins, and one of his friends quickly covered my mouth as I went to scream.

Allen laughed and ran the blade of his knife along my cheek, just hard enough to incite fear but not actually break skin. I squeezed my eyes shut, tugging against the two strangers' grips on me. They laughed at the sight of my horror and rejoiced at my inability to fight back.

Somewhere in the distance, I heard what I thought was a car door closing. I prayed that whoever was there would see or hear the scuffle and come running to help me, but as the seconds ticked by, doubt seeped into my hope. I was alone. No one was coming.

"I'm going to have fun slicing you up. Then Blake can have a turn. Then Jake and Garrett can have a go. Your boyfriend isn't here to save you this time," Allen taunted.

"Think again," Rune snapped.

Rune emerged from behind my car, his eyes alight with sheer rage. He yanked Allen back by his hair before swinging his fist hard against my attacker's stomach. Allen doubled over in pain, and while he was bent down, Rune swung his fist at Allen's face. Allen collapsed beside my car as Rune arched his leg back in the air, smashing his heel in Blake's face. Blake fell backward, landing unconscious on the ground. The other two rushed Rune at once, but he easily dodged them before smashing their heads together with a dull thud. They fell to the ground in a heap until all four lay unmoving on the asphalt.

My body shook uncontrollably, and tears made a mess of my face.

Rune looked back at me. His anger dissipated into a worried frown as he slowly bent down in front of me. He reached for me, but I was so shaken that I recoiled from his touch. My face fell into my hands as I hiccupped my tears.

This was so much more than being scared. This was an almost tangible, paralyzing terror that stole my ability to breathe or think rationally.

"Bria," Rune whispered, his voice laced with concern.

My eyes met his through my fingers.

He reached for me again, hesitating a moment to silently ask for permission to come closer, and I held still as he tucked a strand of hair behind my ear. He slowly came closer to me, and only after gauging if I was okay, he gently wrapped his arms around me. He hugged me to him, and I let him, despite my previous frustration with him.

The sudden feeling of security I got in his arms was like the first rays of sunlight breaking through the clouds after a storm. It was what I needed in that moment, and the unexpected rush of safety filled my eyes with fresh tears. They fell along his shoulder, and he let me cry there. He made no move to push me away, and he made no snarky comment. He held me close, trailing a soothing circle along my back.

After grabbing my phone from the asphalt, Rune scooped me up, bracing me against his side so I could walk on my shaky legs. He turned away from my car and walked through the parking lot until we came to a black McLaren. After opening the passenger side door, he sat me down in the seat. Coming around to the drivers side, he got in before starting the car. He pulled out of the parking space and took off down the road.

"Why didn't you call me and tell me they were chasing you?" His voice was surprisingly gentle as he broke the minutes of silence.

I closed my eyes, swiping at another escaped tear. All I could do was shake my head. I couldn't find the strength to stop trembling, let alone the ability to speak in coherent sentences. Anyone else would have thought I was freezing, but it was pure shock that caused my body to keep shivering. I didn't know if it would ever stop.

I had almost *died*.

Rune gave a heavy sigh. "It's okay. I can take you to the police station to put another report in on those assholes. Or, if you want, we can go to my house until you feel better. Just tell me what you want me to do."

I closed my eyes and tried calming down as we drove. The sinking pit in my stomach made me want to vomit, and my attempts at breathing slowly didn't help. My nerves were rattled. I could still feel that cold, metal blade against my skin.

"I don't want to talk to anyone right now. I'll call the officer later. I just want to get away," I whispered.

He paused, then gave a small nod. "My house it is then."

CHAPTER
TWELVE

When we reached what I assumed was Rune's house, he got out and came around to my door. The home was situated in a private section of land shrouded in the cover of trees. The home was a single-story brick house. It was quaint, peaceful, and not at all what I was expecting.

My legs still felt like jelly as Rune guided me out of the car, so I had to catch myself on the door. He quickly helped me get my footing before walking with me to the house.

As soon as we walked in, we were greeted by a huge smile and Japanese greeting from his friend I remembered to be Akira. When Akira saw the state I was in, though, his face fell.

Glaring at Rune, he put his hands on his hips and snapped, "What did you do to her?"

Rune bared his teeth at Akira as he walked me through the entryway and into the large living room with a very comfy couch. He sat me down and glared back at Akira. "I didn't do anything. Those same bastards from the club showed up at the mall."

"Oh my gosh!" Akira fell onto the couch next to me and hugged me tightly before pulling back to look at me with concerned eyes. "Oh sweetie! Are you okay?"

At that same moment, Rune's other friend from the club came into the room from down the hall. He had his long black hair pulled up in a messy bun on the top of his head, and he looked like he'd just gotten up for the day. As soon as saw me, he looked at Rune. He pointed a finger at me and asked, "What did you do to her?"

Rune groaned and pinched the bridge of his nose. "Again, it wasn't me."

"Bassel, honey," Akira started as he rubbed my back in a reassuring pattern. "She was attacked by those animals from the club again."

Bassel stood in front of me and peered down. "Are you okay?"

Before I could answer, a third and unfamiliar redhead came into the living room. He hesitated when he saw me before finally moving to the high-backed chair, watching me carefully. He glanced at Rune while tugging on his hair in a nervous fit and whispered, "What did you do?"

Rune threw his hands up in the air. "What is with you guys? I didn't do anything!"

Akira rolled his eyes. "Well, you *are* the asshole that's forcing her into being your girlfriend."

Despite myself, I laughed. It was funny, in a way, how everyone here knew Rune's *charming* personality so well that they blamed him without a second thought. After I laughed, all four of them looked at me.

Akira beamed at me and said, "Lookie there! We made you smile!"

"So," I started, looking between the friends. "You guys know about the fake dating deal?"

"We do," Bassel answered hesitantly. His eyes were sympathetic as he continued, "We'll be going on that trip with Rune to his hometown, so we know about his whole plan to pose as a couple with you. It's really great of you to agree to help. I'm sure it sucks being roped into this."

I nodded at the accuracy of that statement. The only thing that didn't suck was the money I'd get from the arrangement.

Akira placed a hand on my arm, turning my attention back to him. "I know our first meeting was unusual. Let me reintroduce myself. I'm Akira, one of Rune's roommates and best friend. That's Bassel," Akira explained, pointing to the familiar face.

Bassel gave me a friendly wave. "Nice to meet you. Officially, that is."

"And that," Akira said as he pointed to the redhead who quickly averted his eyes, "is Marlow, another one of our roommates."

"It's nice to meet everyone," I said as I gave them each a nod.

Akira turned to Rune, who still stood by the couch. "Why don't you go make some coffee or something warm for our sweet Bria here."

Rune shook his head and mumbled, "Yeah. Okay." His honey-colored eyes softened as they met mine. "How would you like your coffee?"

"Black is fine."

He cocked an approving brow at me. "Really? You have good taste. I'll be back in a minute."

As Rune left for the kitchen, Bassel sat down on the other side of me. "So what happened?"

My dismay was quick to resurface at the thought of what had transpired, but Akira quickly leaned across me to slap Bassel on the side of his head.

"Ow! What was that for?"

Akira rolled his eyes and dropped his head into his hands. "Don't ask her what happened. You have absolutely no tact. She can tell us when she isn't still scared shitless."

"I like being scared," Marlow said.

We all looked at him. He was staring at the wall with a deranged smile.

Akira let out a sigh and shook his head. He pursed his lips, looking bored with his friend. "Yes, well, that's because you're a weirdo."

I raised a brow at their odd exchange, and Akira gave me a reassuring look. He patted my knee and said, "Well, if you're going to be hanging out here for a while, why don't we all do something fun?"

Bassel rolled his eyes and asked, "Like what? We each have different ideas of fun, you know."

Rune entered the room with a tray of five steaming coffee mugs. He set it on the coffee table in the center of the room. Three of the drinks were sandy colored, and two were a deep black. Rune stood up straight, and I noticed he took one of the black mugs. I mentally filed that away. He may be questionable in a lot of areas, but he at least drank coffee the correct way.

The boys started suggesting different ideas for ways to pass the time, and while they did, I noticed a text from Dallas. She thanked me for the photo I took of her and Rance sleeping, and I let her know that I was hanging out with Rune, to which she sent a winky face. I rolled my eyes and put my phone away. I wish it was winky-eye worthy, but instead, our time together was a complete one-eighty from my hopes. Dallas would, no doubt, be very disappointed when I came back with no juicy details about mine and Rune's first hang out. Well, other than the attack. *That* she'd flip shit over.

"How about a movie?" Rune asked after Marlow's suggestion of playing Go Fish.

"Great idea!" Akira said, clapping his hands eagerly.

Rune smirked. "Good. I'll pick it out."

Akira stopped clapping and clutched his forehead again. He shook his head. "Not a great idea."

"Why not?" I asked.

Rune was already picking a movie off the shelf and sliding it into the DVD player. He glanced over his shoulder and asked, "Do you like scary movies?"

Akira rolled his eyes and threw his hands in my direction. "She literally just got done being scared over something traumatic! Why the hell would you pick a scary movie? Are you seriously that demented?"

A scary movie? While I didn't prefer scary movies, the idea was actually appealing right now. If I was too busy being scared of the film, I wouldn't have to dwell on what had happened. Replacing one scary event with a different kind might be the perfect distraction, and I wondered if Rune had secretly thought that, too.

I swallowed hard and said, "No. It's fine. I need to learn about Rune anyway. Watching his kind of movie will help me do that. I can see what kind of sadistic mind he has."

Akira chuckled at that and said, "I like you, Bria-chan!"

I accepted the compliment with a small laugh, and he handed me my coffee mug. He got one for himself as he moved to the love seat. Rune took his spot by me as the movie lit the dark living room. I swallowed hard and found myself involuntarily drifting closer to Rune throughout the previews.

Yup. I *really* hated scary movies.

Rune glanced at me and whispered, "Don't come closer. I'm allergic to scaredy-cats."

Bassel scooted closer to me on my other side and smiled. "I can protect you."

Marlow scooted to the edge of his chair and said, "No! Let me. I can be brave too."

Akira rolled his eyes and held his arms open wide. "Bria-chan, come over here with me. Those two idiots next to you are way too girl-crazy. I'm your safest and funnest option here."

Bassel pointed a finger at Akira. "Excuse me, I'm not *just* girl-crazy. I'm boy-crazy, too. Rude."

Marlow waved a small finger in the air. "I was just going along with Rune and Bassel. I'm not girl or boy crazy."

Akira gave Marlow a comforting nod. "I know you're not, buddy. Don't worry. That's why I didn't include you in that."

Laughing, I got up from the couch and went over to the loveseat.

Akira welcomed me as I fell into place next to him.

He wrapped his arms around me and whispered, "I'm scared of horror movies, too. I don't like being alone through them, either."

After the exchange, Akira and I turned to the TV as the movie got started. Akira made funny comments or faces while we sat huddled in a nervous bundle. He constantly had me smiling or laughing, but we made sure to giggle quietly so we wouldn't disturb the movie for the others.

At one point, I glanced at Rune and found him watching me instead of the movie. I quickly averted my eyes back to the TV and kept them there for the remainder of the film, refusing to wonder why he'd been watching me. Well, trying not to.

CHAPTER

THIRTEEN

Bassel stretched his arms high above his head as the end credits rolled on the TV. "That was a good movie."

I couldn't tear my eyes away from the now black TV. The idea of going into a dark place alone was suddenly more foreboding than usual. You could forget standing anywhere near the edge of my bed, either. Something would most definitely reach out from under it to grab me. Beside me, Akira matched my expression. We were still clinging to each other, and I didn't think either of us would ever let go. That movie had been an hour and a half of agonizing horror. How the hell did anyone enjoy scary movies?

That being said, my hunch was right. Not one time did Allen or any of the others make it into my thoughts. I was too focused on the anxiety inducing images of the movie to dwell on what had happened earlier. It provided the perfect distraction, and I mentally thanked Rune for suggesting such a film.

Akira looked at me as Rune turned the lamp back on and whispered, "This is why I hate watching movies with these guys. I'm not going to be able to go to the bathroom by myself anymore."

I laughed, and Akira smiled at me. He patted my head and said, "At least I had a fellow scaredy-cat with me. Usually they pick on me when it's just the four of us."

"Because you scare easily," Rune said. He drank the last of his coffee and held the mug out to me. "Do you mind getting me more? I'm going to take the DVD out."

Still in a freaked-out daze, I slowly nodded. When I rounded the corner into the kitchen, I fumbled for the light switch on the wall near me. The room erupted in light, and I let out the breath I'd been holding. The coffee pot was still on and hot, so I poured the brew into the cup. The steam rose from the top while I made my way back.

When I made it to the living room, I noticed Rune was missing. I glanced between the trio, who were still discussing the movie, and started, "Hey. Where did Rune—"

"I'm right here."

Still feeling the scary movie's effect, I jumped at the sound of Rune's deep voice right behind me, not expecting him to be there. The sudden movement had the hot coffee spilling all over my hand. My skin immediately sizzled from the hot liquid, so the mug fell from my fingers and shattered on the hardwood floor at my feet.

Rune came around from behind me and bent down to look at the broken pieces. "Dammit. That was a good mug."

"You scared me! Why didn't you say something sooner?"

He glanced at my hand, which I had clutched to my chest. When he met my eyes again, he asked, "Did you burn yourself?"

I shook my head in frustration and yelled, "No! It's fine!"

He narrowed his eyes and grabbed my arm. He pulled me back to the kitchen and turned the sink on cold water. Looking back at me, he said, "Come stick your hand under the water."

I glared at him. "It's fine. It doesn't even really burn anymore."

His exasperation was clear from his sigh. He walked over to me, grabbing my arm once more, forcing me to stick my hand under the stream of cold water. As soon as the cool sensation touched my skin, the stinging immediately subsided. A wave of ease and calm flowed through me. I could stay there with my hand under the water forever.

"I didn't mean to scare you. I thought you knew I was there. I'm sorry," Rune said, his eyes trained on the floor.

I looked up at him. "What?"

He glared at me. "You heard me. I won't repeat myself."

A teasing grin tugged at the corners of my lips. "Wow. Even Rune can apologize and feel sorry for doing something."

He scoffed, shoving his hands in his pockets. "Of course. I *do* have manners."

He had manners? Where?

I looked back at the water rushing over my hand. The cool splashes nearly made me forget what I was so mad about. "I'm sorry for breaking your mug and for yelling at you. I guess I might have overreacted. I'm still pretty rattled from the past few days and the movie."

He was quiet for a moment. At his sudden silence, I looked at him, and his gaze held mine. His amber eyes sparkled like liquid gold, and I had to catch my breath at the way they burned into me. Time seemed to slip away from us under the hold of each other's eyes. The air stilled, the earth stopped, and all that was left were those golden eyes.

He opened his mouth to say something, closed it, then tried again. "I guess I wasn't thinking about that when I suggested the movie. Or rather, I was trying to make *you* not think about it. A fast-paced movie with a ghost haunting an unsuspecting family leaves little room to think about anything else. I was just trying to, I don't know, distract you."

The implied apology was appreciated, and the sincerity in his words more so. We fell silent again, our gazes never wavering from each other. A warmth started to spread along my skin at the intensity of his stare, but it was shattered when he snickered and said, "You really are a scaredy-cat, you know."

I rolled my eyes and turned off the water. "Thanks."

I made my way back into the living room with Rune following closely behind.

Akira turned around on the couch to face me as soon as I walked in. "Are you okay? Hot coffee spills are the *worst*."

I gave him a reassuring smile and patted his shoulder. "I'm okay. Just a small mishap thanks to my lovely *boyfriend*." I glared at Rune, and he sank down on the cushion of the loveseat, completely unaffected by my words.

"Speaking of boyfriends," Akira said, patting the spot next to him on the couch.

I sat down, and he leaned in close. "Was that guy who confronted Rune on the dance floor at the club a boyfriend of yours at one point?"

I gave a half-hearted chuckle and looked down at my hands. I shrugged and said, "I guess he technically was, but I don't know if you would consider it a real relationship."

"Why not?" Marlow asked.

I glanced at him, then back at my hands. "Well, we never actually went out or had a real, meaningful conversation. The only time he'd ever come see me was to give me his homework assignments."

"Why were you with someone like that?" Akira asked.

"It's a long story."

"Aw, come on! You can tell us."

I sighed and shook my head. "Well, I liked Dax for a long time. Me, him, and Dallas all went to the same high school, so I knew him from there. Being young and stupid, our fleeting conversations between classes and exchanged glances made me develop a crush.

"When we found out which college we'd been accepted to, I couldn't believe we were going to the same one. Dallas told me it was fate, and at first, I didn't believe her because Dax had never really paid attention to me like that before. But then one day, at the end of senior year, he came up to me and told me he'd had a crush on me all this time but was too nervous to ever tell me. He officially asked me out, and of course I said yes. The rest is history."

Biting the inside of my lip, I met Akira's eyes. That was the end of the story, but he watched me as if he were waiting for me to keep going. Sure enough, he gestured for me to continue.

"So?" he asked. "What happened with you guys? What made it fall apart?"

Shaking my head, I looked up at the ceiling. "I guess the fact that it was never real?"

Ha.

I wanted to let out a bitter laugh and give Rune a pointed look. It seemed I'd found myself in yet another fake relationship. That stung, but at least this one would serve me in a good way. *This* one would be different.

Taking a deep breath, I recounted my relationship with Dax in detail. Rune and the other guys watched me patiently as I told them of the manipulation, the cheating, and the lies. Akira squeezed my hand gently as I talked, and the gesture helped me to get the words out. Rune was stoic throughout the retelling, but there were times when I saw something shift in his face. It was subtle, like a tick in his jaw, when I spoke of Dax's unfaithfulness or a sharp inhale when I mentioned how Dax used me.

As if Rune was any better.

Bassel scooted closer from his side of the couch once I'd finished and said, "Maybe we shouldn't have pulled Rune away from the fight that night. Sounds like that guy deserved a good ass-beating."

I laughed and said, "It's fine. Really. I mean, at first, I was upset about everything, mainly at myself for giving in to such an obvious lie, but right after Dax dumped me, I had this crazy—"

I stopped. I couldn't tell them about the fox. Crazy experience indeed. I barely knew these guys, and although they were very easy to talk to, they'd probably have me committed for talking to a fox as if it were a human being. Granted, I wasn't actually talking to it specifically. I was talking myself through the situation, and he just happened to be there to listen with nonjudgmental ears. Convincing them of that was more trouble than it was worth, though.

"What?" Rune asked. Amusement played at his lips. "What happened after that?"

I swallowed hard and gave a dismissive wave. "Nothing. I would probably sound crazy if I told you guys."

Marlow beamed at me. "We like crazy. I'm the biggest lunatic here. You can tell us."

Akira gave me an encouraging nod.

I let out a long breath, debating whether I was actually going to say my next words. Under all of their expectant gazes, I finally relented but decided to omit some details.

"Okay, well, I went to this creek, and I saw this ... this fox. He was hurt, so I helped him. After that, he stayed. He didn't seem afraid, and he sat with me for a while. An actual fox. I spent the time reflecting and soaking up the weird experience.

"After that, I felt better. I can't explain why, but he just made me feel like things were going to be okay. That was when I realized I was better off without Dax."

Taking a deep breath, I dared to look around at all their faces, expecting to see surprise, shock, or, worst-case scenario, concern for my sanity. Instead, every single one of them smiled. Everyone except for Rune. He stared off at the drawn curtains along the windows.

I swallowed and gave a nervous laugh. "See? I sound crazy, huh?"

Akira shook his head and said, "I think that sounds amazing! It sounds like you and the fox had something really special for him to stick around. Do you think you'll ever see that fox again?"

I shrugged. "I'd like to. Who *wouldn't* after something like that? It was so dumb now that I think about it, but before I left, I actually put my favorite necklace on him, kind of in hopes that if we did meet again, it would still somehow be around his neck. That way, I'd know it was the same fox. Although, even if he did lose the necklace, I feel like I'd still know it was him."

"Why do you say that?" Akira asked as he bit his lip, like he was fighting to hold something back.

"Because of his eyes. They were the most striking eyes I'd ever seen." My gaze flicked to Rune who still stared at the window. "His eyes actually look a lot like yours, Rune."

Rune looked sideways at me then. We held each other's gaze, and the more I stared into his perfect, amber eyes, the more they reminded me of that fox. It felt like everything in the room had suddenly slipped into the shadows and all that remained was Rune and me again. I held my breath, waiting for him to break the eye contact, but he didn't. He stared back at me with unwavering attention, and the longer he did, the softer his eyes grew. They no longer seemed judgmental or hard at the edges. They were getting a lightness and tenderness to them, one that both thrilled and confused the hell out of me.

Akira cleared his throat to remind us that others were in the room.

I quickly averted my gaze to my lap as heat swarmed my cheeks.

Akira chuckled and said, "Well, I just thought of a great nickname for you!"

Smirking at him, I asked, "What would that be?"

He jumped to his feet and excitedly threw his hands into the air. "*Kitsune-chan!*"

"*Kitsune-chan?* What does that mean?"

He nodded in approval at his own nickname. "*Kitsune* is Japanese for fox. Cause, I mean, you did hit it off with a fox, so it makes sense. What if you kissed him and he turned into a prince like in that fairytale? That would be pretty interesting!"

I giggled at the idea, but before I could comment, Rune stood up. He gave an annoyed snort. "That would never happen."

Akira made a pouty face. He poked Rune in the chest. "You're no fun."

Rune rolled his eyes, then turned to me. "May I ask you a question?"

I hesitated before slowly nodding. "Sure."

"Why did you save the fox?"

His gaze grew intense, and the question was posed in such a serious tone that it caught me slightly off guard.

I shrugged, thinking it was obvious. "I guess because when I looked into his eyes, the only thing that mattered was making sure he didn't die or get hurt anymore. What animal deserves that?"

Rune darted across the living room until he stood right in front of me. He hovered so close that I was forced to lean back until I was sitting all the way against the couch. He cocked his head to the side, wisps of his white hair falling into his long lashes. "What if that fox really was a man in disguise like Akira said?"

I had no idea what was making him ask such a ridiculous question. Everyone else in the room had large smiles on their faces as they waited expectantly for my answer. Was I missing something? It was like they were all taking the question to heart and expected a real answer. Hell, with the way they all grinned at me, it felt like they may even *have* an answer already in their minds, and I was the only one left out of this seemingly funny loop.

I looked back at Rune. His eyes bore into mine, and they really did mirror that fox's. They were both a crisp amber that promised power and danger.

Finally, I said, "This isn't a fairytale. Magic, animals turning into people, none of that exists. Things like that don't happen in real life."

Rune straightened. His eyes went from sparking with amusement to pinched in confusion. Akira was starting to bounce on his heels, and I could tell that he really wanted to say something. Everyone looked at me, their easygoing expressions replaced with perplexed frowns. What had I done? They were the ones being weird.

Bassel scooted all the way over on the couch until our legs touched. He stared hard at my face as if he were trying to figure something out. He squinted his eyes and said, "Aren't you—"

"Fae!" Akira screamed. He started panting after finally releasing the breath he'd been holding. His excitement went from ear to ear as he said, "You don't have to pretend around us. We're all Land Fae, too."

Eyes wide, I stared at them, waiting for the punchline or something. *Land Fae? What the hell is a Land Fae?* Not following the conversation, I shook my head.

"I'm sorry. I have no idea what you're talking about or what a Land Fae is."

Marlow, Akira, and Bassel all exchanged puzzled glances. Rune was the only one who kept his eyes fixated on me. His brow furrowed as he worked through something in his head. The laid-back atmosphere from earlier was gone, and I found myself suddenly wary of these people as they kept talking about things that didn't exist.

Rune tilted his head to the side slightly and asked, "You're human?"

I stared at them all in disbelief and started to back away from them on the couch. "Yes? What else would I be?"

Rune closed his eyes and let out a frustrated groan. Bassel stood up to stand near Rune and Akira. Marlow followed suit. They all moved away from me across the room and hovered together as Marlow leaned in and whispered, "How is she human? There's clearly an aura around her. I can practically feel the magic radiating from her."

"I thought she was a Salamander Fae like Marlow or something," Bassel said while holding Rune's attention. "I mean, didn't you say she has a thing for water?"

Akira shook his head. "I thought she was Fox Fae like Rune. She and the fox did connect."

"I wondered if maybe she was Water Fae," Marlow offered. "Since she likes the creek so much."

"No way," Bassel argued. "She'd never save a Fox Fae or willingly hang with us if she were Water Fae."

Bewildered and tired, my mind had had enough. I had no idea what was going on, but I did know that I couldn't be here anymore. Something was definitely weird about these guys, and even though they had seemed friendly before, they were freaking me out now. I decided it was best to get out of there as quickly as possible and back to the real world where things made sense.

I jumped to my feet and ran for the front door. I was only a few feet away when a ring of fire erupted all around me. Panic swelled in my chest as I became blocked in by the fiery cage, and my mind raced to piece together what was going on. The orange flames licked at my skin, and a scream lodged in my throat as I prepared for the inevitable burn. But that searing never came. The flames weren't hot, which only spurred more of a panic within me.

What the hell was happening?

The fire suddenly went out, and when it was gone, Rune stood in front of me. He was leaning against the front door with a snarled lip and narrowed eyes. That look of contempt wasn't what had me quaking, though. The flames had moved from around me to dance above his upturned hand.

He *held* the fire, and he was not happy.

CHAPTER

FOURTEEN

Instinctively, I leapt away from Rune, but I collided with something cold and wet. Whipping around, I came face-to-face with something that looked like Marlow, only now his face was painted gold and brown. His eyes were large and glassy, and his skin had a wet layer to it. He looked like a man that was turning into some sort of animal.

Screaming, I darted to the side of the living room, away from him and Rune. The high-backed chair put enough space between us for me to run for one of the bedrooms. My plan was to lock myself in and hopefully get out of a window, but when I reached the entrance to the hall, I crashed right into what looked like Bassel.

Except now he had yellow-striped ears on top of his head and sharp teeth peeking out from his mouth. His hands and the edges of his face were furry and striped like his ears.

My stomach lurched into my throat, and I wheeled around to race back into the living room. Akira came out of nowhere. He caught me with a frown and hugged me close to him. He still looked like himself, but I no longer trusted him, either.

Tugging and shoving at him to get loose did nothing. His alarmingly strong grip held me firmly in place. Bassel, Marlow, and Rune approached us. Bassel and Marlow still looked like half-human, half-animal creatures. My heart thumped against my chest, and I was sure I was five seconds from hyperventilating.

"Bria," Akira said, his voice calm and gentle.

Daring to look at him, I found him frowning.

"Please calm down. Look, we obviously have some explaining to do. Granted, those two morons," he said, glaring at Bassel and Marlow, "should have waited to transform until after you'd heard our explanation."

Bassel shrugged. "I was following Marlow's lead."

Marlow mirrored Bassel's nonchalance. "Rune did his fire thing, so I thought that was code for we could change."

Akira rolled his eyes and muttered, "*Baka*."

There was a slight tremor running through my body, despite my attempts at keeping my fear at bay. "What's going on?"

Akira sighed and stepped away to give me space. He gestured to Bassel and Marlow before starting, "As you can see, we aren't exactly human. In fact, we aren't human at all. We're something known as Land Fae."

The four of them were now congregated in front of me, so I took a nervous step back. "What's Land Fae?"

"We're basically magical beings with special abilities. We can take on human form, Fae form, or animal form. Bassel and Marlow," Akira explained, gesturing to the two of them, "are currently in Fae form. They look human with a few traits of their individual animals."

Bassel stepped forward and flashed his now deadly sharp teeth in a smile. I swallowed hard as he said, "I'm a Liger Fae, originally from Egypt. Don't ask me to speak Arabic, though. I haven't lived in Egypt in centuries, so I lost touch with my native tongue."

Had he just said centuries?

Marlow stared at the floor and hugged himself. He refused to meet my eyes or speak, so Bassel nudged him in the side with his elbow. Marlow's skin shimmered as he glared at Bassel. He mumbled, "She's human."

Bassel rolled his eyes. "Marlow is a Salamander Fae. His—"

"That's Northern Two-Lined Salamander, Bassel. Not just any Salamander. How rude!"

Bassel's eye twitched. "Right. Northern Two-Lined Salamander. My apologies. Anyway, his kind aren't too fond of interacting with humans, hence the reason he never joins us when we go out somewhere."

Marlow glared at him and started arguing that Bassel made him sound lame. Bassel yelled back, and as I took in their exchange, I couldn't help but think they were still the same. Granted, they were some kind of animal freakiness, but they still acted the way they had before. There was an undeniable air of friendliness around them. My concern over the situation was still very much present, but I couldn't deny I saw the same people who had made me laugh and feel included all day long.

Akira stepped in front of me and said warmly, "Now for me! I'm a Raven Fae. I'll gladly transform for you, but only if you're okay with it. I don't want to frighten you any more than the idiots behind me already have."

Seeing that familiar face, I knew there was no way I could ever be afraid of Akira, so before I knew it, I was nodding. I wanted to see each of them for what they really were.

"Okay. I'm ready. Go ahead."

He slipped off his shirt, which I didn't understand until

after he transformed. His brown eyes began to glow an iridescent color before the pupils consumed all the color in his eyes, turning them solid black. At the same time, tiny black feathers began to sprout and grow along the edges of his arms, and his nails sharpened into talons. There was a loud snap then pop as massive black feathered wings shot from his back.

I held my breath, heart racing a mile a minute. Watching him change into this creature was horrifying, but once it was over, his eyes grew warm like they always did.

Akira threw his arms open wide and jumped around in circles, singing, "Huh? Whatcha think? Whatcha think? Aren't I amazing?"

My voice cracked as I joked, "No beak?" I was trying to make light of this situation because if I didn't say or do something, I would commit *myself* to an insane asylum.

Laughing, he waved his taloned hand. "No beak. When we're in Fae form, we don't have *all* the traits of our animals. Just a few! For example, birds like me get our wings, our talons, and feathers in a few places. Canines and felines, like Rune and Bassel, get their tails, ears, sharpened canines, and things like that. Some get a little bit of fur on parts of their body, like Bassel, who has a little of his liger's fur on his arms and chest. Others get less fur, like Rune, who only has fur on his fox ears and tail."

Unease placed it's hand on my shoulder as I really took in Akira's gaze.

Noticing my stare, Akira said, "I know my eyes may seem a bit creepy considering they're pitch black, but I'm not scary. I'm still the same Akira as before. Friendly and totally loveable! We all are."

I took a deep breath and nodded as I processed this information and tucked it away. It was best to gather all the info I could to provide to whoever would check me in at the mental hospital. They needed to know how to treat my delusion because that's definitely what this had to be.

I glanced at Rune then, who was still standing away from the rest of us with a bitter scowl. He looked human for now, but based on all I'd heard, I knew there was more to him. Akira called him a canine, and before, they'd mentioned he was a fox. Briefly, I thought of my fox in the woods. I quickly stomped out that notion, though. There was no way they were one and the same. They were far too different in their behavior. My eyes found their way to Rune's neck as I searched for my necklace but came up empty.

This still seemed far too absurd to believe, but when I tried pinching myself, I didn't wake up. I wasn't dreaming, which meant this was very much real. These guys were Land Fae, magical creatures that looked like animals combined with humans. They were each incredibly beautiful yet terrifying. I mean, how could this happen? This kind of stuff didn't exist.

I glanced over at Rune once more, and curiosity made me wonder what he looked like in his Fae form. Was he just as beautiful as the rest? Was he grotesque, frightening, or alluring? I tried to picture it as he stood there with his arms crossed over his chest, staring at the floor with his face pinched tight.

Akira noticed where I was looking, so he jumped in front of me to block my view.

"Rune over there is Land Fae, too. That being said, his kind can be quite scary when they're angry. He looks pissed right now, so it may be best to leave him alone." Akira looked at Rune and said, "I won't ask you to transform for her, but I'm still going to explain what you are."

Rune glared at Akira from underneath his light blond hair. Chills ran down my body after seeing that gaze. His eyes contained a darkness as he turned his glare from Akira to me. I held my breath, and my knees buckled the more he pinned that look of fiery hatred on me.

Akira moved closer to my side, and he gently wrapped me in his wings. "I don't know what you're so mad at her for, Rune."

Rune stood up straight, meeting Akira's glare head on. "How could she have fooled me? There's no way! She shouldn't have been able to make any of us believe she was Land Fae if she was a mere human."

He glared at me again as his eyes began to glow a bright gold. A trail of flickering flames burst from his hand, and it circled up and around his body. As it passed over his lower half, a large, fluffy, black tail swished behind him. His fingernails sharpened into pointed claws. The flame traveled up farther, circling his upper half. When it disappeared above his head, my eyes went wide. He now had pointy, black ears on top of his head that faded into white to match the shade of his hair. He sneered at me, giving me a perfect view of his canine teeth, which had elongated into fangs.

Akira gave a frustrated sigh and waved dramatically towards Rune. "As you can probably tell, Rune here is a Silver Fox Fae. That's why he's so pissed. You made him think you were a Land Fae like us because you emit the same magical essence as one of us. Fox Fae are supposed to be the wisest and most cunning, so he's irritated that you tricked him. *He's* usually the trickster."

I looked at Akira and pleaded, "I didn't mean to. I wasn't trying to trick anybody. I didn't even know that you guys existed."

"Exactly!" Rune roared. A flame erupted around his hand. "So how the hell could I have been tricked into thinking you were a Land Fae all this time? That's the reason I picked you!"

Bassel took a step in my direction as Akira's wings went tighter around me. If I thought I was afraid before, that fear had nothing on how I felt seeing Rune so livid.

My body shook in Akira's arms, and when he felt my trembling, he clenched his teeth and glared at Rune. I didn't even think it was possible for Akira to genuinely be angry, but I was proven wrong.

Akira narrowed his black eyes on his friend. "Calm down, Rune! You're not helping her feel safe with us."

Bassel stood by me and stared Rune down. "Yeah. There's no need to act this way, man. Just calm down, and put out your fire. Damn. You Foxes are always so hot-headed."

Rune's eyes met mine. They dripped with what could only be described as pure venom, and I really didn't want to find out what would happen when he turned that silent rage into action. Not wanting to see that look in his gaze anymore, I squeezed my eyes shut. I wanted him back to his old self. I wanted the teasing smirk, the sincere moments of honesty, and eyes that grew softer with time instead of harder with contempt. This wasn't the same Rune from before.

There had to be something I could do to turn this around.

Instinctively, my mind went to water. Water always soothed me and calmed me down. I didn't think it would necessarily do the same for Rune, but I had to do something to get him to stop looking at me with such malice.

With a semi-plan in my head, I shoved myself out of Akira's arms and ran for the kitchen. Akira, Bassel, and Marlow protested, but Rune laughed. Was my running from him amusing? His laugh sent chills along my spine as I dug in the cabinets, trying to find a cup. When I found a glass, I held it under the faucet to fill it up. As soon as I turned around, Rune stood in the center of the kitchen. The entryway to the kitchen was blocked by a wall of fire, so Akira, Bassel, and Marlow were shouting from the other side of it.

Something akin to mocking amusement danced in Rune's eyes as he glanced at the glass of water in my hand. He chuckled and said, "That water won't put out my fire."

Taking a deep breath, I dared to take a step forward. He watched me with a curious pinch of his eyes, and when I was an arm's length away, I held out the glass to him. He looked from the water to me as one of his dark fox ears twitched in confusion. Any other time, I would've laughed at such an outrageous sight, but right now, I was too on edge to find any humor in this.

I tried giving my best smile but was sure he could see right through it. "Water always helps me when I need to clear my head. I don't know how to calm you down, so I figured I'd get you some water."

He straightened and narrowed his eyes at me. His full tail flicked behind him as he asked, "Why are you not afraid?"

I swallowed as tears pricked the edges of my eyes. I held back that sign of weakness. "I am. I'm terrified, actually, but I don't want to see what will happen if I make you any angrier. If I tried to leave or escape, that would just make things worse I'm sure, so here I am, trying to make things better. None of this makes any sense to me, and to be honest, I still feel like this is a dream or that I'm hallucinating.

"If that isn't the case, though, and this *is* real, I want to understand. I'm sorry for making you so angry and not being what you thought I was. Whatever I have to do to make you calm down and not be so angry, I will do it, Rune. Just, please. Calm down."

His guarded eyes watched me carefully, and I took the chance to look over his fox features again. His fluffy, black tail reached the floor, and from this close, the white tips on each individual hair were clearly visible. The pointed fox ears on top of his head twitched slightly as he watched me. I glanced down at his fingernails. They were still sharpened to deadly points. My stomach churned at the idea of him using those claws to shred my skin, which I wasn't dismissing as a potential result of this meeting.

He glanced down at the glass, then turned his attention back to me. Finally, he narrowed his eyes, and the corner of his mouth rose in a grimace, exposing his fang-like canines. He gave an irritated flick of his wrist over his shoulder, and the flames barricading the door went out.

Akira, Bassel, and Marlow all came running into the kitchen. They were still in their Fae forms, and when they saw that I was alive and well, they gave a unanimous sigh of relief.

Akira's relieved hold of his shoulders quickly straightened as he glared at Rune. "What the hell? I can't believe you kept us out with your fire."

Rune rolled his eyes and left the kitchen.

Marlow dashed over and took me by the shoulders. He gave a relieved sigh after looking me over from head to toe. "He didn't burn you or kill you. That's good."

My eyes went wide, so Bassel punched him in the arm.

Marlow pouted as he clutched his arm. "Ouch! What did you do that for?"

Bassel gestured to me with his furry, striped hands. "Why would you say that to her?"

Marlow rolled his eyes. "Well, I mean it *is* Rune we're talking about. He's a Fox Fae after all. They aren't exactly known for being nice."

Akira joined us, and he hugged me tightly. He let me go and used his feathers to brush away at my clothes, despite there being nothing to brush away. As I watched the three of them interact, I became confident in my earlier decision to still trust them.

Rune was another story.

CHAPTER

FIFTEEN

"**C**an you please explain this to me?" I finally asked. Passing my gaze between the three of them, I took a deep breath. "I don't understand any of it. How is this even real?"

Akira nodded and said, "Of course. Why don't we go sit down in the living room? It would probably be better if you were sitting."

I hesitated. "What if Rune is in there?"

Akira shook his head and rolled his narrowed eyes. "Rune may be scary, but he's all bark and no bite. He won't actually hurt you."

Akira took my hand and led me back into the living room. Rune was leaning against the far wall, glaring at us as we walked in. Akira sneered at him and dropped my hand. He quickly turned, flapping his wings hard. The single beat of the feathers sent a giant gust of wind soaring in Rune's direction. Rune merely rolled his eyes and twirled his hand in the air. At the same time, a funnel of fire met the wind halfway and sliced it down the middle, causing the wind to move out and away from Rune.

Rune glared at Akira. "Why would you try to fight me? First of all, that pathetic human is no reason to pick a fight with your best friend, and secondly, you know that I won't fight back. Not with you at least."

Akira led me to the couch where he had me sit down. My cautious gaze was locked on Rune the whole time. He stared back at me, his eyes dripping with fiery venom.

Akira stood in front of me with his hands on his hips. "She's not a pathetic human. She's your girlfriend for the next two months, so you'd better start playing nice."

My eyes went wide. I was about to argue against him and explain that I wasn't going to do it anymore, but Rune beat me to it.

"That plan is off now. I can't take a human to my house. She isn't Land Fae. Everyone will know she's human. Plus, I don't want to spend any more time with her now that I know the truth."

I tapped Akira's arm. He looked at me, his dark bangs falling into his solid black eyes.

I swallowed hard and whispered, "I don't want to go anymore, either. This is all a bit much for me, and plus, if his family is anything like him ..." I glanced at Rune again.

He narrowed his eyes at me.

Looking back at Akira, I finished, "... I really don't want to go."

Akira threw his hands in my direction and yelled at Rune, "Look what you've done. You've scared her. Now she's going to think that Land Fae are scary, evil creatures. She won't trust any of us anymore, and it's all your fault. Apologize!"

The cool temperature from the glass of water settled my nerves while they bickered. Passing a look around the group, I asked, "Can you explain what you guys are again? Maybe a bit slower this time?"

Akira sat down on his knees in front of me as he said, "Of course. Sorry about that. So, we're all Land Fae, which are magical beings from the land. There are Fae for almost everything, but the two largest classes are Land Fae and Water Fae, which are made up of animals, plants, and, of course, water. That being said, Land Fae and Water Fae don't get along, to put it nicely, so unless you have specific questions about Water Fae, I'd rather not talk about them. Is that okay?"

I nodded. I needed to focus on one thing at a time. Land Fae. I needed to know about what was right in front of me.

"Great! So, Animal Fae make up the majority of Land Fae. You, of course, already know what kind of animals we are. Raven, Liger, Fox, and Salamander."

"Northern Two-Lined Salamander," Marlow threw in quietly.

Akira shot him a quick look before turning back to me with forced patience. "Northern Two-Lined Salamander. Right." He cleared his throat. "We aren't really something you would've heard too much about. Not exactly. There are certain countries and cultures with myths and legends about our kind. They have different names for us and are mistaken about certain aspects of who we are, but it's still interesting to see humans try to figure us out."

A small smile tugged at the corners of my mouth, and I tried not to let on how lost I was. Good Lord, was anything going to be normal after all of this? Probably not. I was most likely going to end up in that psych ward I'd envisioned.

"I know this is pretty hard to believe, but it's all true," Akira started. "We each have special abilities, some of which you've seen. As you can probably guess, the ability of Fox Fae, along with any Fae belonging to the canine family, is fire. They can control everything about it, including what they want it to actually burn, hence the reason our house is not ablaze right now." Akira glanced at Rune with an accusatory look.

I couldn't help but toss a pointed look at Rune, too.

Akira turned back to me and continued, "My ability as a Raven is the creation and manipulation of wind. I attempted to knock Rune down as punishment for being a dick, but as you saw, he deflected it easily. Fox Fae are among the strongest of our kind, especially in regard to will and intelligence."

"They're also full of themselves because their skill goes straight to their egos," Bassel mumbled.

Rune's glare shot daggers at his friend. "I heard that."

Bassel laughed and flipped him off.

Rune sneered at Bassel, exposing his fangs.

Marlow giggled and clapped as he said, "I love it when you two fight. Show me more of your fangs!"

Akira shook his head as he mumbled, "Salamander Fae, along with other smaller amphibians, are extremely weird. They don't interact with humans at all, which is one of the reasons they're so bizarre. Sometimes you have to ignore Marlow. He can be a creep without meaning to be."

Marlow leaned forward eagerly, rubbing his finger over the gold patches on his arms. They shimmered beneath his touch as he asked, "Would you like to see what I can do?"

I didn't have time to respond. He raised his finger, and at the same moment, the water in my glass rose into the air and spun above me. Mesmerized, my eyes were glued to the shimmering liquid. It danced in the air, rising high and dipping low, whisking around in a circle. I could've watched the way it moved all day, but he sadly lowered the water back down into my glass.

My eyes widened in wonder. "That was amazing, Marlow!"

His eyes sparkled. "You think so? It isn't much. Sadly, Northern Two-Lined Salamander Fae can't manipulate a lot of water because we're from the land. Water Fae are Fae who are literally *water* or live within water. I can maybe control the amount of water that would fill a bathtub, but that's pretty much it. That's one of my personal reasons for hating Water Fae. They can control huge bodies of water. It isn't fair!"

Marlow crossed his arms over his chest as he began to pout.

Bassel stood up and approached Marlow to pat him on the back. He gave him an understanding nod. "I know, buddy. It sucks. But we all hate them, so it's okay."

I inclined my head at Bassel and asked, "What's your ability?"

He shrugged. "It's nothing fancy. I can't control some element or anything like that. My specialty as a Liger Fae is enhanced strength and athleticism. I have superior fighting skills, I can jump higher than most, and my claws can cut clean through pretty much anything."

Marlow glanced at Bassel's hand, which still rested on his shoulder. He carefully grabbed one of Bassel's fingers and lowered it. "Yes, so why don't you keep them away from me?"

Akira chuckled and met my eyes again. "As you can see, even though we're a bit scary looking at first, we actually don't mean any harm. Not all Land Fae are bad. Granted, there are some who are evil, but then again, there are humans who are evil, too. We don't want you to be afraid of us, and we're sorry we sprung it on you like this. It was our mistake for jumping to conclusions."

"It's okay. You all don't seem as frightening as I originally thought. Don't get me wrong, you're still pretty terrifying. Just not as much. What exactly gave you the impression that I was Fae to begin with?"

His jaw was rigid, and his eyes hard as he explained, "Every Fae has an aura about them that basically acts like a light. The more powerful the Fae, the brighter the aura around them. You have one of those magical auras. Most Fae conceal their auras for security ever since the war between Land and Water Fae. I assumed maybe you were newly introduced to your powers or that you were so confident in your abilities that you didn't need to hide your aura."

That bit of information was a lot to digest. There was absolutely no reason I should have any sort of magic around me. I was human through and through. There was nothing special about me, at least not in that regard. So why did they sense that from me?

"I'm human, so why would I have an aura?"

"That's what I'd like to know," Rune said.

His amber eyes swept over me like he was looking for an answer or something that would explain the aura around me.

Part of me hoped he'd find something because I was wondering the same thing myself.

Akira fidgeted and asked, "So since you're not too scared of us, would you still consider hanging with us and being Rune's fake girlfriend?"

Rune stepped forward then, shaking his head. "I said no. We can't take her anymore. I *won't* take her anymore."

I ignored him and asked, "Is there more to that whole story, too?"

Akira shrugged. "His mom is a very powerful Fox Fae. She wants Rune to marry and breed with another Silver Fox to keep the purity of their bloodline. That being said, our dear ladies' man over there would never marry, especially not someone of his mother's choosing. Even more than that, he doesn't want to start popping out babies with any woman. Bringing a Fox Fae as his present girlfriend would show his mom that he's thinking about a future with someone, but it's someone of *his* choosing."

I glanced at Rune then, but he refused to meet my eyes. He turned to stare out the window again.

"But I'm not a Fox Fae," I said.

"Exactly," Rune suddenly snapped, looking back at me. His black ear twitched again. "So, I won't use you anymore. You're off the hook. Lucky you."

"Actually," Akira said, rising to his feet. He clapped his hands excitedly. "We happen to have a good friend nearby who is the queen of magical transformations. She could totally turn you into a Fox Fae! At least appearance-wise."

Bassel smirked as he looked at me from head to toe. "I could totally picture you like that. I bet you'd look sexy as hell."

Rune shot an icy glare at Bassel and let out a low growl.

We all looked at him as Bassel chuckled and said, "What? Afraid I'm trying to steal what's yours, Fox?"

What's Rune's? Did he mean me? I was *not* Rune's by any means. Firstly, I wasn't an object to be owned by anyone or anything. Secondly, he was among the least likely people that I'd ever actually be with now that I knew him.

Irritated by the exchange, I crossed my arms and looked away from Rune, mumbling, "I would much rather be Bassel's fake girlfriend than yours."

Rune glared as he stalked across the room, heading right for me. He leaned down close as he trailed his claw down my cheek and said, "Well, too bad. You're my girlfriend, so get over it."

I met his glare head on, forgetting my fear of him. Like the guys said, they would take care of me. I got in his face and spat, "So what? Now you want to go along with the plan all because you're an over-reactive, jealous dickhead? Hell no! I have no idea what I'd be getting into if I went with you to your family's house. Screw you."

As soon as the words left my mouth, I wanted to eat them. I suddenly remembered why I needed to do this. If I didn't go along with the plan and see this through, I wouldn't be able to study abroad. My dream would be crushed alongside my chance to work under the greatest painter of my time. The idea of not being able to do those things when they'd felt *so* close made my insides burn in wretched agony. I needed to do this, regardless of how unpleasant Rune was or how intimidating I found all of this new info.

Akira got down on his knees and made a puppy dog face. "Please come! It would be so boring without you there! All of us will be there with you, so nothing will happen!"

I took a moment to look between them before shaking my head. "This is all too much to take in right now. I mean, I just learned that everything I thought was reality, isn't, and what wasn't reality, is. I need time, and I need to think about what I want to do."

I knew what I wanted. I wanted my future, the one I'd craved since I first picked up a paintbrush. It was just a matter of coming to grips with this new reality and understanding how to navigate it safely.

Akira, Marlow, and Bassel nodded. Rune scoffed and sauntered back to the other side of the room with his tail dragging behind him. That in itself was beyond bizarre. I needed to process everything from today. I mean, how was I supposed to believe all of this and be okay about it? This was huge! It still had me on edge, and my entire body felt heavy with the news of it all.

"Well," Akira said, standing up straight. "Will you still meet Rune every day to prepare? Just in case you decide to come?"

My eyes met Rune, who now regarded me with a blank expression. Turning back to Akira, I slowly nodded. "But it has to be in public. More so now than ever."

"Understood. I'm glad you're being so cool about this."

I held up my glass of water. "The effect water has on me. It's always soothing and helps keep me calm."

Akira patted my head as his eyes glowed iridescent once more. His wings retracted, and his eyes were back to their normal brown. Marlow and Bassel followed suit, transforming back into their human forms. I was glad to see them looking normal again, at least on the outside.

They were far from normal.

All of them.

Including Rune.

Pushing past the shakiness in my legs, I stood up. "I should really head back to my dorm now."

Akira nodded and ran a hand through his dark hair to make it settle back down. Rune stepped forward, his eyes glowing gold again. A flame wrapped around him as he approached us, and when it was gone, he looked human again.

He crossed his arms. "Your car is still at the mall."

I closed my eyes and hung my head in frustration. With a sigh, I met his eyes again. "Crap. You're right."

Bassel shrugged and raised a hand. "I could drive you back to get it if you want."

"No," Rune said, grabbing his keys off the coffee table. "I'll drive her back to get it."

My nerves kicked up a notch, and I took a step away from him. "No. I'd rather Bassel or someone else take me."

Rune glared at me. "You'll either let me take you or you can walk there."

Italy. Luca Romano. Think about the big picture, Bria.

I swallowed hard before slowly picking my bag off the floor. I pulled it onto my shoulder and mumbled, "Fine."

Looking at Akira, Bassel, and Marlow, I gave each of them a half-hearted smile. "Bye guys."

They all waved at me while giving Rune curious glances. They felt uneasy about him driving me, too, which didn't do a whole lot to make me feel better. I turned to follow Rune to the door, but I stopped when Akira called my name.

He fidgeted and said, "I'm sure you already knew this, but please don't tell anyone about us. We don't really want anyone to know about our existence. Since we messed up and said too much before confirming who you are, you're in the knowing club, but others don't need to be."

"Don't worry. Your secret is safe with me."

He nodded, his eyes warming. With our gazes locked, he said, "Take your time figuring everything out. We understand that it's a lot."

A frown was quick to form, despite my attempt at hiding it. Not wanting him to see it, I looked away from him. It was a lot, and I didn't think it was going to be easy to grasp. I mean, I could still see myself spending time with them and coming to terms with everything that they had shown me today, but that didn't mean it was going to be easy. Especially with Rune because he seemed to hate me now, which threatened my chances at getting his money. I had to get on his good side to make sure Italy was still on the table.

With my back to Akira, I gave a quick nod before walking the rest of the way to the door.

CHAPTER

SIXTEEN

Rune and I rode to the mall in silence. My body leaned as far away in my seat as the passenger door would allow, and I glanced at him every few seconds to make sure he wasn't going to lunge at me. His eyes remained fixed on the road in front of us, and his knuckles were white from where he gripped the steering wheel so tightly.

I swallowed hard, trying to think of something to break the tension. Looking at him out of the corner of my eye, I said, "So, you're a fox. That-That's cool. I like foxes."

I like foxes. Nice one, Bria. Real smooth.

He glanced at me but didn't say anything. If the silence wasn't bad enough, his face stayed devoid of all emotion as he drove, making it hard to gauge exactly what was going on in his head.

I let out a nervous breath and leaned my head against the cool window. The passing street lights moved by in a blur, and I tried to make myself focus on something besides the past hours' events. It hurt my head to dwell on what had happened.

Land Fae existed. Magical creatures with special abilities. How could anyone easily cope with that?

They weren't the only magical creatures, either. Water Fae were real, too. It was bizarre to think about. Did that mean vampires, werewolves, and mermaids were real? It felt like my whole world had been turned upside down in a matter of hours.

Daring to look at Rune again, my body relaxed some. He seemed calmer now that time had passed. He drove with one hand, staring intently at the road as he absent-mindedly played with the collar of his shirt. Looking at him like this, I thought he seemed approachable and less aggressive, but I knew that if I pushed the wrong button, that mask could easily turn dark. He wasn't a normal guy. He was a freaking fox.

The reminder of who he was drew up the memory of the fox from the creek yet again. I chewed on my lip as the idea of Rune and my fox being the same person plagued me. The only similarity between the two was the fact that they were both Silver Foxes with golden eyes, but nothing else about Rune pointed to him being the fox. There was no injury to his wrist, which would've been his paw in fox form, and he didn't have the necklace. Still, the uncertainty was driving me mad.

"Can-Can I ask you something?" I whispered.

He looked sideways at me, but he didn't say anything.

I took a deep breath and decided to ask anyway. "Are you the fox I met that day at the creek?"

He sighed and rested one arm on the edge of the door. He planted his chin on his fist. "Maybe. Maybe not."

I groaned, not wanting any half-ass reply after this day. "Why do you have to answer like that?"

He gave a slight smile. "It's more fun that way. Makes it a mystery, and who doesn't love a good mystery?"

I threw back my head against the headrest of my seat and huffed. "Well, Agatha Christie, it's frustrating for me. Are you him? Or do you know him at least?"

He gave a noncommittal shrug. "I might know him."

"If you know him, can I meet him?"

He looked me in the eye briefly before turning his attention back to the road. He shook his head and asked, "Why would you want to meet him?"

I pondered this and bit the corner of my lip. It probably was an odd request. Twirling a small strand of my hair around my finger, I said, "I don't know. To see how he's doing maybe. I would just really love to see him again. He, in a way, is special to me. He was like a beacon of light when I was in an over-whelmed place."

Rune remained quiet for so long that I thought he was done with the conversation. He kept his gaze locked dead ahead on the road with his brow furrowed in deep thought.

My stomach turned in knots. Maybe I'd said too much?

Growing more embarrassed by the minute, I was prepared to let it go when he finally sighed and said, "He might be at the party in my hometown."

My heart skipped a beat, and warmth flooded my veins. "So, you do know him?"

"Maybe. Maybe not."

I rolled my eyes and fell back against the door in defeat. He wasn't going to give me a straight answer, but that was fine. He said I'd get to meet the fox eventually. I couldn't help but feel a little excited about that fact. It was a mystery to me why the thought of meeting him again made me so happy, yet it did. Maybe it was because of how he seemed to really *care* when I needed someone to listen. Whatever the rea-son, fantasies of what he'd be like flitted through my mind.

I hoped that he was kind and warm, the way he'd seemed at the creek.

Then again, I didn't even know if Rune was still going to let me be a part of this, so I might not even get to meet him. A bitter pang hit me in my gut at the thought. Sure, Rune had calmed down now, but that could easily change. What if his family was like that too, or what if they were even worse than Rune? It would be a nightmare, and that could put me in danger for all I knew. Akira, Bassel, and Marlow would be there, but they said that foxes were among the most powerful of the Animal Fae.

How could they protect me against a family of Foxes?

I shook the thought from my head and closed my eyes. There was still so much to think about, and I needed to figure out more about Rune and the other guys. Good thing I had roughly two months to sort through it. All I could do now was learn about them.

When we finally reached the mall, the parking lot was nearly empty. It was dark by now, so the only cars left were either employees' or last-minute shoppers'. Rune parked next to mine. The sound of the idle engine was all that could be heard in the small space.

My eyes were glued to the asphalt next to my car. The rough gravel against my back flashed vividly in my mind, along with the rush of panic that had flooded my senses as Allen and the others attacked me. The aching sting of helplessness and rage were still there, simmering beneath all my emotions, begging to explode.

"Are you okay?"

The quiet tone of Rune's voice startled me. Glancing over at him, I found him watching me with soft, worried eyes. Not expecting to see that expression on him or to hear the gentleness of his voice, I swallowed hard and looked down at my hands in my lap.

"You know," I started, pushing past the emotion clogging my throat, "back in high school, I hated gym or any class that required physical abilities instead of intellect. Sports, not my thing. Running, absolute hell for me. Strength, none to speak of. I didn't see the point in really honing those skills. You never think that one day you might be in a situation where you need to be strong or quick on your feet. Or at least, I didn't."

My emotions were starting to show, so I forced myself to stop and take a deep breath. "You never think you might be attacked one day and need to fight back."

"Hey," Rune whispered.

I met his blazing eyes.

"None of that stuff was your fault. You know that, right? You were being held at knifepoint. There's no way you can be at fault for not fighting back. Same with today. It was four against one, Bria. No one could fight against that."

"You did."

His mouth turned up ever so slightly. "That's because I'm not human. My abilities supersede many things, so that doesn't count."

Turning back to the spot where they'd ganged up on me, I took another steadying breath. "I don't want to be weak anymore. I want to know how to protect and defend myself so that I don't have to rely on anyone else to do it for me."

Glancing back over at him, I made up my mind. "Do you think since we're gonna be spending so much time together anyway, you could train me? You know, to fight?"

He dragged a hand up the side of his face, shaking his head. "Self-defense isn't really my fighting style. I know actual combat techniques and hand-to-hand fighting for opponents on my same level."

"Please?" I turned to face him fully, my eyes practically pleading with him. "If I can learn half, no, even a quarter, of what you guys know, I won't have to feel weak. I won't have to be scared anymore."

His eyes held mine. They were piercing, as if they could see right into me. See the deepest parts of me, see the bitter insecurities as well as my greatest desires. His amber gaze was all-knowing, and for a brief moment, the air in my lungs stilled. I froze, lost in those endless depths, drowning in him.

Finally, he took a breath and nodded. "Okay. We can work on teaching you self-defense."

Warmth flooded my chest, and my earlier fears seeped away, replaced with a new found eagerness. "Thank you. I appreciate it. I also want to thank you for how you helped me earlier with, you know..." I looked out the window at my car.

He understood what I was trying to say, so he shrugged and said, "It wasn't a big deal. Just try to avoid any strangers until you know a few things."

I rolled my eyes and mumbled, "Sure thing, *Dad*." I opened my door and stepped out of the car.

Rune leaned across the console to look at me through the open door. "What time do you get out of class tomorrow?"

"My last class ends at four."

"Then we'll meet after that. Where would you feel safest meeting me, since, you know, you're supposed to be frightened of me now?"

I ignored the slight smirk that played at his lips as he said that last part. I shrugged and glanced at the mall. "We can meet here again."

He nodded and asked, "What time will you get here?"

"Probably around five."

"Then I'll see you tomorrow at the coffee shop at five."

"Five," I repeated.

I dug in my purse for my keys as I stood by my car. Once I got in, the car roared to life, and I stole one last glance at Rune, who still hadn't pulled away. It was odd that he was sitting there, but I chose to not worry about it.

Pulling out of my parking space, I made my way to the exit of the mall. Glancing in my rearview mirror, I found Rune's car following right behind me. My dorm was in the opposite direction of his house, so it was weird that he was going out of his way like this. I shrugged and kept going. Maybe he was heading to the strip near campus to get some food. After a few minutes, I glanced in the mirror again and found him still following me. My eyes narrowed. What was he doing?

When I reached my dorm parking space, Rune circled around the parking lot to face the way out. It hit me then that perhaps he'd come all this way to ensure I made it back safely.

When I stepped inside the glass front door to my dorm, I turned to look at where Rune sat. Not even a second later, his car pulled away. I was rooted to the spot as my eyes followed his red taillights as they grew smaller.

He really *had* been making sure I got in safely. The rush of warmth filling my chest was impossible to stop. He had his sweet moments. If only he would stay that way all the time. The chances of that were slim, though.

I pushed the thought aside and went to make my way up the stairs but stopped short. My eyes were drawn to a shadowed figure lurking in the parking lot. It wasn't odd to see people hanging around so late, but something felt off. This figure was too dark, almost like an inky black shadow covered them, obscuring their features. Not only that, but they seemed to be staring at the dorm, and a shiver ran down my spine as I realized it almost looked like they were staring right at me.

Unease blossomed in my chest, so I quickly spun away from the door. After reporting the weird person to dorm security, I headed upstairs. Even as I got closer to the safety of my own room, there was something I couldn't shake after seeing the dark figure.

I briefly recalled this same feeling of unease when I'd seen the stranger across the club, the one from the tattoo shop. Worry pricked at my insides, but there was no way it could be him. It had to be someone else—or some*thing* else. After learning all I had today, there was no telling if the figure outside was a person, a Fae, or if it was my mind playing tricks on me.

CHAPTER

SEVENTEEN

Since it was late when I got back, I opened the door to my room quietly. The dark silence greeted me, and I kept my steps measured to avoid waking Dallas. I could see her sleeping form lying beneath her blankets, but what really let me know she was already asleep was her snoring. I giggled softly as I shut the door behind me.

I placed my purse down at the foot of my bed before falling back onto the mattress. My eyes were fixated on the ceiling as I dug my phone out of my jean pocket. Flipping through my contacts, I clicked on Rune's name to send him a text.

Thank you for seeing me home.

My phone landed beside me with a muted thud after I clicked send. I pushed myself back up to grab a pair of my flannel pajamas. It was a relief to get out of the clothes I'd been wearing all day and slip into the soft, comfy material. I yanked back the covers of my bed and slid underneath the warm blanket. At the same time, my phone lit up with a text from Rune.

> You're welcome. See you tomorrow ... Kitsune-chan.

I smiled and rolled my eyes, ignoring the warm feeling in my chest, and placed my phone back on the nightstand. I snuggled deeper into the covers, and for some reason, the buzzing giddiness in my chest wouldn't go away. Why was I so happy because of Rune's stupid little text? I wiped away the look and shook my head to clear all thoughts of him. Everything was still too new right now for me to even consider how I felt about any of them, especially Rune.

My mind raced to wrap around everything I'd learned. It seemed so unreal, yet I knew it had to be true because I had seen it with my own eyes. Either it was real, or I was crazy.

I didn't know which of those scenarios I would rather be true.

Somehow, I managed to drift off to sleep, dreaming of the only thing in the world that I could seem to count on. It was still a mystery as to why water seemed to be such a part of me, but it was. Water was my anchor, and in my dreams, it was like I became a part of it. It wrapped me in its cool, easy current, and all the worries of the day slipped away until it was full of nothing but tranquility.

The sound of my alarm ended the peaceful sleep the next morning. Yawning and stretching my arms above my head, I groaned tiredly and climbed out of bed, grabbing clothes. Once I was dressed, I hauled my backpack onto my shoulder and looked at Dallas, who was still lying in bed, snoring. She had an hour before her first class, so I left, hoping she would wake up to her alarm this time.

When I got to my art class, I took my usual seat at one of the long, wooden tables. They were stained with paint, and all of them had shapes and words carved into them from years of use. My personal favorite was a note made by some lonely soul who'd carved his cell phone number with a message requesting any "hot, single babes" to text him. The clutter of the table's surface made you really think about how many people created masterpieces in those very same spots before you, or how many were just here for another college credit. I had a feeling Mr. Hot, Single Babe was of the latter group.

As soon as class started, Professor Lichen informed us that the next project we'd be working on would be pottery. Dread filled me with ice at this news. Clay was not my friend. Painting and works of 2D were definitely my strong suit, not 3D pieces. Sighing, I put on my mental big girl panties. I could do this if I tried. The only thing I needed to figure out was what I could screw up the least.

A vase? A mug? Who knew!

The rest of class was spent picking our brains for A-worthy ideas and sketching said ideas in our portfolio pads. Some students went to the library for inspirational references, and others walked around campus, looking for key elements in nature to replicate.

I remained seated and stared at my blank sketchbook. I chewed on my lip as I grabbed a pencil and started making a rough outline of what was supposed to be a bowl. That should be easy enough to make.

I made quick jerks of the pencil, and after a few seconds, I got lost in my own head. Rune and the world of Fae slipped back into the forefront of my brain. That wasn't helping me right now, and by the time I shook away those thoughts, a fox head stared up at me from my book instead of a bowl.

Groaning, I mumbled, "Get it together, Bria."

The fact that I couldn't focus on anything besides Fae made the day drag by. It felt like I'd aged years by the time four o'clock came. I was beyond relieved when I left my last class of the day, but that also meant it was time to get ready to meet up with Rune. I couldn't tell if I was dreading it or actually looking forward to it.

My emotions and thoughts were a jumbled mess.

I went back to my dorm room, knowing that Dallas would be in her usual Monday afternoon science lab. My reflection in the mirror caught my attention, and my eyes were drawn toward the jeans and school-themed t-shirt I wore. For some reason, I felt like changing. I wanted to look a bit more put together for this meeting. Something more professional, since what Rune and I had was a business deal. Hopefully, he'd see I was taking this seriously, and he'd decide to let me play the part of his girlfriend because I needed the money.

The jeans stayed, but I switched out the t-shirt for a nice pale pink dress shirt. I yanked on a jean jacket over it and pulled my hair out of its ponytail. Slipping on a pair of brown ankle boots, I gave myself an approving nod.

I swapped my textbook-laden backpack for my purse before heading to my car. The sun beamed down on me. I still wasn't quite sure what I'd seen the night before lurking among the shadows, but the bright afternoon made me feel braver to traverse the area.

By the time I parked at the mall, it was five minutes 'til our meeting time. I shot Dallas a text, letting her know where I was and what I was doing, before making my way inside.

The crowd of people was heavy as I neared the coffee shop where Rune and I had met before. Rune was just starting to sit down at a table with his coffee. I held my head high and walked straight to his table. I could play nice. He looked up at me, and my triumphant smile could blind the dead.

He glanced at the time on his phone then back at me. Closing his eyes, he shook his head. "It's only 4:59. I said I'd meet you at five."

My grin cracked, and I had to fight to hide my eye twitch. Was he serious? Working to keep the venom from my voice, I bit out, "Are you kidding me?"

He sipped his coffee and kept watch of his phone. He was quiet, choosing not to answer. The anger simmering inside of me reached its boiling point. I was about to shout at him and take the seat anyway when he met my eyes.

"It's five now. You can sit."

Mentally reminding myself that stabbing someone wasn't nice, I sat down with a bitter huff.

He smirked, his amber gaze taking note of my narrowed eyes.

"Why are you smiling?" I snapped.

"Because I find your frustration amusing."

With a groan, I held my head in my hands. "You are such a freaking pain! Can we please just get on with this so I don't have to see you anymore today?"

He nodded and placed a folder on the table. Opening it, he pulled out all kinds of photos. He laid them each out, facing me. Every photo captured different people, all looking every bit as gorgeous as Rune.

My mouth parted slightly at the sight of all the beautiful people, or should I say, Fae.

When he was done arranging them, he looked up at me. "These are some pictures of my family. They'll all be at the party. I'm sure my mom will have some extra guests there, but you don't need to worry about them." He pointed to the picture closest to me and said, "This is my cousin, Ardley."

Picking it up, I studied the photo. It was of Rune and Ardley, both of them in their Fae forms.

I quickly glanced at the people closest to us and hid the photo. My wide eyes found Rune's, and I leaned in close to whisper, "Are you crazy? You can't whip out photos of you guys looking like this. What if people see?"

He chuckled, and the sound warmed something low in my stomach. I hated that my body reacted this way to the sound of his laugh. He leaned in close to me, and I held my breath as our faces were now inches from each other. His amber eyes flicked down to my mouth before slowly meeting mine again. "Do you think people would see these photos and immediately think we're magical creatures?"

Ignoring the way my skin hummed with his nearness, I considered his question. "No, I guess not. They'd probably assume it's a costume or something since things like Fae aren't supposed to be real."

"There you go then. It's fine. Don't stress over it." He leaned back in his chair and sipped from his coffee.

I swallowed my frantic emotions and turned back to the photo. I couldn't get distracted by him.

Ardley had his arm slung around Rune's shoulder while Rune stared away from the camera with a blank expression. Ardley, on the other hand, was captured mid-laugh, exposing his two fang-like canines. He had dark curls that matched the black fox ears on top of his head. He seemed to be built much like Rune, tall with wide shoulders and well-formed muscles. The cousins matched in all black, too. Ardley's forearm was exposed in the photo, showing a tattoo of a fox head.

"You don't seem too happy in the photo," I noted.

"I just don't like taking pictures. Ardley, on the other hand, loves the attention. That's something you'll notice about him. He's a huge people person and a flirt, so be prepared for him to say inappropriate things to you."

I sighed. "Awesome. Can't wait."

"Ardley is probably the one I'm closest to out of my whole family. We're the same age, so we get along rather well when he isn't being obnoxious."

"How old are you anyway?"

Amusement flickered in Rune's eyes. "I'll be turning 223."

My jaw hit the floor as I stared at him in disbelief.

His grin broadened at my astonishment while he sipped at his coffee once more. He didn't look a day older than 22 or 23, which meant their aging was clearly slowed down. I remembered then that Bassel had mentioned something about not being back to his home in Egypt in centuries. That made a lot more sense now. Fae obviously aged differently than humans.

Go figure.

Looking at him, it was hard to think of him as 222, and I struggled to wrap my mind around it. I guessed it was no stranger than anything else I'd learned about him. I wondered how old the other guys were. Most likely, they were around the same age as Rune.

Shaking my head, I looked back at him and said, "This is so insane. I still can't believe this stuff is real."

He shrugged. "Well, it is. You've already seen the proof, or would you like me to give you another demonstration?" Something dark and mischievous flashed across his eyes.

I swallowed hard. I didn't like what he was implying, so I slowly shook my head. "No. That's okay."

His mouth turned down in a mocking pout. "Fine." He pointed at the photo of him and Ardley again. "Anyway, don't be surprised if he asks you really weird questions, including about our more intimate affairs. Just pretend we've had sex."

I recoiled and felt my cheeks warm. "Why? Can't I say that it's none of his business?"

"You can, but he'll probably pry more after that. That's how Ardley is. He's a curious dickhead."

I groaned and shook my head. "I'll just tell him that we haven't, then."

Rune rested his cheek on his fist as he looked away from me. "He'll know something is wrong if you do that. It's going to be odd enough that I'm bringing home a girlfriend considering I don't date. At all. If you say that we haven't slept together, it's going to be even more obvious that it's fake."

"Why? Do you sleep with every girl?" My heart clenched as the words left my mouth. It took me a moment to realize that the bitter twist in my stomach was because I didn't want him to say yes. Which was odd. Who he fooled around with wasn't my business.

He didn't look at me. His gaze remained fixated across the mall as he scratched nervously at a chain around his neck. He pursed his lips, mumbling, "Not *every* girl."

I frowned at him. "So, if you don't date, that means you just hook up?"

He sighed. "Lots of Fae, and people for that matter, sleep with loads of partners. It's how some choose to operate. I don't want to form any personal or emotional connection with anyone. I'm only ever in it for one purpose, and that's not to form a relationship. Period."

I looked down at my lap, and for some reason, my stomach twisted into knots again. I refused to meet his eyes. It hurt to think that he'd slept with loads of other girls, but I didn't understand why. It's not like we were actually together or that I had any sort of feelings for him. Maybe it was concern for a friend? Yeah, that was it. Concern that he'd get an STD. Or maybe I was hurt because he'd intended for me to be one of those girls initially.

A one-night stand.

"Can we please move on? I don't even know why we're talking about this," he said, rubbing his creased forehead.

I glanced at him and mumbled, "Well, I need to learn about

you, as well as life as a Fae since I'm pretending to be one. It's best I know things like that, otherwise I would've told Ardley that I was a virgin, and that would've ruined the whole plan."

I wasn't sure how I felt about pretending to be sexually experienced with Rune's family. That was something I'd always thought of as personal information, but I guessed it was different in the Fae world. I'd have to practice giving off that kind of confidence and intimacy with Rune.

He met my eyes briefly before looking away again. "Let's move on." He pointed to another photo as he explained, "These are Ardley's parents. They're my aunt and uncle on my mother's side. My aunt's name is Sinopa, and my uncle is Crevan."

Ardley stood in the middle, laughing once more for the camera. His mother, Sinopa, had long, midnight-colored hair that matched the shade of her fox ears and tail. She was tall and slender, and she wore what looked like a Regency-era navy and white dress. Crevan stood on the other side of Ardley. His hair was dark like his son's and wife's, with ears and a tail to match. He was a bit heavier, his belly sticking out slightly. He, like Sinopa, wore Regency-era garb. They almost looked silly wearing such clothes with Ardley standing between them in modern jeans and a fitted tee. Even more jarring was Ardley's vibrant laugh on full display, while neither of his parents even so much as smiled.

"As you can see," Rune began, "my aunt and uncle are very traditional. My mother and grandparents still wear clothes like that, too. They would prefer that girls wear dresses and men wear suits, which is part of the reason that neither of them are smiling in that picture. Ardley is very much a free spirit who does what he wants. The rest of them aren't very progressive."

"Do you dress like that when you go home?" I asked, looking him in the eye. A laugh bubbled up my throat as I pictured Rune in Regency-style clothing.

"Hell no. Like Ardley, I do as I please."

"I figured as much," I said, sarcasm laced into each word.

He rolled his eyes and pointed at the next photo. "These are my mother's parents. My grandmother, Lilith, and my grandfather, Devoss. If you go, don't speak to them. You only speak to them when spoken to first."

I sighed and mumbled, "Great. Everyone just keeps sounding better and better."

I gazed down at the photograph, shocked. Its two subjects didn't look a day over 50. And in the Rune family fashion, neither were smiling.

Why did no one except Ardley smile in this family? Were they allergic to joy?

"Everyone except for you and Ardley have seemed quite …" I paused, searching for the right word. Meeting his eyes, I pursed my lips and finished, "Proper."

He nodded. "They've been around for centuries, so they're all old-fashioned. Granted, I've been here for a little more than two centuries, but that's not long at all in terms of Fae years. You could say I'm the equivalent of 22 in human years. Since I'm, as my grandparents like to say, 'young and naive,' I prefer to move along with the times instead of living in the past. I enjoy modern-day amenities whereas my family loathes them."

I looked at the photos once more. My eyes scanned over the ones we'd already looked at, reviewing their subjects' cold, blank stares. They seemed so harsh and unfriendly. It was clear just by looking at them that they were more standoffish than Rune, which was really saying something. If this was them on a daily basis, I didn't want to see what they were like when they were angry, which they'd most definitely be if they found out about this charade.

My eyes moved to the next picture in line.

Rune explained, "That's my mother, Myra, my step-father, Alvaro, and my two younger brothers. They're twins, and technically, they're my half-brothers. We don't see each other that way, though. The one with glasses is Newt. The other is Greshim."

Myra stood in the back with Alvaro, a dark and handsome man whose frame was quite large. It looked as if he might burst from the seams of his suit. Myra's long, blonde hair just reached the ground, and it matched her fox ears and tail. The nearly white color of her hair stood out brilliantly against her black Regency gown. There was an undeniable beauty about Myra.

As I moved on to the next subjects of the photo, my world froze. The chatter of the mall, the smell of brewing coffee, the thought of Fae. It all dissipated the minute I saw them.

Standing next to Myra was Rune, who wasn't looking into the camera. He smiled down at two small boys, who stared back up at him. Bright grins lit their faces, and their eyes shimmered with unhindered joy. The looks that the three of them wore, the way their faces were turned up in pure bliss. The amount of unconditional love between the brothers captured right there in one small photo. It was enough to make my breath hitch in my throat.

I beamed at Rune. "Your brothers look so excited and happy to be with you."

The corners of his mouth lifted ever so slightly, but it was a look that I couldn't help but think seemed a bit sad. "I guess so. They liked having me around to watch out for them."

"Liked?"

He nodded. "Myra doesn't allow me to come around without her invitation. I haven't seen the boys in three years now."

A deep ache formed in my chest. "Your own mom doesn't let you come over?"

"Family is different with Fae. At least, it is with Foxes. We're selfish by nature, even with our own blood. It's very rare for a Fox to get to the point where they love someone else more than themselves. Myra just doesn't see me or the twins that way. She keeps me away as a way to torment the boys ... and me. She thinks it will help toughen the boys by not letting me 'coddle' them."

I looked back down at the picture, studying his mother again. She looked so young, no more than 40. Despite her beauty, something about her gave me chills, and it wasn't just the information I was hearing from Rune. It was the way her hint of a smile didn't quite reach her eyes, or how her brown gaze seemed to freeze me in my seat through a mere photo. I swallowed hard. Pleasing her must be a huge challenge—one I hoped I could manage.

"Your mother seems—" I hesitated, trying to think of the right word.

Rune filled in for me. "Horrifying."

I looked at him.

He was staring off into the distance again. He nodded and said, "She's cold and cruel to everyone." He paused, swallowing hard and picking at the lid of his coffee cup. "Especially Newt."

"Why Newt?" I asked, looking back down at the picture.

Newt's smile was large as he stared up at Rune, his small hands reaching out towards his older brother. His glasses sat crooked on his face, and his dark suit was ruffled, no doubt from an afternoon of playing.

"Newt has a stuttering problem—something Myra sees as an imperfection. She despises him for 'tarnishing our family name.' She rarely speaks to him or even acknowledges him. She'll purposely try to pamper Greshim in front of Newt to 'punish' him for simply existing. When Akira told you there were evil Fae in the world, he was right. Myra is one of them. She's the one I'm most worried about you meeting, especially since you aren't really Fae like us. She'll most likely pick up on it fairly quickly if we aren't careful."

I swallowed hard. My hesitation was slowly morphing into

bitter rage. The more he talked about her, the less I wanted to go. My blood simmered when thinking about how she treated Newt, and my heart broke for him. I did *not* want to meet that woman. I looked back down at her picture, her dark eyes staring back at me. I felt like she was going to reach right out of the photo to tear at my flesh with her sharp canines and claws.

"You don't have to worry about her doing anything to you," Rune said.

I looked up at him.

His eyes were surprisingly understanding as they held mine. "If you go, I'll be there by your side the whole time, so nothing will happen to you."

Heat rose to my cheeks at the sincerity in his words, so I quickly looked back down at the picture. I cleared my throat, trying to think of something to say to change the subject. "So," I began, looking at the pictures on the table. We had gone through all of them. "Where's your dad and his side of the family? Don't I need to know about them, too?"

He shook his head as he downed the last of his coffee. "My father, Balgair, died 20 years ago. My mother always hated his family, so she doesn't allow them to come around us since he's no longer here. You don't need to know them since they won't be there. It's just Alvaro in the picture, and his family doesn't come around much."

My heart sank. "I'm so sorry."

"For what?"

"I'm sorry you've lost your father and his family."

Rune looked away and shrugged. "It doesn't bother me."

I watched him, mentally repeating his response in my head. He watched other people as they walked around the mall, traveling in and out of shops, carrying loads of bags. His eyes tracked them, but at the same time, he didn't seem to actually see anything. He felt distant and alone in that moment.

My frown deepened as I whispered, "You're lying."

He glanced at me, his brow furrowed. "What?"

I gave him a sad, knowing smile. "You're lying. I know because I tell myself the same thing, too. I was adopted, you see. I tell myself it doesn't bother me that my real family gave me up. After all, it was a long time ago, and I didn't even know them. Why would it bother me, right?" I looked down at the picture of Rune and his family. "But it does. It bothers me more than I can even say. I don't understand how I can hurt so much over people I don't even know. You knew your father. You had so many years with him. It's okay to miss him."

Silence fell between us for a few moments.

I wiped at a tear that threatened to slip down my cheek. I figured he would say some snarky comment about me being a crybaby.

Instead, he said, "You're right."

It took everything in me to keep my jaw from hitting the floor.

His eyes were turned down to the tabletop as he nodded. "It does bother me. Not the part about his family. We were never all that close. But the fact that he's gone. He's never coming back. That part—" He glanced at me, then looked out into the crowd of people once more.

Silence gathered, and I waited, knowing how hard it was to find the right words over something like this.

He finally sighed and whispered, "That part bothers me."

Understanding the sentiment, I nodded and looked at my lap as I fought against the tightness in my chest.

"I'm sorry about your parents."

My gaze found his, and I watched as his eyes softened at the corners.

"I didn't know you were adopted," Rune continued. "That must be hard sometimes."

Clearing my throat, I took a deep breath and fought against

the tears trying to escape. "It is. Some days it's harder than others. Like when I found out about the chance to go to Italy. It would've been nice to call home and tell them the news, but ...."

Our eyes locked, and the air in my lungs stilled. We were being so open with each other, and the usual façade he put up was slowly slipping away. Him being so vulnerable made me feel raw and exposed, as did my own honesty. This was something I never talked about, and I had a feeling Rune didn't either. We had laid ourselves bare in such an honest way. It stirred something within me, something I couldn't give a name to.

Suddenly, he narrowed his eyes. "Don't you dare tell anyone I said anything sentimental like that."

I sighed. The usual Rune was back. "Sure thing. I won't tell a soul. Except for maybe Akira. And Bassel. And Marlow."

He glared at me.

Holding my hands up in surrender, I laughed. "Kidding, kidding."

His features smoothed with my reassurance. Glancing at his phone, he said, "It's only six, but I think we've covered everything that we needed to in regard to my family. I warned you about the important stuff, and you know their names and faces. I know I don't need to go over them again since you have that handy-dandy photographic memory."

"Correct. I have each of them memorized. Speaking of memorizing," I said as I pulled out my prepared document from my purse. "Here's the questionnaire you need for me."

He smirked. "Thanks. Give me a day or two since I can't remember stuff the way you can. For now, we can end things here today. Tomorrow, after you get done with classes, we were all hoping you could come back over to the house. Our friend, the one who specializes in transformations, will be there. She's going to do a test run on you to make sure she can make you look like a Fox Fae."

The thought of being in a house alone with all of his

roommates and this new stranger after learning what they truly were still made me kind of nervous. I preferred to meet somewhere completely public like this, but I figured it would be pretty odd if I suddenly sprouted ears and a tail in public. It would be best to do that in a more private setting like their home.

I finally gave a small nod. "Okay. I'll be there after class gets out."

Rune gathered up all the photos. I realized I was still holding onto the one of him with his mother and brothers, so I begrudgingly gave it back to him. He studied me as he took the photograph from my hands. I stared after the image, feeling a twinge of sadness. It was odd, but that photo had struck a chord within me. Not so much for Myra, but for Rune and the twins. I loved seeing the way Rune looked at his little brothers and them back at him. It captured what I had always wanted in a family.

He closed the folder once all the pictures were inside, and then stood up. "I'll see you tomorrow then. What time?"

Now knowing Rune's nitpicky personality, I said, "*Around* five. Not exactly five, but somewhere around there."

Approval glittered in his gaze. "You're learning. Good girl. I figured we could do some self-defense training tomorrow after the whole transformation thing if you wanted."

Perking up at the suggestion, I nodded. "That would be great! Thanks."

"Wear something that's easy to move around in. Sweats, leggings, whatever." He reached into his pocket, pulling out a small, pink cylinder. "Until you're trained, it might be a good idea to carry this around to put yourself at ease."

Taking the canister, I realized it was pepper spray. "Wow," I started, looking back at him in surprise. "Thank you. I kept meaning to get some but never found time."

"Well, now you have some. And in case anything ever does

happen again and you can't get to that, just remember to always aim for the goods."

I quirked an eyebrow at him. "Excuse me?"

"You know," he said. He glanced down at himself, *way* down, before meeting my eyes with a meaningful look. "The goods. Aim for them."

Cheeks heating, I looked away and waved a hand at him. "Oh, right. Yeah. Will do."

"Well, I guess I'll see you around," he said.

I bit my lip, ignoring the smile in his voice.

"See you tomorrow, Bria."

Rune started to walk past me to leave but abruptly stopped. He looked down at me with his brow furrowed and his eyes searching. Glancing at his folder of pictures, he opened it. I watched as he took out the picture of Myra, Alvaro, him, and the twins.

He watched me carefully as he held the picture out for me. "Do you want to hold onto this one?"

I stared up at him in disbelief. "What? No! I couldn't take your picture. That's a precious photo of you and your brothers."

He laughed. "It's fine. I want you to hold onto it for me for the next two months. Maybe having that picture will help you look forward to the trip, because I still want you to come."

Our gazes locked in an unbreakable hold. The sudden happiness that blossomed inside me was so unexpected, I had to fight the urge to smile. How could his words make me this happy and nervous all at once? I couldn't believe he'd actually said he wanted me to come with them. That was almost like a compliment coming from him, and it sent my emotions into an unrestrained frenzy. I tried blaming all those reactions on the fact that this meant I still had a chance of getting my five thousand dollars.

Nothing more.

I tore my gaze from his and looked at the photo in his

outstretched hand. I was immediately met with the image of Newt's and Greshim's large grins. I slowly reached out to take the picture, and my attention traveled to Rune in the photo. His smile was so genuine, and it was rare that I got to see that kind of look on him. This photo had captured it, allowing me to see the beauty of it for as long as I wanted.

Beaming up at Rune, I said, "Thank you. I'll take good care of it."

The smile he now wore was contagious. Had I inadvertently given my official agreement to go along with everything? I think I had. I prayed I wouldn't come to regret it, though I doubted I could ever come to regret a decision that made him look at me the way he was right now.

He turned and resumed leaving.

My eyes followed him as he walked away. I sank down in my chair, and I couldn't help but notice the tightness that grew in my chest as I watched Rune leave. We had only met to discuss his family and their pictures, but it felt like so much more had gone on and in such little time, too. We had let our guard down and shared intimate emotions. It had gone by so quickly, and I wished that it hadn't. Despite how I had felt when I first arrived, I actually wanted more time with him.

CHAPTER

EIGHTEEN

My eyes were glued to the photo Rune had given me. My cheeks hurt from smiling at it all day. I had brought it with me to art class the following morning, hoping the elated faces would give me inspiration for the piece I was working on. So far, all it had done was fill my head with more thoughts of Rune.

I'd been having trouble getting him out of my head since yesterday.

Which couldn't be a good sign.

Forcing myself to focus, I sketched out a coffee mug in my notebook after abandoning the bowl idea in favor of a coffee mug. Mugs were something I had experience with from high school, so I hoped it would be the easiest to complete. The only thing holding me up was deciding the design.

I looked back at the photograph. My eyes immediately went to Rune. His fox ears stood erect on top of his head, and his fluffy tail was draped to the side. His fang-like canines flashed brilliantly at the camera, revealed only because of his warm smile. Inspiration sparked somewhere in the back of my mind. I glanced at my blank mug sketch, then back at the photo.

Suddenly eager, I got to work with my sketch. I didn't know why I hadn't thought of this before. My head had been full of nothing but this new, fascinating world ever since I'd learned about it. It should've been obvious. My inspiration had been in front of me all along.

I drew out a fox head on the front of the mug, and on the opposite side, I sketched the handle. I labeled each section with the color it would be once I glazed it. The mug itself would be blue, Rune's favorite color, and the fox would be the same beautiful black with white tips as his ears and tail.

My plan was complete, and excitement rushed through my veins. I was actually looking forward to making the mug, and I wanted to try my absolute hardest to make it perfect. Since Rune's birthday was coming up, I figured I could give him the mug as a present. He drank coffee like it was water, so it felt like a good gift for him. I hoped he wouldn't think it was silly.

The rest of the day dragged on. I found that paying attention in class was far harder now that I knew there were bigger things in life than how to write a character analysis essay or the difference between mitosis and meiosis. I mean, things of myths and fairy tales were real. It was hard not to walk around campus, see a squirrel darting by, and think that that little guy could actually be a sexy hunk of a man. Or when I was forced to listen in on a dull lecture about people from history and secretly wonder if that person was actually a mighty Fae. Nothing felt the same anymore.

When my last class of the day was finally over, I walked across campus to my dorm room. Dallas was inside, highlighting in her textbook, while sprawled on her bed. She beamed at me when I came in before jotting down a note.

"Hey you," she said as her smile disappeared, and she grimaced at her pointer finger.

I tossed my backpack onto the bed and nodded at her. "Hey to you, too. What's wrong with you?"

"Stupid ass paper cut. I hate getting those!" she complained, as a vibrant drop of blood dripped down the side of her finger.

I gave her a sympathetic look. Paper cuts truly were things of nightmares.

I turned my attention to my mirror. Knowing I'd be doing some training later today, I already wore a pair of leggings and fitted white tee. After pulling my hair up into a messy bun, I reached for my purse.

"Woah, woah, woah. Hold your horses. Where do you think you're headed off to?" Dallas asked with a smirk.

I shrugged and tried to keep my tone casual. "Oh, you know. I'm just going over to Rune's for a bit."

Dallas gave me a knowing look as she tossed aside her textbook and notes. She scooted to the edge of her bed and stared at me with eager eyes. "Rune, huh? Haven't you two hung out every day since Sunday?"

"Yeah, we have."

After our initial meet up at the mall, I'd planned to confide in Dallas about Rune's plan, but I'd ended up deciding against it. I was worried that revealing too much about Rune and the fake dating would provide room for me to slip up and tell her about the Fae. It wasn't that I didn't trust Dallas with such a secret, but I'd promised not to tell anyone. Plus, that kind of secret wasn't mine to share. So I decided to keep quiet and pretend that he and I were actually hanging out due to our growing feelings.

"So, do you like him?" she asked.

I looked out the window, avoiding her gaze. That was an excellent question, one I was beginning to wonder myself. Did I like Rune? Nibbling on my lip, I looked back at her and took a deep breath.

"Yeah, I do."

As soon as I said it out loud, I knew I wasn't only answering for the sake of the fake relationship. There was some truth in that answer, too, which terrified me. My emotions about him no doubt had more to do with curiosity in figuring out who he really was, than me having genuine feelings for him. At least, that's what I was telling myself. Even so, I had to rein in those feelings before they could take root and turn into something more than intrigue, because if I fell for him fully, I knew I'd get my heart broken in more than one way.

Rune wasn't interested in being with me for real, something he and his friends had made clear. He wanted us to stay professional, so if he thought I couldn't handle the "just business" approach, he could decide not to have me join in on the plan, which would destroy my chances of getting the money for Italy. I'd be left with a rejected heart and my shattered dreams.

Dallas squealed in a way only she could. "That is so awesome! Y'all would be so cute together. Plus, he's like your knight in shining armor since he rescued you at the club."

I laughed and scratched nervously at my scalp. "He's definitely something."

That something being a Fox Fae.

She fell back against her pillows before picking up her highlighter and textbook once more. She pointed her finger at me and said, "I won't keep you or your lover waiting anymore, but I want all of the juicy details when you get back. It'd better not be PG either. I want either PG-13 or R, you got me?"

Flaming bright red, I shook my head and started to walk to the door when I paused.

"I thought you had a paper cut?" I asked, quirking a brow at her. Her peach flesh was unmarred and devoid of blood.

Her eyes went wide as she looked at her finger. Laughing, she looked up at me again. "I guess it wasn't as deep as it felt. Yay for me!"

"Lucky you. Whenever I get them, my fingers take forever to stop bleeding."

She flipped her red curls over her shoulder. "The perks of being me, I guess."

Laughing, I gave her a final wave and raced from our room.

A smile was plastered to my face as I weaved my way through the stairwells. I found myself almost enjoying this game of pretend that Rune and I were playing. It was nice picturing us hanging out because we actually liked being around one another. Part of me wished that were the case. I wished that we were a normal girl and guy going out and getting to know each other instead of a human and Fae faking a relationship. It was nice, in part, because the pretending was what allowed Rune and me to get closer. If we weren't pretending, would we have had sex and been done after day one? Would we have had this chance to hang out and explore what it meant to be together? While I wanted us to be seeing each other under normal circumstances, pretending would have to be enough.

The afternoon sun was bright as I exited my dorm. Up ahead, Dax was kissing some redhead at her car. He had her pinned against it as they made out with an intensity that wasn't appealing to the public eye. My stomach coiled in disgust, and I looked away, intent on getting to my car. I had figured seeing him with another girl like that would hurt, even just a little, but oddly enough, it didn't. The knowledge made me hold my head higher. I had happily moved on.

As I approached my car, Dax yelled, "Bria!" He waved bye to the girl with whom he'd just been tongue tied. He turned back to me as he jogged over.

"What do you want?" I asked, disdain seeping into my voice.

He shoved his hands into his pockets. "Look, I'm sorry for being an ass Friday night. I guess I got a bit jealous when I saw you dancing with that loser."

I glared at him and crossed my arms. "His name is Rune, and I don't want your apology. I want you to leave me alone."

He chuckled and nudged me with his elbow. "I know you don't mean that. You and I are good together. We had something special."

I gave a bitter laugh as I sneered at him. "You and I had nothing special. It was a mistake to ever be with you, and I still don't understand what I ever saw in you. I've moved on, Dax, and I'm much better off without you. So now if you'll excuse me, I have somewhere to be."

I turned to climb into my car, but he grabbed me tightly around the arm. He yanked on me, pulling me close to him. I glared at him and tugged against his hold, but he didn't let go.

He glowered at me as he asked in a cold voice, "Are you with that guy?"

My words were venomous as I repeated, "His name is Rune. And yes, I am."

He scoffed and yanked on my arm again.

I cried out at the burst of pain that trailed up my arm, and I tried prying off his hand. His grip had gotten so tight, and my arm was beginning to throb. I frantically looked around for someone who might be walking by, but there was no one. Where the hell had that redhead gone? Something dark had come over him, and it was beginning to scare me.

"You're mine," he said, grabbing my hand to stop my attempts to free myself. He squeezed my fingers hard as he leaned close to my face. "Don't think you can go to someone else. You're mine, and no one else's."

Dax had never acted this way before, and it was startling to see. I squeezed my eyes shut, taking a calming breath. "Let go of me."

He scoffed then shoved me away from him, making me fall back against my car. He stepped forward, pressing against me, so I put my hands on his chest and tried to push him away. Frantic, I realized my pepper spray was in my purse, but I couldn't get to it with him pinning my arms between us.

My heart raced as he bent close to my ear and spat, "You. Are. Mine."

Lit with a raging fire inside, I shoved him hard.

Not expecting my outburst, he stumbled back enough for me to rear up my knee, nailing him hard right where it would hurt most. He doubled over instantly, clutching his groin.

I didn't stick around after that to see what else he'd do. I quickly opened my car door and climbed in, locking it behind me. Tears pricked at my eyes as I started the car. Dax was hunched over next to my window with a face pinched in raw pain. Not caring, I peeled out of my parking space, throwing gravel on the asshole as I sped away.

CHAPTER

NINETEEN

My tears felt like a weakness as they fell, and my hands shook against the steering wheel. I was so *angry.* The way Dax spoke to me, as if he had a claim over me, was revolting. *He* was the one who didn't want to be together. *He* was the one always seeking pleasure from other girls. *He* was the one who hadn't wanted to be mine—until now apparently. How dare he grab me and tell me I was his when he'd ruined his chance at us having a relationship. I wanted to wipe away all memories of him and pretend the toxic relationship had never existed.

By the time I got to Rune's, it was already 5:10, but I refused to go inside crying. I closed my eyes and rested my head on the steering wheel. It took effort to make my breathing even, and I wiped my eyes with the back of my hand. My heart was finally starting to beat normally, and my breathing had calmed down.

I sighed and pulled down the visor above my head. My eyes were still a bit puffy and red, so I decided to wait a few more minutes before going in. I didn't want any chance of the others knowing I'd been crying.

I leaned my head back against the headrest and looked over at the house. As soon as I did, my eyes met Rune's. He leaned against the front door with his arms crossed and stared at me with an unreadable expression. I knew if I stayed in the car with him watching me, it would be obvious that something was wrong, so I took a deep breath before opening the door.

I climbed out and mustered the best smile I could.

He watched me with his brow furrowed, never moving from his position.

I shut my car door and forced myself to walk. It took everything in me to keep my legs from shaking.

"Sorry I'm so late. Traffic," I lied. Once I reached him, I looked down at my hand and pretended to study my fingernails. I couldn't meet his eyes because I knew he'd still be able to tell I'd been crying.

"Funny," he said. "I didn't realize traffic could bring a person to tears."

I glanced up at him.

He stared down at me with expectant eyes, waiting for me to tell him what was up.

Instead, I mumbled, "I wasn't crying."

"I was standing here the whole time. I saw you crying and trying to wait it out. So tell me. What's wrong?"

I looked away from him, my eyes brimming with angry tears again. My mind flashed back to Dax's painful grip and misguided words. Where was his drive to be with me when we'd *actually* been together?

I forced a laugh and said, "All right. You got me. Traffic makes me cry."

"Was it Allen again?" Alarm suddenly laced Rune's words.

"No, no. It wasn't him. It was—" I paused to take a deep breath.

His worry was so clearly etched in the crease of his brow and frown. His mind was probably going to the worst-case scenario after everything that had happened lately. Even so, I wasn't sure how to explain why I was crying. I wanted to tell him. But how? Part of me was embarrassed that I had been brought to the point where I was so livid that I had started crying.

Rune was quiet for a long moment before asking, "Is it me or something I did?"

My head snapped up to meet his guarded gaze.

"What?" I asked incredulously. "No. You haven't done anything. I promise."

The concern embedded in his features now mixed with guilt and remorse. The look was so foreign on Rune, and seeing it made the ache in my chest expand to new lengths.

With a final second to steel myself with courage, I told him what happened. As I recounted what Dax did, all of the looks previously in Rune's eyes were overshadowed by a thick coating of venom. His jaw clenched, and I saw loathing simmer in those golden orbs. When I told him of how I'd done exactly as he instructed and aimed for the goods, a new emotion warred with the anger.

Pride.

He was proud of me.

I waited to see what he'd say or do. There was no telling with Rune. As a Fox Fae, he had primal instincts that came from his nature, so I was never sure which side was going to win out with him—the animal or the human.

"I'm glad you put him in his place," Rune finally said through clenched teeth. "But I'm still gonna go pay him a visit."

He brushed past me to head to his car, and I quickly turned to go after him.

I clutched onto his arm. "Don't go, Rune. It's fine."

"It's not fine!" he yelled as he turned all the way to face me. He looked down at me with his face scrunched in disbelief. "He hurt you after you made it very clear you weren't interested. He talked to you as if you were an *object*. So now I'm going to teach him a lesson, in addition to the lovely precursor you've already delivered."

He started to turn away again, so I let go of his arm. Instead, I wrapped my arms around his waist and hugged myself tightly to his back. He grew rigid under my touch, but I didn't care. I pressed my face into his back as I begged, "Please Rune, don't. I just want to go inside with you. I already handled it, remember? Let's go inside together. *Please.*"

He stood there frozen for a moment. Being so close to him like this made some of the dark emotions fade away. I felt safe, warm, and at ease. It was so strange how he could make me feel that way. I still didn't understand it, but I didn't need to. The way he made me feel was enough.

He was enough.

He turned around to face me, so I let go. My arms hung down by my sides, and I looked away before he could meet my eyes. I had held him so tightly and for so long that I was sure he was going to say something snarky to me about it, so when he crooked his finger under my chin to tilt my face up, my body froze. My eyes went wide as I soaked in his gentle touch.

"Are you okay?" he asked.

I nodded. "I am now."

Taking a deep breath, he brushed a strand of hair that had fallen loose from my bun back behind my ear. His fingers lingered on the edges of my jaw before slowly trailing to my chin. His thumb barely brushed against the skin below my mouth, igniting a fire deep within me. I swallowed hard, and his eyes locked onto mine. Something in his gaze changed. A flash of swelling desire blossomed in those endless depths, but then he looked away. When he met my eyes again, the fleeting emotion was gone.

Clearing his throat, he took a few steps back and nodded at the house. "Well, if you're sure you're okay, then we should get inside. Our friend, Avana, is going to be here soon."

Nodding, I followed him to the house. My nerves were still rattled from having him so close, but I couldn't think about that right now. Or at least I tried not to. That didn't work out too well.

My heart pounded. I wasn't sure how to label my feelings for Rune, but there was definitely *something* there, some flickering flame in my chest, trying desperately to ignite. I wasn't blind. Rune was clearly an attractive man, so I could admit that I was definitely attracted to him. But did it go beyond that?

Every time he got close to me or touched me, it got harder to tell what either of us was feeling, and if it really was affection blossoming, I *had* to stamp it out. Having either of us acknowledge it would only add gasoline to that flame, making it consume me. That was something I didn't want and couldn't afford right now. Not with my trip to Italy on the line.

Or my heart.

CHAPTER

TWENTY

Bassel, Akira, and Marlow sat around the living room. As soon as they saw me, they greeted me with enthusiastic voices.

"Bria, good to see you." Bassel said, his dark eyes meeting mine. He patted the empty space next to him on the couch. "How was school?"

I smiled, accepting the offer for the seat. "School was school. Not much to say. Honestly, it's been hard to focus ever since I've found out, you know, the truth of the world. I keep trying to figure out if my peers or professors are actually something besides human."

Akira laughed at that from where he sat on the love seat. "I highly doubt they are. All Land Fae within a certain area try to take note of others so we can watch each other's backs. I don't know of any that go to Brinkley or work there."

My relief was instant. "That's good to know."

"Avana should be here soon." Akira skipped over to the window, peeking out the curtains. "You're going to love her, Bria. She's amazing!"

Rune dropped into the high-backed chair, and Marlow crawled across the floor to sit next to his legs. There was a lazy, contented hold to his mouth, and he hummed a song faintly.

Strange.

"So, Avana knows that I'm human, I take it?"

"Yeah, we let her know what was going on," Rune answered.

"She totally understood why we needed her since it's Rune we're talking about." Akira laughed. "No way can Mr. Ladies' Man over there actually have a girlfriend to take home. She thought it was hilarious."

"Yes. Ha. Ha. So funny," Rune mocked, shaking his head.

"She's here!" Akira squealed, dashing to the door.

Suddenly nervous, I fiddled with the hem of my t-shirt. A warm, female voice with a heavy accent flooded into the room with Akira's laughter. I was quick to get to my feet, turning to the door to greet the new presence.

"Avana," Akira said, waving his arm at me. "Meet Bria. Bria, this is our good friend, Avana."

"*Salama*, Bria! It's so nice to finally meet you."

Avana was stunning. Her dark brown skin was flawless, as was her long, black braids, which had gold ribbon threaded in them. None of that compared to her smile though. It was so welcoming and kind that all my nerves instantly melted away.

Matching her excitement, I shook her outstretched hand. "You too. So, you're a Land Fae?"

"I am. I'm a Chameleon Fae, originally from Madagascar, hence my accent. As a Chameleon Fae, I have the ability to change a person's outward appearance, which is what I'm here to do today."

"Her transformations are amazing," Bassel said, tossing a grin her way. "Give Bria a demonstration."

Avana looked in my direction, her gaze becoming focused and steady. Her brown eyes studied me as she took in every inch of my body. After only a few moments, patches of her dark skin began to lighten. Her black and gold braids unraveled and redid themselves until she sported a blonde messy bun. Her off-the-shoulder shirt and maxi skirt shrunk against her body until she wore black leggings and a white t-shirt. Her features and skin continued distorting until I was left staring at an exact image of myself.

My eyes went wide, and a surprised gasp left my lips. "Holy shiz," I mumbled, approaching slowly.

She beamed, twirling for me to take in all of her. Or rather, all of *me*.

"Pretty neat, huh?" she asked, her voice still her own.

"It's incredible! It's almost freaky how much you look like me."

She laughed as her body and clothes began fading and re-shaping until she stood before me as herself once more.

Still in shock, I stared at her. She was going to do that to me—change the way I looked. Granted, it wasn't anything on the same scale as to what she'd done to herself, but the idea was both fascinating and disturbing.

Placing her hands on her hips, she addressed me with an eager twinkle to her dark eyes. "Are you ready to turn into a Fox Fae?"

I swallowed my nerves. "Is this going to hurt?"

"Not at all," she said, waving away the idea with her hand. "If anything, it tingles and tickles a little bit."

Rune came up beside me and addressed Avana. "You need me to change, right?"

She nodded. "I want to make sure I cover everything and get it looking just right. Being able to see what I'm trying to replicate will make it look better."

An orange flame erupted around Rune's body then. It traveled the length of him until he stood next to me with his fox ears, tail, and claws. Glancing at me, he smirked, which made his sharp fang peek out from beneath his lip.

I swallowed hard, trying to ignore the curling heat his grin caused. Instead, I tried to mentally prepare for what was about to happen.

"Perfect!" Avana clapped her hands. She studied Rune, walking in a slow circle around him. When she stood in front of him again, she pointed at his mouth, which he opened so she could evaluate his canines.

Avana faced me then and watched me intently. She held her chin, mumbling, "I'll have to alter the color slightly, but that's fine. Shouldn't be too hard."

She stood up straight, and her eyes bore into mine. After a few moments, tingles erupted along my spine and traveled down, ending where my back and rear met. It was such an odd sensation, especially there, and I desperately wanted to scratch at it to make the tingling stop. I fought the urge and remained still as the tips of my fingers began to buzz, followed by my gums. Last came the ticklish vibration on the top of my head. It felt like bugs crawling around on my scalp, and I had to ball my hands into fists to keep from clawing at my head. But when I closed my fists, sharp nails bit into my palms.

"Okay! All done! What do we think, boys?" She grabbed my shoulders and spun me around so that everyone could see me.

"Holy shit," Bassel laughed. "You look exactly like a Fox Fae."

I smiled at that, my sharp canines now exposed.

Approval melted into Bassel's dark eyes, and he nodded. "You look hot, *Kitsune-chan*."

"God, you can't tell that you're a human at all. You're stunning." Akira beamed at me.

Giggling, I glanced over at Rune. His eyes were fixated on me, traveling the length of my body. Heat pooled in my lower abdomen at the intensity of his gaze, and the world seemed to slip away. There was just him, taking in all of me. Drinking in the sight of me. A warm tension started to build between us, and when his eyes locked onto mine again, my breath stilled in my throat. His cheeks had grown rosy, and fire lit his amber eyes.

Rune was blushing.

Someone cleared his throat, ending whatever had been happening between us. My cheeks flamed, and Rune quickly turned for his room, striding away from us. My heart sank a bit as he disappeared. Whether I wanted to admit it or not, I had been hoping he'd compliment me. It was clear that he liked what he saw, but it would've been nice to hear it from him, too.

Avana nudged me gently. Chuckling, she whispered, "I think he likes it."

"Pfft," Akira teased. "Liked it? He loved it. He probably has to go cool off, if you know what I mean."

I let out a laugh, my stomach suddenly in tight knots. Heat crept up my neck and across my face, and I ducked my head. "Yeah right," I mumbled. "I doubt it."

I ran my tongue over my new set of pearly whites. It felt weird talking with two elongated, sharp canines, almost like my mouth was too full. I'd definitely have to practice talking naturally with them before we went to Rune's home. I refused to fail just because I wasn't used to talking with some extra sharp teeth.

Akira nudged Avana with his elbow and asked, "So, Avana, have you decided if you're gonna come with us or not? It would be a lot easier to pull this off if you were there to keep her disguise from wearing off."

"You're coming, too?" I asked, suddenly a bit more enthusiastic.

"We all thought it would be a good idea since I'm the sole Fae who can keep up your ruse. I had to pull some strings over at my shop, but yes, I'll be tagging along."

Smiling, I let out the breath I'd been holding. "That's a relief. I'm glad you'll be coming."

"What, Bria?" Bassel asked. "Not excited to be going on a trip with all of us boys?"

"You guys are great, but it will be nice to not be solely surrounded by testosterone."

"I hear that," Avana laughed. She placed a hand on my shoulder, turning my attention back to her. "You still haven't seen your new look. Why don't you go take a peek in the bathroom?"

Realizing she was right, I made my way down the hall. My nerves were an absolute mess the closer I got. I could see my nails, which had turned into claws, and I could feel the fangs poking at my lip. The thought of actually seeing the entirety of my transformation was enough to send my mind reeling. Flicking on the bathroom light, I closed my eyes and took a deep, steadying breath. I was at a loss when I opened my eyes to my reflection.

Two pointy ears sat erect on my head. They blended seamlessly into the colors of my hair at the base and faded into a rich black the higher they went. The strands of hair sticking out of my bun teased the edges of my ears, tickling them. I choked on my budding laughter when I realized I could feel with these things. They weren't merely an illusion for the eyes but used for touch, too. They twitched at the sensation, and I nearly gasped, watching the motion.

I stood on my tiptoes and turned to the side, bringing my tail into view. The black fur was thick, and my tail was large. I let out a breathy laugh, and I reached behind me to grab it. I nearly leapt out of my skin when my fingers brushed the extremity.

Not only could I feel the contact through my hands, but I could feel it through the tail itself, too, which was an odd sensation. It left goosebumps on my arms.

They were all mine. The claws, the fangs, the ears, the tail.

I was a Fox Fae.

At least appearance-wise.

Movement in the mirror caught my attention. Rune stood in the doorway, leaning against the frame with his hands shoved in his pockets. His eyes met mine in the mirror, and we held each other's gaze. Heat still simmered in his eyes, and I couldn't ignore the ache that settled low in my abdomen as he regarded me.

I had all his attention.

I was the reason a fire blazed in his amber eyes.

I was what he wanted.

At least, I was right now.

Suddenly feeling exposed, I fought for something to say. "What do you think? Do I make a convincing Fox?"

He pursed his lips, studying my guise in the mirror. Pushing off the door, he came right up behind me. He was so close that the warmth from his body wrapped around me. It sent shivers running down my spine, and the urge to let myself drown in his warmth was hard to resist.

He cleared his throat and scratched at his chin. "Yeah. Looks good."

He reached up and stroked behind my fox ear. I let out a gasp at the feel of his fingers brushing across the fur, still so shocked over the physical sensations coming through these foreign parts. He went rigid, and his eyes snapped back to mine through the mirror. Running his fangs over his lip, he shook his head as if to clear it of the need that suddenly clouded his gaze.

He turned back to the ears atop my head with a cheeky grin. "I'm surprised you can feel. Avana's pretty great at what she does."

I cleared my throat and picked at the hem of my shirt, trying not to acknowledge how warm his touching my ear had made me grow in very sensitive areas. "It's weird being able to feel that stuff. I kinda feel like I've grown a second head."

He laughed, the sound deep and rich. He met my eyes in the mirror again. "No second head. Just a nice set of fox features."

"So, do you think this will work then? No one should suspect I'm human?"

"They definitely shouldn't suspect you're human," he mumbled, glancing down at my tail. His eyes lingered there, which made my face heat all over again.

The two of us, standing side by side in our Fae forms, was enough to make my heart and mind wander. We looked good together. Like, *really* good. It was easy to picture his arms wrapped around me, my hands intertwined with his, his lips on my skin. Part of me—the part that enjoyed us pretending we liked each other—wanted that. Wanted this to be real.

What a fool that part of me was.

I turned to face him. There were mere inches between us, and it would be so easy to close that distance. But I wouldn't and neither would he.

"What will happen if they realize I'm a lie? What if they do figure out I'm human? And don't sugar coat it. I need to know what I'm getting into."

He was quiet for a moment, his amber eyes searching mine. When he found whatever he was looking for, he took a deep breath. "Humans aren't supposed to know Fae exist."

The unspoken meaning was clear. If they discovered I was human, I'd be dealt with.

Permanently and indefinitely.

The threat was like a weighted chain pulling me down. I trusted Rune and his ability to be there should anything happen, but that didn't stop me from wondering what if. What if he couldn't be there, or what if he was too late? My life could be in danger if I went through with this, but my life's passion was also on the line.

Swallowing hard, I kept my determined eyes locked on his. "Then we'll have to do a damn good job of convincing them otherwise."

His lips lifted. "We will." A ring of fire erupted around him, trailing his body and removing his fox features. "Let's have Avana remove your transformation, and you and I can get started on some training."

Instantly perking up, I said, "Yes, please! I'm beyond ready to get started."

He turned to leave the bathroom but drew up short. Facing me again, he quirked a curious brow. "Actually, can you do something for me first?"

"What?"

He turned to fully face me and spread his toned arms wide. "Punch me."

I blinked. "Excuse me?"

"Punch me. And don't hold back, either. Give it all you've got."

Stunned, I recoiled from him and folded my arms. "Why would I punch you?"

"I want to gauge how much work you'll need. It's fine. I'm giving you permission."

"Rune, that's—"

"Punch me!"

Biting my lip, I fidgeted. This was the last thing I wanted to do, but then again, if part of my self-defense training was going to be sparring, I'd have to get used to throwing punches at him. Taking a deep breath, I reared my fist back before slamming it hard into his bicep. Pain instantly flared behind my knuckles, as well as in the palms of my hand due to the claws. I realized too late that I may have gone a bit overboard.

"Shit," I mumbled. "That was too hard. I'm so sorry."

He blinked once, then twice. Looking at his arm, then back at me, he laughed. "That's it? I told you not to hold back. It's really fine. Punch me like you mean it."

I frowned. "What do you mean? That was my punch."

His smile fell. "Are you serious?"

Now my guilt was turning into something red hot that tasted bitter like anger. Narrowing my eyes at him, I drew my hand back again and swung it even harder at his arm. He didn't flinch, while I had to bite the inside of my cheek to keep from crying out.

He gave a low whistle and turned on his heel. "Okay. So, gym first, training later. You clearly need to build some upper body strength."

Offended, I went to make a retort, but deep down, I knew he was right. I wasn't toned for fighting. It was no wonder he laughed at my punches.

We met the others back in the living room. Avana changed me back to my human-looking self, which felt just as bizarre as it had the first time. Then it was off to Hell, or as Rune liked to call it, the gym.

CHAPTER
TWENTY-ONE

My biceps ached as I threw another hard punch at the focus mitts Rune wore. Sweat beaded my brow, and my breathing came out fast and heavy. Fatigue settled into the muscles of my arms, and before long, I felt my swings getting less and less powerful. Rune's concentrated stare, no doubt, read the tired look on my face, and there was no missing my weakened hits.

I swung again, and as soon as I made contact with the mitt, Rune swung the other one at my middle. I was supposed to dodge the attack as we'd practiced for the past two days, but I was too slow. He hit me right in the gut, just hard enough that it didn't hurt but did make my legs give out from exhaustion. I fell backward and landed hard on my butt. My body rejoiced at the feeling of resting, so I laid back, shut my eyes, and worked to calm my ragged breathing.

"Are you okay?" Rune asked. His shadow fell over my face, and I knew if I opened my eyes, I'd find him hovering over me.

"I'm—" I gasped, "dying. Welcome ... to my ... funeral."

He chuckled, and I opened my eyes at the warm sound. He flopped down beside me and leaned back on his hands. His long, white hair was in a ponytail at the base of his neck, but a few strands had fallen loose across his forehead. I tried not to focus on how sexy he was when he looked this way or how it made my insides curl tightly with heat.

"You're not dying," he said. "You're doing a really good job actually, and it will get easier the more you use those muscles and improve your techniques."

"When exactly will it get easier?"

"That depends on you."

I took a deep breath and shook my head where it rested against the blue mats. "I don't think I can handle this."

"Yes, you can."

Rune grabbed my arms and pulled until I was forced to sit up.

I turned so that we sat directly across from each other with our knees barely touching.

He didn't let go of my arms. Instead, his palms traveled down my forearms, over my wrists, and settled in my hands. A euphoric buzz immediately erupted in my stomach at the intimate gesture. Rune and I didn't touch skin to skin too often, but when we did, it elicited such a warm feeling inside of me, one that could only be described as desire.

Rune's golden eyes held mine as he said, "I know it's hard right now, but you can do it. You've faced down knife-wielding criminals and stood your ground against a Fae like me. If anyone can do this, it's you. Believe in yourself, because I know I do."

Emotion clogged my throat. His words, his encouragement, his belief in me were something precious. They made me feel empowered, and the doubt inside me finally started to seep away.

"You really think I can do it?"

"Of course. Your punch has already improved. It doesn't tickle anymore."

"Shut up, you jerk," I laughed, punching him in the arm.

"Ow!" His laugh was deep and smooth, and he rubbed at his arm. "See? I actually felt that."

I rolled my eyes and got up to get my bottle of water. As I watched Rune down his own drink, I couldn't help but wonder what he was like when first learning to fight. Was he quick-tempered? Did he have moments of doubt? Akira had mentioned a war between their kind and Water Fae, and Rune had mentioned his experience in combat. Did that mean he'd seen real battle? He was no doubt a fearsome creature.

"What was it like the first time you had to fight someone?" I asked.

He paused in the middle of readjusting his hair tie. His gaze was glued to the floor, but it was unseeing. I could tell my question had transported him to a different place, and I wondered what it had resurfaced for him.

"My first fight," Rune mumbled. He shook his head and gave a humorless laugh. "What a day that was."

"Was your first time against Water Fae?"

"Yeah." He nodded and finally met my eyes. "Yeah, it was. It was a day that really changed my attitude, and it's one I'll probably never forget."

"Can you tell me about it? If it's not too painful. I'd really like to know more about Fae and—" I paused, unsure if I should continue. I decided since I was asking him to open up, I should do the same, so I finished, "And about you."

Rune's eyes didn't waver from mine, and there was no retort or brushing off my words. That surprised me but also seemed to poke at the feelings growing in my chest. It could be because he saw this as an opportunity to show me more of himself for the sake of the charade we were preparing for, which is really why I should've asked. I think we both secretly knew there was more to it.

"I was really naive back then," Rune started. He moved to the center of the mats and rested his arm against his knee as he sat down. His amber eyes were on mine, but they also held a solemn look as he thought back to that time.

"I was already a century old, but up until that point, war hadn't been a part of my personal life. I'd, of course, seen humans fight and witnessed struggles between small classes of Fae. But I'd never been actively involved in full-blown combat until that day. It was something I had trained for because Land Fae sensed a battle coming with Water Fae. I was young and dumb, though. The idea of finally being able to fight and show off my skills was what I cared about. It almost didn't feel real when word spread that war was on our doorstep. All I was focused on was being powerful and strong."

He paused and swallowed hard before finishing, "I wanted to make my dad proud."

The sentiment was bittersweet. There had been so many days I'd wanted the same thing. I had wanted to make Greg and Wendy proud, to show them my art wasn't pointless. After a while, I had given up on that. I had realized they'd never be proud of what I loved, but maybe—just maybe—my real parents would've been. That became my new drive. Even if they weren't there to see all the work I'd done, I could regale them with stories and pictures one day. I'd find them and give them a reason to be proud of me. Or so I liked to dream.

"Not that I needed to fight to make him proud," Rune

continued. "I can't even tell you how many times he told me, strength or no strength, power or no power, win or lose, he would *always* be proud of me."

Rune stopped to take a deep breath. Talking about his dad was never an easy task. I knew how hard that could be.

I moved closer to where he sat and found my place directly beside him. Wanting to provide support and comfort, I grabbed his hand and squeezed.

His eyes found mine again, and they warmed at the edges.

"Anyway, my day of battle came sooner than I expected. There was a small village of Dove Fae in the forests along the East Coast. They were peaceful beings who wanted harmony and balance. They always stayed out of trouble and had no urge to fight. The Water Fae, whom they'd welcomed into their village at that point, didn't care.

"Water Fae soldiers wiped out that entire community. There wasn't a single Dove Fae left alive. Babies, children, mothers, fathers, grandparents. When we found the town like that, the air polluted with the stench of blood, we knew we had to avenge those innocent lives. We had to stop that group of Water Fae before they slaughtered more communities.

"We tracked them until they made camp. As soon as their guard was down, the group of Fox Fae soldiers I was a part of moved in. I must've killed a handful of Water Fae within minutes. It put my power on full display, but it also made me feel sick. I didn't like taking lives after all. It was harder than I thought it would be, watching a person's life fade from their eyes and knowing it was because of me."

A heavy weight settled on my chest. While Rune and I were training, it was simply for self-defense. I couldn't imagine ever taking a life. The burden that must cause and the guilt you'd no doubt feel had to be indescribable. I couldn't ever begin to fathom how Rune dealt with it all.

"So, what did you do?" I asked after some silence had passed. "Did you decide you couldn't fight anymore?"

"I didn't know what to do. I couldn't stop because there were other Fox Fae with me who needed me. I decided I'd figure out what to do once we all made it out of there safely. That was before I discovered what awaited in the Water Fae captain's tent."

Dread pricked at my insides like shards of ice. I swallowed hard and leaned forward. "What was in there?"

"We had been wrong. There was a life left from the Dove Fae village. The captain of the Water Fae soldiers had taken a trophy. A woman named Mei, and she ... she was actually a family friend. The captain laughed when he saw how surprised I was. He told me that she was there for the taking and that he had every right to indulge in his 'spoils of war.'

"When I saw her and the state she was in, I snapped. I wiped out at least a dozen more Water Fae, including the captain himself. My team spared no life that day, and I haven't since. Not when it comes to Water Fae."

My blood ran cold. This had been Rune's first taste of combat, and it had been devastating. It made me sick even listening to the summarized, less-graphic version. To have actually been there, to have witnessed a friend being held and tortured, must've been traumatizing to say the least. It had left such a profound mark on him. To him, the Water Fae were creatures who seemed to take what they wanted with no regard for others. What a dangerous way of life. I hoped I never had to meet a Water Fae, at least not one like that captain.

It was also hard to process how much loss of life Rune had witnessed and been a part of. What kind of scars had it left on his heart? I knew he did it out of loyalty to his kind and to protect those he loved, but it still had to leave wounds behind. Perhaps that was part of the reason he was always so guarded and distant. He'd seen so much devastation in his life that it was hard for him to see and indulge in the goodness out there.

"What happened to Mei?" I asked when he didn't continue.

Rune hung his head, and his eyes slipped closed as his shoulders slumped with his next words. "She was the only prisoner. Her husband of two centuries was killed during the Dove Fae village raid. Mei had been pregnant at the time. She was supposed to have a daughter, but due to all she'd endured when the captain held her, she miscarried. The grief was too much for her without her husband and child. She ended her own life."

My stomach churned. What a nightmarish and heartbreaking tale. Only it wasn't a tale for Rune. It was real life. It was a real occurrence he'd lived and witnessed, a real friend he'd lost. That fact made my next inhale hard to take.

So much pain. So many innocent lives lost. So much devastation.

Those wounds clearly ran deep for Rune, and even though his story was hard to listen to, it really helped me to understand him a little more. He had painful memories and a dark past. He had a good group of friends now and seemed to be in a better place, but that didn't change all he'd gone through to get to this point. No wonder he sometimes got frustrated, easily angered, and overprotective. It was from years of seeing people he cared about killed and abused by Water Fae.

I placed my hand on his shoulder. His golden eyes drifted to mine, and when they did, I saw the misery. I saw the burden, rage, and suffering that he always kept locked away. He was letting me see this side of him, and I couldn't be more grateful for that. But it also made my stomach sour. I wanted to wipe away that pain. I wanted to hold him close and reassure him that everything was going to be okay. He didn't have to hurt anymore. He didn't have to go through it alone anymore.

"I'm so sorry, Rune. I can't imagine all you've been through. I know it's not much, but if you ever need to just talk, I'm here to listen."

In an instant, the mask he always wore was back in place, and all the long ago memories were tucked away. Any trace of vulnerability was gone.

The corners of his mouth lifted a fraction. "Thank you. Enough talking now. We have some fighting to get back to."

I glanced over at the discarded focus mitts and gloves. My heart fell with a different kind of dread as I sighed. "Yippee."

After two weeks of classes followed by working out at the gym and then sparring, I was completely beat. My entire body felt like it had been shoved in a grinder and beaten to death. The flaring pain and muscle soreness was finally tolerable, but it still sucked when I started working out new muscles.

That being said, the time with Rune was interesting to say the least. We were both learning each other's quirks and personalities more and more each day. He loved to tease me every chance he got, and I worked to one-up him with as many retorts as I could. He got under my skin, and I got under his, but I also liked to think both of us were secretly enjoying the other's company.

When we weren't doing weights or throwing punches and kicks, we were spread out on the mats, side by side, just talking, although it wasn't ever as heavy as when Rune told me about his first experience with battle. Instead, it was random stuff.

We talked about how shell macaroni was a thousand times better than the noodle version. We also argued over which bending ability was best from *Avatar: The Last Airbender*. He, of course, said fire, and I was a hard supporter of water benders, though we both agreed it would be cool to be the Avatar.

While we worked out and trained, I still found myself second-guessing my ability to get better or to keep going. Every single time, Rune stayed patient with me. He pushed and encouraged me, always expressing that he believed in me.

Today was the first day in over two weeks that I hadn't seen Rune to train. He thought I deserved a break since it was Saturday, plus I needed to do some major butt-whooping on my homework. It was odd not seeing him. I had grown so used to his company.

Seeking some solitude from the hustle and bustle of campus, I spread out a blanket by the creek bed behind the campus property. It was the perfect place to get some work done, and a large part of me hoped I'd run into my fox again. My backpack sat next to me, spilling its contents out over the blanket, and I had my Art History textbook pulled into my lap as I stole glances around the trees for him.

Biting down on a carrot from the snacks I'd brought, I mumbled, "Trying to kick Rune's ass is way more fun than this."

Jotting down a note from the text, I froze. An eerie feeling crept over me, and the hairs on the back of my neck stood. It was the sort of feeling you get when you know someone's watching you. Peeking up without trying to make obvious movements, I scanned the trees surrounding me. Shadows lingered in certain spots, and I held my breath, waiting for signs of lurking life. To my right, the shadows along the tree line seemed thicker and foreboding. My eyes were glued to the darkness between them, and for a split second, I could've sworn I saw movement mixed into the blackness.

A twig snapped to my left. Whipping my head around, my heart leapt into my throat as I prepared for some sort of attack. When my eyes met his, I instantly felt silly. Standing a small distance away was the Silver Fox, and he watched me with those friendly gold eyes.

Letting out the breath I'd been holding, I willed my heart to calm down. "Oh, it must've been you I felt. Hi again."

The fox took a small step backward as if he were scared of me.

Frowning, I held my hand out. "Wait! Please don't go. You're Fae, aren't you?"

The fox watched me, and slowly, he dipped his head in a nod. My emotions skyrocketed as he washed away any lingering doubt.

"I thought so. I'm actually—" I paused.

Rune said this fox, whoever he was, would be at his birthday party. I'd already confided in him about things that wouldn't line up with our story, so I wasn't completely sure how to go about interacting with him. With no way of knowing what this fox knew about the situation, I decided to play it safe and go along with the ruse. I could answer the hard questions about my behavior from before later.

"I'm Rune's girlfriend."

Guilt pricked at me. I didn't like lying to him, but I had no choice. I had a job to do, and a trip to Italy that relied on me doing it well, so even though lying to the fox didn't feel right, it was a necessary pain.

I turned to set aside my textbook and veggies, and when I faced him again, I nearly jumped out of my skin. The fox had made his way over to me and was sitting directly by my side now. "You startled me. You moved so quietly."

He stared up at me, tilting his head slightly.

Raising an eyebrow, I bit the corner of my lip. "You know, you could transform into your human form. Then we could actually talk, and you could tell me your name since Rune won't."

He shook his head.

"Fine." I caught a glint of something around his neck. When I looked down, a warm grip wrapped around my heart like fire eating away at a stack of paper. He was still wearing the necklace I'd given him. Smiling wide, I nodded toward it. "You still have it. I'm glad."

He tilted his head back slightly as if to show me that the necklace was still in good condition. Seeing him again, with my necklace on, was like basking in the sun.

Clearing my throat, I looked out at the creek, toeing loose a pebble near the stream. "Rune said you'll be at his party. Hopefully you'll be, you know, less furry and more fleshy for that."

He looked down at his fur covered body, trying to find something wrong or out of place.

Laughing, I gently poked his forehead, and he looked up at me. "I didn't mean that in a bad way. Your coat is beautiful. I'm just excited to actually see you face-to-face and talk to you."

The lighting in the woods was starting to grow dim with the approach of evening, so despite my hesitancy to leave the fox so soon, I started to pack up my belongings.

"Well, Mr. Fox, I should head back to my dorm. It was good to see you again, and I look forward to our next meeting, too."

Smiling at him, I stood and swung my backpack over my shoulders. His eyes followed me as I waved and walked back toward campus. When I was no longer able to see him through all the trees, I was left feeling cold and alone. It would've been so easy to turn back around, but it was getting late. I'd have to wait another month and a half to meet him in his human or Fae form instead of his animal one.

I could totally wait that long.

Maybe.

CHAPTER
TWENTY-TWO

The sketch of Rune's mug taunted me. It was a beautiful design, one that would make a great mug, but clay was my enemy. I didn't want to screw this up.

Mustering my focus, I worked the clay, molding it. Once the shape was right, I grabbed a needle tool to draw out the fox on the front of the mug, biting my lip as I concentrated. It spanned almost all the way around to the handle on both sides. By the time I finished drawing in all of the details, I released the breath I'd been holding, more than happy with the way it was looking so far.

As soon as I finished glazing my fox with color, class ended for the day. I gathered all of my things and made my way outside. As I headed to the English and Language Arts building, my phone vibrated. Rune's name lit up the screen.

> Come to the house tonight around 5. We're gonna be reviewing everything you've learned, and we're gonna go over some new stuff.

A nervous and giddy buzz filled me at the sight of his text. More and more each day, I found myself looking forward to Rune's texts and meetups. He was stirring something inside of me with each of his jabs, his smiles, and his endless encouragement. I wasn't used to feeling whatever this was, but I refused to pay any more mind to it. He and I were just pretending. Knowing it wouldn't lead anywhere due to his no-dating policy, I couldn't fall for him. I just had to play the part.

When all of my classes were done for the day, I headed straight to Rune's. Once there, I approached the house with the sound of my heart pounding in my ears, and it felt like I was trying to walk through quicksand. I really needed to rein in my emotions so that no one could tell what I was starting to feel.

When I knocked on the front door, it was only seconds before Marlow opened it. He stood there in his Fae form. His brown and gold skin shimmered, and I could see the moisture that had gathered on his skin. His eyes were glassy like a salamander, and each eye stared off in opposite directions, making me recoil slightly. To make matters worse, he didn't speak. He puckered his lips in an imitation of a fish, and he started making strange gurgling sounds.

Bassel came up behind him and pulled him back away from me. "Go back inside, Marlow. What would you have done if it wasn't Bria at the door?"

Bassel shook his head and rolled his eyes as Marlow walked away from us. Marlow wobbled further into the house, leaving drops of water in his wake.

When Bassel looked at me, he gestured over his shoulder. "Sorry about that. It's supposed to rain later, and when rain is in the forecast, Marlow acts extra weird."

I shook my head and gave him a small grin. "It's okay. At least you're never bored with him around."

He stepped aside to let me in. I walked past him into the living room. Akira appeared from the kitchen hallway, carrying a tray that held a plate of cookies and five coffee mugs. Upon seeing me, his eyes brightened, and he set the tray on the coffee table.

"Hey Bria," he said. "Look, I made homemade cookies."

I perked up at the mention of sweets, and my stomach growled at the sight of the oatmeal raisin deliciousness.

"Why don't you go get Rune so we can start?" Bassel said to me as he flopped down on the couch. He reached for his coffee mug before looking at me again. "He's in his room."

I glanced down the hall. My heart quickened with where my mind went at the mention of his room. The combination of me and Rune alone in his bedroom, made me feel exposed and flushed. I'd never been inside the private space, and the thought of going there now brought on nerves I didn't know I had.

Rune.

Alone.

In his *bedroom*.

Looking back at Bassel, I found myself nodding despite my sudden nerves. I spun on my heel and approached Rune's room. The door was cracked, so when I reached it, I slowly pushed it open. "Rune? Bassel told me to come get you."

My eyes went wide when I stepped into the room. I froze as every inch of my skin flooded with warmth. Rune stood in the middle of his room, dripping wet. He was completely naked, and he stood there, drying his hair with a towel. I couldn't help but notice his sculpted stomach, firm chest, and toned arms. His golden body was mouth-watering, and when my eyes traveled down of their own accord, I felt my knees grow weak. I could definitely see why girls loved to sleep with him.

He looked over at me as he continued to dry his hair, not even fazed by the fact that he was naked in front of me. "Okay. I'll be ready in a sec. You can come in if you want."

I finally shook myself from my wide-eyed, frozen state. Quickly covering my eyes with my hands, I shouted, "Why the hell would you leave your door open and unlocked if you were in here naked?"

I started to back out of the room, but he suddenly gripped the front hem of my jeans. My protest stuck in my throat as he pulled me into the room. The click of the door shutting sounded behind me. My heart hammered in my chest, and the idea that he was about to try something flashed through my mind. Maybe he was feeling pent up, and he was about to offer a more physical deal, something I wasn't sure I'd pass up if given the chance.

Instead, he groaned and said, "Don't leave the door wide open. I had it shut for a reason. I don't know why you're hiding your eyes, either. You just got an eyeful anyway."

His soft hands grabbed my wrists. He pulled my hands away from my eyes, but I squeezed them shut. What was he doing? My heart raced so fast and loud, there was no way he couldn't hear it. He let go of one of my wrists before placing his fingers under my chin, tilting my face up to look at him. Despite this, I left my eyes closed. I couldn't look at him like this. I knew my eyes would betray me, just as my legs were beginning to.

He stepped closer to me, his wet, naked body pressing against me. My nerves skyrocketed, and my knees wobbled. You'd think a girl would argue against him at this point, but I wasn't. I knew why, but it was hard to admit, even to myself, that I didn't want him to stop. I wanted to kiss him. I wanted to see what it felt like to have him hold me and touch me. Those thoughts sent another wave of excited nerves through me, causing my knees to finally give out.

Before I could crumble, Rune grabbed underneath my butt to pick me up. He wrapped my legs around his waist, and I clutched onto his broad shoulders, not wanting to fall. A dizzying buzz filled my head from how hard my heart was beating. It only intensified when he headed in the direction of his bed.

Was he actually about to do this? Was I? Part of me wanted him so much that I was willing to explore things with him, but the other half of me knew that if I gave that to him, his rejection would only hurt even more.

Because let's face it. My crush was one sided and stupid. His blunt and clear warning that he only hooked up should have been enough to keep me from getting too close or comfortable with him, but I was. I'd come to lean on Rune, trust in him, and even call him a friend.

We collapsed onto the bed, and my eyes shot open. Our gazes locked, and he grinned down at me. I swallowed hard and tried to fight off my blush. There was a look in his eyes, a glimmer of something tender and almost like longing. That, paired with the subtle curve of his lips, made me want him all the more.

The orange flame I'd come to associate with his Fae transformation trailed up and around him. I watched with pure fascination as the flame moved higher and higher until it disappeared above his head. He now had his fox ears and fangs. I looked over his shoulder, seeing his fluffy, black tail swishing back and forth, at which I nearly laughed.

Was he wagging his tail?

Not even a second after I met his eyes again, he leaned down, placing tantalizing kisses along my neck.

I shut my eyes, and my stomach flipped as he kissed all along my throat.

His canines scraped against my skin, and his hands moved from where they had been on either side of my head to trail up and under my shirt.

I took in a sharp breath as his hand traced a warm path from the bottom of my stomach to the base of my bra. My toes curled when his teeth nipped at the skin on my neck, and at the same moment, his fingers slipped beneath my bra to coast over the sensitive tips of my breasts. A jolt of want instantly rippled down my spine, and I had to bite back a gasp as he sucked and teased at my throat. Liquid fire slicked down my middle while his wicked fingers taunted and circled my budded nipples.

My breathing came out in small gasps as I fought to say, "R-Rune. We— I—" I couldn't finish my words. I didn't even know what I was trying to say. He'd turned my mind and words into incoherent mush.

He raised up to look down at me, and he tucked a strand of hair behind my ear. "What? You don't want to do it?"

The gentle touch of his fingers brushing my hair back and grazing my ear sent shivers down my arms. Heat pooled in between my thighs at the intimate caress, fueled by the way he'd just been touching me.

Blushing, I bit my lip. "I didn't say that. But-but we aren't actually together, remember?"

Minutes must've ticked by while he stared down at me.

My heart was still beating a mile a minute, and it felt like I had just gone down a hill on a roller coaster. Him watching me with those eyes didn't help any, either.

I waited. I waited to see what he'd say. Had he decided he wanted a physical relationship with me in addition to the business one? Had he changed his mind and wanted to give a real relationship a try, choosing to express so via physical means? My heart nearly exploded while I waited with bated breath, hoping his answer would be in line with my own swelling desire.

He cocked his head slightly to the side as one of his fox ears twitched. Leaning down close, he asked, "Then why aren't you fighting me off?"

Not wanting to meet his eyes, I looked down. That was a mistake, though, because when I looked down, my eyes fell upon the very large, hard part of him that was not helpful for me to see. I quickly averted my gaze, looking at the pillows next to me. I could tell from his question and comment that he was onto me. He knew I was starting to feel things for him, which posed the question of whether he was doing all of this to mess with me or if he wanted me in some sort of way.

He nodded to himself and climbed off of me.

I didn't watch him since he was still naked. My eyes remained fixated on the pillows. I listened to the sound of him opening his closet and shuffling the clothes around. That had really been a close one. I had nearly given in.

"I wasn't actually going to do anything," he said.

I glanced at him as his words sliced into me.

He had just finished pulling up his pants over light blue boxers, and I noticed he looked human once again. He looked over at me, his mask suddenly back on, hiding whatever emotions had previously been there. "I was seeing something, I guess."

Yup. He was totally onto me.

"Besides," he continued, "I don't sleep with virgins, which you are. I wouldn't want to be responsible for taking that or worrying about being gentle. Don't worry. You and I are still strictly business."

Closing my eyes, I shook my head and sat up on the edge of the bed. His words left me feeling like a balloon that had lost all its air. The fact that he didn't want me like that shouldn't bother me. This was strictly professional between us. I knew that. Sadly, my heart decided it didn't care.

Even more gut-wrenching was him using this tantalizing moment only to see if his hunch was right. It wasn't because he enjoyed his skin on mine or because he enjoyed seeing how I reacted to his touch. It was all for the sake of seeing if I'd give in to the temptation and cross that "just business" line. I wanted to be sick just thinking about him realizing there was more to this for me. If I couldn't keep things professional and stoic the way he wanted, he'd get rid of me. He could decide to take back the deal, and in turn, rip away my chances at getting my money for Italy. I couldn't let that happen. I couldn't let him know I was falling for him.

I decided to ignore the last part of what he said since there was nothing I could say to that without giving him the wrong idea and further risking my chances of staying on his good side. Instead I went with, "You shouldn't mess with people like that."

"Why?" he asked, watching me. "It's not like this relationship means anything to either of us."

A wave of disappointment overtook me. If it hadn't been obvious before, that should've made it. This meant nothing to him. I was here for one purpose and one purpose only: to be Rune's *fake* girlfriend. Nothing more. His words were a bitter reminder that my feelings were futile.

"You're right. It means absolutely nothing." I shot to my feet and marched to the door. Flinging it open, I headed into the living room without looking back.

CHAPTER

TWENTY-THREE

Akira and Bassel sat on opposite ends of the couch, watching the TV. Marlow was lying on the floor between the TV and coffee table. He stared up at the ceiling as he whispered the word *rain* in a chant-like fashion.

When Akira saw me, he smiled until he read something on my face that I was trying desperately to hide. Embarrassment. Anger. Disappointment. Sadness. I was a tangled ball of emotions with a shitty poker face.

"Bria, sweetie. What's wrong?" Akira asked, getting up from the couch to guide me next to him on the loveseat.

Shaking my head, I put on a happy face and sighed. "He's a lot to deal with sometimes. That's all."

"Do you want me to beat his ass?" Bassel asked.

I laughed. "That's definitely a tempting idea, but no. It'll be okay."

"What did he do? Or should I say what did he do *this time*?" Akira asked, giving me a pointed look.

I shrugged, not wanting to talk about whatever it was that just happened between us. "Nothing. Don't worry about it."

Before they could respond, Rune walked in. I didn't look at him as he sat down across from me in the high-backed chair. My eyes were transfixed on the window, watching the sky turn gray as the clouds flooded it with a promise of rain.

Akira glared at Rune as he offered me a warm mug of coffee and a cookie. After he took some for himself too, he set the plate back on the coffee table and said, "Rune, didn't you have some stuff that you wanted to go over with everyone here?"

He nodded. "A few things. First, I finally talked with Ardley. He's in on what's really going on, so he'll act as an ally over there. He's also going to vouch for us and pretend he's met Bria and me for get-togethers before. He's already making up stories to feed his parents about Bria, which will no doubt get to my mother eventually."

The idea of Myra and the rest of Rune's family already knowing about me was enough to make me want to rock in a dark corner. It made this feel real, more so now than ever. But it was also a good idea. Showing up randomly without them ever hearing about me would surely cause some suspicion. Ardley was doing us a favor.

"Sweet," Bassel cooed. "Even better since it's technically not a lie, either."

Ears perking up, I turned to Bassel with a curious brow raised. "What's not a lie?"

Those were lies. We hadn't met Ardley for any get-togethers, so how was it technically not a lie that we'd met him?

"Bassel," Rune warned.

Glaring at Rune, I repeated, "What's not a lie?"

"Anyway," Rune started, completely ignoring me. "Next we need to decide how long Bria and I have been together, as well as how we met. You know my family will ask questions like that."

"Why don't you tell the truth about how you guys met? You met at the club," Bassel suggested.

Still pissed that they were leaving me out of the loop in certain things, I chomped angrily on my cookie. I didn't like being left out. It was my charade to pull off, too.

Rune shrugged. "That could work, but I'd obviously have to change the story some. I wouldn't want them to know about her almost being robbed and us intervening. It needs to be something else."

"Fine," I said, wanting my voice to be heard after Rune had blatantly ignored me. "I asked you to dance, so we did. After we danced, we spent the remainder of the night together, and the rest is history, as they say."

"That's a good story," Akira said. "I like the sound of that."

"Okay," Rune said. "That's our story then."

My attention turned to the cookie I held. They continued discussing a believable amount of time that Rune and I could have been dating, as well as other intricacies of the plan. My mind strayed as I twirled the cookie around in between my fingers. Images of earlier tonight flashed in my head. I could still feel Rune's lips on my neck as if his kiss were branded there. My skin still felt hot where his hand had trailed up my shirt, caressing my breasts.

He was such a dick for playing me like that. He said he wasn't going to do anything with me, yet he did stuff with every other girl. He'd even planned on doing that same thing with me at the start, so what was stopping him now? Had my personality made me unappealing to him? Or was he afraid of crossing the "strictly business" line we'd drawn? Whatever the reason, it ached like a punch to the gut.

I snapped the cookie in half, listening to the loud pop as it broke down the middle. That's what I felt like. Torn. There was so much on my plate. Between school, training, the weird shadow that kept popping up, and studying to be a Fae, I didn't know how to also sort through these feelings about Rune. It was leaving my mind a confused mess.

"Bria," Akira called softly, placing a hand on my arm.

"Hmm?" I turned to look at him.

He quirked a brow. "Did you get all that?"

Quickly pushing all thoughts of my relationship troubles aside, I nodded. "Ah, yeah. Sorry. I just spaced out for a minute. I still paid attention, though. Y'all decided we've been dating for two years. Since Rune hasn't been home in about three years, two seemed the most believable."

"How did she get all that if she wasn't actually listening?" Bassel asked, watching me with wonder.

"I was listening."

Sort of.

Rune downed the last of his coffee before jumping to his feet. "Well, since the planning party is over, Bria and I are going to head out."

His gaze found mine, and my heart tripped over itself. It was the first time we'd *really* looked at each other since earlier. I hated that he had this effect on me. With one look, he had my skin flushing and nerves rattling. My heart clearly didn't understand that it was supposed to be mad at him.

Stupid heart.

"Come on," he said.

I placed my now-cold coffee on the table and stood to follow Rune to the door. "Are we doing more training today?"

"No training. You've gotten the basics of fighting down, so we're doing something else today."

"Really? What?" I asked, thrown off guard.

"It's a surprise," he said before grabbing my hand.

I reluctantly followed him to his car. The rain was just starting to come down, so we rushed to get in, and once we were settled, Rune took off down the road.

I laid my chin on my fist and rested my arm on the armrest of the passenger side door. I sighed and asked again, "Where are we going?"

"It's a surprise. I already told you that. I'm not giving you any details. That's the point of a surprise."

I frowned but didn't ask any more questions, knowing by now it was futile to argue with him. I stared out the window at the falling rain, counting the drops that trailed down my window. We drove for a good twenty minutes before he pulled up outside of a large brick building. My jaw fell open as recognition flared. It was called *The Paint Palace*, a well-known place for dating couples to paint together.

Dumbfounded, I turned to Rune. "What are we doing here?"

He smirked and gestured at the building. "Isn't it obvious? We're here to paint. I know how much you love painting. You're putting up with all of this Fae stuff just so you can paint professionally. I thought this could be something fun we did together. You've been working hard, training and putting up with me. You deserve some fun, don't you think?"

My heart warmed, and I had to work hard to keep the happiness off my face. "But this is a couples painting class. You know, for like a date night."

He glanced sideways at me, his mouth turned down slightly. Furrowing his brow, he mumbled, "Well, we're a couple, aren't we? Fake or not. I can still take my fake girlfriend out on a fake date."

I tried my absolute hardest to keep from smiling. Pinching myself didn't wake me up, but I had to be dreaming. A date with Rune? Dax never even took me on a date, yet he had been my actual boyfriend. For Rune to want to do this, to take me painting no less, was like a sweet dream that I never wanted to wake from.

I beamed at him, and he glanced at me again. When he saw me smiling, he quickly looked back at the building and asked, "Can we please go inside now?"

I nodded. Despite the fact that he looked slightly annoyed, I knew it was a façade. Rune tried to put out an air of unconcerned arrogance, but after spending so much time with him, I knew better. It was a way of keeping himself guarded. According to Rune and the others, Fox Fae had trouble loving others. They were selfish creatures by nature who thought of themselves above all else. Rune's attempts at being unaffected by me were his way of ensuring that nothing took root inside of him. Based on his bringing me here, I wondered briefly if it was already too late for that.

But then, of course, common sense reminded me that he didn't get involved emotionally with partners. To him, this was just a part of preparing for the ruse.

We made our way to the building, side-by-side. The rain didn't even bother me. I could hardly focus on anything besides Rune. Not only was he taking me out on a date, he was taking me to do something he knew I loved. I was eager to paint beside him.

When we walked in, the smell of acrylic paint greeted me. It was the best welcome, and it smelled like home to me—a place where I belonged. I couldn't wait to pick up a paintbrush and feel it glide across the canvas, bleeding the colors onto its surface. It had been a while since I had done an actual painting outside of the fox painting, which I'd barely gotten started on due to my limited free time.

"Welcome!" a young girl announced from behind the counter.

It was placed directly in front of the doorway that led to the space where you painted.

I tried to peer past her into the room, hoping the class wasn't already full, but everything was blocked from where I stood.

Rune stepped up to the counter. "Reservation for Rune Beckett."

"All right. I've got you and your date listed right here. There are two easels set up for you in the next room. The class will start in a moment. You two have fun!" she said with a bright smile. She waved her hand behind her to let us know to go in.

My worry dissipated, replaced by uncontrollable excitement. Rune had this all planned out, and I wondered how long he'd been arranging this little date.

When we walked in, almost every table was taken. Each couple seemed to be in their own worlds. They leaned in close to one another, and I saw most of them holding hands or joking. Putting some pep into my step, I followed Rune to our easels, where he sat looking around the room nervously. He fidgeted with the end of a paintbrush on the table, and he stared down at the palette, which held red, blue, yellow, white, and black paint.

I leaned sideways and nudged him with my elbow. "What's wrong? Do you not want to be here? We didn't have to do this, you know."

He sighed and shook his head. "It's fine."

"Then why do you seem like something's bothering you?"

He glanced at me, then turned to the canvas that sat on the easel in front of him. His frown deepened as he mumbled, "I can't paint. I'm going to look stupid in front of you."

My mouth opened slightly as I stared at him in disbelief before bursting into a fit of laughter. I covered my mouth with my fingers, fighting against my mirth. "That's what's wrong? You're worried about looking stupid because you can't paint?"

He narrowed his eyes. "Looking foolish is not something I particularly enjoy doing."

Mouth still lifted in amusement, I shook my head. "You aren't going to look foolish. I think it's going to be fun to paint together. I'm honestly really excited and happy that you brought me here."

Rune looked at me with an intrigued glint in his eye. My cheeks grew warm under his stare, so I turned away. At the same time, the instructor for the class waltzed in. He was an older gentleman who wore an apron, which was stained with paint in every color. His glasses sat on the bridge of his nose, and he smiled at everyone in the room. He carried a canvas depicting a lake at the base of mountains, which he placed on an easel at the front of the classroom.

It was a simple enough picture for beginners, but as I gazed at the picture, my mind began to see other possibilities for my own painting. I would still keep the idea of the example piece, but mine would be original to me.

The man at the head of the room gave us a warm greeting. "Good evening, everyone! Welcome to *The Paint Palace*. I'll be your instructor for the night. My name is Harris Lancer, and it's lovely to meet all of you fine couples. Tonight, we're going to work on a landscape piece. While I have an example piece to work on with you, we are artists in this building. Your picture can be your interpretation. Do not hold back, dreamers. Paint as you see fit! Now then, to begin our class—"

I tuned him out as he explained to everyone how to start the painting off with the background color. Picking up my paintbrush, I dipped it into the white paint. I brushed it out into my mixing tray before getting a small dab of the yellow to mix with it. Once I had the color I wanted, I began to make soft, gentle brushstrokes across the canvas. It took hardly any time to finish coloring the canvas.

The outer edge of the room had tables with hair dryers set

up so we could dry the paint quickly and move on to the next part of the painting. I got up to join the others who were already working on drying their wet paint. When one of the dryers became available, I grabbed it and started drying my canvas.

Rune came up next to me and looked over my shoulder at my yellow painting. He looked down at his blue one then back at the front of the class at the one we were replicating. Its sky was blue as well.

Rune looked at me again, and he pointed to my canvas. "Are you color blind?"

I stopped drying mine to hand him the dryer. Smiling at him, I shook my head. "No. I know it's not the same color as the one up front, but I'm doing something a bit different."

His mouth was set in a deep frown, his brow furrowed as if he were trying to solve an impossible puzzle. "But the sky isn't yellow."

I laughed. "I told you. Mine is going to be a bit different."

I made my way back over to our table as he began to dry his paint. When I sat back down, I didn't wait for further instruction. I cleaned my brush off and started to mix colors and let the image bleed from inside me and out onto the canvas.

When Rune sat back down, he had blue paint smeared on his hands. He was trying to blow some stray strands of his hair back from his eyes without touching it with his stained fingers.

Giggling at his failed efforts, I reached into my purse, pulling out a spare hair tie.

"Here," I offered, standing up. "Want me to pull your hair back for you?"

He glanced at the hair band then met my eyes with a bashful grin. "Please. As much as I love blue, I'd rather not have blue hair."

Laughing, I stood behind him. My heart started thundering in my chest as I slowly reached forward. His hair was even softer than I thought it would be. It slipped through my fingers like pure silk. I'd secretly wanted to run my hands through his long hair before, and now that I actually was, my heart twisted with excited nerves. It felt intimate to comb my fingers through his hair, and it made my skin prickle with desire for him.

I couldn't let that happen.

Clearing my throat, I finished raking back the strands and secured his hair in a small ponytail. "All done."

One corner of his lush lips lifted as I sat back down on my stool. I swallowed hard seeing him with his hair pulled back. It wasn't the first time I'd seen him like this since he always put it up when we trained. Still, I didn't think I'd ever get used to how attractive it made him look.

It took me a minute to focus on my painting again, but once I did, I got lost in the vision. I was constantly getting up to dry the paint so that I could keep going. Every time I began painting again, Rune would glance at mine, then his, then the one up front.

Rune was fun to watch. Anytime he finished something, he would sit there and wait for further instructions from Mr. Lancer, and as Mr. Lancer spoke, Rune's brow would furrow as he concentrated. When he painted, he leaned close to the canvas and moved his hand ever so slowly so that he wouldn't mess up. It was hard not to smile while watching him. He was trying so hard to replicate the example picture, and I found myself leaning over to help him at moments when he seemed disheartened.

I had just gotten focused on adding the stream to my painting when Rune's voice broke my concentration.

"Hey," Rune said.

"Hmm?"

I turned to him, and at the same moment, he swiped his paint brush across the bridge of my nose. Instantly, he bent over, clutching his stomach as his deep laugh rocked his body. My mouth hung open, and it took me a second to recover from the shock. Laughing, I quickly grabbed my own brush and smeared black paint across his jawline.

This was war.

Rune made a move to come at me with his purple paint brush, and I held his wrists, trying to fight off his advances and my own laughter. As he was about to reach my neck, Mr. Lancer cleared his throat from behind us. My stomach dropped as we whipped around to face him.

"Children, this isn't that kind of paint class." He gave us a pointed look and cast another around the room. After ensuring no one was eavesdropping, he leaned in close and whispered, "But I do have a class of that nature. See me afterwards for details if interested."

He walked away briskly. Rune and I met each other's eyes, and in an instant, we broke out into fits of laughter again. It was minutes before we calmed down and got back to the task at hand.

By the time I finished my painting, it was still a landscape with water, but it wasn't a lake with mountains in the background. Mine depicted what had become one of my most treasured places. It was the stream behind my campus dorm room. It showed the stream with the trees beyond it during sunset, so gold light streamed through the trees, reflecting upon the water's surface. Not only was it the picture of the stream and surrounding forest, but in the center of the painting, at the edge of the stream, I had also painted the fox and me sitting side by side. We were facing the water, our backs to the viewer.

I beamed at my completed painting, then turned to look at Rune's. He stared at his painting with a solemn look. He had tried so hard on his painting, yet it looked like a blue half circle at the base of two purple triangles with white lines every now and then. I bit my lip to fight the giggle that was trying to escape, finding it oddly adorable.

"Mine looks like a third grader did it," he pouted with a

huff.

I laughed and shook my head. "Well, I love it."

He looked at mine for the first time since its completion, and when he did, something in his gaze changed. It sharpened and became alight with some unreadable emotion. His eyes flicked to me, then back to the painting. He slowly raised his hand, pointing at the piece. "Is-is that—"

I turned back to my own work and gave a satisfied nod. "It's the creek where I met the fox."

Rune stared at the painting, his amber eyes shining. The way his gaze traced every detail of the picture made my heart want to leap from my chest. He seemed so captivated by the painting, and that warmed me from head to toe. Besides my art teachers, no one had looked at my works the way Rune was. Granted, it looked good, but he seemed utterly fascinated by the picture, as if it held answers to some unknown question. He looked at it the way I looked at the picture of him with his brothers.

After a few more moments, he shook his head and looked away from the picture. He cleared his throat and said, "Well, I guess we should go now since the class is over."

We gathered our paintings and made our way back outside. Luckily, the rain had stopped by this point, so our paintings didn't get wet. Rune wanted to throw his in the garbage, but I wouldn't let him. He frowned as he placed it in the backseat, along with mine.

"Thank you for taking me," I said, the bliss bleeding into my words as we drove back to his house. "I really enjoyed it."

"You're welcome. I have to admit, I liked it a bit, too. Not the painting part. I hated that, but it was interesting watching you work."

Crimson lit my cheeks as I looked out the window. He had been watching me that much? I mean, I had watched him, but knowing he watched me that intently made the giddiness in my stomach dance wildly. He said that it was interesting. Was that a good or bad thing?

Being alone with Rune after a fun-filled evening, my insides tightened with fresh nerves. My mind drifted back to earlier in the day when we'd been in his room. The memory felt far away, almost like a dream. My cheeks grew warm when I remembered the way it felt to lay beneath him or the way it had felt when he ran his fangs across my skin and touched me in sensitive areas.

"I want to apologize." His voice was so soft, I almost thought I'd imagined it.

I looked at him, my train of thoughts coming to a standstill. "For what?"

"For what I did earlier. You know, in my room. That was wrong of me to mess with you like that."

Refusing to meet his eyes, I turned back to the window. It wasn't something I wanted to talk about. I feared it would spark a conversation about my feelings for him. There was no way I was going to admit how I felt, so I kept quiet and continued to watch the passing trees. I did appreciate his apology. It was only the second time he'd openly apologized after doing something he knew was wrong.

Neither of us spoke the rest of the way back to his house. Despite my better judgment, I couldn't stop thinking about what it felt like to do normal things with him. We had laughed and made jokes while painting, and it had felt so natural. So *real*. To anyone there, it would've looked like we were an actual couple. Then, when I thought back to his words after the incident in his room, I was given a painful reminder that we weren't actually anything. None of it was real or had any meaning.

At least not to him.

By the time we made it back to his house, it was already dark out, and the lingering rain clouds obscured the moon. We stepped out into the silent darkness, and I watched as Rune went to the back to grab our paintings.

"I want to thank you again," I said as he handed me mine.

"For taking me out this evening."

He gave me one of his usual sarcastic grins. "Don't get used to it. Unless you'd want to take Mr. Lancer up on his offer. I wonder if those other kinds of classes are just as interesting."

Rolling my eyes, I glanced down at my painting. As I examined the picture through the dark, the memory of Rune's face lighting up upon seeing it flittered by. Glancing back up at him, I realized he was looking down at the picture, too.

Smiling, I held it out. "Here. You can have this."

He looked at me with a hint of surprise on his face. I was well aware by now that he didn't like to show any signs of emotion other than boredom, sarcasm, or confidence, so it was nice to see him so surprised. He looked from me to the canvas. "But it's yours."

I shrugged. "I don't need it. I want you to keep it. I don't know who the fox is yet, but you know him. That means it's a picture of someone you're close to and the girl who saved your ass from needing to have a *real* girlfriend."

He stared down at the picture with the faint trace of something warm playing at his mouth. Finally, he reached out and took it from me. The motion made a happy buzz stir in my chest as I watched the way his hungry eyes traced over the image. Maybe that fox was dearer to him than I had realized.

Rune looked down at his own painting, then back up at me. He gave me a nervous smile, something I had never seen on him before. It made him look even more charming than usual. "I would offer you mine, but I don't think anyone would want it, especially a painter like you."

I laughed before reaching out to take his canvas. I hugged it to my chest and said, "I'd love to take it. I think it's one of my favorite abstract pieces."

"Abstract," he repeated, shaking his head. "I think even that is being a bit too kind."

He looked at me with a glimmer of something sincere in

his eyes. It was that genuine smile of his that seemed to turn my knees to rubber and heart to mush. I had only seen it in the picture of him with his brothers, so seeing him look at me that way made the lid on my feelings crack down the middle. Trying to avoid letting him see my cheeks glow red, I looked down at his painting. Despite what he thought, I really did love it.

Meeting his eyes again, I gestured over my shoulder at my car. "Well, I should probably get going since it's getting late."

"Wait." He cocked his head to the side, revealing his ponytail. "You're forgetting your hair tie."

"Oh, right."

I held out my hand, waiting for him to give it back, but he didn't move. He smirked as he waited, still tilting his head. I realized he was waiting for me to take his hair down for him. Swallowing hard, I reached out with my free hand and slowly pulled the band from his hair. Our bodies were inches apart, and the close proximity paired with the intimate action made my breath hitch in my throat. I bit my lip as the tie came loose, and his heated eyes dropped to my mouth. His white hair spilled around his shoulders, and I swallowed hard as I combed my fingers through the soft strands. He shifted a little closer, his head angling down slightly toward mine. My eyes fell to his full lips of their own accord, and my hands slipped through his locks until my palm rested on his shoulder.

The air between us was suddenly thick, and it vibrated with need. All I had to do was lean closer and give in to that incessant desire. I could see in the way his eyes burned a trail along my lips, my neck, my body, that he wanted this just as much as I did.

But I was scared.

Scared of his eventual rejection.

He didn't do relationships. He did hook ups, and as much as I wanted him, I didn't want to be just another one-night stand. I'd want something more while he'd only be offering a physical connection.

Clearing my throat, I stepped away and dropped my hand to my side. I clutched his painting to my chest as if it were a shield that could protect me from my attraction to him. Daring to glance up at him, I gave a sheepish grin. "Thanks for the hair tie back. I should probably get going now."

He stared at me a moment, as if he were trying to process what happened. Finally, he nodded. "Right. Well, I guess I'll see you tomorrow for some more training."

I nodded and started to turn away when he called, "Oh yeah. Before I forget, don't worry about coming here on Friday night. I'll pick you up at five."

I looked at him sideways. "Really? What for?"

He shrugged as amusement lit his golden gaze. "I guess you'll just have to wait and see."

I rolled my eyes and fought my smile. "Fine. Be all mysterious."

I felt his eyes on me as I walked away, and it made my stomach twist in desperate need. I wondered what he saw or what he thought about when he looked at me. Was I just a girl who was easy to use, or was I someone he was beginning to enjoy having around?

CHAPTER

TWENTY-FOUR

My eyes kept traveling to Rune's painting while driving back to my dorm. When I thought about how focused and determined he'd been at the class, I couldn't help but dance on the inside. This was a painting he'd given his all on, and the experience was a memory I got to share with him. No other girl had ever gotten to say that about him based on what he and the guys had told me about him. It had only been sex for them, and even though we weren't doing that, I still felt grateful for the amazing thing he *had* given me: the honor of being each other's first date.

I was on cloud nine when I reached the dorm. It was dark, and very few students were out when I managed to skip my way across the parking lot. My eyes were still glued to Rune's painting, and my head and heart were in a blissful blur when an ominous shiver traveled down my spine.

I stopped dead in my tracks, knowing by now that this feeling was someone's eyes on me. Scanning the cars, my eyes lingered on a black SUV. The shadows near it were inky and dripping with rancor. I took a step away from the car when the shadows started to move. The darkness shifted and swirled together until it was no longer a shadow but a man in front of me.

His dark hair fell in waves to his shoulders, and he had a neatly trimmed goatee around his broad, eerie smile. "Finally. You're alone! It's been quite irritating trailing you with so many people around."

Swallowing hard, I stood my ground. Two weeks of self-defense training wasn't much, but it made me feel a bit braver than I would've before. If this guy tried anything, I could defend myself. As I stared at him, I realized he looked vaguely familiar. My mind raced to pinpoint where I'd seen him before, and that's when it hit me.

He was the man I'd run into on my first day here outside the tattoo parlor as well as at the club.

"Who are you?" I demanded, wondering if he had been stalking me since that moment outside of the tattoo shop. Maybe that phone call I'd overheard really *had* been about me.

He quirked a bushy, black brow. "You don't seem surprised about the way I appeared from the shadows. I thought you were oblivious to this world."

It dawned on me that he was right. I hadn't even batted an eye at him turning from shadows to a man. Once you saw one Fae, you'd seen them all. His little magic trick wasn't anything special at this point.

Raising my head in defiance, I said, "You're Fae."

He laughed, clapping his hands. "Bravo. Interesting. I was told you had no idea about us. Well, whatever. It makes no dif-

FIRE OF THE FOX

ference to me if you know the details or not. I only care about getting the job done and being rid of you."

My brain was starting to hurt. I had no idea what this guy was saying. Who had told him about me? Why had he been tailing me? And by "rid of me," did he mean he wanted to kill me?

All of this was going through my head when his bulky body suddenly stiffened. He whipped his head toward our dorm room and let out a low growl. Turning his glare back to me, he hissed, "Always around someone. Well, I guess that means we'll be meeting again soon. Look forward to it."

Without another word, he burst into a cloud of shadows, and from the shadows emerged a bat. The small creature hovered in the air, then turned and flew off. Not even a second later, the dorm building's doors opened, and Dallas came running out.

"There you are! Finally! Please tell me you got some tonight."

Heart still pounding furiously, I watched Dallas run across the parking lot. I definitely hadn't gotten any, but I had received a strange visit from a Fae. And I was pretty sure he didn't spell good news.

"So, what happened?" Rune asked.

We were sitting on the blue mats of the private studio we'd been using for self-defense training. We'd just finished sparring, and I was gulping down my bottled water.

After running into that weirdo last night, I had sent Rune a text telling him about it. His response was immediate. He wanted to talk more in person, thus resulting in this little session.

Swallowing the liquid goodness, I caught my breath and met his eyes. "A Fae showed up. A bat. He said someone sent him to get rid of me."

His amber eyes narrowed. "A bat? Did he have long black hair and a goatee?"

"You know him?"

He let out an annoyed grunt, leaning his forearms on his knees. "Jonah. He's kind of a recluse among the Fae. Keeps to himself usually, and he isn't against doing shady stuff. Why would he come after you?"

I shrugged. "That's what I want to know. He said someone told him I was ignorant of Fae, and he was tasked with getting rid of me. Whatever the hell that means. Do you think he has me confused with someone else? I mean, I'm clearly not a part of this world unless you count my helping you out, so why would he need to get rid of me?"

His head tipped back, and he stared at the ceiling as he worked through something in his head. This Jonah guy had to be mistaken. Unless it was a way to keep me quiet since I knew about Fae, but even if that was the case, he'd gone into this thinking I was oblivious to Fae. So that still posed the question of what could he possibly want in coming after me?

Rune met my eyes again. "It doesn't make sense, but then again, neither does you having the same magical aura as a Fae. I'll have some people look into Jonah and see what his deal is. Until then, don't go anywhere by yourself in the dark. Bat Fae use it and shadows to travel. He can blend in with it and manipulate it to his advantage."

I swallowed hard. My simple life was becoming more and more screwed up with each passing day. I had so many questions, and it was moments like this when I really felt the absence of my parents. Most people could seek solace in their moms and dads when faced with trying issues, but that wasn't an option for me. Instead, I was left feeling overwhelmed and wondering if things would ever go back to normal.

CHAPTER
TWENTY-FIVE

Friday's art class was a good distraction from the week's earlier events, because it was the day we got back our clay pieces. I needed it after all the stress. Dallas had been so excited about the possibility of my sleeping with Rune that she didn't notice the funk I was in all week. I was glad for this because I didn't know how to tell her about Fae.

By the time class was winding down, my mind buzzed with the anticipation of seeing my creation. Professor Lichen hadn't let any of us see our projects after she fired them, but instead, went straight to grading the pieces. I crossed my fingers that mine turned out the way I'd wanted it.

"I was very impressed by your mug, Bria," Professor Lichen said, coming up behind me. "I could tell you put a lot of thought and care into making it, especially the fox. He looked absolutely incredible! I felt like I was actually looking into the fiery eyes of the creature!"

I smiled at her before finding my mug on the previously covered table in the back of the room. It had turned out even better than what I'd pictured. The blue around the mug was vibrant and the exact shade of Persian blue I'd envisioned. The black and white fox stood out in bright contrast against the color, too. You could see each strand of fur I'd etched into the fox, and the texture helped to bring the vision to life. The thing I loved most was the eyes. The vivid amber orbs shone as though embers blazed wildly within them.

"Are foxes your favorite animal?" Professor Lichen asked.

I paused as I weighed the question. I was crazy about Rune, who was a fox, and I felt a strong bond with the one I'd met at the creek those few times. I hadn't given it much thought until now, but I nodded and replied, "I'd say so."

I accepted my A with a grateful heart and went to leave, but not before Professor Lichen asked if I'd made up my mind about Italy. I told her it wasn't set in stone yet, but things were looking good in that department. She reminded me to have the money to her no later than November first with the paperwork, and I promised I would. The trip to Rune's hometown was the third week of October, which would put me really close to the deadline. But I'd still have it to her before the first, which was all that mattered. All I had to do was keep with the plan.

My mind had been so distracted by the mug and Professor Lichen, I never had time to think about my plans with Rune for that night. While in my following classes, my mind drifted off, trying to come up with possible scenarios for this evening. My readiness to be with him again made the day trail on at a snail's pace.

By the time my last class ended, I bounded out of my desk. I was eager to get ready for this evening, but I hesitated.

How would I know what to wear? I had no clue what we were doing.

Dallas would probably have an answer, so I put a bit more pep in my step. When I got to our dorm room, she was busy getting ready for something, too. She wore a blue shirt with a tight, black miniskirt. Her high heels made her look even taller than normal, and her long red hair fell down her back as she leaned down to look in the mirror, applying her makeup.

She turned to smile at me when I came in. "Hey! You wanna come to a party with me tonight?"

I shook my head. "I'm going out with Rune. I actually wanted to ask you what I should wear because I have no idea what he has planned. He said it was a surprise."

She looked at me with her face lighting up. "Wow! What a romantic gentleman. Rune's such a better boyfriend than Dax ever was. I still can't believe you actually wanted the painting he did, though."

I looked at Rune's painting, where it hung above my bed. I'd put it there after our night at *The Paint Palace*, despite Dallas's arguments.

I shook my head at her. "Instead of making fun of his hard work, why don't you help your best friend figure out what to wear?"

She sighed and flopped down onto the edge of her bed. She pursed her lips and looked at me from head to toe, taking in my leggings and hoodie I'd worn to class. She mumbled, "Well, definitely not that."

I laughed and rolled my eyes. "I knew that much."

She tossed her red curls over her shoulder. "Why don't we go to one of the shopping outlets? We can buy you something cute to wear. I still have a few hours before I have to meet Rance for the party anyway. What time do you need to be ready?"

"He's picking me up at 5, so if we run to that strip in town, we should have plenty of time."

"Sweet!" Dallas sang. She hopped up and raced for the door, her purse flung over her shoulder. "Hurry up, slowpoke!"

Once we made it to the strip in town, we strolled along the sidewalk and peeked into boutiques for any signs of cute clothes.

"So," Dallas started. "You guys came close to being *intimate*. Are you sure you didn't do anything else?"

"I'm sure. I honestly have no idea what even happened there," I said, thinking back on the events in his bedroom.

I hoped she couldn't hear the disappointment in my voice as I answered her. It wasn't that I was looking to do that stuff with him right now, but it did make me feel a bit dejected since he'd given that to other girls so easily, especially since it felt like there was *something* in his eyes every time he looked at me now.

"Well, that's depressing," Dallas said with a frown.

I smirked at her and cocked an eyebrow.

She shrugged and said, "Hey! Let's swing into that book-shop really quick. It just opened, and I want to see if they have anything good."

Laughing, I followed her into the shop. I was thankful for the change in topic, plus I loved wasting time looking at books. Who didn't?

A small bell chimed above the door as we entered. A beautiful woman with dark hair turned to welcome us. She had been placing books on a shelf when we came in, and a small dark-haired boy was holding onto her pants leg.

"Hello there!" she greeted with a bright smile. "Welcome to our shop!"

"Hi," I grinned back.

Her round stomach showed she was far along with child, and based on how closely the small boy clung to her, I assumed he belonged to her as well. His bright blue eyes followed Dallas and me as we roamed the store. I gave him a friendly wave, at which he gasped before hiding behind his mother. She patted his head gently as the two of them went behind the counter.

"This book sounds good," Dallas sang as she plucked one from the shelf. "I love a good romance, which is why I wish you'd get on with it already with Rune."

Rolling my eyes, I glanced over the various titles on the shelves. There was a large variety to choose from, which was great. We didn't have too many good bookstores around here. Maybe they had some on Fae?

"Raven, honey, where do you want this display?"

A man with jet-black hair emerged from the back of the store, carrying a metal stand. The woman, Raven, gave him a pointed look before flashing us an apologetic smile. "Kaden, we have customers," she muttered to him between her teeth.

"Oops," he laughed, rubbing the back of his neck. "Sorry, ladies. I hope you guys find some good books! If there's a title we don't have, let us know. We can order anything you want."

"Thank you!" Dallas said. "That's so awesome of you."

Kaden gave his wife a peck on the cheek before retreating into the back once more.

Giving us another apologetic look, she said, "Sorry about that. We haven't had too many customers yet since we just opened."

"No problem," I said with a dismissive wave.

Dallas practically hopped to the front counter with three books in her hand.

Raven scanned the titles and met Dallas's smile with a matching one. "Angel romance stories, hmm?"

"Yes. I love stories like that."

Raven laughed softly. "Me too."

"Do you by chance have any books on folklore?" I glanced at Dallas. Not wanting to ask for books specifically on Fae since that may raise questions from her, I cleared my throat and added, "I'm doing a project on folklore for English and was looking for some good reference books. You know, something that has a variety."

Raven paused, pursing her lips. "Hmm. I don't think we have any on hand, but I can definitely order some in for you. Any specific titles you want?"

"No. Just whatever you find that has a good variety of stories in it."

"Will do! I'll look tonight and order some. Give me a week or two."

We finished up our book purchases and waved to the woman and her son, promising to come back again soon. Only a few shops away, we found the perfect clothing boutique. After trying on a few items, I decided on a pair of dark jeans and a white top that was littered with flowers.

Dallas and I still had some time left, so we also stopped for coffee. Dallas continued to shower me with questions about Rune, and I managed to sneak in some questions about her and Rance. She got a spark in her eyes every time she talked about him, which I loved. It made me happy to see her so elated.

By the time we made it back to the dorm, it was 4:15. I put on my new outfit, curled my hair, and touched up my makeup. After I was done, I checked my phone for the time. It was three minutes until five, and since I knew Rune would be here at exactly five, I decided to make my way downstairs to wait for him outside. I practically oozed excitement, constantly readjusting my shirt or pulling my hair over my shoulder before tossing it back over, only to pull it forward again. It was hard to contain the intoxicating rush of nerves.

My feelings were becoming undeniable, but I had to fight it before Rune realized. While there had been some sort of spark for both of us recently, I didn't know what inspired his.

Lust? Sexual frustration? Or maybe something real and new was developing for us both. I just didn't have that answer yet.

Until I knew where he stood and how he *actually* felt, giving in to my feelings would only put my money to Italy in jeopardy because then he'd see this wasn't fake for me anymore. If he only wanted to explore a physical relationship like he'd done in the past, if this didn't go beyond that for him, he could take the deal off the table. That was something I couldn't afford.

CHAPTER

TWENTY-SIX

The clock struck five. As soon as I looked up from my phone, Rune's car pulled next to the curb, and he looked at me through the passenger-side window. I got in with excitement flooding my system.

His eyes roamed over me as I buckled. My cheeks heated under the intensity of his gaze. It was like he was taking in every inch of me, tattooing it into his memory. When he finally met my eyes again, he asked, "What would you have done if I were taking you to play paintball or something?"

"I guess I would've been in a sticky situation. Why? Is that what we're doing?" I asked. I looked over his own outfit. He wore khakis with a dark blue button-up shirt. I was going to assume that meant the paintball idea was out the window. Thank God.

He pulled away from the building and made his way for the exit on campus. "I thought I'd take you out somewhere nice to eat."

My heart grew warm, but my worries about where we stood still plagued me. Staring forward at the passing scenery, I picked at the hem of my shirt. "Can I ask you something?"

"Depending on the question, I may or may not have an answer, but sure."

I looked at him out of the corner of my eye and asked, "Why did you never take other girls out on dates?"

"I've told you before. I don't date. Every girl I ever—I guess you could say 'hooked up with'—knew beforehand that I had no interest in being serious with her. I wasn't going to take someone out when I had no interest in building a relationship with them. That wouldn't be fair to them, getting their hopes up for something more than what it was, and dating would've done exactly that."

My heart stopped. Dating meant there was something more in his mind. And here he was, taking *me* out. Did I dare to get my hopes up?

"Then why are you taking me out?"

"Because you and I are pretending to be a couple, are we not? We need to do the things a real couple would. That way it'll feel more genuine and believable when the time comes for us to put on the show."

"Right. That makes sense."

It did make sense, but it hurt, too. I knew what I was signing up for when I agreed to do this. Two months of fake dating. That was it.

Looking down at my curled hair and new clothes, I mentally slapped myself. I had tried so hard to look nice tonight, all for him. I was so embarrassed over my pointless efforts. Was he making fun of me on the inside, too? *Silly, Bria. Trying to get all dressed up for someone who would never like you back.*

I sighed and mumbled, "Will I ever find someone who actually likes me for me?"

"What?" he asked, glancing at me.

I waved a dismissive hand. "Nothing. I'm just talking to myself."

"You probably shouldn't do that. People are going to think you're weird."

I rolled my eyes. "Thank you for the advice. You'd 100 percent be the head of that weird club, though."

He looked at me aghast and gave a brief laugh. "Excuse me? I'm perfectly normal."

"Right, right." I nodded, exuding as much nonchalance as I could muster. "Except for the whole Fae thing. And magical powers thing. Oh, and the bad personality. Did I mention the Fae thing?"

"Wow," he dragged out the word. "Are you trying to hit below the belt?"

Laughing, I met his eyes. Leaning in close, I dropped my voice. "You wish I'd go for below your belt."

Surprise flickered in his gaze for a brief minute before being replaced by an intense, almost pained flare of something I knew all too well. Desire. Longing. My heart quickened as I caught a glimpse of that look, but he quickly recovered and turned away from me. In a daze, I leaned back in my seat and turned to look out the window. Maybe that joke had gone a bit too far.

"Have you started packing for the trip yet?" he asked after a few moments of silence. I was glad for the sudden change in topic. "Since we leave next week, it might not be a bad idea to start getting all your stuff ready. Depending on what you have clothing-wise, we may need to go shopping before we leave. Like I said, my family is *very* traditional."

The reminder that it had already been nearly two months of being with him was difficult to stomach. It seemed like only yesterday that we met at the club. The time had passed quickly, and more than anything, I wanted to slow it down. I wasn't ready for our time together to come to an end. My chest tightened when I thought about losing him and the other guys. They had wiggled their way into my heart in such a small amount of time, and the thought of not seeing them again ached like a physical wound.

"No, I haven't packed yet. I'm not too worried about the clothes, either. I have some dresses I can bring. Honestly, I haven't even told Dallas I'm leaving yet, but I'm sure she won't mind me being gone. It means she and Rance can have our dorm room all to themselves."

"That's something I've been meaning to talk to you about. It doesn't make sense to me," he said, his eyes narrowing.

"What do you mean?"

He sighed and explained, "When we first met you, we thought you were Fae because you emit the same magical aura as us. That wasn't all, though. When Dallas and Rance were outside the club with us after the attempted robbery, we could faintly sense that same aura on them. I brushed it off, thinking they'd just been around a Fae inside the club, but I'm not as convinced anymore."

I frowned. There wasn't anything weird about us. We were all human. Dallas and I had been friends since freshman year of high school. I would know if there was something odd about her, and I'm sure she would've figured out if something was up with Rance by now or if he was Fae. So then why did all three of us give off that aura?

I turned back to Rune as he continued, "I considered the possibility that you were Water Fae since you love water, but if you were, you never would've saved the fox at the creek since Water Fae don't help Land Fae. Also, you seemed way too surprised and shocked when you found out that Fae even existed, so I've somewhat ruled that out."

"Well, you can rule it out all the way. I'm 100 percent human. Yeah, okay, I like water a little more than the average person, but I'm not some magical being like you guys."

"Have you ever been able to manipulate water?" he asked, glancing at me with an inquisitive look.

I shook my head. "I've never tried. Why would I?"

He raised his chin and said, "Maybe you should. It's also possible that you're descended from someone who had Fae in them. You could have an ancestor somewhere down the line that decided to get freaky with a Fae, and the Fae in you got diluted by humans with each generation."

Considering that theory, I nodded. "I guess that makes sense. Still, it's hard to believe I could have any Fae in me. It would be a lot easier to figure out if I could ask my parents what they knew." I paused and forced myself to take a deep breath. Closing my eyes, I shook my head and mumbled, "Too bad that can't happen."

Silence filled the car, and I realized too late that maybe that was too heavy of a comment. I clearly didn't know how to read the room, but it was something that genuinely frustrated me. Ever since Rune and his friends had mentioned that I had a magical aura, I'd so badly wondered if my real parents would've had an explanation for that. Would they have laughed and told me I had a great-great-great-great grandmother who really had gotten freaky with a Fae? Or could there be another explanation entirely? I didn't have those answers, and that killed me.

"Do you want to talk about it?"

The gentle tone of Rune's voice had me turning to look at him. He glanced at me before focusing on the road again.

I swallowed hard. "Talk about what?"

"Your parents."

My chest tightened. Having him ask me about my parents was like a huge breath of fresh air. I never talked about them, and no one ever asked how I felt about the subject. Not even

Dallas. My birth parents had always been a topic I kept hidden, only to fantasize about them when I was alone. Maybe talking would help lessen the pain a bit more, and Rune was someone I didn't mind confiding in.

"When I was little, I would secretly stay up all night with a flashlight and my sketchbook. I'd hide under my covers and draw their faces for hours. I obviously didn't know what they looked like, but that was part of the fun, I guess. I got to make up what they looked like, what they did for a living, where they were in the world. I'd draw and draw and draw until my hand cramped."

"I bet they're really good people."

The faintest touch of a smile graced my lips as I stared out the window. Emotion clogged my throat as I said, "I hope so. I hope they're good people, still alive and well. Even if I can't see them, I just want them to be okay."

Rune reached across the console to take my hand in his. Our fingers intertwined, and his thumb brushed over the top of my hand in soothing circles.

My eyes slipped closed, and I focused on the warmth of his hand in mine and the gentle pattern he trailed along my skin. The touch grounded me, and his spicy, woodsy scent wrapped around me. I inhaled deeply, and with his presence, peace settled in my core once more.

Rune was here.

He was here with me.

He was here *for* me.

And he was all I needed right now.

After a few moments of silence, I cleared my throat and sought for a change in topic. "Why are Land Fae and Water Fae enemies? You mentioned it briefly before, but what exactly happened?"

Rune thought about it for a moment before answering slowly. "It wasn't necessarily a single event that made us not get along. Water Fae live in the water, but they could also survive on land. They'd come up to the surface every so often, and the more they did, the more they decided they preferred land. Water Fae started getting the idea that they could rule both land and water, which we didn't take too kindly. Land Fae wanted their territory to stay theirs, and Water Fae wanted control of both. Thus began a century's worth of war and slaughtering each other. We finally stopped a little less than twenty years ago."

"Why did it stop? Did one side win?"

"Land Fae did. We're stronger than the Water Fae, which is obvious to anyone. Land Fae all have different abilities, depending on what kind of Fae they are, and there's a lot of us. Water Fae have some varying abilities, like Water Fae can control water, Jellyfish Fae can shock people by touching them, and so on. Still, it's not enough of a diverse arsenal to defeat Land Fae.

"They knew it was a losing fight, so after the Land Fae killed nearly all of the Water Fae, the Water Fae King and Queen hid their son from us roughly eighteen years ago. Ever since then, most of the Water Fae that were left disappeared from our radar, most likely awaiting the Prince's return to help them try to defeat us. They'll still lose, of course, but they can have their hope, I guess."

I looked up at the fading sun, my mind trying to process all of this new information. "Fighting for more than a century?" I looked at Rune and was hesitant as I asked, "So, you killed a lot of people, then?"

He suddenly glared at me, anger rolling off him in waves. "They aren't people, Bria. They're evil beings with no regard for anyone other than their own kind. But yes, I killed a lot of them, and in the end, it was a losing fight for them. A Water Fae with centuries under his belt wasn't able to stand a chance against me or any Canine Fae.

"Some Land Fae weren't powerful enough to win against the Water Fae. For a high-ranking Canine Fae, like a Fox, the only ones who stood a chance against us were elite soldiers and those of royal birth. The royalty were obviously the most powerful among the Water Fae. Not even their own people could use their water magic against them. It came from centuries of breeding the most talented of Water Fae together to continue the strongest, purest line of raw power. Still, in the end, the king and queen knew there was no chance for their kind, so in a last attempt to save the Water Fae, they hid the prince. The remaining Water Fae followed suit, hiding like the cowards they are."

Trying to picture the two classes of Fae going to war with each other was bizarre to think about, yet it had really happened and had only ended eighteen years ago, all because the prince was hidden away. Rune had even participated for a majority of it. That was a bitter idea to swallow, but he was from a different world than me. A lot of this stuff was hard for me to fathom, despite the fact that humans had plenty of war, too. This war felt much closer to home for some reason.

I turned back to Rune. His eyes seemed so far away, and I could tell his mind was elsewhere. I had no idea what he was thinking about, but he seemed almost wistful. This was one of the few times I'd seen a truly somber look on his face, and it pained me. I wanted him to smile, even if it was one of his mischievous or sarcastic grins. I didn't want him reliving the pain, blood, and loss of life from long-ago nightmares.

I was looking for something to say that could lighten the mood when he mumbled, "The Water Fae King was the one who killed my father."

My heart ripped open at the grief laced in his voice. Rune clutched the steering wheel so tightly that his knuckles turned white. His gaze was fixated on the road, but his eyes were still unfocused and bleary. His kind hated the Water Fae due to their own issues, but now, I realized his personal reasons for hating them ran deeper than I'd previously thought. They had taken something precious from him.

Not knowing what to say or do, I whispered, "I-I'm so sorry."

His eyes grew dark then. I had seen his eyes cloud over before, but this was something completely different. It was as if an actual dark veil came over him as he sneered, "The king got what he deserved."

Fear brewed deep in the pit of my stomach. I had been afraid of Rune before, but this was entirely different. He seemed so far away from me at that moment. It felt like no matter how far I reached or how loud I called, I'd never be able to get him back from wherever he'd gone. He was corrupted by a need for vengeance, and it was chilling to see.

As soon as the look was there, it disappeared just as quickly. He shook his head, as if coming out of a trance. He glanced at me and gave me a small, forced smile. "Sorry. I bet that scared you a little. The guys say I seem different when I talk about Water Fae."

I tried putting on a pleasant face, but it fell short. I was still too shaken by that drastic change in character, so I just looked out the window. I could understand that he wanted to avenge his father, but that anger-fueled side of him was frightening. Akira, Bassel, and Marlow definitely had it right—he was a completely different person when it came to Water Fae, and it wasn't someone I wanted to meet again.

CHAPTER
TWENTY-SEVEN

The air became more lighthearted as we finished the hour's drive to the restaurant, although I didn't know if I could call it a restaurant. When we pulled up to a river's edge, my breath caught. A large, white river-t sat docked in the water in front of me. Lights were strung g the upper railing, casting a beautiful glow upon the deck. mall ramp connected the entryway to the dock, allowing ple to board, but the only car I saw was Rune's.

I looked from the boat to Rune, my face still fro- in complete wonder. Rune's eyes brightened as he ched me, which sent my heart reeling. It was that uine smile of his again. My cheeks colored, but dn't care. I suddenly wished that I had dressed r for such a place.

I looked back at the boat and shook my head. "We can't eat here, Rune. It's probably crazy expensive!"

He gave a small laugh, the sound so foreign. It, like the delight painted on his face now, was so real. My heart wanted to dance to the sound and commit it to memory. He looked away from me with a nervous glint in his eyes, and something in my chest tightened, seeing how charming he looked when hesitant.

Was it getting hot in here?

I swallowed, trying to keep my own nerves out of my voice. "What? What's so funny?"

He gave me a sheepish grin. "It won't be expensive. I own the boat."

My wide eyes traced the large vessel, then met Rune's again. Now I was the one with the nervous laugh. He owned a freaking riverboat? Something I'd started picking up on was that money didn't seem to be an issue for Rune or the others. Bassel owned a gym, which is where we trained. Avana was an entrepreneur who owned dozens of clothing boutiques, mystic shops, and all-natural spa services. And that was just the start.

My eyes were transfixed on the giant boat, so Rune nudged me with his elbow. "Are you just going to stare at it all night, or would you like to actually get on?"

I nodded my head, a bit too eagerly. "I'd like to get on."

"Then try opening the door and getting out. You'll be able to board better that way."

Rolling my eyes at him, I was quick to open the door and jump out. My gaze was still trained on the boat as we approached it together. Its clean body gleamed a beautiful white, and all the railings and borders shined in a sleek black. It was a stunning vessel that demanded attention and reverence.

When we reached the ramp, Rune let me go first. I smiled at him before slowly walking up the inclined wood until I was inside the second floor of the boat. I gasped the minute I laid eyes on the interior. The room was large and open, spanning from one end of the boat to the other. A set of beautiful marble steps led onto the upper deck to my left and another set went lower into the boat on my right.

The floors were a beautiful and intricate design, made up of gold and red patterns. Brown leather chairs sat throughout the room in small arranged seating areas. Across from me, in the center of the room, was a 360-degree mahogany bar. An array of brandies and wines stocked the shelves. A large, crystal chandelier hung above it. Its gold branches swung out and upward, allowing strands of crystals to hang down. On the other side of the bar sat a couch that faced a large wall made of glass, which allowed people to look out onto the river.

My mouth practically dragged across the floor as I walked further into the room. Rune watched me with amusement playing at his lips. I beamed at him as I spun around in slow circles to take in the room.

"This is incredible."

A mixture of pride and relief flooded his features. "I'm glad you like it."

"*Lord Rune.*"

At the sound of someone's voice, I turned to the stairs that led onto the upper deck and tried to keep my snicker hidden at the use of the formal title. An older gentleman who was dressed in a black butler's suit stood by the stairs. He had one arm draped behind him while the other was hugged to his stomach, and he stood in a bow.

"Ah, Charles." Rune said, greeting the man.

Charles stood up straight. He pushed his glasses up his nose before stepping sideways. He gave a wide sweep of his arm to gesture up the stairs. "Your table is ready."

Rune nodded, then turned back to me. "Are you ready?"

I nodded, and together, we made our way up the stairs. When I stepped out onto the deck, goosebumps broke out along my arms, and it wasn't from the sudden chill in the open air.

The only light up here came from the moon, stars, the small lights that had been strung around the railings, and the candles. A single table with two chairs waited in the center of the polished, wooden deck. A white table cloth decorated it, and two candles sat in the middle. The plates, silverware, and glasses had already been neatly arranged with a bottle of wine and a basket of bread.

"Well," Rune said, approaching the table as he shoved his hands in his pockets. "I told Charles to prepare a nice dinner table for two, and he definitely delivered."

I gave a small laugh, my eyes still roaming over everything. "Yes, he did."

As if on cue, Charles came around me and pulled out a chair. Looking at me, he said, "My lady."

Nothing could wipe the smile from my face. There was a soft breeze that blew as the boat pulled away from the dock, moving into the gentle flow of the river. My shirt had long sleeves, but it was loose and thin. There was a slight chill growing on my arms, but I didn't care. I couldn't believe Rune did all this for us.

For me.

Even if it was fake.

Sinking into the chair, I thanked Charles, and Rune took the seat across from me. Charles plucked the bottle of wine from its place on the table and tilted it toward me.

"Would the Lady care for a glass?"

I started to decline, explaining that I didn't drink nor was I old enough to, but Rune nodded to Charles and said, "We'd both like some."

Charles bowed slightly and poured the wine in each of our glasses. Rune gave me an apologetic smile from across the table. His gaze paired with the twinkling lights and flickering candles was making my heart do crazy things, and my skin flushed a warm pink. I looked down at my glass of water, which had already been set out. Reaching for it, I took a few sips to calm myself. Rune always had a way of making me nervous and excited all at once.

Charles placed the wine back in the bucket and gave Rune and me small menus listing different *expensive* foods, such as filet mignon and lobster. I swallowed hard, trying to pick something. How was I supposed to choose from this stuff? Did he or I have to pay for it, or was it taken care of since he owned the place? I glanced up at Rune, who watched me with a curious glint in his eye. He didn't even glance at his menu, but then again it was his boat, so he most likely already knew what he wanted.

Meeting Charles' patient gaze, I let out a nervous breath and said, "I'll take the parmesan chicken linguine."

He nodded and took my menu. He turned to Rune who shrugged and said, "The same thing as always."

Charles bowed. "Yes, my lord."

He turned on his heel and walked away, retreating back down into the lower level. That's when it started to sink in that Rune and I were alone in such a romantic setting.

My nerves spiked to uncharted territory, especially since he kept smiling at me as if *he* were the lucky one. He looked so good in his dark, long-sleeved button up. The wind caught the end of his long hair, tossing it gently around his shoulders, and his eyes had a shine to them. It made my voice get stuck in my chest.

Clearing my throat, I looked down at the wine. When I met his eyes again, I said, "I've never actually had wine before. Or alcohol of any kind."

He nodded, picking up his own glass. "I know, but you'll be expected to when we go to my mother's house. This will be good practice. Just try it. You may end up liking it. Plus, it's best if someone drinks it now that we opened it. Don't want it to go to waste."

I glanced warily at the glass before picking it up. Out of curiosity, I asked, "How much was it?"

He shrugged and leaned back in his chair. "I bought it at an auction, so just shy of $2,000."

My eyes went wide, and I nearly dropped the glass of dark liquid. He had paid $2,000 for this? Money really *wasn't* an issue for him. I figured as much since he was giving me five grand in exchange for my help.

I met Rune's eyes over the top of my glass. "I hope this was made with gold to be $2,000."

He laughed. "Maybe it was. I'll let you be the judge if it's gold worthy."

I sighed before bringing it to my lips. It was sweet, something I wasn't expecting. The taste was unlike anything else I'd ever drunk before, but I rather liked it. That was definitely a good thing considering the price.

"Well?" he asked.

I nodded. "It's good."

"Told you that you might like it."

Swallowing another sip, I twirled the stem of the glass. "Have you heard anything back about Jonah?"

"Not enough. As far as my guy can tell, he's working for someone who's tasked him with tracking you down. We already knew that, of course. He doesn't meet up with whoever has hired him. They just make calls, and he hasn't said why he's after you."

That wasn't what I wanted to hear. "So, we still know nothing?"

Rune watched me, mulling over something in his head. Leaning forward, he crossed his arms over the table. "The only reason he'd want to take someone out is either if he had something personal against them, which he doesn't in this case since you didn't know him, or if they were Water Fae."

"But I'm not Water Fae, either. I'm not Fae at all. I'm human."

He pursed his lips. "Are you sure?"

Narrowing my eyes, I clenched my fists. "Yes. I think I'd know if I were some kind of magical creature, Rune."

Taking a deep breath, I worked to calm my frustration. Sure, it was weird that a Fae was after me, and it didn't make sense that I had some sort of magical aura. But I *was* human.

Doubt crept in despite my reassurances. There was no reason for me to question who or what I was, but what if someone in my blood line really came from Fae? I could have this whole other side to myself that I didn't even know about, all because I didn't know who I was. Not knowing who I came from or where had always left a hole in my heart, but now it drew up even more questions. I'd never been more frustrated about it than I was now.

Chewing on my lip, I met Rune's patient eyes. "Is there a way to see if I come from Fae? If Jonah really is after me because I descend from Fae or something like that, is there a way we can test it?"

He rubbed a hand across his jaw. "You want to test yourself? To see if you're Fae?"

"I don't know. Yes? I'm so confused, and I want definitive answers for myself to prove I'm normal."

His brow furrowed, and he took a minute to think it over. His eyes never left mine. "If you did have some sort of Fae in you, it would most likely be related to water judging by your attraction to it. I guess there's a way we can test the theory."

I swallowed hard. If that were the case, if I had Water Fae in me, that would make me Rune's enemy. And not just his. I'd be Akira's, Bassel's, and Marlow's, too. I'd be the enemy of my fox. These were probably irrational fears since I was 99.9 percent sure I was human, but until I was certain, doubt was going to weigh me down.

I had to find out who I was.

Rune pulled out his phone and sent a long text to someone.

He locked his phone back and set it to the side. Meeting my eyes again, he gave me an encouraging smile. "We'll figure it out. Just give me a bit to set some things up."

"I wish Jonah could be here to witness the test. Maybe then he'd see he's made a mistake and leave me be."

Rune shrugged and glanced across the river to the dark trees. "Who knows. He may be watching from the shadows right now."

The idea sent chills down my arms. Neither of us spoke for a while. Rune stared off into the passing treeline as if he actually believed Jonah was out there. I was busy trying to sort out my own mess of worries and thoughts. It seemed that mound of emotions kept getting larger and larger.

Rune's phone buzzed on the table, bringing us both back to the here and now. After reading whatever it said, he took a deep breath and looked at me. "Test time."

Slightly nervous since I didn't know what the test would actually consist of, I was slow to stand.

He walked over to the railing of the boat before looking back at me. He waved for me to join him, so I forced myself to move and walk over to him.

Standing beside him, I peered down into the dark water as the boat moved through it. When I looked down at the rushing current, something deep in my core wanted to reach out and run my hand through the cold waves. That part urged me to be calm, but it was also that part of me that sent a jolt of terror through my heart.

What could those feelings and desires mean?

Rune turned me to face him. He put my back against the railing, and before I could even register what he was doing, he grabbed me by the waist. He lifted me up, and I gasped as fear took hold of me. He sat me on the edge of the railing, so I clutched tightly to his shoulders. My breath hitched in my throat as dark water churned below. Was he out of his mind?

With frantic eyes, I shouted, "What are you doing? Let me down before I fall!"

He shook his head. "I can't do that. You wanted to test it. This is how."

Before I could respond, he pried my fingers off his shoulders. I watched in horror as he pushed me backward. I went to grab onto his hands or shirt or anywhere that I could before I fell, but he stepped out of my reach at the last minute.

The edge went out from under me, and I plummeted toward the cold, turbulent water.

CHAPTER

TWENTY-EIGHT

I fell backward, the security of the railing rushing away from me. Cold wind whipped at my skin as the water rose up to meet me. Panic seized my heart, and I squeezed my eyes shut in an attempt to block out the inevitable smack of the hard waves crashing against the side of the boat.

Before the crash could come, two hands wrapped around my waist. They jerked me upward, and my eyes shot open. Whipping my head up to see what had ceased my fall, I marveled at the sight of Akira in his Fae form. He held onto me while his large wings beat the air. He flapped them hard, taking us up higher. He looked down at me with his dark eyes, and his hair whipped around in the wind.

Relief flooded me. I had never been happier to see him.

When he made it over the deck of the boat, he hovered a moment before carefully descending. My body shook from both the chill and the adrenaline that coursed through me.

Rune approached us as Akira brought us lower. When I was within reach, Rune grabbed me around the waist. Akira released his hold on me, so Rune lowered me the rest of the way. As soon as my feet touched the ground, my knees gave out. They were like pure jelly, and I couldn't force myself to stand. Rune wrapped his arms tight around me, holding me to him.

I clutched onto the front of Rune's shirt with my head buried in his chest. My body wouldn't stop shaking, and my breathing came out hard and erratic. I wanted to shove him away and scream in his face for what he did, but he was the only thing holding me up at the moment.

"I'm sorry for doing that to you," Rune said, his voice quiet and gentle. "I know that scared you, but we needed to know if you were Water Fae, yeah? I couldn't give you any warning for what I was planning, because we wanted to get a genuine reaction from you."

Akira stepped closer to me and explained, "Fae powers are tied to our emotions, especially when we're first learning how to control our abilities. If you were Water Fae, the fear of plunging down would have scared you into manipulating the water to cease your fall. You would've involuntarily controlled the water to aid you."

Shaking my head, I fisted Rune's shirt tighter. "I told you I wasn't Water Fae. I hope you believe me now."

"I know," Rune said gently. His cheek rested on the top of my head, and he rubbed my back, trying to soothe me. "That's why I secretly had Akira at the ready. To catch you if you were truly human."

I looked over at Akira, who smiled apologetically. Seeing his completely black eyes didn't help to settle me, so I buried my face in Rune's chest again. I focused on the warmth he gave off and the feel of his arms around me. I was still mad at him and a little on edge since he had pushed me off, but his closeness managed to mollify me somehow.

"Akira," Rune said. "I think you're good to go now."

I glanced at Akira as he smiled and nodded.

"You two enjoy your date. I hope you got the answers you wanted, Bria, and please don't be mad at me. I never would've let you hit the water."

A burst of black feathers shot out around Akira. When they cleared, a raven flew where he had been standing. He hovered there for a moment before flying off in the direction that we had come. That left Rune and me alone once more. He didn't let go but kept his hold on me and rocked me gently side to side until I finally stopped shaking.

"Are you okay?" he asked.

I nodded, not able to find my voice yet, so he leaned back some. Shaking my head, I took a deep, steadying breath. "I understand why you did what you did, but I still wish you'd done it a different way."

He sighed, his face pinched in what looked like pain. "I know. I'm sorry. The only other way to test you would've been to physically hurt you somehow. If you healed quickly, that would've meant you were Fae. I didn't want to go that route, so I went with my Plan B."

I mentally pictured Rune taking the knife on the table and slicing open my skin to see if it would stitch back together. Swallowing down the nausea, I glanced at my wine glass. "I think I'm gonna go finish that drink now."

He laughed and followed me back to the table. I sank down into the chair and reached for my glass of wine, taking small sips of the sweet drink. He got out two breadsticks from the basket and offered one to me, which I gladly took. All the adrenaline left me feeling hungry.

"The food should be out soon," Rune said, watching me with careful amber eyes.

I swallowed the bite I'd just taken and looked around for something to say that was easy. While the test had proven Jonah couldn't be after me for being Fae, it had also been a jarring moment. My nerves were shot, and I craved a simple topic now, one that didn't make my heart thunder with anxiety, fear, and worry. I wanted to start a conversation to distract myself from the event that had taken place.

Waving my hand about us, I asked, "How did you get the money for all of this?"

"A lot of Fae end up quite wealthy since we live far longer than humans. In fact, you'll notice that the wealthiest of people are Fae, not human."

"Really?" I asked, tearing off another bite of bread. "Like who?"

He winked, a playful smirk tugging at his mouth. "Sorry. I can't tell you. It's secret information that only fellow Fae know."

I faked a pout. "Stingy." I took another sip of wine and peeked at him over the glass. "How do you update your legal stuff since you don't age like humans? You know, IDs, birth certificates, college transcripts, things like that."

"Fae have connections with people in those legal fields to get updated documents or updated college transcripts and degrees. That being said, I personally like to go back to university every few decades. I find learning enjoyable, and there's always something new to learn when I retake classes."

I soaked that in, impressed and oddly scared of what Fae lurked in the high ranks of our country. "Interesting. So, then what's your job now?"

"Right now, I'm focused on funding and running my non-profit. We provide financial support for single-income families in need, funding their education, making sure they get school supplies, clothes, things like that."

My eyes went wide, and I set my glass back on the table. My gaze drank in Rune as he sat casually across from me, and there was no denying the warmth that blossomed in my chest. Smiling, I said, "Wow. That's absolutely incredible. I bet you help a lot of families."

His smile was soft and genuine, not at all smug or proud. "I hope so. There are so many people out there who require it, and if I have the money sitting around, why not help them, you know? They need it more than I do."

My chest swelled at the generosity in this man's heart. Wanting to know more, I leaned forward. "Out of all the jobs you've had, which one was your favorite?"

He looked up, twirling his wine around in his glass as he thought about my question. His eyes found mine again as he answered, "Probably being an architect. I enjoyed planning out and designing something, then seeing it come to life before my eyes."

Smiling, I pictured that. "I bet that did feel pretty amazing."

"Is it the same for you?" he asked, taking a bite of his own bread. "You get an idea in your head, and when you paint it into something real, you feel, I don't know, alive?"

I thought about it, then nodded. "You're right. I've never tried putting it into words like that before, but that's exactly what it's like. When I hold a paintbrush, when the air smells like acrylic or oil paint, when I stain a new pair of clothes, it's like my mind, my heart, even my very skin comes alive with my passion for painting."

Discussing our passions. Holding each other's gazes. It was enough to make me want more. More deep conversations. More alone time with him under the stars. More days, more seconds. It was moments like this when my feelings sparked in my core, and picturing us together became easy. I was at my happiest with him, and I didn't want it to end. Unfortunately, I knew the clock counting our time was ticking down.

Soon, there would be no more of anything. I'd have my money, he'd have his life back, and we'd both go our separate ways.

Looking back at him, I asked, "Will you be glad once we're back home from the trip?" His gaze was fixed on mine as I finished, "No more having to pretend with all this stuff or trying to get along with each other."

The corners of his mouth turned down slightly, and his eyes dropped to stare into his glass. Something churned in his gaze, as if he were trying hard to form an answer. If I had asked a few weeks ago, his answer would have been yes without a moment's hesitation. Did the fact that he had to think about it mean he was starting to feel something, too?

Maybe he didn't want this to end, either.

He looked at me again, but before he could answer, Charles walked out onto the deck. He carried a tray with two plates of hot food.

I was glad to have our meals, but I was also disappointed.

After Charles set our plates in front of us, he went along his way. Rune didn't try to answer my question. He changed the subject and told me how Charles was a butler, but that Rune had hired him to take charge on the boat since he didn't need a butler. While Charles knew that Rune was Fae, he had no ties to Rune's family back home. He had served other Fae in the past, as had his family before him.

I glanced down at Rune's plate of food as he spoke. It only had one thing on it, and the sight made my stomach lurch. It was a steak, but it was completely and entirely raw. The blood from the meat swam beneath it, and I felt my appetite dwindling.

It was practically mooing.

Rune looked from his steak back to me. Color barely hinted at his cheeks, and he said, "That's something I forgot to mention.

When we eat steak at my mother's home, which we definitely will, it'll be raw like this. A lot of Fae don't mind raw meat. At least, not the ones who are omnivores and carnivores."

I swallowed the bile rising up my throat. "What will I do when we eat that? I obviously won't be able to eat steak like that."

He gave a dismissive wave of his hand. "Don't worry about that right now. I'll handle it when we get to that point."

I wanted to argue that we needed a game plan *now*, but I decided to keep quiet. He knew how to handle his own family, so if he said it wouldn't be a big deal, I believed him. A key to being successful in this ruse was trusting Rune and the others, something that I'd grown far more accustomed to over the past few weeks. I'd be in danger should his family discover I was a fraud once we were in Massachusetts, but I also knew that I had a whole group of people who had my back, including Rune. Plus, worrying about tomorrow's problems wouldn't help me in the here and now.

We spent the rest of dinner eating and talking about different aspects of his home or family. I wanted to know as much as I could about them and life as a Fox Fae, since I had to be one for a whole week.

When we finished dinner, we were almost back to the dock where the night began. It had grown chillier on deck, so Rune and I decided to move to the lower floor. I flopped down on the couch that faced the large wall of windows. He sat down next to me, catching my eyes briefly as he did.

"So," I said, meeting his eyes. "Do you think your mom will figure us out?"

He glanced at the windows to watch the passing water. He shrugged. "She's definitely the one who would pick up on it the easiest if we aren't extremely careful. Luckily, you give off the same magical aura as us. Even if we aren't quite sure why, it's a good thing that you do. That'll keep her from figuring it out quickly.

"Just try to avoid her as much as possible when we're there. Don't engage in conversation with anyone else unless either me or one of the others is around. If you say something wrong, which I feel is likely to happen since there's so much to learn, we need to be there to clean up any mess."

I glared at him. "I'm not a screw up. I'll be careful with anything I say."

He sighed, laying his head back. "I didn't mean anything bad by that. Anyone would have potential for slipping up in this situation. Another big thing to be wary of is games. If anyone challenges you or offers to play a game, you tell them no and leave immediately."

I swallowed hard. "Why? What does that mean?"

He shook his head. "Just do it. Please. It wouldn't be a game for you. It would be a death sentence, and I can't lose—"

He stopped, taking a deep breath. His amber eyes had found mine again, and they bore into me with some deep-rooted truth that told me what he wanted to say, even if he didn't finish the sentence.

My heart quickened. That look. The way his eyes traced my face, scanned my mouth. The way his chest rose and fell in a heavy breath, like he was struggling to breathe when looking at me. The way his eyes lit up with an undeniable fire that begged me to give in to him as if I were the gasoline fueling his need.

I was familiar with all of it. Those raging, explosive emotions that threatened to take over everything else. I knew them all too well, because it was how Rune made me feel. He wanted me, and I craved him.

Leaning closer with my breath caught in my throat and cheeks flushed, I whispered, "Rune."

His name was all I could utter, but it was enough to push him over the edge. He closed the space between us on the couch. His warm hands trailed up the back of my neck and into my hair, urging my face closer. He pressed our foreheads together, and with only inches between our lips, he pleaded in a quiet voice, "Can I?"

I didn't hesitate. "Yes. Please."

His lips were on mine without another second's hesitation. It started slow and easy, his lips gently prying mine open, his tongue grazing mine.

My hands pressed into his chest, and his erratic heartbeat matched my own. My skin warmed as the kiss intensified, and suddenly, we were both so hungry for the other, nothing else seemed to matter. I was drowning in him, never to resurface for air.

There was no more space between us, but it still wasn't close enough. Rune sensed my need to be closer, and he broke away just long enough to pull me onto his lap, my legs straddling his hips. As soon as I was nestled against the hard mass in his pants, I wrapped my hands into his hair and pressed my mouth to his again.

He groaned as my tongue brushed his, and his grip tightened on my hips after I involuntarily rubbed against him. He was quickly losing control, urging me and begging for me with his hands and lips and breathy moans. It made my body come alive knowing *I* was doing this to *him*.

"Rune," I breathed in between kisses.

His lips moved from my mouth to my jaw, traveling down the skin on my neck. I bit my lip and let my head fall back as his mouth and teeth caressed my skin just enough to make my toes curl and my lower abdomen to warm with an incessant need for him.

As his fingers teased their way up the hem of my shirt and onto my skin, a horn blared from the boat. I jumped, and Rune pulled back, breathless. We looked at each other, both of us trying to catch our breaths. His eyes were still hungry and full of want, and mine no doubt matched his.

He took a deep breath and closed his eyes. With his hands still on my hips, he leaned forward and rested his head in the crook of my shoulder. "We're back at the dock."

Swallowing hard, I nodded. Not trusting my voice to say anything coherent, I slid off his lap and prayed I wouldn't tumble over my weak knees.

Rune stood up, adjusting his pants and clearing his throat. He beamed at me, as if he'd just won the lottery. "Come on. Let's get you back to your dorm."

I slowly followed after him in a daze, lips tingling, and heart pounding.

Did–did I just kiss Rune?

CHAPTER
TWENTY-NINE

Rune pulled onto campus, stopping in front of my dorm.

"Thanks again for tonight," I said, flashing Rune a teasing smile. "Well, besides the part where you threw me over the edge of the boat."

Glancing at me with a devious glint to his eyes, he said, "It was a pretty fun night. Well … besides the part where I threw you over the edge of the boat." He paused and looked up at the ceiling. Shaking his head, he grinned. "No, actually, that was kind of fun, too."

I rolled my eyes and gently punched his arm. He looked at me with his eyes alight. Neither of us had stopped smiling since our heated moment on the boat. My lips still tingled with the memory of his on mine, and I was so high off the giddiness coursing through me I didn't think anything could pull me back down to earth.

I finally looked at the large brick building of my dorm, and a small wave of disappointment hit me. More than anything, I wanted to spend more time with Rune. I wasn't ready to leave yet.

I cleared my throat and turned back to him. "I guess I'll see you tomorrow."

He nodded. "We can hang out around the house if you want. Maybe get in a few hours of sparring."

"Sounds great. I'll be there around noon."

He nodded, warmth tugging at his mouth again. He glanced over my shoulder at the dorm, then back at me. His gaze was searching, like he was looking for a reason to not leave yet, either. Part of me so badly wanted to lean across the console and claim his mouth again, but the other part knew better.

Doubt and insecurity made me wonder if the kiss on the boat was a lapse in judgment on his part. Who knew how long it had been since his last hook up. He could've been taking the chance to fulfill some of those urges. I knew he wanted me physically, but I couldn't be as sure when it came to him wanting me on a deeper level. As much as I wanted to give in to the temptation to stay with him, I knew it was best to leave. I needed to regroup with myself and evaluate how I was feeling after tonight. He probably needed to do the same.

With a final goodbye, and sadly no kiss, I climbed out. He waved, and I returned the gesture before heading to the dorm. My entire body buzzed with the need to turn back around and run toward him, but I kept that desire in check.

Smiling like a fool, I pulled open the front doors to the dorm as my phone buzzed in my back pocket. I dug it out as I glanced through the door's glass to see if Rune was still out there. He was pulling away from the curb, and the happiness I felt only spread further until I was bathed in its glow from head to toe. He had waited until I made it all the way inside before leaving.

Feeling on top of the world, I finally looked at my phone to read the text. My mood instantly soured at the name lighting up the screen.

Dax.

I scoffed, reading his text.

> We need 2 talk. Im a dick. I want 2 make things right btwn us. Meet me @ the creek u luv behind ur dorm. I got donuts - ur fav & made a picnic.

Donuts. It was almost laughable how little he truly paid attention.

I didn't want to deal with Dax and his drama, but if I knew anything about Dax, it was that he would keep bugging me until we finally put an end to whatever was going on. I had to put him in his place and explain to him in clear terms that I wanted nothing to do with him anymore. Any chance we'd had at reconciling went out the window when he grabbed me like I was his property, something I'd definitely make him pay for tonight should he cross any boundaries again. I wasn't weak anymore, and I could take care of myself without fear of him.

Turning on my heel, I went back out the way I came and made my way into the trees behind campus. I was quickly becoming frustrated with how this perfect night was turning out, and my footing turned sloppy as I stomped through the dark woods. After nearly face-planting over a fallen tree limb, I forced myself to stop and take a calming breath. I didn't need to go into this with a mind clouded with anger. That wouldn't solve anything. Dax and I could talk like mature adults and resolve this civilly over donuts.

While I worked to calm my boiling rage, I started to notice how dark the woods were. Moonlight barely broke through the treetops, making everything eerie shades of black and gray.

Swallowing hard, I remembered Rune's warning.

Don't go anywhere by yourself in the dark.

I was already halfway to the creek where Dax should be waiting, which meant I wouldn't be alone soon enough. Even so, to be smart about this, I decided I'd better call Rune to have someone aware of my location in case something happened.

I dialed his number, and it had just started to ring when the shadows in front of me began to shift. Coming to an abrupt stop, I swallowed hard and glanced down at the screen of my phone. It said we were two seconds into the call.

He had answered.

Looking back up at the shadow that now looked like a man, I slipped my phone into my back pocket with the mouthpiece up and said a silent prayer that Rune could hear. It was risky to stay here with Jonah alone, but this also gave me a chance to get the answers I'd been seeking. It was an overdue confrontation, and should it take a turn for the worse, Rune would have the information he needed to get here.

My eyes narrowed on the Fae. "Jonah."

He laughed, the sound deep and ominous. "Bria. Fancy running into you here."

My heart was racing, and I fought against the terror that was threatening to take over. I wouldn't get scared. I had to be strong and stay smart so that I could get my explanations.

Swallowing my fear, I asked, "What are you doing in the woods behind my dorm?"

There. Now Rune knew where I was should I need help. At least he would if the call was still going. Too bad I couldn't whip my phone out to check.

"I told you I'd be coming back. You should've expected me sooner or later," Jonah said.

"Oh yeah. I've been super excited. Figured we could watch movies and make friendship bracelets together."

He glared at me. "Your sarcasm isn't cute."

"Neither are you, yet you keep showing up."

Smirking, he nodded. "I do. It's because I have something I need to do, and it starts with this."

I didn't even see him move. One second, he was fifteen feet away, and the next he was right in front of me, swinging his arm fast and hard. His fist cracked into my cheek, and the force of the blow sent me crashing to the ground. Pain erupted in my cheek, and I cried out from the searing heat that exploded there. The coppery taste of blood filled my mouth. I glared up at him as he towered over me, and the jerk actually threw his head back and laughed.

Fighting through the pain, I pushed myself onto my hands, ready to fight this bastard, but he moved too quickly for my eyes to track again. He kicked my hands out from under me, and the loss of support knocked me back down. My head smacked on a rock that jutted up from the earth, sending a wave of dizziness rushing through me. Something warm trickled down the side of my face.

Tears pricked at the corners of my eyes, and my head felt much heavier than normal. Sucking in a sharp breath, I started to push off the ground again.

Jonah laughed and stomped on my outstretched hand, scraping it into the twigs and rocks.

I winced, biting back a whimper.

Think, Bria, think. You aren't *defenseless anymore.*

Gritting my teeth, I yanked my hand out from under his boot and kicked out my leg. It hit the back of his knees in the weak point, and he collapsed. Without hesitation, I smashed my elbow into his cheek, and his head snapped to the side from the blow.

Knowing when to stop fighting and make your escape—especially if you knew it was a losing battle— was one of the most valuable lessons I'd learned in self-defense. As confident as I was in my newfound strength and as much as I wanted answers, I knew I couldn't win this fight. Jonah was Fae. He had a huge advantage on me in terms of strength and power. Seeing that he was momentarily impaired and stunned, I knew it was now or never. This was my chance to play it smart and run.

Rushing to my feet, I took off in the direction of the dorms. Not even five steps later, Jonah grabbed my hair and yanked me back against him.

"That hurt," he spat into my ear.

"That was the point, bastard!"

Jonah threw me to the side, and I landed hard on my back. The impact knocked the wind out of me, and my body went rigid as it tried to recover from the jolt that shot up my spine. I didn't have time to recoup either, because Jonah knelt over me, and with an evil tilt to his lips, he drew back his fist and smashed it into my right eye.

I yelped and clutched at my face. Blood seeped through my fingers, and my head instantly began to throb.

"You know," Jonah laughed, getting to his feet again. "This is so funny to me. You're going to die tonight, and you don't even know why. Isn't that the best kind of torture? You, lying there in agonizing pain, thinking to yourself, 'Why me? Why me?' Oh, I just love thinking about it!"

I opened my lips, wanting to reason with him, to explain that he had the wrong person. If it was a Fae he wanted, he had the wrong idea about me. But no sound came out, despite my efforts. I couldn't bring myself to think or talk anymore. Things were getting too fuzzy. My eyes started to drift shut, but that seemed to reignite his fury.

He brought his foot down hard onto my side.

My scream caught in my throat in a tight choke. I clutched at my ribs and rolled onto my knees. Nausea rocked through me as pain overtook all my senses.

"Are you scared?" Jonah laughed.

I took a deep breath to calm the urge to vomit. Glaring up at him past my bleeding eye, I shook my head defiantly. I was scared shitless, thinking this would be my last moment on Earth, but I'd never give him the satisfaction that he wanted.

Roaring with a newfound anger, he kicked me again and sent my body rolling back over the dirt. I barely had time to suck in a breath through the pain before he grabbed me by my neck. I clutched at his hand as he yanked me up by my throat. My legs wobbled as he forced me to stand, and I dug my nails deep into his hand. He ignored it, as well as the blood now seeping from his hand, and he slammed my body back into a tree. It sent another shock of agony through me, and the jolt made my hands fall limp at my sides.

Darkness seeped into the edges of my vision. No air filled my lungs despite my desperate gasps for it. Pain laced every inch of my skin, muscle, and bone.

This was it.

This bastard's ugly, malicious sneer would be the last thing I ever got to see.

"Bria!"

Jonah whipped around and dropped me.

I collapsed at the base of the tree, too broken to move. I didn't need to move to see the owner of that voice, though.

Dax.

CHAPTER

THIRTY

It took everything in me to speak and turn my head in Dax's direction. "Run, Dax."

Jonah's piercing glare turned on Dax, who stood a distance away from us. It looked like he'd come from the direction of the creek. I had been so close to another person, to safety. And now that Dax was here and had seen Jonah, I only feared for what that might mean for him, despite all our history.

Dax met Jonah's glare with a confident sneer of his own. "How dare you! You filthy Land Fae."

My mind stilled.

Had he just said what I thought he did?

Blinking past the fog in my head, I cried louder, "Dax, get out of here. He'll kill you!"

Dax laughed, stalking closer. "He can't hurt me, Bria. And he won't hurt you anymore, either."

What was he talking about? Too lost in my own agony and the fear of what was about to happen in this Dax versus Jonah showdown, I pushed all of the confusion about his words aside. Dax needed to get out of here, maybe even go get me some help.

"I'm going to enjoy killing you," Dax sneered at Jonah.

The sound of rushing liquid headed in our direction from the creek. All of a sudden, a wall of water formed behind Dax like an impenetrable fortress. My eyes went wide, and Jonah took a step back. Dax shot out his arms, and the water rushed at Jonah in the exact same moment.

Jonah jumped to the side at the last minute, narrowly missing having his head blown off by the force and speed of the deluge.

He let out a frustrated and angry roar, glaring once at Dax then at me. "I'm not done with you yet, girl."

His body evaporated into black shadows before slithering away into the night. He was gone. For now.

"Bria!" Dax rushed to me and crouched beside me, looking over my bloody and dirty body. Meeting my confused eyes, he groaned, "Damn. You look bad. It's okay, though. I'm here now."

A sharp pain erupted in my side when I tried to ask him what was going on. He was a freaking Water Fae? How could I not have known something like that? I sucked in a sharp breath as another tear slipped down my cheek.

"I know. Shh." He cupped my cheek, my *swollen*, *battered* cheek. I cried out at the ache that flared under his touch, but he didn't seem to understand. "I'm so glad I made it in time."

He was smiling at me, and for the life of me, I couldn't understand what he was so damn happy about. I was still lying here, bleeding and in excruciating pain. He should be helping me get medical attention, not smiling down at me like we were skipping through a meadow of flowers and fucking rainbows.

"Help ... me," I croaked.

"Of course! I'll always be here to help you. It's me and you. Forever."

Groaning, I shook my head against the ground. "Not ... not me and you. Get ... get me help."

His brow furrowed, and the worry in his eyes seemed to morphe. "What do you mean, not me and you? We are a couple, Bria. We will *always* be a couple."

Squeezing my eyes shut, I pushed my face into the cold dirt. Ah, the cool sensation felt so good on my aching body. I wanted to wrap myself up in it and fall asleep.

Sleep.

That sounded so easy and nice.

Taking a deep breath, I glared sideways at him. Why was he still hung up on our relationship? Why was he not getting me out of here and helping me? He was egotistical, as always.

"Fuck ... you."

He narrowed his eyes. "Don't you mean thank you? I just saved your ass. I'm your hero. You should be praising me!"

His voice rose higher as his yelling increased, but I stopped hearing him. For a moment, I stopped hurting. I went numb to everything. My mind slipped away to a place that was warm and soft, a place I had come to love.

Rune's arms.

The sound of Dax struggling brought me back to my senses. His breathing was labored, and I could hear him trying to fight off something. Taking slow and easy breaths in order to keep the pain at bay, I tilted my head back and forced my eyes open. My body went rigid when I saw who was battling Dax.

Rune stood there in his Fae form, fangs bared and claws digging into Dax's throat. He sneered at Dax, rage rolling off him in waves as his knuckles turned white from his tight grip.

Rune's eyes narrowed with unhindered loathing. "I'm going to rip you apart, you bastard. How *dare* you touch her. Your death will be slow, agonizing, and I can promise I will enjoy every fucking second of it."

Rune threw Dax's body like it weighed nothing, and he crashed into a tree that was a good ten feet away. Dax's face morphed from anger to pain as he slumped to the tree's base. His eyes barely flicked open before drifting shut again.

Rune's glare was venomous as fire erupted in each of his hands.

My eyes darted from the man I loved to the one I once thought I did. Dax was a dick. He was pure scum for what he'd done. Even so, I couldn't let Rune kill him. I wouldn't be able to live with myself knowing Dax had died at Rune's hands.

Pushing myself up from the dirt, I groaned at the electrocuting pain that shot down my back and through my limbs. At the sound of me moving, Rune whipped his head in my direction. As soon as our eyes met, his face fell until he looked as if he were the one in pain.

"Rune." I cringed, my voice hoarse and shaking.

He rushed to my side, extinguishing the fire from his hands. He was slow to reach out to me, careful of where he touched me.

With shaking hands, I grabbed onto his arms and looked up into his eyes. "Don't. Don't hurt him anymore. It was Jonah who did this, not him. Leave him be. Please."

"Why?" he asked in a quivering breath. "Why do you defend him after everything he's done to you?"

I reached up and cupped his cheek before realizing how bloody and dirty my hand was. I went to pull it back, but he covered my hand with his own, holding it to his cheek. His desperate eyes never once wavered from mine.

Dax didn't deserve to die just for being a dirtbag. And Rune didn't deserve yet another mark marring his soul with another life taken by his hands. There had been enough death.

Taking a steadying breath, I whispered, "Please don't. Let's go. I want to go home with you. I don't want to go back to my dorm."

My mind and body were exhausted. More than anything, I just wanted to wash the grime off, collapse in a soft bed, and fall asleep with some type of pain medicine. But, more than that, I wanted, *needed*, Rune by my side. The comfort of his nearness was my safe haven right now.

Rune glanced over his shoulder at Dax, who was still passed out. He glared at Dax's unmoving body, then turned back to me with eyes radiating concern. I could tell he wanted to fillet Dax in a bed of fire, but he cared more about me in this moment than his hate for Dax.

"Okay," he said, an orange flame circling around him. The fire didn't burn my skin, despite brushing over me where I held onto him. When it disappeared, he was in his human form.

He gently scooped me up, bringing me close to his chest. Intense pain still gripped me, but the warmth coming off him was soothing. He cradled me to him as he retreated from the woods. His car was in the middle of the cul-de-sac lane, driver's door flung open, and the car still running.

"Bria?" a familiar voice called.

Peering over Rune's shoulder, I found Dallas standing by the dorm doors. As soon as she saw me, her green eyes went wide, and she raced to us in a stumbling mess of high heels.

"Oh my God! What happened? You're bleeding everywhere!"

"There was an accident, that's all."

I couldn't tell her what happened. She didn't know Fae existed, and I couldn't bring her into this ridiculous world where humans who knew the truth got tracked down by psycho Fae.

Rune walked around her to the passenger door. He knelt down to open it, taking care to not jostle me around. Once the door was open wide enough, he carefully placed me in the seat.

My head lolled to the side, and I peeked around him at Dallas.

Tears slid down her cheeks.

She threw a skeptical and icy glare at Rune.

Sensing what she was getting at, I explained, "It wasn't him. I had a run in with some mugger." Sure, that sounded convincing. "I'm going to Rune's for tonight. See if Rance can come stay with you, okay?"

Rune stepped back once I was buckled. Dallas knelt down next to me and gently wrapped her hand around mine. Instantly, I was hit with a whiff of alcohol. She'd been partying, so I wasn't surprised to see her so drunk. Even so, the strong smell of booze had the contents of my stomach roiling.

"I'm so sorry," she sobbed.

My eyes slipped closed, and it was hard to get them back open. "It's not your fault. Go inside. I'll be okay."

She said something else, but I didn't hear her. I was drifting, floating to somewhere warmer and less painful. My breathing had become soft and shallow. I was falling sideways as the world fell in the other direction. Before I knew it, everything had gone dark, leaving me to dream and float.

I dreamed of Rune. His kiss, his touch, his protective hold. I was surrounded by him and his light. No pain. No sadness, frustration, or confusion. Just him and me in our own little world made of light.

CHAPTER

THIRTY-ONE

My eyes slowly fluttered open. My right eye was swollen, so I couldn't open it as far as the other. Even so, I knew where I was. A small light illuminated Rune's room in a soft glow. Akira stood next to me, gently pulling the covers up to my chin.

When he saw I was awake, his eyes warmed, and he whispered, "Hey. Sorry, I didn't mean to wake you."

I shook my head to tell him it was fine, but I quickly regretted it because the motion made a terrible throbbing start where I'd busted my forehead on the forest floor. I squeezed my eyes shut and brought my hand up to the wound. It was then I realized my hand had been wrapped with gauze. There was a small piece also taped to the spot where my head had split open, but it still hurt beyond the soft material.

"Is your head hurting?" Akira asked, his eyes looking all around the spot I held.

Taking a few steadying breaths, I nodded.

He frowned, his eyes full of understanding. "I washed out the gash and put some gauze on it, but I was waiting until you woke up to see if you needed any pain reliever. We weren't sure if you would want to go to the hospital or not, so Rune decided to bring you back here until you came to. I went ahead and assessed your condition. You have a lot of bruising but no broken bones, which is good news."

"Pain reliever would be nice."

I tried taking a deep breath, but that sent a pang across my ribs and sides. My stomach and back were killing me from where Jonah had mercilessly kicked me. Everything felt bruised and battered.

I was honestly still in shock over the fact that I managed to come out alive. When I'd decided to stay and confront Jonah for answers, I'd underestimated his drive to get the job done, as well as his supernatural speed. I'd expected to have time to talk rationally, but I guessed Jonah wasn't of sound mind.

Looking back at my friend, I said, "No thanks to the hospital. I'd rather take some medicine and get sleep here."

Doctors and needles were not my friends.

Akira nodded and turned to leave the room.

"Where's Rune?" I asked.

He turned back to me as his brow pinched slightly with worry. Not meeting my eyes, he fiddled with the bracelet he wore. "I guess you could say Rune's taking some time to cool down."

"Cool down?"

He let out a heavy sigh and walked back to the bed. He sat down on the edge, and he chewed on his lip with a furrowed brow. "He's pretty upset about what happened, obviously. We all are, but I haven't seen him so angry in a long time. When he came back with you, he had me fix up all your wounds, and I changed you out of your bloody clothes."

I looked down. The covers obscured what I wore on my lower half, but judging by the comfort, I could tell it must be loose-fitting sweatpants. I also sported a large, black t-shirt. The clothes were no doubt some of Rune's. The fact that I was wearing his clothes and lying in his bed should've made my heart dance, but I found it hard to be happy at a time like this.

My eyes met Akira's again as he continued, "When I took you from him, he turned back into his Fae form before going on a rampage about what happened. You could have a bonfire for days with all the shit he's setting on fire. I think he partially blames himself for what happened. He wishes he had gotten there in time to stop Jonah."

I shook my head and closed my eyes. "He got there as soon as he could. He doesn't drive a jet. It's not his fault."

"He's proud of you, you know."

My heart kicked up a notch. "He is?"

Akira nodded. "You were sneaky, smart, and a badass. Calling him and feeding him details like where you were and who was there. Standing your ground against a Fae and refusing to give up. He's proud of you. But still pissed and upset. He's a confused ball of feelings right now—something he's not used to."

I swallowed my emotions. I'd made Rune proud? That in itself was like a hearty dose of medicine. At first, I'd viewed tonight as a failure on my part. I hadn't been strong enough to hold my own. I'd needed help. Rune didn't see it that way. He was *proud*. He'd seen my strengths tonight, not my faults. He'd seen me as brave and strong, not helpless and weak. Biting back a sob, I realized he was right. Sure, I'd gotten beat, but by no means had I been weak.

Akira leaned back on his hands and looked at me for a moment. Pursing his lips, he was hesitant to say, "He said you told him to stop when he was attacking Dax."

I met Akira's eyes and nodded.

He gave me a small smile. "I think that's something else he's mad about. The fact that you defended Dax after everything he's done to you. I think he's pissed at himself, too, for actually listening."

"I know Dax has done a lot of messed up stuff, but he didn't deserve to be killed. I mean, do Fae usually kill humans when we piss them off?"

Akira stared at me, bewildered by what I'd said. His brow furrowed, and he gave a small laugh. Nodding, he said, "Human, hmm?"

Oh right. Dax wasn't human. That was going to take some getting used to. I felt so blind for not knowing, but then again, how could I have known? All this time, he'd been Water Fae, and I partially wondered if he somehow knew something about me. Could he know why I had a faint magical aura? We'd been around each other for years. Surely, he knew or suspected something.

"Not human," I sighed. "I'm still trying to wrap my head around him being Fae."

"That's understandable. Honestly, there's more to explain regarding that—things we realized tonight—but I'll leave that to Rune."

"What do you mean?" My head was starting to hurt, and not just from the physical pain.

Akira rubbed my gauzed hand gently. "He'll explain. Anyway, I think you were right to stand up for Dax. Sure, he's absolute trash, but he didn't need to die. Just a nice ass-beating."

I raised my brows. I hadn't expected a Land Fae to take a Water Fae's side. "Even though he's Water Fae?"

He laughed, but there was no humor in it. "I think it's a bad idea to generalize anyone, including Water Fae. To say *all* are bad and deserve to die is ignorant and spiteful. You'll find I'm not big on the whole Land versus Water Fae feud. I don't say anything around the others because they've been through a lot with the fighting. I can understand the guys' sides, even if I don't agree with it."

Curious, I asked, "Why aren't you against Water Fae like they are? You know, besides the whole generalizing is bad thing?"

His dark eyes lost some of their usual spark, and the edges of his mouth fell. He picked at nonexistent lint on his jeans. "Like the others, I lost someone important to me because of the feud. Only, the person I lost wasn't Land Fae. He was Water Fae. We were forced to choose sides when the war began, and we both ignorantly sided with our own kind." He gave a sad laugh, shaking his head. "I regret that every day."

Coming back from the torture of a long-ago memory, he smiled again and patted my knee. He got to his feet and went to the door. "I'll go get you pain medication."

I wanted to ask who this someone was and if Akira was okay, but I knew better. Akira would tell me if and when he was ready.

"Okay. Thanks, Akira."

His exit left me alone. I hated that this feud took so much from everyone I cared about. Rune's father; Akira's special someone. What was the point of it anymore? Did they even know at this point?

Too tired to think about heavy stuff, I looked around Rune's room. My eyes traced the walls but paused on one thing in particular, something that hadn't been here before. Gasping, my heart stopped. Across from the bed, hanging on the wall, was the painting I'd done of the fox and me. He'd hung it up in the middle of his room.

An absurd amount of joy took root in my chest. Rune loved the painting so much that he'd actually hung it up. It made me proud and happy to know he adored the picture. Even after the two months were over, a part of me hoped he'd keep the painting hung up. Even if we were no longer in touch, that painting would keep us connected in some small way.

Because let's face it, there was a chance that once this was all said and done, we'd end up going our separate ways. I mean, would he really be willing to give up his cherished lifestyle of freedom to pursue whatever was happening between us? And would he want to when I left for Italy? Those were questions I didn't have answers to right now, but I hoped to soon.

My eyes began to drift closed as the weight of everything hit me all over again. Before I could fall asleep, the sound of the doorknob turning made my eyes flicker open. I expected to see Akira coming in with the medicine, but instead, it was Rune.

He closed the bedroom door behind him and leaned against the frame, holding a glass of water. We watched each other in silence for a minute, and the fury still simmered in his eyes despite his return to human form. When he pushed away from the door, a muscle ticked in his jaw as he attempted to rein in those feelings. He didn't say a word as he held out the glass of water, and he opened his other hand to offer the two pills.

My eyes found his again, and I tried to push myself up in bed. I winced and bit my lip at the aching protest in my arms and abdomen.

Rune, seeing my distress, set the glass of water on the nightstand and helped me sit up with gentle hands. His touch was so different from the heat in his eyes. He seemed so furious on the inside, but I knew it wasn't directed at me. I think that was the only reason he was able to keep his composure.

Once I was sitting, I took a moment to get my breathing under control. The pain made me nauseated again, but the feeling subsided after I sat there for a moment. Rune held out the two pills and water again. I accepted the pain relievers with a mumbled thank you. When I was done swallowing the pills, Rune took the glass from me to set it back on the nightstand.

When his eyes found mine again in the dimly lit room, I couldn't help but feel self-conscious. Because of the horrible way I must look, I suddenly didn't want to meet his eyes out of fear that I'd see pity there. My eye was no doubt swollen and purple, and I imagined my cheek must be, too, from where Jonah punched me. My face throbbed as if his fist were still connected with my skin.

The bed sank down as he sat on the edge next to me. I glanced up at him, but he wasn't looking at my face. His brow was furrowed, his mouth drawn in a tight line, as he stared down at my stomach. My breath fluttered as he pulled the comforter back from my lap. He grabbed the hem of my shirt and began to lift it up.

"What are you doing?" I asked in a breathless string of words as I gripped his wrists.

"Please," he whispered. His eyes squeezed shut as his frown deepened. "Please let me see how bad it is."

"Why? What good will knowing do, Rune?"

I didn't know what kind of marks painted my skin, but if they looked anything like how they felt, it wasn't going to be pretty. I didn't want those images in his mind.

"Because I'll know how much pain to return to Jonah." His golden eyes were charged with loathing as they met mine. "I will return what he did to you tenfold and then some. Please, show me how he hurt you."

I swallowed hard and finally relented. Releasing his hands, I held my breath as he slowly pulled up the shirt. When my stomach was exposed, he froze. My eyes were glued to his face, but he was focused solely on my abdomen. His face fell. I glanced down. Large purple bruises covered my stomach and ribs in an ugly pattern. The pain behind each mark was impossible to ignore.

"Are you sure you don't want to go to the hospital?" Rune asked carefully.

"I'm sure," I insisted. "I don't want to deal with all the questions or prodding and poking. Akira has me covered."

Rune sighed and mumbled, "So damn stubborn."

Rune reached for me then, and I instinctively closed my eyes as if that would protect me from the hurt his touch would invoke. No pain came, though. The tips of his fingers danced across the skin of my stomach in feather light touches. It was warm and soothing, and the sensation stilled the air moving in my lungs. It amazed me that someone's touch could be so gentle.

His face scrunched up, and he let out a heavy sigh. Turning away, he fell back onto the bed and draped his arm over his eyes. "I don't understand at all. I hate not understanding something."

"What don't you understand?"

"There's so much I don't understand when it comes to you. I don't understand why you'd want to defend Dax after everything he's done to you. I don't understand why I actually listened when you told me to stop. Stopping isn't in my vocabulary when it comes to Water Fae. The last thing I don't understand is how everyone around you is a Water Fae, yet you don't appear to be one yourself."

I furrowed my brow, confused by that last part. "What do you mean everyone around me is Water Fae?"

He moved his arm behind his head, and his eyes found mine. "Exactly what I said. Everyone around you is Water Fae."

CHAPTER

THIRTY-TWO

"Dallas and Dax are both Water Fae," he started.

"Wh-what?" I asked, incredulously. The suggestion was utterly impossible that it made me want to laugh, but I fought against the notion, seeing as it would most likely be hella painful.

"We've mentioned it before, how Fae have a way of making their auras harder to pick up on. We didn't realize it at first because the few times we'd seen them, Dallas and Dax had been concealing their magical auras for the most part to look human. You were the only one we sensed anything substantial from at the start. Dallas wasn't able to hide hers tonight, most likely due to how drunk she was. Then, of course, Dax gave a demonstration of his true nature. Both are Water Fae."

This was ludicrous. Dax I'd seen with my own two eyes, so I knew he had to be, even if it was hard to believe, but Dallas? She couldn't be Water Fae. There would've been signs before now, signs I would've most definitely picked up on considering we'd been best friends ever since high school. The air felt like it had been punched from my lungs all over again. Wouldn't she have told me? Wouldn't I have noticed something odd after all these years?

Rune sat back up and leaned in close. My cheeks warmed at his sudden nearness. His eyes roamed over me, studying me closely. I didn't know what he was looking for, but finally, he met my eyes again. "Are you Water Fae?"

Narrowing my eyes, I leaned back away from him. "No! We've already been through this. I thought after what happened on the boat, you'd know I wasn't."

He sighed and leaned back, running a hand through his white hair. "I know. I just wanted to ask point blank. You're very hard to figure out, more so now than ever since all your friends are Water Fae."

"That's where you're wrong. Some are Land Fae, but does that make me a Land Fae, too? No, it doesn't. I. Am. Human. I mean, if I were Water Fae, I'd theoretically hate you and all the guys, right?"

He looked at me sideways. "Theoretically."

"Well, there's your proof." I looked down at my hands and felt my cheeks warm. I couldn't believe I was about to say this. I swallowed hard and continued, "I couldn't be Water Fae, because I actually enjoy being with you. All of you. At first, I hated it because I thought you were a blackmailing, douche canoe, but now, I—well I—"

"I get it," he said, and I looked up at him through my lashes. He stared off away from me with tightly shut eyes. "You aren't Water Fae."

I looked back down at the comforter and silently cursed myself. Now was not the time to be discussing our feelings, but it was important that he understood what I was and what that meant for my feelings. He no doubt knew what I was trying to say, so he'd stopped me. They weren't words he wanted to hear, especially not right now. We could figure out our relationship later.

"We'll have definitive answers come tomorrow anyway, so there's no point in trying to talk it out right now." I gave him a questioning look, and he finished, "Your wounds. Like we've explained before, Fae heal much faster than humans. If your wounds are gone by tomorrow, no one will be able to deny what you are."

I knew I had nothing to worry about. Even if Rune had his doubts, I knew I wasn't Water Fae. I had never controlled water or healed extremely fast. I was an average Jolene.

As I sat there and thought about what he'd said, something dawned on me. In high school, Dallas had burned her forearm on her oven while baking cookies. I knew it was a really bad burn because I'd witnessed the whole thing. You could even smell burning flesh. It should have scarred or at least lasted for a few weeks, but by the next day, there was no sign of a burn. She was completely healed.

That wasn't the only strange healing incident, either. Once, Dallas got in a fight at school with another girl, and since she was suspended for a week, I went to her house every day to see her. The day of the fight, she had a black eye. The very next day, her eye was fine. When I asked her how it had healed so fast, she'd laughed and told me it was magic. I thought her answer was her being witty, but now I knew that she'd been telling the truth.

Even more recently was her paper cut. Gone, mere minutes after she'd gotten it.

Rune could obviously tell by the look on my face that I'd realized something because he asked, "What is it?"

I met his patient eyes and explained, "Dallas has always been able to heal way faster than she should. I guess ... I guess, she really is Water Fae."

I squeezed the blanket tightly between my fingers as the burn of betrayal settled in my throat. Why had she never told me? I mean, I knew it wasn't something you'd randomly tell someone, and it would've been hard to believe at first. Still, we had been best friends for so long. She knew she could trust me, and with time, I would have accepted it. It was such a large part of herself to keep hidden, and it made me question if she truly trusted me. It made me doubt if I'd been a good enough friend to her. That insecurity made emotion clog my throat, and I had to swallow hard to keep it from rising to the surface.

It also begged the question of why. Why was everyone I'd been close to Water Fae? What did that mean for me? Did I just happen to choose friends who were Water Fae? Or was there another reason? My head was spinning with all these questions, and they were only serving to make it hurt more.

While lost in trying to accept the reality of who Dax and Dallas were, something else occurred to me. Fear took hold of my heart, and I leaned toward Rune. "Wait! Even if they're Water Fae, you-you aren't going to hurt them, are you?"

He narrowed his eyes. "I've already told you I want all Water Fae dead. I don't care who they are."

Panic blossomed, sinking its icy claws in me. Shaking my head, I reached out and touched his arm. "No, Rune. You don't need to hurt them. Th-they aren't bad."

"To you. You aren't Land Fae, so you don't understand."

I stared into his eyes, my heart sinking with dread. He wanted my dear friend dead, and it didn't matter what I said. She was Water Fae, so that was reason enough for him. He wanted every Water Fae gone, despite who they were. Or so he said. But how true was that?

Swallowing hard, I gazed into those amber eyes I'd come to love so much. Ones I knew belonged to a man who was capable but scared of love. "What if I were Water Fae? Would you want me dead, too?"

He seemed thrown off guard by my direct question. His wide eyes were locked with mine for a few endless moments. After seconds of silence, I was going to repeat my question, but finally, he looked away from me with a bitter frown. He stood up and said, "You aren't Water Fae, so it doesn't matter."

Anger ignited my veins like a match being thrown into a tub of kerosene. I wasn't going to let him dodge my question this time. As he started for the door, I threw off the blankets. I braced myself for what was probably about to hurt and swung my legs over the edge of the bed. Pain ricocheted up my limbs, but I ignored it as I stood up to go after him. As soon as I tried taking a step forward, the ache in my abdomen became too much. My knees gave out just as Rune looked back at me from the door.

Before I could collapse, Rune was at my side, keeping me from smacking into the ground for the dozenth time tonight.

"What are you doing?" he said, his tone a mix of urgency and firmness. "You don't need to walk yet."

"Then don't walk away from me," I demanded as he carried me back to the bed. My arms were tight around his shoulders, and I rested my head in the warm crook of his neck. With a heavy sigh, I repeated softly, "Don't walk away from me."

He carefully laid me back down in the bed. He guided my head to the pillow, but I kept my eyes shut and turned away from him. I was tired of this game where he refused to reveal anything about his feelings. The walls around his heart were tall and steep, but I was trying my damnedest to mount them.

He pulled the covers back over me, and when I expected him to leave, he surprised me by crooking his finger under my chin and tilting my face up. My eyes shot open, and our gazes locked. For once, his expression was undeniably clear. There was an immeasurable amount of affection buried in those depths, and it was directed right at me. "I'm not walking away from you. I just don't like the answer to your question."

A sinking pit formed in my stomach. I swallowed hard and confirmed, "So you would kill me."

He frowned, his face torn. "No. That's why I don't like the answer. I've *never* hesitated when it comes to killing Water Fae, but if you were one—" He paused, looking down at me with soft eyes. He shook his head and finished, "I couldn't bring myself to hurt you, let alone kill you."

My heart took flight on the wings of relief at his words. Here we were, a girl and a boy, pretending at love but somehow actually falling in head first. I was supposed to find him infuriating, and he was supposed to find me impossible. And while we definitely did, something heated and alive still managed to blossom between us. He was my greatest ally, my constant supporter, and I was the girl changing the way he looked at the world. This wasn't a confession by any means, but it was the most honest he'd ever been about how he felt.

I wasn't the only one falling in love.

Rune was, too.

He must have realized how open and vulnerable he was being, because he quickly pulled away his hand and turned to look anywhere that he could, except at me. He cleared his throat and said, "You get some sleep. If you need anything, I'll be in the living room."

He turned for the door, so I frowned. "You're sleeping in the living room?"

He glanced over his shoulder at me. "Yes. Why?"

A wave of guilt washed over me. I was essentially kicking him out of his room, even after he'd helped me.

"You don't have to sleep in there. There's enough room for us both to sleep here. I don't mind."

A seductive smirk pulled at his lips. "Don't tempt me. I know my limits, and being in the same bed isn't a good idea."

My body heated with need at what his words implied. Suddenly, all I wanted was for him to crawl beneath the sheets with me and show me what it meant for him to lose control. Our intense kissing session was still fresh in my mind. It left me feeling raw and antsy. He had to be feeling that way, too. The thought was quickly crushed by the logical side of me. With the shape I was in, I needed to rest, not test Rune's boundaries or my own.

Swallowing hard, I cleared my throat. "Fine. You sleep in here. I can sleep on the couch."

He shook his head. "Don't worry. I'm fine on the couch. I want you to sleep in here. What kind of boyfriend would I be if I put my injured girlfriend on the couch to sleep?"

I blushed and gave a small laugh. "Okay. I owe you, though."

"You don't owe me anything. Just rest and get better. That will be enough for me."

His words made me warm inside. He was so different now than when we'd first met. He was far more open and honest at times, and I enjoyed seeing that side of him. It was hard to think that the man who tried so hard not to care about others cared about me so openly.

I couldn't help but wonder what we'd be like if our relationship were real. No pretending for the sake of maintaining his freedom and closed-off lifestyle, no spending time with him in exchange for money. If we had more time, could things become real? Because time was slipping by. It had already been nearly two months, although it felt like a lifetime.

I wanted two more months with him.

I wanted *always* with him.

"Good night, Bria," he whispered, his voice deep yet gentle.

"Good night, Rune."

He shut off the lamp, and the room flooded with darkness. There came the soft click of the door shutting behind him, and then, I was alone. Part of me wanted him to lie with me or stay and talk. His presence had become such a part of my life that, without it, I felt exposed and lonely. I wanted him here with me.

Sleep came surprisingly fast after Rune left. My body and mind were exhausted, so rest was much needed. Unfortunately, my dreams had another idea. I tossed and turned in a fit, my mind taunting me with images of Jonah and his torment. His eerie voice filled my head with promises of pain and death, haunting my waking and sleeping thoughts.

You're going to die tonight, and you don't even know why.

My eyes shot open, and I gasped for air. My body flared hot with a renewed burst of pain. It was as if Jonah had hit me all over again. I didn't know how long it had been since I'd taken the pain medication, but it was still dark outside. I couldn't have been asleep very long at all, which didn't surprise me given what waited for me in dream land.

The dark room suddenly felt too small. Chills swept down my arms. I didn't want to be in here by myself, so I slowly pushed away the covers. After my failed attempt to walk the first time, I decided to take it slower and easier this time. It still hurt, but I managed to get up and stumble to the dresser. I braced myself on it and quietly opened the door.

The faint sound of the living room TV came from down the hall. All the lights were off, but there was a glow from the TV. Figuring Rune was still awake, I decided to go sit with him instead of trying to fight off invisible demons in his room.

I leaned on the wall for support as I crept down the hall. Rune was lying on the couch, covered with a throw blanket.

He was in his Fae form, so his tail peeked out from beneath the blanket, draped over the edge of the couch. His fox ears twitched slightly as he lay there in a sound sleep. His chest rose and fell with his soft breathing.

Seeing him sleeping, my chest bubbled with warmth. He looked so peaceful and beautiful. More than anything, I wanted to crawl up next to him and fall asleep in his arms, but I knew I couldn't do that. I didn't want to wake him.

Still, I didn't want to go back into his dark room alone, so I tiptoed further into the room. Gripping the back of the love-seat, I maneuvered around it. The soft cushion welcomed me, and I reached to grab the throw blanket that was draped across the back.

I covered myself up and snuggled into the cushions. My eyes found Rune as I got comfy. Even though I wasn't right next to him, I still felt more at ease falling asleep so close to him, and his presence helped me drift off to sleep and kept the nightmares away.

CHAPTER

THIRTY-THREE

My eyes fluttered open. Immediately, I was face to face with Marlow, who stood directly above me in his Fae form. He stared down at me with his glassy eyes. The brown and gold skin along his face shimmered with a fine layer of moisture. Caught off guard by his close proximity, I nearly jumped out of my own skin.

"You're funny when you're scared," he said, leaning in close to me. His eyes roamed from my head to toes, where I was still stretched out on the loveseat. When his eyes found mine again, he cocked an eyebrow and asked, "Why did you sleep in such an uncomfortable place?"

I glanced at my makeshift bed. "It's not uncomfortable."

Peeking over at the couch where Rune had

slept, I saw he was no longer there, and the pillow and blanket he'd used were gone.

When I looked back up at Marlow, I found his face mere inches from mine. I jumped back a little, not expecting him to be even closer.

He studied my face and mumbled, "Your eye and cheek are so puffy. Can I touch them?"

I grimaced and tried to think of a gentle way to tell him no. Talking to Marlow sometimes felt like talking to a child. He said strange things and acted unusual, but he never meant anything callous by it.

Luckily, Bassel came into the room from down the hall. When he saw Marlow crowding over me, he rolled his eyes and said, "Hey, goober, leave Bria alone."

Bassel was in his Fae form as well. Not only that, but he was shirtless, too. Gold and brown striped fur ran along his hands, trailing up his dark arms. The fur went over his shoulders and just barely started down his built chest before stopping. His striped ears peeked above his sleep-tousled hair, and when he yawned, I could see all of his sharp teeth. If I didn't know Bassel as the softy he was, I would've been terrified.

Marlow frowned at him. "I just wanted to touch her eye."

Bassel growled, deep and throaty. The sound was eerily similar to a tiger who was seconds away from pouncing on its prey. His sharp teeth were bared, and he stalked closer to Marlow.

Marlow, knowing he was in trouble, backed away from me. He glanced at me with a pout, then turned to go sit in the high-backed chair across from me.

I turned back to Bassel as he came all the way into the room. He smiled at me and approached the loveseat. I moved my legs aside to make room for him. He flopped down next to me, his liger's tail landing in my lap.

His brows pinched in concern as he asked, "How are you feeling?"

"Somewhat better after sleeping all night."

"That's good. You looked really bad last night when Rune showed up with you. Both of you guys were covered in your blood. I can't believe Jonah did that to you. As soon as we find him, he's going to wish he never set foot near you."

Chuckling, I said, "Oh no. He's invoked the wrath of the mighty Bassel. Whatever will he do?"

Bassel laughed, ruffling my hair with his large hand.

A sweet aroma began to fill the air. I inhaled its sugary scent, and my mouth instantly watered. It was the sweet mixture of baking cinnamon rolls and brewing coffee.

Bassel smelled it, too, because he looked at Marlow and asked, "Who's cooking?"

Marlow crossed his eyes, which I was starting to realize he did often when speaking. "Rune."

Bassel scoffed. "Yeah right! Rune never cooks."

At that exact moment, Rune came down the short hallway from the kitchen. My breath caught when I saw him. He must not have been awake long because he was shirtless, giving us a delicious view of his toned stomach, chest, and arms. He was still in his Fae form like the night before, and I was beginning to gather that perhaps they all slept in that form. Those incredible, golden eyes found mine, and he walked toward me, carrying a tray that held a plate of cinnamon rolls, two cups of coffee, and a glass of water.

Rune bared his canines at Bassel and growled.

Bassel, in turn, held up his hands in surrender and said, "Calm down there, Fox. I'll move."

Bassel relocated to the couch. Rune, looking appeased, carefully lowered the tray onto my lap, after making sure the weight wasn't too much for my bruises. A mound of cinnamon rolls stared up at me from the plate. My stomach growled at their delicious smell, which paired nicely with the coffee. Rune had done this for me? I was overwhelmed by the thought he'd put into this. Little things like this made it hard not to fall in love with him.

I thanked him as he sat beside me. He looked at his two friends, then gestured toward the kitchen. "There's more in there if you're hungry."

Marlow immediately jumped up after hearing the news that breakfast awaited him.

Bassel sat there for another moment, grinning knowingly at Rune. "What? Aren't you gonna bring it on a tray for all of us?"

Rune returned the look with a snarky smile of his own. Suddenly, the end of Bassel's tail caught fire. Bassel's eyes widened in alarm, and he roared as he jumped up in a panic. Before he could make any move to put out the fire, Rune had already extinguished it. He laughed as Bassel turned to glare at him.

Tension rolled off Bassel, which made Rune chuckle. A fight was sure to ensue, so I was more than grateful when Akira came into the room. He was in his Fae form like everyone else, and his black eyes darted back and forth between Rune and Bassel.

"What's wrong with you two so early in the morning?" Akira asked.

Bassel pointed a finger at Rune. "He set my tail on fire!"

Rune took one of the cinnamon rolls off the stack on the tray. He bit into it and chewed slowly. "I didn't burn you. I chose to keep it as an unheated flame. You should thank me, not yell at me, silly liger. I hope you learned your lesson. Don't tease me."

Akira sighed and approached Bassel. "You *do* know better than to tease him."

Bassel rolled his eyes. "How could I resist when the big bad fox actually made breakfast for Bria and even brought it out to her?"

Rune studied his cinnamon roll as he flicked his hand at Bassel. Bassel let out another cry as his tail caught fire once more.

Akira gasped and turned around, flapping his wings at the flame to put it out. Unfortunately, the wind only made it grow larger. Rune laughed at his friends' efforts and shrieks as they fought urgently to put out the fire. Bassel held onto his long tail, beating it against the couch in an attempt to extinguish the flame. After having his laugh, Rune gave another wave of his hand, putting out the fire.

Bassel panted as he glared at Rune. He took a step toward him, but Akira grabbed onto his arm. He pulled Bassel away and said, "That's enough playtime. Let's go to the kitchen, Liger. *Yoshi, yoshi.*"

Bassel begrudgingly followed.

Akira looked over his shoulder at me and winked. "Glad to see you're still all beat up, Bria."

Momentarily confused by such an odd statement, I quirked a brow at him. Being glad about my injuries didn't make much sense, but then it dawned on me—if I had healed, that would've meant I was Water Fae.

Finding my voice, I met Akira's gaze. "Thanks. Me too."

He laughed and turned back around, heading toward the kitchen with Bassel.

I was glad my bruises served some sort of purpose. It showed Akira and the others I was human, unlike Dallas and Dax.

My chest tightened, and I swallowed hard.

Dallas.

There was so much that needed to be talked about between us, so many answers I needed from her. I was scared, though. What if I talked to her and didn't like the answers I got? She could confirm my worst fears and reveal that she hadn't told me who she was because she didn't think our friendship was strong enough. That alone had me freezing up when I even considered answering her numerous texts and calls. I needed more time to sort through my feelings and the fact that she … she was Water Fae.

With Akira and Bassel's exit, Rune and I were alone in the living room. I looked down at the cinnamon rolls, my heart in my throat with sudden nerves. He sat so close I could feel the heat radiating off his bare skin.

"Thank you for making me breakfast."

He shrugged and looked at me. "It's not a big deal."

I bit into the warm, gooey roll. The hot icing made my taste buds dance. Never had anything tasted so good. I swallowed the bite I'd taken and looked at him. "They said you never cook, though."

He rested his chin on his fist and mumbled, "I wouldn't call it cooking. All I did was take them out of the tin container and follow the directions."

I laughed. "Well, even so, thank you. It means a lot to me. Cinnamon rolls are my favorite."

Smirking, he said, "I figured there was something about them you liked. I mean, when Dallas offered to get some that first night we ran into each other, you practically turned into a firetruck."

Glowing bright pink at the reminder of that memory, I cleared my throat and shoved another bite in my mouth. "Oh. Yeah. Right."

Leaning in close to me, a playful gleam danced in his eyes. "What was that about anyway? I've never seen someone react that way to food. What actually had you so flustered back then? Could it have been—"

Quickly turning, I shoved the rest of my cinnamon roll into Rune's mouth. His eyes went wide, the gooey bun hanging halfway out of his mouth. He met my eyes past the food and started chewing. Taking a deep breath, I turned back to the plate and willed my face to cool down. It was even more embarrassing now than it was then. The irony of this moment, eating cinnamon rolls with Mr. Cinnamon Roll himself was not lost on me.

"No deeper meaning," I said past my roll. I glanced at him as his tongue slowly blazed a trail across his lip, licking up some stray icing. Warmth trickled through my body, settling between my thighs, and I had to quickly look away again. "I just really like cinnamon rolls."

Laughing, he shrugged. "If you say so. Anyway, how are you feeling? Want some more pain reliever?"

"I'm feeling okay given the circumstances. Still pretty sore. Some medicine sounds really nice."

"Thought so." He pulled a bottle out of his sweatpants pocket and held it out to me. "Take some after you finish eating."

I did just that. I wolfed down all four of the remaining rolls, downed my coffee, and took two extra-strength pain killers. Rune made me an ice pack to help the swelling on my eye go down. After making me move to the couch, he put on *Jurassic Park*, which happened to be our shared favorite movie. He had me lie on my side, head in his lap, and an ice pack on my ribs and back. We spent the entirety of Saturday morning like that. Him rubbing soft strokes along my back and keeping my ice pack in place, me commenting on my love for all things dinosaur.

The day felt so normal. So natural.

"So do you want to go back to your dorm tonight?" Rune asked. "Or do you want to stay here?"

Turning my head to look up at him, I shrugged. "Dallas is going to be there tonight. I'm honestly not sure if I'm ready to see her yet."

He brushed a strand of hair back from my forehead, tucking it behind my ear, and my heart ignited under his touch. "You can stay here then. None of us mind."

Smiling, I tried to keep at bay how happy that made me. "Really? Are you sure?"

He nodded. "We leave in a week anyway. You can stay here

until then. Plus, I don't think any of us feel comfortable with you being alone while Jonah is still out there somewhere."

At the mention of his name, fear lodged its way into my chest. I couldn't feed into that emotion. If I did, he'd win. I had to keep moving forward and not let what happened paralyze me.

Meeting Rune's eyes again, I nodded. "I'd like to stay here then. As long as you promise it's okay."

Rolling his eyes, he poked my forehead. "I already said it's fine. Now that that's settled, let's get some lunch."

After Rune made lunch—a simple turkey and cheese sandwich with chips—he had me flip over. I lay on my back with ice pressed firmly under me and on my stomach. His thigh was a comfy pillow, and I was so content that I ended up closing my eyes and releasing a breath I didn't know I'd been holding. His fingers gently combed through my hair, and after only a few blissful moments, I was drifting off to sleep.

CHAPTER

THIRTY-FOUR

"**I**'m so glad all that sleep and ice helped the soreness go down," Akira said.

My back was pressed against the love seat, and Akira sat behind me, brushing my hair. It was relaxing having him run a brush through the strands and play with different hair styles.

"Me too. It feels a bit easier to walk now, thank God."

It was Sunday morning, and everyone was still asleep, except for me, Rune, and Akira. The three of us were sitting in the living room, drinking coffee and enjoying the normalcy of an early Sunday morning.

"So," I started, looking in Rune's direction. It was time to address the elephant in the room. "What are we going to do about me looking like this? If Fae heal quickly, your family's obviously going to wonder how I'm beat up. We leave in six days, which isn't enough time for me to heal."

"I wondered the same thing at first," Rune said. He stuffed his hand into the box of Cheerios he was holding and tossed me a few, which I happily popped into my mouth. "After talking to Avana, she assured me she could make you look normal."

"Really?"

He nodded. "It's just appearance-wise. She can't actually heal your wounds, so while you'll look fine, you'll still be injured under all that magic."

I processed that information. So, I'd look fine and dandy, but underneath that, I'd still be a pummeled grape. Good to know. Hopefully, no one wanted to hug me too tightly. That thought had me wanting to giggle, because that would never happen. His family? Wanting to hug me? Yeah, not gonna happen. I'd be fine.

My phone buzzed on the floor next to me, and guilt settled in the pit of my stomach. It was the thirteenth text from Dallas since Friday night. After telling her I was fine Saturday morning, she'd been blowing up my phone with calls and texts, all of which I'd ignored. It didn't take much imagination to guess that she was trying to convince me to come back. I wasn't ready to talk things out with her yet, so I kept ignoring her like a coward.

"There!" Akira beamed, putting the final touch on my hair.

He settled on a high ponytail, and even put in a bow that he had lying around.

Smiling up at him, I thanked him.

"Looks good," Rune said. "I like the bow."

Cheeks flushing and heart warming, I ducked my head to hide the massive smile plastered on my lips. "Thanks."

"Whenever you're feeling up to it, I can drive you back to campus to get all your bags."

I downed the last of my coffee and nodded. "I'm ready to go now. It'll be nice to wear my own clothes, no offense."

Smirking, he stood up. "I like you wearing my clothes, but I get it. Give me a second to get changed, and we'll head out."

Akira helped me stand while Rune put on some real clothes. Rune reappeared in a dark t-shirt that fit his body beautifully and some low-hung jeans that made my imagination run wild. I had to look away quickly, otherwise I'd risk being caught drooling.

After hugging Akira and promising we'd do nails with Avana when I got back, I followed Rune to the door. My body was still stiff in places, the pain a faint-but-constant reminder that I needed to take it easy. The aching wasn't as defined as yesterday; so as long as I didn't go running any marathons, I'd be fine. That didn't stop Rune from walking right next to me, just in case I had any trouble getting to the car.

It was only nine on a Sunday morning, so if Dallas stuck to her usual Sunday routine, she'd still be over at Rance's place. I prayed that's where she was, because my mental state could not handle seeing her yet. I mean, what would I say? *Hey, Dallas, you're Fae? That's awesome! Thanks for hiding it all these years! Want a cookie?*

She'd no doubt also wonder how I was so understanding of Fae, which would bring up Rune and the others. Seeing as how they were sworn enemies, I couldn't have her finding out my boyfri—er, friend, was Land Fae.

But what if it was too late?

If Dax still had his memories after being slammed into a tree, he'd recall that Rune was Fox Fae. I still didn't know if Dallas and Dax were in on each other's real identities, but if they were, he may have already told her about Rune.

What if Dallas wanted to hurt Rune now?

I let out a frustrated sigh as we pulled onto campus.

Rune glanced over at me, his eyes concerned. "What's wrong?"

Pursing my lips, I shook my head. "Just a lot on my mind, I guess."

Parking the car in front of my dorm, he turned to me. "Want me to help you gather your stuff?"

"It's fine. I need to do a few things before I head back to your house anyways."

He frowned. "Are you sure? I can wait if you want."

"You hate waiting on things. I'm fine, really. You head home. I'll see you later."

He looked warily at the building. He swallowed hard and found my eyes again. "Your room isn't on one of the upper floors, is it?"

Confused, I cocked an eyebrow at him. "It is. Why?"

"Then at least let me help you get up the stairs. I don't trust you not to fall in your condition."

Narrowing my eyes, I pointed an accusatory finger at him. "You're acting like you don't want to leave me."

He scoffed and turned off the car. He got out and came around to my door. Opening it, he held out his hand for me. "Fine. Maybe I don't want to leave you yet. But it isn't because of some deeper meaning. Like I said, I just don't trust you to walk up a flight of stairs on your own."

Laughing, I said, "Three. It's actually three flights of stairs."

He didn't hear me. He was looking around the building, his eyes searching for something. I realized then that he was genuinely worried, and I felt a bit guilty for trying to joke about it.

Walking to the dorm with him by my side, I kept my tone gentle as I said, "Nothing is going to happen, Rune."

A muscle in his jaw ticked, and his eyes narrowed into thin slits. "I didn't think anything was going to happen the other night, either. Look how that turned out. I'm not making that mistake again."

We walked through the glass doors. The stone steps were directly ahead, and we carefully made our way up them together. He held onto one of my arms in guidance, while I used the other to grip the railing. I was suddenly glad he'd decided to help. The stairs were a painful bitch.

Glancing in his direction, I finally said, "It wasn't your fault."

He looked at me briefly but wouldn't meet my eyes. Guilt was like a poison, infecting the usual carefree glimmer in his eye. He didn't deserve to feel that way. There was nothing he could've done to prevent what happened that night.

Finally, we made it to my floor, and after a short walk down the hallway, we were there. I glanced at Rune and unlocked my door. When it was open, I walked in with Rune right behind me.

Dallas's bed was empty. I let out a relieved sigh.

"Since I made it in safely, you're okay to go now," I said, turning back to look at him.

As soon as I saw his face, I froze. He stared away from me with his mouth slightly agape. His eyes were wide with a mixture of bewilderment and fascination. I followed his gaze to see what had him so speechless. It was his painting, which was hung proudly above my bed.

I looked from him to the painting, then back. "Rune? What's wrong?"

His eyes remained transfixed to the canvas, and he raised his finger to point at it. "Why-why did you hang it up?"

I laughed and went over to my closet. I bent down to grab the large suitcase that rested at the bottom. "What do you mean, why? I told you I loved it. I wasn't lying when I said that to you."

He looked over at me, suddenly confused. "Why? It looks like a kid painted it."

I smiled and walked closer to the picture. My eyes traced every inch of it, remembering the way he had leaned so close, trying to be as slow and careful as possible. "You may see something that looks childlike, but I see something that someone important to me put their all into, working harder than anyone else in that room. I see a precious memory with someone special."

I swallowed hard, my gaze trained on my suitcase now. I had gotten so lost in his painting that the words left my mouth before I could stop them. He was important to me. He was special. He was most definitely already aware of my feelings for him, but neither of us had verbalized it like that before.

I glanced over at him, trying to gauge what he thought about what I'd said. He was still standing by the door, but he was finally looking at me, his amber eyes searching mine. I couldn't hold his gaze for long, because I was so embarrassed by what I'd said.

I cleared my throat and blurted, "All right, well, I have to change and pack. You can probably go now. Like I said before, I'm fine and need to do some stuff. I'll see you later tonight."

He looked at the door, then back at me. I couldn't actually look him in the eye, but I saw him nod. He left without another word, leaving me standing alone with my thoughts. I wanted to collapse. So much was going on inside my head. Nervousness. Excitement. Terror. Determined restlessness. Euphoria. It was all so much piled on top of everything else. I didn't understand how to sort it all out, so I was thankful to have some time to myself, even if that time proved to be pointless. I was no closer to understanding the new world I found myself in, or my own feelings.

CHAPTER
THIRTY-FIVE

It was time to get down to business. I had to pack my suitcase for the trip, as well as a duffle bag for Rune's house this week. The duffle bag was easy since I could wear all my comfy t-shirts and leggings. Throw in some panties, socks, toiletries, and violà. It was the bag for the trip that I had to really think about.

I went through my closet and dresser, thoughtfully picking clothes I hoped would work. As I was digging around, I found a large pink and black Victoria Secret bag at the bottom of the closet. I slowly pulled it out to re-examine its contents, which I hadn't seen since Dallas first gave it to me after Dax and I got together.

Inside was a black lace thong and a matching bra. She'd bought it since I didn't own any "sexy" panties or bras. I'd told her I didn't plan on needing them anytime soon, but now for some reason, knowing that I was going to be in the same house as Rune for two whole weeks had me wanting to bring the set.

I looked from the bag of seduction to the open suitcase. I felt silly for even considering taking the two garments, yet my feet moved on their own, guiding me to the suitcase. My stomach twisted with excited nerves as I pictured what I would need them for. My exposed skin teasing Rune with only two black coverings concealing the most intimate parts of me. His naked body pressed against mine. Dallas would have a fit if she knew I was packing them.

Ah. Dallas. My heart pinched tightly, but I quickly shook off my emotions.

I needed to focus on packing, so I continued to dig around, throwing anything I thought I might need into the suitcase. With only two dresses in my closet, I figured a trip to a boutique might not be a bad idea since Rune's family expected me to dress in what they found proper.

Once I'd packed everything that I could, I grabbed a pair of jeans and a sweater to change into. Before leaving for the shower down the hall, I noticed the mug I'd created for Rune sitting on my desk. I made a mental note to pack it when I got back. Carrying my clothes to the bathroom down the hall, I stood under the heat of the water, letting it wash away the lingering memories from the encounter with Jonah. This was the one constant in my life. The gentle stream of water trickling down my skin seemed to soothe any remaining ache in my body. I felt energized and at ease once more. With so much turmoil going on around me, the water's caress was like a breath of fresh air.

When I got back to my room, I gathered up my belongings but paused. Seeing as how I wasn't going to meet Dallas again before I left for the trip, I decided I needed to put on my big girl panties and at least reach back out to her. I pulled out my phone and was instantly struck with guilt. I had seventeen texts now, plus the ignored voicemails she'd left.

I finally read the texts and listened to all of the voicemails. Her tone was frantic, telling me to come back to the dorm immediately or to give her Rune's address so that she could come get me. She didn't want me around Rune anymore.

The more I listened to her high-pitched voice, the more my fears were confirmed. Dax had told her. She knew what Rune was, and her distrust of him was evident in how she spoke. My heart pounded with this new issue. Two of the most important people in my life hated one another, and they both most likely wanted the other dead. What was the right answer in this scenario? How did I tackle this?

I decided not to text Dallas, but instead got out a piece of notebook paper to write her a note that she would only find after I was already at Rune's.

Dallas,

    I'm sorry for not telling you sooner about this trip, but I'm leaving for awhile. Two weeks. I need some time to myself. Plus, it's Rune's birthday, so we're going to his hometown next week. I'll be perfectly fine. You don't need to worry about me. I trust Rune, so you should, too. Please do not be angry or worried. I'm recovering from the other night nicely, so you don't need to worry about that, either. I will come back home safe and sound. I love you. ALL of you.

                              Bria

Biting back my emotions, I laid the note on her pillow. I probably could've said something more about being aware of the truth, but I wanted to talk about that in person with her, not through a note. Still, I felt physically sick doing something that would worry her so much. I didn't want to cause her any grief, but I knew I was safe with Rune, even if she didn't believe me. I had nothing to worry about when it came to him. His family, on the other hand, was a different story.

That was another problem for another day, though.

I had to make two trips to my car between my suitcase, duffle bag, backpack, and purse. Traveling the stairs numerous times while still recovering from my beating was exhausting, and by the time I loaded the last bag in my car, my sides were throbbing. After resting on my hood for a few minutes, I braced myself and headed on foot to my English teacher's on-site housing. Not all of the teachers here lived on campus, but a few of mine did, which was convenient.

When I made it to my English professor's house, I knocked, and within seconds, she opened the door with a wide grin. Her black hair was twisted in an elegant bun at the top of her head, and her purple-rimmed glasses sat on the tip of her nose.

"Hi, Professor Dobbins," I greeted her with a smile of my own.

Her previously bright face fell as she let out a gasp. Her mouth fell open, her concerned eyes raking me over. "Dear Heavens, Bria! Whatever happened to you?"

I sighed and touched the bottom of my swollen eye. It was sensitive to the touch, and I had to fight back a wince. I realized then that I should've covered the injuries with make-up, but the idea hadn't occurred to me while I was still in my dorm.

Drawing my hand away, I said, "I, uh, got in a pretty bad car accident the other night. I'm still a bit traumatized by the whole thing, so I'm actually going home and staying there through fall break next week. Since I won't be here, I wanted to let you know."

I hadn't planned on skipping this whole week, but after getting pummeled into a disgusting sight, I decided it would be best to avoid campus. Plus, I wanted to avoid Dallas at all costs until I'd come to terms with that secret she'd kept from me all this time. Weak or not, I wasn't ready to face that battle yet.

I waited, hoping Professor Dobbins bought my lie. When I'd first thought up the story, it sounded believable in my head.

I must have been right, because she gave me a soft smile and said, "Of course. I'm so sorry that happened to you! Take all the time you need. I can email you the PowerPoints and assignments for this week, so just do them when you feel up to it. You can turn them in after we come back from fall break."

Smiling, I thanked her. I repeated the process with the other professors who lived on campus, with a plan to email those who didn't live here. It was a good thing fall break was the week of Rune's trip. Two weeks of missed work would be a bit much, even for me.

Glancing at my phone, I saw it was now 10:45. Dallas would be getting back any minute, so I quickly headed back to my car and made my way to the mall. Not only did I need to get more dresses, but I wanted to get Rune something for his birthday, in addition to the mug. My plan was to find him a scary movie. Granted, I had no idea what horror movies were actually good, but hopefully, there would be someone I could ask.

I pulled into the mall parking lot, but this time, I chose to park in a populated area, near the front. No way was I going anywhere near where Allen and his goons had jumped me. The thought of something like that happening again made ice settle in my veins.

As I made my way into the mall, my phone vibrated in my purse. I dug it out and looked at the screen. It was Dallas. I knew she must have found my note, so she was probably calling to scream at me to get back. She'd no doubt say or try anything to get me away from Rune now that she knew what he was.

"Sorry, Dallas," I mumbled before hitting decline.

My phone started buzzing once more. Dallas again. I took a deep breath and squeezed my eyes shut as I turned off my phone. I dropped my phone back into my bag and continued on my way. I hoped she wouldn't keep calling all week and next. If she did, I'd have to keep my phone turned off, otherwise I'd feel compelled to answer.

The film and music store was thankfully near the entrance of the mall. It had dozens upon dozens of shelves and tables, all piled with movies and CDs. The store was organized by genre, so I followed the signs until I found the horror section.

I was completely out of my element as I scanned the titles. Frustrated at my lack of horror knowledge, I looked around for someone to help me.

A voice came from behind me and asked, "Can I help you find something?"

I froze, and my skin crawled. I knew that voice. *I knew that voice!* I slowly turned around to look at the person behind me. As soon as he saw my face, his friendly expression fell. I swallowed hard, looking at his blue shirt and khakis. A name tag was pinned to his shirt.

Blake.

CHAPTER

THIRTY-SIX

Blake looked around us frantically.

"What are you doing here?" he whispered, growing a sickly shade of white.

Instinctively, I backed up a step. "I'm not here to fight with you. I didn't even know you worked here."

Our last encounter resurfaced in my mind, and I realized I'd made a grave mistake that day. After Allen and his friends tried to finish what they'd started, I'd meant to call the officer who was handling the case to give him an updated description. That was the same day I'd discovered Fae and the truth about Rune and the others.

I'd been so focused and overwhelmed with that discovery, it had completely slipped my mind to call the officer back. Then things with Jonah escalated, and it seemed like reporting Allen and the others took the back burner. Now here I was, staring down one of my assailants who *worked* here.

Blake approached me, so I quickly stepped back again. I couldn't go far with the shelves behind me, so I pressed as far as I could into them, watching him closely. Fear and guilt seemed to cloud his eyes. He glanced over his shoulder again, crossing his arms.

When he looked back at me, he asked, "Is your boyfriend with you again? I don't want any issues. I actually need this job."

I shook my head. "No. It's just me. Although, I should tell your employer what you've done. Do you know how terrible of a person you are?"

He recoiled as if I'd physically hit him, and his eyes fell to his sneakers. "Don't tell me what kind of person I am. You don't know me."

"I know enough. You're a coward who watches as people get attacked, right?"

He quickly turned to look around the store. No one was paying us any mind, but then again, there was only one other person in here—a young girl, who was engrossed in browsing DVDs on the other side of the room.

He whipped his head back up to meet my eyes and pleaded, "Please, keep your voice down."

My eyes shot daggers his way, and I noticed him staring hard at my face. As I was about to tell him off, he asked, "What happened to you? You're pretty beat up."

I fumed at his question. He really had the audacity to ask about my injuries when he'd watched his friend threaten me with a knife? I fought to stay calm, quickly turning around to find a movie so I could get out of here. "I don't have to tell you anything."

He walked around me, standing to my left. I glanced at him as he studied me. He nodded at the shelf of movies. "What are you looking for?"

"A horror movie, obviously. I don't watch them, so I don't know what to get."

He nodded and pulled one off of the shelf. "If you want one with a good plot line and made by a pretty good crew, I would go with this one."

I glanced at him and slowly reached out to take the movie from his hands. I didn't like him being so close to me. This *was* Blake after all. I felt pretty sure he wouldn't do anything right now because he wanted this job, but that didn't do much to ease my wariness.

I knew I couldn't trust him.

At least not as a person, but for now, I'd have to trust in his choice of movie. I wanted out of there, so I accepted the suggestion.

"Thank you," I mumbled and turned to walk away.

He followed behind me, which made my heart rate spike. Why the hell was he following me?

I speed-walked to the counter to pay for the DVD. I wanted out of here and away from him as quickly as possible, but I realized too late that no one was behind the counter. I felt my stomach twist as he came up behind me, but instead of stopping, he went around me and behind the cash register. He held out his hand to me. I looked at it.

He sighed and said, "The movie?"

"Oh," I said, handing him the DVD.

Relief and a bit of stupidity hit me as he took the movie from my hand.

"$21.84," he said.

I noticed his eyes scanning the marks on my face again, and it made me want to hide. My cuts and bruises were vivid, and the attention was making me self-conscious. It didn't help that the onlooker was Blake of all people. He didn't even bother telling the girl who'd been browsing thank you as she exited the store, leaving the two of us alone.

As I handed the cash over, he asked, "Were you in a wreck?"

"No," I snapped.

He moved at a sloth's pace as he gathered my change. "Did you get in a fight?"

"No," I forced out between clenched teeth.

"What happened then?"

"What does it matter, Blake? Do you somehow care about others now? It's none of your business."

His eyes went wide, and hurt took root in them. As soon as I saw the sting register on his face, I couldn't help the biting guilt pricking at my insides. Blake was a criminal. He'd stood by and watched his friend try to rob me and then again threaten to kill me. He'd watched and done nothing to help.

"I'm sorry," Blake whispered.

His voice came out so low, I thought I'd imagined it at first. But as he handed me my change and his eyes found mine again, I saw the tears pooling in the corners, and I knew I hadn't imagined anything.

The memory of his hesitation, his attempts at convincing his friends to walk away, and the threat made to him about being homeless again rang through my head. He clearly felt bad about his part in what happened, but remorse didn't fix things. He'd still made those mistakes, and they were his to live with. I didn't need to pity him.

Though, knowing I didn't *need* to didn't stop me.

He sniffled and repeated, "I'm so, *so* sorry."

"What you did is not okay."

"I know. I know it's not. There's no excuse for what I did. Still, I am so sorry."

Perhaps one day I could forgive him, but not yet. Instead, I nodded to acknowledge his apology and placed my wallet back in my bag.

"I get that you don't want to tell me what happened, but can you at least tell me if you're okay?" I looked up at his sudden question, and he nodded towards my face. "Allen didn't get to you, did he?"

A shiver ran down my spine at his phrasing. Was Allen trying to "get to" me? Could that imply he was actively pursuing me to finish the job and silence me? I wouldn't put it past him to do something like that, and the very notion made unease settle in my gut like a cinder block in water.

"No. Allen didn't find me. Is he trying to?"

"I'm not sure, to be honest. I cut ties with him after, well, after that day."

I raised a brow in surprise before I could stop myself. I wasn't expecting to hear that from him. Allen had definitely felt like a fierce leader, and Blake was a loyal, if not fearful, follower. To hear that Blake had managed to break away from the toxic friendship was good to hear. I hoped that meant he was on his way to a better lifestyle, one that wouldn't have such dire consequences.

There was no need for me to stick around and congratulate him, however. I started to turn to make my leave.

"So was it your boyfriend, the one who helped you at the club and here? Is he the one who did it?"

The idea made me recoil. Rune would never ever hurt me. The mere suggestion made my defensive tongue lash out.

"No. It wasn't Rune. He'd never do that."

Blake nodded as he twirled a rotating display. "So that's his name. Rune. What's your name?"

I narrowed my eyes. "Why would I tell you my name?"

"You know my name. What's the harm in me knowing yours?"

I rolled my eyes at the ridiculous question.

"It's Amber," I lied.

The corners of his mouth barely hinted at a smile. "Wrong. I know that's not your name."

"And how would you know?"

"Because you're clearly stubborn, so you wouldn't give me your name that easily."

"Then why bother asking?"

"You're right. I guess I was trying to start over. You know, show you I'm not that kind of monster. It's why I want to know what happened to you, too. I care about people. I'm not a ... a heartless criminal or whatever. I'm trying to make amends for what I've done."

His eyes pleaded with mine to understand, and deep down, I knew he probably was a good guy who'd just made some really bad choices. Everyone was flawed. He was trying to be friendly and express his sincere regret, but I wasn't sure where I sat on the matter yet. There was far too much going on in my life right now. Adding Blake and his struggle to redeem himself to the list was too much at the moment.

Exasperated at his attempts to persuade me to trust him, I decided to come across like a lunatic who wasn't worth convincing.

"You really want to know what happened to me?"

His green eyes brightened with the light of hope. "Yes. How'd you get hurt?"

I motioned him closer, and he turned his ear toward me. Cupping my hands around my mouth, I whispered, "A magical bat creature attacked me and then tried to kill me."

I leaned back with a smirk glued to my face, and I crossed my arms. That outrageous, yet true, answer would have anyone rolling their eyes and moving on, but after a second, I realized that didn't happen. He stood frozen, ear still tilted toward me, eyes bugging out of his head.

Finally, he took a deep breath and turned to me. With a firm nod, he walked to the entrance of the store where he flipped the sign to *Closed* and set the clock sticker to say he'd be back in ten minutes.

When his eyes found mine again, he said, "Come on."

That wasn't the reaction I was expecting.

"What? What do you mean? I'm not going anywhere with you."

He ignored me as he opened a door at the back of the store, revealing a sink and toilet. My stomach tightened with nerves as he waved for me to follow.

"You've got to be kidding me, right?" I yelled. "I am *not* going back there with you!"

"I'm not going to hurt you. I told you that's not who I am."

"As if I'd believe that. I would *never* trust you."

He ran a hand through his hair and went into the small bathroom. I watched him turn on the sink before stepping away from it. He looked at me again and said, "I promise you that I'm not going to do anything like what you're thinking. I'm going to do something to help your injuries."

I narrowed my eyes and crossed my arms. "There's nothing you could do to help my injuries."

The corners of his mouth lifted, and despite my better judgment, this smile was not malicious in any sense of the word. It was a real one, full of warm emotion, something I didn't think Blake was capable of. "Don't be so sure. Please. Come here. You can even have your phone out with 911 on speed dial if it makes you feel better. I swear, I mean you no harm."

Even with the sincerity in his voice, I knew he couldn't be trusted. He was insane if he thought I'd fall for whatever this was. With my resolve to leave and be done with this mess, I turned to make my escape.

As I moved for the door, something stopped me in my tracks. A faint whisper, like a lullaby in the back of my mind, hummed and calmed me to my core. Something deep within me told me to go. Go to Blake. Go to the sink full of water.

Water.

My body moved on its own, turning until I faced the bathroom. I felt myself take a step forward.

Then another.

And another.

I continued in small, slow measured steps until I was finally in the bathroom. My brain was firing warning signals, but my feet wouldn't listen. It was as if my body and mind were no longer communicating. Blake regarded me warmly, but again, it wasn't a threatening expression. He stepped around me, shutting the door behind us. Whatever weird spell I'd been under evaporated at the sound of the latch catching, and my guard instantly went back up.

My heart raced, and I frantically dug in my purse for my pepper spray. "What are you doing? Open the door, Blake! I swear to God, I will scream, and people will come running. You'll rot in jail. But not before I douse your ass in pepper spray."

He held up his hands, trying to put me at ease. "Shh! Calm down! I only shut it because I can't let anyone see what I'm doing."

My mouth fell open, and my breath quickened as panic set in. I whipped out my spray and pointed it at him. "Is-is that supposed to make me feel better? Newsflash: it doesn't!"

Groaning, he clutched his forehead. "I'm just going to stop talking now since I'm an idiot." He met my eyes briefly then looked at the water that poured out of the spout on the sink. When he looked at me again, he let out a heavy breath. "Close your eyes."

My body moved away from him until my back pressed against the wall. My lip quivered as memories of the knife being held to my throat came rushing back. Cold, sharp metal. The threat of it slicing my neck like a warm blade through butter. Bile rose up my stomach.

Frowning, Blake whispered, "I'm not going to hurt you."

I shook my head. "I don't believe you!"

"Please. Just close your eyes."

I shook, terror sinking its claws into my chest. My stomach was in knots, and I was seconds away from being sick. I had to use the wall for support when my knees buckled slightly. Raw fear pumped through me and shattered my mind, reaching deep within me to tear at my sanity. It chilled my skin and stole my ability to breathe and think calmly, but I had to try to focus. I had to push past my panic so that should I need to put up a fight, I could.

My eyes fell to the tiled floor, and I gripped the pepper spray canister with trembling hands as if my life depended on it. While fear begged me to dart from the room, another more alluring sound called me to remain calm and to listen.

"P-please don't hurt me. If-if I close my eyes, don't come near me, or else I won't hesitate to use this."

I glanced up at him and watched him nod. My heart hammered in my chest. I didn't trust this bastard as far as I could throw him. Still, I let my eyes flutter shut with that soft lullaby creeping its way back into my mind. I held my pepper spray out, waiting for something. I didn't know what I was expecting. The feel of a knife slicing through me? An evil laugh before a declaration that I'd been tricked?

I could have never expected what did.

With my eyes still firmly shut, I heard the gentle sound of moving water. The trickling whisper of it drifted closer until I felt the cold touch of the water kissing every inch of my face. It cupped my cheeks and forehead, clinging to me. Instantly, its riveting current soothed the pain from my face. It didn't stop there. The liquid traced along my skin and under my clothes, relieving all the pain in my ribs and back. Finally, the water dripped away, falling from me in small drops.

My eyes fluttered open. I expected to see Blake standing before me with a hose or something he could've used to run the water over my face, but he stood on the other side of the room

FIRE OF THE FOX

by the sink. His grin was large and bright as he took in every inch of me.

"There's that beautiful face," he said. He stepped away from the sink and gestured to the mirror hanging on the wall above it. "Come look."

At a loss for what had happened, I watched him carefully. I chose to ignore his calling me beautiful, and instead, approached the mirror. When I peered into it, my eyes went wide. The canister of pepper spray slipped from my fingers as my hands flew to cover my mouth in astonishment. All the bruises, cuts, everything was gone. I was completely healed.

Blake stood behind me, looking at me through the mirror. His smile never faltered. "I told you I could help your injuries."

I was so shocked to see myself healed and to feel no pain that my mind stuttered as it worked to process how this could happen. I looked down at the water, which was still running, and my heart stopped as it dawned on me.

Water.

Ability to heal.

Slowly, I turned around to face Blake. My hands fell back down to my sides, and my voice caught in my throat. "This can't be happening. You're Water Fae, aren't you?"

CHAPTER

THIRTY-SEVEN

It was Blake's turn to look at me in surprise. The look was quickly replaced by excitement. "So, you are Fae, right? I knew it! I always thought there was something special about you. After what you said back there, I wasn't sure, but seeing as how you know what I am, you must be Fae, too."

I gave a nervous laugh and leaned against the sink for support. Was the room spinning, or was that just me? "Sorry to disappoint, but no. I'm not Water Fae, but apparently, everyone else around me is."

He frowned. "You aren't? I could've sworn you were."

I sighed and shook my head. I couldn't believe this was happening. "I'm human."

"Why'd a Bat Fae attack you then?"

I shrugged. "That's the million-dollar question. Maybe because I have a lot of friends who are Fae?"

His eyes went wide. "You're friends with other Water Fae? Is Rune one? I couldn't sense if he was Water Fae when I saw him."

Curious, I narrowed my eyes at him. "What did you sense he was?"

"Nothing. As far as I could tell, he was just a human with a wicked right hook. A lot of Fae conceal their magical auras to avoid being detected by the enemy, so it's hard to tell if someone you meet is Fae or not. You, on the other hand, I could vaguely sense your aura, so I thought you were maybe one of us."

No wonder Dallas and Dax hadn't figured out that Rune was Land Fae before Friday night. He'd concealed his aura to avoid being caught.

Coming back to the conversation at hand, I shook my head and said, "Well, yes. I'm friends with Fae. Although, I'm on the fence about Water Fae at the moment, and considering you're one, it kinda paints a bad picture of them for me."

He sighed and leaned back against the wall on the other side of the room. He raised his hand in front of him, and I tried to keep my composure as a trail of water flew from the sink behind me toward his outstretched hand. I stood there in shock, watching the water come together into a single ball. It twirled in the air in front of him like my very own water show.

"I used to have a happy little family. A mom who gave way too many hugs, a dad who chased away everything bad in the world, and a little sister who looked at me like I was her hero. They were all taken from me. My entire world, my reason for breathing, was stolen in a war that wasn't even ours to fight."

Swallowing hard, I asked, "The fight between Land and Water Fae?"

His watery eyes found mine, and he nodded, wiping at a tear. "Yeah. We wanted no part in that fight, but I guess citizens don't really get a say when their leaders decide they want war. During the evacuation of our kingdom, I got separated from my family. There was an ambush, and, being the coward I am, I hid ... I hid, not even knowing my family was out there being slaughtered."

He hung his head low, sobbing into his hands. No words could comfort him, and I wasn't sure if it was my place to try. I stayed quiet, letting him get his emotions out. Something told me he'd never said this tale aloud before.

Finally, when he could speak through his tears, he continued, "I've been alone ever since. A century alone, wandering, lost, hating myself for not dying with them. When I met Allen, I just wanted a place to belong to again, a family to belong to. My need for that blinded me from seeing what he and his friends were actually like. By the time I realized they were up to no good, I was already in deep. I didn't want to lose them, too. I was terrified of being alone again, waiting all by myself for the day our Water Fae Prince finally came out of hiding to take us all home."

Meeting my eyes, he said, "I'm not asking for your forgiveness because I know I don't deserve that. I stood by and watched, doing nothing to help. These are my mistakes, and I have to carry them with me forever. I just wanted you to know why and that I'm really sorry. I tried telling Allen that mugging you wasn't right many times. He chose to ignore me, and the threat of being homeless again was too hard for me to ignore. That doesn't change what I did, but I've regretted it ever since. I have a lot to regret since I can't seem to stop making mistakes."

Frowning, I turned and placed my hands on either side of the sink. Water was still pouring out of the spout, so I turned it off and stared at the drops on the drain. It was surprisingly hard to listen to Blake's story and not sympathize with him. Earlier, I was convinced he deserved to feel that much pain. Now, I couldn't help but feel bad for him.

I couldn't picture living for as long as he had without having something or someone to hold onto. What would that be like? Had Rune or Dallas ever felt that way? I hated to think that any of my friends had been that lonely. Their happiness meant everything to me, and to picture them in that much agony made a sliver of pain slice open in my chest.

I turned to look at Blake again. His eyes were glued to the ball of water that he'd been playing with while talking. Clearly, I wasn't the only one who took comfort in water. It spun above his hand as I probed, "You said the Water Fae Prince was in hiding. Is that why all Water Fae are, too? You guys are waiting for the Prince to come back?"

He nodded before making the water burst into hundreds of droplets. They floated all around us in a beautiful, sparkling dance. "Eighteen years ago, he was hidden away. It's when the war came to a sort of standstill."

I nodded. "Right. Land Fae killed your King and Queen, who hid their only son to keep him safe from the Land Fae. Or at least, that's what I've heard."

He gave a small laugh before replacing the drops of water back into the sink where they went down the drain. "Did your Water Fae friends tell you all of that?"

I gave a small laugh of my own and ran a nervous hand through my hair. "Not exactly. My, uh, Land Fae friends did."

His face fell, and he stared at me with distraught eyes. "W-what? Land Fae? You're friends with Land Fae?"

I nodded. "I'm friends with Water and Land Fae. Everything is still pretty new to me, but I have a basic idea of the history between the two of you."

He narrowed his eyes. "Is Rune a Land Fae?"

I looked into his eyes and saw a hatred building up in them. If I said Rune was Land Fae, would he try to hunt Rune down to confront him? He said he wanted no part in the fight, but after losing his family, I wondered if that was still the case.

Loss could change people. It made you desperate, which Blake seemed to understand firsthand.

I couldn't picture Rune losing if they ended up fighting, but still, I answered, "No. He's human like me."

He nodded and looked away from me. His cheeks grew rosy as he glanced at me and asked, "So-so is he actually your boyfriend? I know I've called him that, but is he really?"

I quirked a confused brow at him, not sure what that really had to do with anything. I shrugged. "He is."

Sorta.

Not really.

His lips turned down. He stared at the floor and shoved his hand into his pockets. He wouldn't meet my eyes as he asked, "Are you guys serious?"

I narrowed my eyes at him. I parted my lips, trying to figure out what to say. His behavior and questions were throwing me for a loop. This side of Blake was so different from what I'd seen before. He seemed timid, almost shy.

First, he had wanted to talk with me, then he healed me, knowing that doing so would reveal what he was to me. He had no way of knowing for sure that I knew about Water Fae and such, so why would he do that? I had a feeling I knew why he was being so strange with me, as well as why he was so curious about my relationship with Rune.

"Blake," I said, taking a tentative step toward him.

He looked up at me, his cheeks still rosy.

With that, my suspicions were confirmed. I frowned and said as gently as I could, "Blake. I'm with Rune. Even if I wasn't, after what you did—"

He shook his head and closed the distance between us as he pleaded, "That wasn't me. Yes, I did go along with it, and I didn't do anything to stop them. Even so, I never wanted to be a part of that. That's not who I am! I-I want you to give me another chance to show you who I really am. I've never opened up about being Water Fae to anyone, but with you—" he paused, taking a deep breath. He looked down at the floor as he finished, "With you, I feel that spark again. I feel that sense of purpose I've been longing for. I can't explain it, but it's like this invisible pull tugging me toward you."

Speechless, I stared at him. No one had ever said something like that to me, and it was hard to swallow such a strong confession. Although, it was more likely *confusion* on his part than a real confession. As he'd said, this was the first time he'd been honest about who he was, and it felt like he needed someone to fill the void he'd had for so long. I wasn't the person who could do that for him, and I think he knew that deep down, too.

I couldn't return his feelings. Besides the fact that Blake had made too many mistakes for me to trust him like that, my heart already belonged to someone else—someone who was waiting for me as we spoke. Sure, Rune's feelings were a puzzle I was still trying to solve, but I almost had those pieces put together. It was hard for him to blatantly say the kind of things Blake was trying to, but I couldn't deny the fact that I wanted Rune and Rune alone.

Blake's eyes were glued to the tiled floor, his mouth turned down.

Gently, I tapped his arm.

He looked up at me, his green eyes shining.

I took a deep breath and said, "If things were different, I honestly think I could forgive you for your part in what happened. The rest of your friends, not a chance. But you ... I can tell you're sincere about regretting what happened, and I guess, in a weird way, I can see why you tried doing it. It's the same with humans and peer pressure. Although, your case was a bit more extreme."

His face beamed with newfound hope. "So you'll give me a chance?"

I sighed and shook my head. "I could consider a friendship. Nothing more. Look, Rune and I aren't actually together. We haven't been this whole time. It's a long, crazy story, but the point is, even though we aren't actually anything, I really love him. A lot."

My heart raced, and color rose to my cheeks. This was the first time I'd admitted my feelings out loud to someone. I couldn't believe that the person I chose to confide in was Blake, but then again, he had confided in me, too. Maybe he really wasn't that bad.

Blake's head fell in defeat, his eyes turning back to the floor. He gave a long sigh, and he nodded. "I understand. But—" He looked at me again, "But if things don't work out with him, could you maybe—"

"I can't promise anything more than friendship. I know where to find you now, so if you can prove to me that you truly aren't anything like the person I thought you were, we can try being friends. Okay?"

Optimism bled into his features once more as he said, "Of course. I'd like nothing more. It will be nice to have a friend again."

I grinned and glanced at the door. "I should probably get going now, and you should get back to work. You've definitely been gone longer than ten minutes."

He shrugged with a dismissive wave of a hand. "It's fine. It would be worth it for the sake of healing you."

My lips turned up slightly, and I looked down at my feet. I didn't know what to say to him, but I didn't have to say anything. My body locked up when he wrapped his arms around me in a gentle hug, and only after feeling the way he trembled did I finally hug him back.

When he pulled away, tears streaked down his cheeks again, but there was a flood of hope in his eyes amidst the pain. "Sorry.

It's been a really long time since I've hugged anyone. I'm also sorry for causing you so much trouble."

My mind was in a daze. How sad that a small hug from me could bring so much emotion to the surface. Dallas and I hugged almost every day. That small act between us was like a promise that everything was going to be okay, because I had someone on my side who loved me. Right now, she and I weren't in a good place, but that didn't change the fact that I loved her and our friendship. To know he'd been without that yet craving it was gut-wrenching.

"One other question," I said.

"What is it?"

I paused, remembering that odd sensation that drew me into the bathroom. It was like I was under a spell. "Did you hypnotize me or something? You know, to get me into the bathroom?"

He burst into laughter, clutching his stomach. "What? No. I don't have that sort of power. I don't think any Water Fae does. Why do you ask?"

Frowning, I shook my head. "Nothing. Never mind."

We walked back out into the store together. When I made it to the entrance of the store, I waved goodbye to him, which he returned with a smile.

I turned to leave, but before I could exit, he yelled, "Wait!"

I froze and looked back at him.

"Um, do you-do you think I can know your name now?"

Pursing my lips, I considered his request. "Do you promise to keep away from Allen and choices like the one you made?"

"Absolutely. I'm never going back down that road again."

Taking this into consideration, I nodded. After learning all I had and seeing more of who Blake was, I decided to give him a second chance. Mistakes were unavoidable, and his were inspired by his trauma and desperate need to find a place to belong again. I could understand how that need blinded him for a time, but he could see that now. This made my decision to let the troubled and lonely Fae in easier.

"Good. I'm glad you're seeing the error of your ways. In that case, my name is Bria."

"Bria. Well, it was nice to meet you, Bria."

"It was nice to meet you too, Blake. The real you, that is."

CHAPTER

THIRTY-EIGHT

"**W**elcome!"

The bell chimed as the bookstore door swung shut behind me. Smiling at Raven, I waved. "Hey! I was stopping in to pick up those books you ordered for me a few weeks ago."

After leaving the mall, I'd decided to stop by the bookstore to pick up the books I had ordered. This was my last week to really study up on Fae before the big trip, so I wanted some reading material to go through. I'd come back alone after mine and Dallas' initial visit to ask Raven to order a specific title. Avana had informed me of a book that was written by an Owl Fae regarding their world. To most, it seemed like a book full of fiction and fairy tales, but Avana assured me it was actually non-fiction. I was hopeful it would give me some more insight into this world.

Raven's face lit up, and she clapped her hands. "Yes. I have them right here. I ordered three different titles, including the one you asked for. They had the best ratings from what I could find, and they contain a plethora of stories and legends."

I paid for my new books, thanked Raven for her help, and continued on my errands. By the time I turned into Rune's driveway, I'd successfully gotten three more dresses for the trip and a gift bag for his presents.

My mind was still mulling over what had happened with Blake as I made my way to the front door. It was a lot to process. I mean, before today, I thought he was some scumbag, but now I saw something deeper than what was on the surface.

When he let Allen try to rob me, all I saw in Blake was a monster. When he told me his story and hugged me back there, he was so different. It didn't excuse his actions. It didn't make him a good person or warrant him forgiveness, but it did give me something to think about.

Shaking my head, I pushed thoughts of him from my mind. It didn't matter what he was like now. I wouldn't give him the relationship he wanted. I still only cared for Rune, and I honestly didn't see that changing. The closer I got to his front door, the more excited I got because I knew he was on the other side, waiting for me.

As soon as I stepped up to the door, realization struck me hard. I was healed. There wasn't a single injury marring my body now, which was going to pose a major question for everyone when I walked into this house. Dread filled my stomach with nerves as I took a deep breath, preparing for the painful sting of the band aid I was about to rip off.

I knocked on the door, and it wasn't long before it opened. Akira greeted me with a bright smile, but then the look quickly vanished. His face paled, and his dark eyes clouded with fear.

I plastered on a reassuring grin. "Hey. I can explain."

His mouth opened slightly, and he looked at me from head to toe. When his eyes found mine again, he stepped to the side and said in a small voice, "Come on in."

I bit my lip and shuffled inside.

He held his hand out and nodded at my bags. "I can take those for you."

Fighting to stay calm to avoid alarming everyone, I let him take my suitcase and duffle bag. I followed closely behind him into the house. When we made it into the living room, I found Marlow and Bassel sitting on opposite ends of the couch. Rune sat in the high-backed chair, watching the show playing on TV.

Akira backed away from me, his eyes never leaving mine. He cleared his throat, which made Bassel and Marlow look in my direction. As soon as they saw me, their eyes went wide, and their calm demeanor melted away as their mouths fell open.

Bassel shot up off of the couch and stuttered, "R-Rune."

Rune looked at Bassel and followed his line of sight to me. I met his eyes, watching them go from surprised to empty voids. He stood up and faced me, his eyes roaming every inch of my body. All of them were looking at me with wary, searching gazes, which I had expected.

Rune narrowed his eyes, and his voice came out with an edge to it. "Looks like someone heals fast."

The blood drained from my face. I knew this was going to be a shock for them. No human could go from looking the way I had earlier to suddenly all shiny and new. To them, it looked like I was Fae, and I had to quickly put those suspicions to rest.

Groaning, I gave each of them a meaningful look. "It's not what you guys think. I'm not Water Fae."

"Then how did you heal like that, sweetie?" Akira asked gently. "It seems pretty hard to believe you aren't Water Fae when this morning you were completely beat up."

"I know. But I'm not Water Fae."

My mind went back to earlier with Blake, and I fought for a good way to explain this. I doubted it was going to go smoothly when I broke the news that a Water Fae healed me—and not just any Water Fae, either.

I looked back up at them, but I wouldn't meet Rune's eyes. I was too afraid of what I might see in them. "Can you guys heal other people besides yourselves, or is that something only Water Fae can do?"

Bassel's brow furrowed, and he asked, "A Water Fae healed you? Who? Was it your friend?"

That was a great lie, one that would go over a lot better than the truth, but I didn't want to lie. Not to them.

I shook my head. "No. I, uh, ran into one while I was out. He healed me when he saw me."

"He?" Akira asked. I looked at him sideways. "Who is 'he,' Bria-chan?"

I bit my lip and looked anywhere besides at Rune. "Um, do you remember those two guys from the club? It was one of them. Blake. He's Water Fae apparently."

"You ran into him again?" Rune asked, urgency laced in each word. His hands clenched into white-knuckled fists, and his eyes were ablaze with raw outrage.

I nodded.

Akira set my suitcase down and raced toward me, his face now pinched with worry. "*Maji ka*! Are you okay? Did he attack you again?"

"No, no. I mean, he shut me in his store's bathroom with him, which is when he healed me. But he didn't, you know, do anything like before. He isn't actually like that."

Rune narrowed his eyes, searching my face. "Why do you seem defensive of him?"

"I'm not defending him. He showed some different colors today, that's all. I mean, he healed me after all, and he apologized."

"Ha!" Rune fumed. "An apology? That somehow makes it better? That makes what he did okay?"

I narrowed my eyes. "No, Rune, it doesn't. He knows that, and I know that. But he was sincere, and he helped me."

Rune's eyes went dark, and he took measured steps across the room until he stood directly in front of me. He towered over me with his chest rising and falling in furious breaths. "He was going to let his friends murder you, Bria. He beat you for the fucking fun of it. I don't give a shit what he did to help you. He doesn't deserve your forgiveness. No Water Fae does."

"So *that's* it?" I yelled. The others were quickly backing away from us, sensing the rising tension of a heated argument. "You're pissed because he's Water Fae, not because of everything else he did. His past actions were wrong, but it isn't about that, is it? It's about him being Water Fae."

"Of course it's about how he treated you! Him being Water Fae is just the cherry on fucking top of reasons why he's nothing but a piece of shit."

I scoffed. "Watch it, Rune. My best friend happens to be one of those things you're calling a piece of shit."

Akira cleared his throat and grabbed Marlow and Bassel. "We're gonna give you two some privacy."

Akira quickly ushered them out the front door, leaving Rune and me to our venomous stare down. Rune's jaw clenched so tightly, I was surprised his teeth didn't break.

The amount of frustration pumping through my veins made my breathing come out fast and heavy. Rune was so blinded by his hatred for an entire group of people that he refused to even consider that there could be good amongst them. Not Blake, not Dax, not Dallas.

"You can't lump all Water Fae together as evil. I know they've taken a lot from you, but to say they're all evil is ignorant."

"You know nothing," he fumed. "You aren't part of this world, so how could you possibly understand?"

I inhaled sharply. Those words cut deeper than expected. True, I wasn't a part of *this* world, but I was a part of *his* world. Or so I thought. To have that door slammed in my face was almost like a physical punch to the gut. He was shutting me out, all because he was angry and refusing to see the truth.

He shoved his hands in his hair and paced a few steps away. We were both silent for a long time until, finally, he grabbed his car keys from the entryway table and said, "I think I need some air."

He walked past me, slamming the door on his way out.

My feet were rooted to the spot where I stood. This had turned into such a mess. It was impossible for me to really grasp what he and his kind had been through, but Blake's words also made it hard to see all Water Fae as evil.

We wanted no part in that fight, but I guess citizens don't really get a say when their leaders decide they want war.

How many other Water Fae felt the same way? How many had lost their families in a fight they didn't even want any part in? That wasn't evil. No matter what Rune said, I couldn't be convinced that Water or Land Fae were malicious with no ounce of goodness. Not when I knew Dallas was one, and not after hearing what Blake had to say. It just didn't work that way, not in that world or the human one. There were always two sides to a story, and to generalize an entire group of people was wrong.

I took all my belongings and dumped them in Rune's room. After a few seconds of tortuous silence, I realized it was uncomfortable being alone at his place after having fought. I didn't really know where to go, so I sat in my car, parked outside his house. The late October nights were chilly, so I had the heat turned on and music playing.

There was no point in fighting with Rune over Water Fae. It was something he'd have to figure out and come to terms with on his own, which would probably be best anyway. After all he had gone through, it was no wonder he regarded Water Fae negatively. I hoped one day he could see they weren't all like that because I knew Dallas wasn't. She couldn't be.

Rune wasn't wrong to get upset about the whole Blake thing. It was stupid of me to go along with his charade, even if something else seemed to control me for a split second. That part still didn't make sense to me, which is why I chose to leave it out of the story for the guys. Blake said it wasn't him, which could've been a lie. But if he was telling the truth, it begged the question, what else could it have been?

CHAPTER THIRTY-NINE

After about twenty minutes of jamming to K-Pop alone and reading through the book Avana had recommended, I watched Rune pull back into the driveway. I took a deep breath, hoping he was in a better mood, and I made my way over to his car. He climbed out with grocery bags in each hand.

"Welcome back," I greeted, trying to remain stoic. "Kill any Water Fae while you were gone?"

His jaw ticked as he clenched his teeth. "No, I didn't. Thanks for asking."

I filed that information away. Considering Rune's heated temper when he left, I was surprised to hear that he didn't go handle Blake, something he wouldn't have hesitated on before. Interesting.

I wasn't quite sure why he chose not to seek out

Blake, but I wasn't going to question it. Maybe it meant Rune's habits, ideas, and views were slowly changing.

Rune pointed at my car with the grocery bags shuffling in his hands. "Were you waiting outside?"

"Yeah. It didn't feel right hanging out in your house without you guys, especially after how we left things."

He frowned. "You're always welcome, whether I'm here or not. Let's get inside."

We were quiet as we filed into the living room, and it wasn't until I made no move to follow him to the kitchen that he looked back at me. "I'm gonna get started on dinner. Are you going to stay here and watch TV?"

I raised an amused brow at him. "You're cooking?"

He smirked and rolled his eyes. "Yes, I am."

I bounced after him. "Now this, I have to see."

We reached the kitchen, and he dropped the grocery bags on the table. He pulled out the various ingredients, and after putting the pieces together, I realized he was going to make spaghetti. Easy enough.

He drew his long, white hair into a ponytail at the base of his neck, and he set about the kitchen. He put the ground beef in a skillet to brown it, and set a pot of water aside to boil the noodles. I stood close by and nibbled on my lip to fight my grin as I watched him work.

He glanced over at me and nudged me gently in the side with his elbow. "Why do you look so amused? Spaghetti can't be that exciting."

"Any kind of pasta is exciting, but that's not what I'm smiling about. It's so interesting watching you cook."

"Are you doubting my noodle-making abilities?"

I held my hands up, laughing. "Oh, I'd *never*."

He narrowed his eyes and pointed his greasy meat-stirring spoon at me. "Liar. Fine then. I guess I'll just have to wow you with my fine noodle skills."

He poured each of us a glass of wine, which I happily accepted when I realized it was the same kind we'd had on the boat. We sipped at our drinks as Rune got busy. He was, in fact, good at making spaghetti. When the pasta seemed ready, he dangled a noodle in the air for me to try. When I went to grab it, he threw it in my hair at the last minute. He burst into a deep, rich laugh, and it took me a minute to recover from my shock. When I did, I ripped the noodle from my hair and threw it back at him, giving him a unibrow. This only sent us both into fits of laughter that didn't stop until we realized the water was boiling over.

We took our plates and wine to the small table by the entrance of the kitchen. The space smelled like well-seasoned tomato sauce, fresh pasta, and Rune.

Smiling, I met his eyes. "Thanks for making dinner. The guys and I stand corrected. You can cook."

Rune tugged his hair loose from the band holding it in place and pride blossomed in his features. "Told you."

We dug in, and after a few minutes of silence, Rune cleared his throat. "I'm sorry for blowing up on you earlier. I'm glad you're not in pain anymore. I just hate that you had to be around Blake again."

I swallowed the wine I'd just drunk. "Me too. It was stupid of me to go near him, even if things turned out fine in the end. I should've been smarter about it and left as soon as I saw him. Sorry for not being more understanding as to why you were upset."

"It really wasn't about him being Water Fae. I mean, yeah, I hate that part, but I care more about what he did to you. That's the part that made me upset. I still shouldn't have reacted the way I did. It's kinda in my Fox nature to lose my shit when something I care about gets threatened."

My pulse quickened, and a flutter broke out in my stomach. I tried not to get hung up on him saying he cared about me, but it was so hard not to. Hearing that he may, in fact, feel the same way about me as I did him was enough to have me teetering on the edge of giving in to him and my feelings.

By the time we were done eating, I'd had a glass and a half of wine, and I was really starting to feel it. My cheeks and ears were warmer than normal, and everything in the room looked brighter. Sitting down on the couch with Rune was also a trip since I misjudged where I was sitting and nearly collapsed in his lap.

"Woah," Rune laughed, holding me upright on the couch. His arm was warm and strong around my waist, and his face was a breath away from mine. "I think that wine is doing a number on you."

I waved a dismissive hand. "No, no. I'm fine. Better than fine. I'm swell."

Cocking a brow, amusement glittered in his eyes. "Swell?"

I nodded, which I'm pretty sure ended up looking like an out-of-control bobblehead. "Yessir. Swell." Dipping my head, I stared down at his other hand, which rested on his thigh, close to me. I swallowed my nerves and reached forward, tracing each finger like I was sketching it out for a painting. "Did you mean what you said?"

"When?" He flipped his hand over at my tugging, letting me trace small lines into his palm.

"When you said you cared about me."

He was quiet, but I heard him take a sharp breath. Meeting his eyes, heat pooled deep in my belly. There was a raw desire burning bright in his eyes, and I felt that same need all the way to my very core. I'm not sure if it was the alcohol or if I was feeling brave today, but I was tired of trying to deny what I was feeling. I was tired of lying to myself about how I felt. I gave in to that need we both had.

Leaning in, I pressed my lips softly to his, and he groaned as I swept my tongue in and placed my hand on his chest. His arm around my waist tightened, pulling me flush against him, and I deepened the kiss, begging for all of him. His taste, his breath, his touch. I wanted it all.

Gripping the back of my neck, he urged me closer, and the urgency in his touch had me aching for him. In one swift motion, he had my sweater up and over my head, and he discarded the material somewhere behind the couch. His hungry gaze trailed from my lips, down my neck, over the swells of my breasts, and back to my eyes.

My cheeks warmed, and excitement curled in my stomach. I didn't care about the embarrassment of being seen in my bra by him. I was too caught up in Rune and the way he looked at me like I was the most beautiful thing he'd ever seen.

I crushed our mouths together again, my inexperienced fingers fumbling to get his shirt off as smoothly as he'd removed mine. His tongue swept against my own as he grabbed at my hands. I was about to protest until I realized it was because he was taking his shirt off for me.

It was my turn to study his bare skin. I'd seen him shirtless before, but I wasn't able to openly take in my fill then. I made up for that now. His sculpted chest and stomach felt like pure gold under my fingertips, and a new hunger brewed inside me.

"Rune," I cried breathlessly, reaching my hands up into his hair and grinding against the hard mass in his pants.

His cheeks flushed, and he quickly pulled me firmly against him as he got to his feet. His mouth was on mine without another second's hesitation, and he held my legs around his waist as he headed for his room.

I was breathless with my heart hammering in my chest as Rune sat me on the edge of his bed. His warm hands moved from my hips, up my sides, and across my back. In one single move, he unclipped my bra with one hand while using the other to pull it off.

Blushing, I went to cover my bare chest but stopped when he got down on his knees in front of me. I was dizzy from all the emotions rushing through me, but more importantly, I was breathless from Rune and what he managed to do to me with his gaze alone.

"God, you're perfect," Rune whispered.

He leaned forward and placed small, feather-light kisses along my collar bone, trailing lower until he reached my breasts.

My eyes slipped shut, and I bit my lip to keep my gasp of approval at bay. Suddenly, I felt his canines scraping teasingly across my sensitive skin, and when I opened my eyes, he was in his Fae form. A wicked and seductive glint was in his eye, and I was desperate to give into his beast.

Coaxing me out of my jeans, he pushed me gently back against the bed. His tongue traveled up my cleavage as he got on his hands and knees over me.

I shuddered and was unable to contain my whimper.

That sound triggered something in him because he leaned down and kissed me with an all-new desire.

His hands ran up the inside of my legs, spreading them apart so he could settle in between them. My skin was on fire everywhere he touched me, and my breathing was becoming erratic in anticipation of his fingers and caress. A sweet heat pooled in between my legs where his hands rested on my inner thighs.

"You drive me crazy," he groaned, grabbing my hands and pinning them above my head.

His lips burned a trail from my mouth to my neck and down to my peaked nipples. The tip of his tongue swirled around the sensitive pink bead of my breast, and I moaned under the jolt of hungry need building under his mouth.

"You've got it backward," I said breathlessly. "You're the one always driving me crazy. I can't get you out of my head."

He sucked at the puckered tip of my breast, and his hand swiped in a teasing trail down my slick middle of my panties. "Do you want me out of your head?" His lips tickled the skin around my beaded nipples, and the warmth of his breath sent goosebumps dancing along my arms.

I shook my head, throbbing for him in desperate need. "Never."

I sucked in a breath and held it as his fingers rubbed in a slow, tantalizing caress in between my legs. Turning my head to the side, I arced my back into his touch. My breathing had become labored at the work of his hand. Never had I felt something so hot and frustrating all at once. The piece of clothing separating his skin from mine was an annoyance I wanted gone. I needed to feel him.

Sensing my need, he glanced up at me from where he kissed my breast, and with a seductive smirk, his lips moved down my stomach. I clutched the blanket beneath me when he reached my panties. His tongue barely brushed the material where his fingers had been working, and it sent a tremor through my body. "Please, Rune," I begged. "I want you."

His canines were careful as he latched onto the fabric. He shook his head once to the side, tearing them from my body.

Biting my lip, I watched him as he hovered back over me. The shredded, pink material hung from his mouth the way a fox's prey might.

Tossing the panties aside, he ran his fangs over his bottom lip. "You have no idea what you're asking."

I reached up, trailing my hands over his chest and up onto his shoulders before finally cupping his cheeks. Again, I whispered, "I want you, Rune. All of you."

"What if you regret it?"

I pulled him down to me, kissing him tenderly, telling him with my touch that regret wasn't possible where he was concerned. He pulled back only enough to breathe and rest his forehead against mine.

Swallowing hard, I met his eyes. "I love you."

The golden light in his eyes flared, and his entire body seemed to spark before the light slowly died out. He gave me a small smile, but it didn't quite reach his eyes. "I don't think we should do this."

A sharp pain filled my chest. "Why? Did I do something wrong?"

He gave a humorless, almost sad laugh and brushed the hair back from my forehead. "Of course not. I just don't feel right taking something so special from you after you've been drinking. I'd want you to have a clear mind so that you don't regret it later." His thumb brushed across my cheek and caressed my bottom lip. He met my eyes as hopelessness etched its way onto his mouth. "You're saying things you don't mean. I don't want to do something to you that you don't mean, either."

"But—"

He leaned down, kissing me one last time, and something about that kiss felt final. It left a sting in my gut and an ache in my chest.

"Get some sleep," he whispered against my lips.

He stood and pulled the covers over my bare skin. I was so stunned and embarrassed, I didn't even follow him out of the room. Tears pooled in my eyes and slipped out the corners.

I hadn't said anything I didn't mean.

I loved him.

Why couldn't he see that?

CHAPTER

FORTY

Awkward didn't even begin to describe the air between Rune and me the next day. We could barely look at each other, and talking seemed to be a foreign concept at this point. Even Akira picked up on the weirdness, watching both of us over the rim of his coffee cup.

Bassel collapsed on the couch next to Akira, yawning and ruffling his long hair. "So," he started, smiling at Rune and me. "Did you two kiss and make up?"

My cheeks flushed, and I wanted to bury my head in the sand. *Kiss.* Why'd he have to phrase it like that? Who even came up with that expression? Whoever it was, I hoped they got ten thousand paper cuts.

"Yeah, we're fine," Rune answered, meeting Bassel's smirk with an icy glare. Rune turned to me, and my heart pulsed when our gazes locked. "Do you want to spar today?"

It took a second to find my voice, but finally, I nodded. "That sounds great."

"She's mine when you two get back," Akira grumbled. "We're doing nails since we didn't get to yesterday."

After getting changed and grabbing some waters, Rune and I headed to the private sparring ring we'd been using. The car ride made me restless and jittery. Being so close to him after what happened last night was hard on my scattered emotions. It wasn't the fact that we'd come close to going all the way. It was the fact that I'd told him I loved him. In my slightly intoxicated state, my barriers were down, and I'd actually said the words. Yet he didn't say anything. Instead, he thought I was saying things I didn't mean. It made me hesitate when it came to us. Was he deflecting how I felt because he didn't feel the same way? Or did he really think I was confused and couldn't love him?

"What do you want to start with?" Rune asked once we were at the training facility. "Hand-to-hand? Leg work? Defense?"

"Actually, I kinda wanted to start with something a little different."

He quirked a curious brow. "Go on."

Pulling out the book I bought, I held it in front of my face. Peeking above the top, I smiled. "How about a reading lesson?"

"That's Kushagra Kumar's book. When did you get that?"

"Yesterday," I answered, handing over the large tome.

He flipped through the pages, his eyes glittering with enthusiasm. He went to the index, then turned to a page near the middle. As his eyes scanned the page, the light in his eyes dimmed until he scowled. Scoffing, he slammed the book shut and handed it back to me.

"That's a load of garbage."

Curious, I opened the book to where he'd been reading and flipped through the pages until I got to a heading labeled, *The Fox*.

The text started:

> **Fox Fae are interesting creatures. With their superior intelligence and ability to move swiftly, they remain a fearsome group. That being said, the majority have unpleasant tempers, lashing out at a moment's notice. They can best be described as conceited, temperamental, selfish tricksters, the reasons for which we shall discuss here.**

Laughing behind my hand, I looked up at Rune. "I think he's pretty spot on."

He crossed his arms and leaned against the far wall. "Do you now?"

"I do, Mr. Hot-headed Fox. That passage isn't why I brought this, though. I was skimming through it last night while you were out grocery shopping, and I read something that got me thinking."

He pulled his hair back into a ponytail at the base of his neck and cocked a curious brow at me. "About what?"

"It talked about methods to defeat Fae. Battle strategies. After what happened with Jonah, I realized how weak I am when it comes to Fae. Since he's still out there and I'm about to go on a trip with nothing but Fae, I want to learn those strategies so I can defend myself."

He frowned. "Bria, nothing is going to happen. Not with Jonah or anyone else. I won't let it."

"You can't be there 24/7, Rune. I need this for myself so that I can stand on my own."

He rubbed a tired hand over his eyes and down his face. "Okay. I get it. But with Fae, there is no deflecting the situation and walking away. Fae will come at you again and again until either you've been dealt with or they have. What you're asking means learning how to kill a Fae if necessary."

My stomach dropped. That never even crossed my mind. Kumar's writing had made suggestions on how to combat individual Fae, but it didn't mention killing them. Perhaps the battle strategies were a means to an implied end. Death. I was just starting to tolerate the idea of fighting. To now consider the idea of *killing* someone .... But if it came down to my life or theirs, I wanted the arsenal to be able to make that choice. I couldn't let things play out the way they had when Jonah attacked me.

Squaring my shoulders, I met Rune's patient eyes. "I want to learn. Even if that means learning how to kill."

He studied me, searching for my resolve, and after deeming it unwavering, he took a deep breath. "Okay. But let me go grab something first. Stretch and practice your stances. I won't be long."

It felt good to stretch my muscles and feel that familiar burning. It had been a while since we'd last trained, and I actually missed it. All the times I'd shared with Rune during training where we were both focused, sweating, and pushing each other's limits was like breaking the surface when drowning. He was my reprieve from the crazy world outside.

The door to the private room swung open, and Rune stepped in, carrying something behind his back. I got to my feet from where I'd been doing sit-ups. Rune made no move to cross the room. He stood motionless by the door.

"Rune? What's wrong?" I asked, starting for him.

Without a word, he pulled a long dagger from behind his back. My stomach dropped as he gripped the hilt tightly and brought the blade down, sinking it into his stomach.

"Rune!" I screamed, racing toward him.

He teetered then collapsed on his side. Panic set in when I crumbled next to him, and my hands shook as I reached for him. What the hell was he doing? Was stabbing himself some sort of training? I couldn't seem to take a breath when I felt him trembling beneath my hands.

"Rune," I cried. "What were—"

I froze when I caught a glimpse of his face. He was smiling. It was then I realized he wasn't trembling from pain. He was laughing.

"What?" I asked breathlessly, stepping away.

He rolled over onto his back, laughing in a deep, rich rumble. He held up the dagger and stabbed his other hand for me to watch. The blade retreated into the hilt when he pressed it into his hand.

It was a freaking toy.

"You asshole!" I fumed, punching him hard in the leg. "You scared me!"

He sat up, still chuckling. Shaking his head, he said, "Sorry. I couldn't help myself. A joke presented itself, and I couldn't pass up the opportunity."

Crossing my arms, I refused to return his grin. "Well, it wasn't funny. Why'd you need to leave to go get a stupid toy anyway?"

He held out the toy, and I was reluctant to take it. "We're going to use it to train. You'll need a weapon like a dagger to fight a Fae, but I'm obviously not going to give you a real one to attack me with yet."

Smirking, I grabbed the dagger and jabbed it into his hard pec as he flinched from shock. "That's probably a good idea since I'm still mad at you."

We stood and got in the center of the blue mats.

"Fae aren't indestructible," Rune started. "We heal fast, so that makes us harder to kill, but it doesn't make us invincible.

You have to deliver wounds that kill us faster than we can heal."

"So, like a shot for a major artery?"

He rubbed the back of his neck. "You can do that, but it won't be enough. We can heal something like that if left to do so. You'd need to go for an artery and then deal a final blow. Severing the head; stab and twist to the heart. Something along those lines."

I swallowed hard, trying not to vomit. "Stab and twist to the heart sounds easier. Let's go with that."

He stepped closer and put a gentle hand on my arm. "We don't have to do this, Bria."

"We really do, Rune." I met his concerned gaze. "I'd rather have the knowledge and not need it than to need it and not have it."

Taking a deep breath, he backed away a few steps. Standing up straighter and getting in his defensive stance, he smirked. "All right then. Try to kill me, Bria."

"Wow! So you actually knocked him down?" Avana laughed.

Pride lifted my head high. "Yup. Knocked him flat on his butt *and* managed to get my knife over his heart and twist. Just took, you know, about a dozen tries."

Akira laughed, blowing on his wet, black nails. "I always knew you'd knock him off his feet."

Akira, Avana, and I sat on Akira's bed after a very long day. We were finally doing our mani-pedis together, and we had *Mulan*, aka the best Disney movie ever, playing in the background.

"God, I'm so glad to have you both here," Akira sighed while admiring his nails. "The other guys suck at painting my nails. It was driving me crazy."

"Should we go paint theirs?" Avana asked, waggling her eyebrows. "We can show them how it's done."

"Absolutely not," Bassel yelled, coming to stand in the open doorway. "The last time I let Akira paint my nails, that shit lasted for a week. And, since it was white, it looked like I'd just had too much fun with Wite-Out."

We laughed, and Bassel gestured back down the hall. "The pizza is here if you wanna grab some."

After grabbing our greasy, cheesy pizza, we settled back in Akira's room. The three of us sat around the floor, belting out the lyrics to "I'll Make a Man Out of You" in the worst pitch ever. It was a dangerous sound to the rest of the people in the house, but it was a sweet symphony to my ears. I needed this moment where things made sense and life wasn't full of strange creatures from a magical world. Tonight, it was just me with my two friends.

Time was ticking down until the day we left for Rune's hometown. We'd be leaving in four days now, and while I knew I was prepared for it, I was still hella nervous. Nervous to be in a house full of Fae who disliked humans. Nervous to meet Rune's family. Nervous to finally meet my fox face-to-face. Nervous for our deal to end.

When we got back from the trip, Rune would give me the five grand I needed for Italy. The deal would be over. I'd get to go on my dream trip to study with my idol, and he'd be free of an unwanted marriage and fatherhood. And while that was all I'd wanted at the start of this, my resolve to get my money and run was gone. In its place was a need to *stay*.

I wanted to stay friends with the quirky group of Fae I'd come to cherish.

I wanted to stay with Rune who I'd somehow come to love. Couldn't I have both?

Even if the deal was done and over with, couldn't we still see each other and, dare I say it, be together? And, if that were an option for us, would he wait for me while I studied overseas?

It was all a lot to think about and prepare for, but I knew I could handle it. I was stronger than I'd been two months ago, both mentally and physically. I could face the den of foxes and come out of it okay.

On Thursday, two days before we left, Rune and I found ourselves at the training facility again. We'd managed to squeeze some training in all week.

He'd just deflected one of my hits with the dagger when he randomly said, "You're going to do great."

I paused, trying to catch my breath. "What?"

"You're going to do great this coming week. You've studied hard and worked your ass off to learn what it means to be Fox Fae. Even more impressive, you've learned what it means to deal with me. I'm really proud of you."

Speechless, I held his gaze. My cheeks warmed, but I hoped it looked to him like I was just hot from sparring. Being told he believed in me was one of the biggest compliments I'd been given, and it made my heart ache with the reminder that I loved him but was unsure of how he felt.

He was still smiling at me, and he wasn't in his proper stance. Not wanting to hear anymore compliments or nice words, I quickly dropped down and kicked out. I knocked Rune's legs out from under him, and he smacked onto the mat. I quickly pinned him under my weight with the dagger to his heart.

Smirking, I tsked at him. "You shouldn't get distracted when in a fight. Isn't that Basic Fighting 101?"

Laughing, he grabbed my arms and rolled. Pinning me beneath him, he grinned. "That wasn't fair. We were talking."

The weight of his warm body pinning me to the floor made desire bloom in my chest. He was still gripping my wrists, and

I was still pressing the dagger into his chest. Swallowing hard, I made a show of pushing the blade of the toy in and out against his firm pec.

"You're supposed to be dead. Now who's the one not being fair?"

"Hmm," he said, smiling down at me. He looked like he was actually considering my question as he gently tucked some hair that had fallen loose behind my ear. My skin warmed, and I sucked in a sharp breath at the feel of his fingers caressing my cheek.

He shook his head. "No. You're still the one who doesn't play fair."

Something told me he wasn't talking about sparring anymore. His eyes bored into mine with a flood of burning desire, and I held my breath, afraid if I looked away, that emotion would disappear, too. I was determined to tattoo his gaze into my memory, but before I could get my fill, he closed his eyes and stood.

"That's probably enough practice for the day. My chest hurts from how many times you've stabbed me."

I laughed, accepting his outstretched hand. "Be glad it wasn't a real one."

"Speaking of a real one …" Rune started. He jogged over to the duffle bag we brought, and after dipping down to dig in it, he pulled out a sheathed dagger. "Here." He held it out to me with a smile. "You've earned it after all the work you've done. I can safely say I trust you to have a real one."

Smiling, I studied the beautiful sheath. It was made up of an intricate pattern, swirling in a mix of bright silver and deep blues. Small gems adorned the tip of the sheath and trickled down, following the swirls. The sharp, silver blade was sleek and simple. It was stunning.

Meeting Rune's eyes, I swallowed hard. "You got this for me?"

He shrugged. "I did. It's not a big deal. I thought you deserved a nice surprise after all the progress you've made."

I clutched the dagger tightly in my hands and tried to steady my racing heart. "Thank you. Truly. I really love it."

He waved it off and grabbed his duffle. "I'm glad you like it. Now, let's get back because *I'd* really love a shower."

CHAPTER

FORTY-ONE

That night, after we got back from training, I decided to do a last-minute check of my suitcase, just to be sure I had everything I needed before we left in two days. Clothes? Check.

Toiletries and hygiene products? Check.

Sexy underwear? Check. Not a necessity, but packed nonetheless.

Gifts for Rune? My stomach dropped.

Suddenly frantic, I pulled everything out of the suitcase. The mug wasn't in there. Tugging on the ends of my hair, I groaned. I'd completely forgotten to pack the mug, even after making a mental note to do so.

I never forgot stuff! That just goes to show how messy my thoughts had been that day.

Putting everything back in the bag, I heaved a sigh and grabbed my purse. Rune met me in the living room where he'd come down the hall from the kitchen.

Glancing at my bag, he asked, "Are you going somewhere?"

"Yeah. I forgot something in my dorm that I need for the trip. I'm going to grab it real quick. I'll be back soon."

He followed me to the door. "Be careful. Do you have your dagger?"

I glanced over my shoulder at him and rolled my eyes. "I'm just running to my dorm. I don't need it."

He narrowed his eyes. "Take your dagger. Jonah showed up there before, he can do it again."

Fighting my grin, I went back to his room to get the dagger from my stuff. Making a show of putting it in my bag, I smiled at him. "All right, *dad*. I've got my dagger. Can I go now?"

"Ew," he recoiled. "Please don't call me your dad. That makes things weird. Now if you want to discuss possibly using the name *daddy*, we—"

Laughing, I waved to him and left without listening to the rest.

Since it was Thursday evening, Dallas was most likely in her night class, which meant the coast should be clear. I'd still been avoiding her since I hadn't had time to really process the truth about who she was and why she hid it from me all these years. Every time I went to call or text her, the fear resurfaced of discovering she'd never thought of me as someone she could truly trust. It was that paralyzing worry of finding out our friendship didn't mean as much to her that made me hesitate and always put the phone away.

Barreling up the steps of my dorm, I raced to my room and grabbed the mug off my desk, pausing only briefly to stare at Dallas' messy bed before heading back to my car. The task didn't even take five minutes. I'd just shut my car door when I glanced up and saw *him*.

Jonah stood in the shadows of my dorm building. His wide smirk was eerie, and he narrowed his eyes at me as he walked backward into the woods. I knew that look in his eyes. He was challenging me, daring me to follow.

My heart rate spiked, not out of fear like it would've in the past, but because this was my chance. My chance to get answers and be done with this game of cat and mouse. I wasn't the same weak and defenseless girl I'd been before. I'd trained for this very moment, and my dagger practically sang from where it sat buried in my bag.

I was done waiting.

It was time to be my own hero.

Grabbing the sheathed dagger, I put it in the waistband of my leggings and climbed out of the car. Jonah was no doubt watching me from within the shadows, so I kept my head held high to show him I wasn't afraid. My footing was sure, my body ready and alert, as I treaded through the woods, fallen leaves and twigs crunching beneath my feet.

I didn't stop walking until I found the place I was looking for. The creek trickled gently in its bed, its soft sound telling me to stay calm and ready. My eyes never left the water, not even when I felt the dark presence form behind me.

"Took you long enough," I sighed, turning to face him.

Jonah stood a few feet from me. That same sick grin twisted his face. "That's my line. You've been hiding from me. And healing quickly, I see. Who did that? Your little man who saved you?"

I ignored his taunt about Dax. "I've not been hiding from you. Why would I hide from something that doesn't scare me?"

His ardor faltered, and his eyes narrowed into thin slits. "Your newfound confidence isn't amusing. It's going to be your downfall."

"Actually," I started, taking a step in his direction. "I think your dismissal of me is going to be *your* downfall. But before we get to that, tell me why you've been after me. What was the point of all this?"

"Why would I tell you? That takes the fun out of it."

He rushed at me, but I was familiar with his speed now. Quickly sidestepping, I rounded on him as he appeared where I'd been standing. Now behind him, I was quick to unsheathe my dagger and swipe across the back of his neck. As soon as my blade cut into his flesh, my stomach soured. While I had been prepared for this moment, I never really understood what it would feel like to truly hurt someone, to slice into flesh and bone, to watch someone scream out in pain from a wound I'd inflicted. It left a bad taste of regret and guilt in my mouth.

Roaring, he clutched the back of his neck where blood oozed in between his fingers, and he whipped around to face me.

"Yikes. That looks like it hurts," I taunted with a plastered-on triumphant grin. I couldn't let him see me struggling with my internal conflict. I had to look strong and confident; otherwise I'd lose for sure.

His chest heaved with angry breaths, and he bared his teeth as he bellowed, "I'll kill you, you stupid bitch!"

His body evaporated into a burst of black vapor before materializing right behind me. It happened in a matter of seconds, too quick for my eyes to track. His foot smashed into my back, sending me rolling across the grass and right into the creek bed. My grip on the hilt of my dagger slackened, and the water pulled it from my grasp.

"No!" I cursed, ignoring the pain in my back and splashing around in the dark water for my dagger.

"What? Have you suddenly lost your nerve without your weapon?"

He threw back his head with a hysterical laugh. He burst into a plume of shadows again before reappearing by the water's edge where I was crouched. Without hesitation, he smashed his foot into my jaw. My head jerked back with a painful snap, and I fell onto my back in the stream.

My head submerged into the cold water, but I could still hear his muffled laugh. Pain exploded like a firecracker along my cheek and jaw. Something felt wrong, and I had a suspicion my jaw was broken.

As my aching mouth broke the surface of the stream, Jonah formed above me with a wicked glint in his eyes. He shoved his foot into my chest and forced me back under the water. Panic swarmed my thoughts, and I clawed and pushed desperately at his foot. It was pressed so firmly into the top of my chest, I couldn't raise up enough to get my head above the water, and my strength was no match for his.

My lungs were beginning to burn with the need for air. His disgusting laugh echoed in my ears beneath the surface. It was the worst kind of torture, his taunting being the last thing I'd get to hear before I drowned.

Why hadn't I stayed in the damn car? How stupid of me to think I was strong enough to take him! Now I was going to die.

Blurry explosions of light erupted in my head, and the fire in my throat got to be too much. I didn't want this.

I can't be weak. I can't give up and die. I have to survive. For Dallas. For my new group of friends. For Rune.

For myself.

A new, lower sound began to fill my ears. It drowned out Jonah's laughter and the buzz from lack of air. It started as a hum, gentle and faint. It grew louder as the burning in my chest grew hotter, and I realized vaguely that it was the same odd tune I'd heard when I'd been in that trance at the mall with Blake. Bubbles erupted from my mouth before I unwillingly tried to inhale with a desperate need for release of the pain. Water rushed into my mouth and lungs at the same time the humming reached its crescendo.

Suddenly, I could breathe again. The pain in my cheek and back faded into a distant memory, and strength flooded my limbs. Gripping Jonah's ankle tightly, I used my newfound strength to shove him back. He stumbled into the water, and I was quick to rise to my feet.

He stared up at me from where he'd landed in the stream, and the color drained from his face. "Y-you! You aren't supposed to have your powers yet!"

Powers?

I had no idea what he was on about, but then again, I was confused by a lot of shit at the moment, starting with the breathing under water and healed injuries. Not only that, I was practically buzzing from some new energy coursing through my veins. I felt powerful, strong, and ready to take on the world.

Gritting his teeth, Jonah evaporated into a gust of shadows and darted toward me, but I could see him moving with hardly any effort now. Either he'd slowed down a lot, or my eye-sight had suddenly improved. Either way, I braced myself to block his attack.

Throwing my arms up to block him, I felt my hands grow warm and tingly. At the same moment, water rushed up from the creek, forming a moving wall in front of me. Jonah smacked into it and bounced backward, but in utter shock, I gasped and jumped away from the water. It collapsed, crashing back down into the creek bed.

Jonah roared from where he'd appeared back near the tree line. "I'm over this. We're ending this now."

I didn't have time to process what was happening to me. Right now, I had to protect myself, and even though it was crazy, I had a feeling I didn't need the dagger anymore.

Jonah ran at me, his hands curled into sharp claws. Daring to take a chance, I focused on the water pooled around my calves. I took a deep breath and waited 'til Jonah was almost to the bank before raising my right arm. A wave of water rose with it, and as I swiped my arm toward Jonah, the water barreled at him faster than he could dodge. It crashed into him, sending him flying sideways.

I wanted to laugh hysterically because, *holy shit, I did that!* I could feel the water move as if it were a part of me, and it followed my command as if I actually wielded it like a sword.

"What is going on?" I asked myself breathlessly.

Jonah let out another frustrated snarl and erupted into a mass of shadows. With a burst of cold wind, he darted toward me, but I wasn't letting him get close. Pulling the water again, I sent it rushing forward to meet Jonah's shadow, and within seconds, his cloudy form was engulfed in a watery trap. Sweat beaded my brow as I held still, encasing him. Slowly, his form solidified until he was thrashing in the water, clutching at his throat.

My stomach churned watching him suffer like that. It was him or me, just like Rune said. I knew that. But this wasn't me. I wasn't a killer, and watching another person suffer made me want to be sick.

Squeezing my eyes shut, I slowly lowered my outstretched hands. The rushing water guided Jonah to the ground before releasing him from its watery clutches. As soon as he was free, he rolled to the side, coughing up water.

Taking a deep breath, I held my head high. "Take that as a warning. I'm letting you live, but if you show yourself in front of me again, I won't be as merciful. Do I make myself clear?"

He heaved ragged breaths, flopping over onto his elbows. Meeting my eyes, he croaked, "How did you get your powers? He said you didn't have them yet."

I narrowed my eyes. "Who said what? Who sent you after me?"

His chest continued to rise and fall, slowly getting back to a normal rhythm. Finally, he opened his mouth to answer. A whizzing sound flew past my head, and a scream lodged in my chest when a thin, red line suddenly appeared across Jonah's throat. His eyes went wide as the color drained from his face, and he fell backward, his severed head rolling across the dirt. I quickly turned to scan the dark tree line to see who was there, who had silenced my one source to the truth, but I found no one. Whoever had killed Jonah was gone, which meant the person who was truly after me was still out there.

CHAPTER

FORTY-TWO

After watching Jonah get beheaded by something—I still didn't know what since I found no weapon near his body—I emptied out the contents of my stomach in the grass, but not before watching his body turn into smoke that was carried away on the wind.

If that wasn't enough, I was immediately reminded of my newfound powers when the water seemed to gather me in a bubble as if to ease my panic and nausea. It responded to my need without me realizing it. The water even brought my dagger back to me when I tried looking for it.

I was a complete wreck.

How could this have happened? This morning, I'd been human Bria, living as normal a life as I could given the circumstances. Now I was … what? Fae? Water Fae?

I had no clue, so I focused on getting back to the dorm and taking the stairs two at a time up to my room, which was far easier than it should've been with my short, stubby legs. That was no doubt thanks to the newfound energy racing through what I thought was my human body.

Human. Fae.

How had I become one of them, a *Fae*? Or had I always been one?

Groaning, I paused in front of my room's door and slammed my head onto the wood. I was mentally exhausted. Physically, I felt like never before. There was an undeniable strength and power flowing through me, waiting to be used.

I hated it.

It was a reminder that this was really happening. I wasn't human.

No more hiding. I had to get answers, and I had a feeling I knew who to get them from.

Taking a deep breath, I opened the door to the dark room, and as I swept the space, I realized something I hadn't when I'd only reached in for a second to grab the mug earlier. The room was exactly as it had been when I'd been here a week ago to pack my things. The only difference was that the note I'd written Dallas was now in the middle of the floor.

I frowned, trying to process what I was seeing. Dallas' half of the room was messy with her school assignments, dirty clothes, and unmade bed, which was totally normal. What wasn't normal was the fact that it was the exact same assignments, clothes, and fold of the bedding as it had been a week before. It was like she hadn't been staying here. That wasn't too odd, I guessed, since she and Rance had gotten serious. But still, I was surprised she hadn't stayed here, in case I showed up.

Turning on the lights, I closed the open curtains to give the room some privacy. I quickly pulled out my phone from my pocket, and I dialed Dallas' number. She answered on the first ring.

"Bria?!"

I took a deep breath, trying to ignore the mix of relief and panic in my best friend's voice. "Dallas."

"Oh my God, Bria. Thank God you're okay! I've been so damn worried. You haven't answered any of my texts or calls, and I got your note. What in the hell—"

"Where are you?" I cut her off, ready to get down to the task at hand.

She answered without hesitation. "I'm in our dorm room."

My throat tightened under the weight of her lie. Why? Why would she lie to me about that? Clearing the emotion from my voice, I stared at her empty bed. "We need to talk. I'm waiting in our dorm room right now."

She was quiet on the other end, and I could picture her closing her eyes in defeat and hanging her head low. She took a deep breath and said, "You're right. We do need to talk. I'll be over soon."

I hung up without saying anything else and quickly shot a text to Rune, letting him know I'd be back late. My mind raced a thousand miles a minute with all the questions I had, all the explanations I needed. I wanted to go take a nice, long shower, but I was suddenly so afraid to go anywhere near water. I had no idea how I was controlling it, and frankly, I was terrified of what my powers meant. Water was the last thing I needed right now, which hurt like a dagger to the heart since it had always been my safety net, my lifeline, and now, the one constant in my life was something I feared.

What is my world coming to?

A small knock came at the door some thirty minutes later. I was sitting back against the headboard of my bed, trying to sort through my thoughts.

Clearing my throat, I called, "Who is it?" I wasn't taking any chances with my true assailant still out there.

"It's me," came Dallas' reply.

I got up to unlock the door, and my heart tripped over itself as I opened it. Her usually bright face was a sickly shade of gray, and her vibrant green eyes had dulled. She had dark circles under her eyes and clearly hadn't been sleeping. Even so, as soon as she saw me, her smile went wide, bringing a spark back to her pained expression.

Tears instantly pooled in my eyes. I had done this to her. My avoidance had crushed her harder than I ever thought it would, and knowing the pain I'd caused her had guilt clawing at my insides with razor-sharp precision.

"I'm so sorry," I croaked, the tears finally slipping down my cheeks.

She dropped the grocery bags she had in her hands before throwing her arms around me. I met her hug with the same ferocity, and we sobbed into each other's hair for what felt like hours. Her smell—lavender with a hint of honey—wrapped around me, and I wanted to sink to my knees. I'd missed her smell, her hugs, her smile. Ignoring her had gutted me, and while facing her after doing so wasn't easy, it was also a huge relief. I finally had my best friend back. It wasn't until we heard another door open down the hall that we finally pulled away, and I stepped back, letting Dallas into the room.

Sniffling, she picked up the grocery bags and headed for my bed. Seeing her sudden enthusiasm was already lifting my spirits. "I got some snacks on the way over. It's all your favorites. Sour Skittles, Starburst, the lollipops with gum inside, even a box of Cinnabon Cinnamon Rolls. I also got Debbie Cakes, some doughnuts, and chips. You name it, I have it."

Smiling past the pain, I sank down at the head of my bed

again. "We always did eat our weight in candy and chips when we had serious talks, huh?"

She laughed, pulling out the rest of the snacks and some DVDs. "Don't forget about the Disney movies we always binged. It made the tension bearable."

"Breaking into song while discussing your desire to sleep with our ninth grade teacher definitely made that conversation easier."

She shook her head as she put on a movie. "He was hot! You know he was."

"Yes, but an attraction that means nothing is much different than an infatuation you intend to act upon."

She sighed with a satisfied, far off look. "He was a great kisser."

I grimaced. "That's just as disgusting now as it was when you first told me about your make-out session."

She laughed, and the sound made my chest tighten. This felt like old times, and for a minute, I forgot about Fae and secrets. For a minute, I was a girl about to binge movies and eat junk food with my best friend. But that wasn't what was happening.

Swallowing hard, I grabbed a throw pillow and picked at the tassels on the edges. No more avoiding this. It was time.

"Where were you really when I called?" I asked, having a feeling it had to do with the secrets she'd been keeping.

She took a deep breath. "I was at my team's hideout. We were discussing strategies of locating you and how best to get you to come back."

I flicked a lone tassel and tossed the pillow aside. Hideout. Strategies. It all sounded like some covert military group on a mission. The idea was laughable, but honestly, that could be exactly where she was. Being kept in the dark ended now.

"So," I started before meeting her eyes again. "You're Water Fae."

She didn't seem surprised by my statement at all. She sat down across from me, and her gaze held mine with absolute confidence. "As are you."

There it was. The answer I'd been dreading but knew was true. I was Water Fae. Sucking in a sharp breath, all the questions I'd been planning went out the window. All I could think to ask now was, "H-how? How did this happen?"

Dallas ripped into a bag of chips as she took a deep breath. "There's so much to explain to you. I guess I should start with the most important stuff. You are not just any Water Fae, Bria. You're the Princess of the Water Fae."

My mind stuttered, and I had to take a minute to process that. "Excuse me? *Princess?*"

"It was those Land Fae who told you about Fae and our world, right?" Her voice held so much disgust as she said 'Land Fae,' like the mere words alone made her want to vomit.

"Yes. My *friends*, who just so happen to be Land Fae, told me about their world."

She recoiled, her face scrunching up with hatred. "They aren't your friends, Bria. They are the enemy. They are the worst of the worst."

I narrowed my eyes at her. "Okay, look. If we are going to have this conversation, there's something we need to get out of the way. I love him. Rune. A Land Fae. I get it, you guys have a long history where you slaughtered each other, but that's the thing. *Both* sides lost people. *Both* sides are hurting. *Both* sides have good in them. I won't sit here and let you berate Land Fae, just as I don't let them talk poorly of Water Fae. Because I love people on both sides."

She held my gaze, studying me for a few silent moments. I could see the war between hate and her ability to care about people waging in her head.

Finally, she smiled, her eyes watering with something akin

to pride. "You are so much like your mother. She'd be so proud of you."

The wind was knocked out of me. "My-my mother?"

Dallas leaned forward to wipe a tear from my cheek. "Queen Alesta. She was a fearsome woman who was also capable of great kindness."

Alesta. For the first time in my life, I finally had a name to put to my mother. She wasn't a nameless, nonexistent figment of my imagination anymore. She was real. She was Alesta, Queen of the Water Fae. My mother.

Fresh tears spilled over my cheeks, and I squeezed my eyes closed. It was a relief to know who my mother was, but the next question that formed on my lips broke open a new crack in my heart.

"Is she de—"

Dallas grabbed my hand, and she waited until I met her eyes again before speaking. "Your mother and father made some choices as rulers that resulted in a lot of innocent people dying. They knew they were targets because of it, and consequently, you were a target. Days after you were born, they set a plan in motion, one that resulted in who you are today. They took you to the Queen of the Fae, the great ruler of us all, to ask for her help in hiding you. She bound your powers so that you wouldn't get them unless you were put in life-threatening danger. If all went well, they would awaken on their own on your twenty-first birthday, which is the age at which all Fae mature and grow into their abilities.

"After making sure your powers were bound, they began spreading word of a baby boy being born to the Water Fae Queen and King. They hoped that by spreading a fabricated story of you being a prince, the Land Fae who were targeting them would search for you in vain. The only people who knew the truth were the royal guards and their advisors. That's when they gave you to me since I'm your personal guard and tasked me with seeing you safely to your human family, Wendy and Greg."

Head hanging low, I closed my eyes against this new information. I was given to Wendy and Greg to be protected from those who wanted to do me harm. No wonder they never wanted to get close to me. They knew who I was. They knew *what* I was. They were simply following orders and fulfilling their duty. It was business for them, a task handed over. They didn't need to love me or welcome me as a real daughter when they knew the truth. That bitter realization stung like acid in my throat.

Dallas gave me a minute before finishing, "Your parents died shortly after having you hidden away."

My chest squeezed tight under the news, and time itself seemed to draw to a standstill. A crater formed in my chest, an ache that ran deep within me.

All those years of wondering where they were, dreaming of what they were doing at that exact moment, conjuring up ways they'd come find me suddenly shattered like glass. The shards rained down and pierced my heart until it bled with those long-felt hopes. They weren't coming back for me. I'd never get to know their smells, the sound of their laughs, the way it felt to be wrapped in their arms. They were gone.

Emotion clogged my voice. "How did they die?"

Dallas stared off at the TV for a few minutes. We were both quiet with only the sound of the Disney movie playing in the background. It was clear this was just as hard for her to talk about as it was for me to hear.

Finally, her tear filled, green eyes met mine. "They were in hiding at a cabin. They each had their personal guards and teams with them, but due to certain circumstances, it wasn't enough. They didn't survive the attack." She sniffled and cleared her throat. "I don't think it's best to go into the details. At least, not yet."

My mind was numb by the time Dallas finished the small recounting of that moment. I was glad that she chose not to divulge the details, because the pain that was already strangling me had reached a crescendo. I squeezed my eyes shut, trying to push out the mental image of my parents being killed.

"D-do you have any pictures of them?"

She frowned. "Not on me. I was afraid you'd find them and ask who they were. We've been trying to keep everything a secret from you until your powers awakened, but there are plenty of photos at the palace."

Choking on a cry, I met her gaze. "We? Who is *we*?"

"The team I was with before coming here and, honestly, everyone around you. Greg and Wendy, me and Rance, Dax, some of your teachers. A lot of people around you are actually a part of your personal Fae security team, save for Greg and Wendy, who are just human allies. They've all been watching over you from afar, protecting you. We had set plans for introducing everyone into your life. Rance was a more recent introduction, although he's always been there in the shadows."

"Wait, you knew Rance already?"

She gave a nervous laugh. "Yeah. We weren't close like that or anything, but we needed a way to introduce him to you. We planned to bump into each other and start a 'relationship,' but somewhere along the way, we ended up actually falling for each other. We are dating *for real* now and have been for some time."

"And Dax? He's one of my guards? He sure has a funny way of showing it."

She nibbled on her lip and looked away. "Dax. Yeah. Him. That story may be best left for another day. This is already a lot, I'm sure."

Stunned, I sat in silence. A lot was an understatement. All of this news made me feel like a fool. Nothing was real. My entire world up until this point had practically been one big joke. I could look past a lot of it. The one thing that I couldn't get over, one of the big lingering fears that took root in my chest, was Dallas. The idea of our friendship not being genuine dragged my heart down a deep, dark hole—one that threatened to consume my entire soul in agony.

Laughing through the pain, I shook my head. "So everything was planned. Thought out. Even us." My eyes found hers as new tears slid down my cheeks. "You only became my friend because you had to, right?"

Dallas jumped slightly, as if I'd physically hit her. Eyes watering, she crawled across the bed until she was next to me. She wrapped me in her arms as she said, "That's not true at all. I may be your personal guard, but you're my friend before anything else. That's not what was meant to happen, but it did. So many times, I forgot what I was supposed to be doing because your friendship meant more to me than my stupid title.

"That night at the club, I was too focused on being a normal college student with you, creating memories to last a lifetime. I forgot I was supposed to be guarding you. I forgot my duties. I was so worried about you, my best *friend*, I didn't even keep a constant watch over you like I was supposed to. And that night you got hurt by the Bat Fae, something Dax informed me about, I was too busy being a regular girl, getting wasted and partying because you made me want to be normal. I neglected my duties. *I'm* the reason you were in danger that night. It was my fault, and I haven't been able to forgive myself ever since. If Dax hadn't come to your aid then, I don't know what I would've done."

She pulled back to look at me, her eyes red and puffy. She choked on her tears as she finished, "I forgot my obligations because I love being friends with you. I love being your best friend and your guard. Even if you have doubts about everything else, *never* doubt that our friendship is real."

She pulled me back into a hug.

I cried into her red curls, and I felt her tears falling down my shoulder as she clung to me in desperation. We were both in pain, both hoping for our bond to be real, and I think we were both relieved to know it was. The truth felt like a silver lining amidst all the storm clouds.

At the mention of Jonah and his attacks, I told her about this evening and how he was the reason my powers had awakened.

She processed this information, growing angrier by the minute.

"So someone told him about you." She groaned and clutched her head. "We have a rat among our ranks."

I swallowed hard at the idea, and it was clear that Dallas was already working to piece together what to do. I wasn't sure what I could do to help in that situation, seeing as how I didn't know who the guards were. It was then that I noticed the time. It was almost midnight.

"Shit. It's late. I have to go."

Suddenly alert, Dallas grabbed my arm. "Where are you going?"

"I have to get back to Rune's. He's probably worried sick."

She narrowed her eyes. "You can't go back to him. I don't trust him. He's—"

"What did I say? I don't want to hear that. *I* trust Rune, so please, trust in *me*. I'm safe with him. He won't hurt me."

She squeezed my arm tighter. "Are you still going on that trip with him?"

It was hard to say knowing what I was now. There was so much going on in my head after having this life-altering talk with Dallas, and I still needed to mentally sort through it all. Even so, I'd worked hard to prepare for this trip and earn my ticket to Italy. Plus, with so many feelings between Rune and me, I didn't want to back out now. A thousand new things were being thrown on my plate. I wasn't sure how I'd tell Rune about this or when, but this new hurdle was one I'd have to figure out with time. I wasn't going to let it stop me from gaining the key to my dream or from being with the man I loved.

"I am," I finally answered.

She stood up, following me to the door. "Then I'm going, too. I can stay somewhere else, but I have to go with you. I can't let you out of my reach again, and I most certainly am not letting you go on a trip alone with a bunch of Land Fae. I do trust you, but I also trust in my experience. I'm coming with you."

The idea of Dallas going and hiding in the shadows was actually a pleasant concept. It brought me some relief, surprisingly, and after promising to text her the details about what had really been going on between Rune and me, as well as to form a plan for how this would go, I left the dorm with far more answers than when I'd arrived, but also a thousand more questions.

Rune was waiting right at the door when I walked inside. His arms were crossed over his chest, and his tone was frantic when he asked, "Where have you been? It's past midnight! Are you okay? What happened?"

I closed my eyes at the barrage of questions and clutched my head. Which didn't hurt. I definitely should've had a migraine at this point. But nope. Just a scattered mess of problems.

"Sorry. I, uh, was feeling a bit bad. I drove around and got some fresh air at a nearby park."

"Feeling bad?" Rune asked, his voice suddenly less frantic and more concerned. "Are you sick?"

I shook my head. "Just a lot going on. It's been a while since I've had time to myself to process everything, you know? I thought tonight might be a good time to get away and de-stress before we leave."

The concern etched into his mouth and eyes made my guilt spike. He'd been genuinely worried, probably thinking the worst had happened. Which it nearly had.

I gripped his arm and gave it a reassuring squeeze. "I'm sorry for not calling. That was wrong of me. I didn't even think about what that would do to you. I'm really sorry."

He took a deep breath and pulled me into a tight hug. It was a surprising gesture, and I didn't realize how much I needed it until his warm arms were around me, holding me to his firm chest. Squeezing my eyes shut, I wrapped my arms around him and held on like he was my life preserver. I was drowning in all the chaos around me, but he was here to keep me afloat and to remind me to keep swimming.

"I'm sorry," he whispered. "You've had to deal with a lot these past few months, and I didn't realize it was taking a toll on you. If you don't want to go on the trip, I—"

"No." I shook my head and looked up at him. "I want to do this. It's what we've been working so hard for."

"Are you sure?" His eyes pleaded with mine to be honest. He cared more about what I wanted in this moment than what not going through with his plan would mean for him.

"I'm sure. I just needed those few hours to myself. I'll be fine now." I mentally screamed, knowing that was time I'd never get.

He tilted his head to the side, pondering. "Do you want tomorrow to yourself, too? I'd understand if you did since it's the last day before we leave."

I smiled at him. "Honestly? I think I'd like to do something normal tomorrow. I could really use some normal."

Pursing his lips, he nodded. "Normal. I can make normal happen. All right. Tomorrow, you and me. Normal. It's a date."

CHAPTER

FORTY-THREE

"So where are we going?" I asked, feeling extra giddy inside.

Rune laughed. "You're gonna have to wait and see. I'm not spoiling anything."

Resting back in my seat, I tried to wait as patiently as I could while Rune drove to our unknown destination. He'd been true to his word all day. We had slept in, him on the couch and me in his bed. We had followed that up with a very nice breakfast of cinnamon rolls. After spending the better part of the day lounging around on the couch and watching TV, Rune had announced it was time to get changed. He was taking me out.

It wasn't much farther until we arrived at a large field at the base of some tree-topped mountains. We'd taken my car because Rune had brought secret supplies that couldn't fit in his.

"What are we doing here?" I asked, following him around to my trunk. "Are we hiking?"

He had told me to wear something I didn't mind getting dirty, but it never occurred to me to also wear something comfy, should we be doing a lot of walking. My jeans suddenly felt a bit too snug.

He shook his head and laughed. "Not quite." The lid of my trunk opened, and he reached in to grab a large basket, which he handed to me. He flung a blanket over his shoulder, then reached back in to grab a large, blank canvas and a box of paints and brushes.

Meeting my eyes, he smiled. "I thought a private picnic and painting session sounded nice. Gives you fresh air, privacy, and a chance to do something you love."

Emotion clogged my throat, and I found myself unable to speak. He probably had no idea how much this meant or how insanely happy he made me. He was giving me such a needed distraction, but he himself was the greatest gift. His presence. His smile. His thoughtfulness. He meant the world to me, and after all he'd done, I was determined to tell him just that.

I was done pretending.

I wanted this to be real, for us to be real.

"Come on."

He gestured toward the field, and together, we made our way through the grass. We found a nice spot about halfway to the base of the mountain where the trees started. He laid out the large blanket and unpacked the picnic basket. Waters, a thermos with hot chocolate and marshmallows, sandwiches, a fruit tray—he'd thought of it all, including all the paints and brushes I'd possibly want.

Beaming at him, I set the canvas in my lap. "What should I paint?"

He laid out on his side and propped his head on his hand. Popping a grape in his mouth, he shrugged. "Anything. Paint something *you* want. This is for you, no one else."

With my heart beating faster and my body buzzing with excitement, I grabbed a brush and let my mind and hands do the work. Rune let me paint, nudging me every so often to feed me some fruit or a bite of a sandwich.

"Your paintings are going to get you far in life, you know. You have such real talent, Bria. It's insane watching you paint."

Smiling warmly at him, I said, "Thanks. Painting is my dream. It's what makes me happiest, but it's not realistic, you know? I'm going to be an art teacher instead."

Unless I came out of this week-long trip alive. Then, maybe, I could go to Italy and change my life forever.

He frowned, sitting up more. "Is teaching what you want to do?"

My lips lifted a fraction as I nodded. "Yeah."

He studied me, his eyes trailing over my face. Finally, he narrowed his eyes. "Liar. You don't want to be a teacher."

"Oh yeah?" I laughed. "How would you know?"

"Because your smile didn't reach your eyes. That's your fake smile, the one you put on to look okay when you're not."

Biting my lip, I turned back to my painting. So far, it was the base colors for what would become the ocean, shoreline, and sunset sky. My fingers itched with the need to keep going, to get lost in the colors and brushstrokes. This was what drove me. Creating. Imagining. Painting. This was who I was and wanted to be.

Swallowing hard, I relented. "All right. You got me. I don't want to be a teacher. All I want to do every day is paint, but like everyone has always told me, it's not realistic. There's no guarantee I'd make a living from that. So, I chose a different career path, one along the same lines, just a little different. Being an art teacher will feed me and still let me be an artist. Somewhat."

Rune sat completely up and scooted closer. Leaning in, he held my gaze. "Okay. I've been alive much longer than you."

I snorted. "Sure have. You're an old man."

He smirked and narrowed his eyes. "Do I look like an old man to you? I think not. What I mean is, I've been around for a while, and if there's anything I've learned, it's that life is far too short for humans to not do what they love. It's cliché to say, but it's true. In the grand scheme of things, what's more important? A life of riches or a life of happiness?"

"Yeah, that's true, but—"

"No buts. Your dream is to be a painter. What's the point in dreaming if you aren't going to at least try to make it real? That's what dreams are for. You aren't given that passion or talent just to ignore it. It's there for you to do something with. Don't just dream it. *Do* it."

A flicker of something bright filled me to the brim, and it tasted of hope and desire all mixed into one. He was right.

Smiling at him, I said, "You know, you're pretty smart sometimes."

"Sometimes? I'm always full of wisdom."

We were silent for a moment when I finally said, "That's actually what Italy is for."

"Becoming a painter?"

I nodded, adding the first of the details to my painting. "If I get to study abroad in Italy, I'll be given the chance to learn under my idol, Luca Romano. That kind of opportunity, that kind of connection could open doors for me. It could really help me get the foundation I need to not settle and actually have a career as an artist."

My hand stilled at the sudden silence. I glanced up to find Rune's amber eyes searching my face, and a warm flutter took flight in my stomach at the intensity of his stare. It was as if he were looking for something within my own eyes, or perhaps he was trying to figure out what to say next.

He took a deep breath before sitting up straight. He reached behind him into the picnic basket, and when he faced me again, he held a large manilla envelope. His golden eyes met mine, and he held the small package out to me.

"Speaking of Italy, this is for you."

I accepted the thick envelope, throwing Rune a curious look. When I opened the flap, the air in my lungs stilled. Crisp stacks of hundred-dollar bills sat neatly in the envelope, and I knew without counting that it was the full five grand. He'd just given me the key to my dreams.

My wide eyes found his, and I stammered, "W-why are you giving me this now? We haven't gone on the trip, so I haven't held up my end of the bargain yet."

Tenderness flooded his eyes as they softened at the corners. "You don't have to. I want you to have the money. Trip or no trip. Deal or no deal. Italy is important to you. I want you to go, so no more strings attached. The money is yours, even if you decide not to go on the trip anymore."

Italy.

Luca Romano.

My future.

Rune just made it all possible. He was giving me a choice and no longer holding his cards close to his chest. They were spread out before me, and it was my move.

I could take the money and wish him well on his trip without spending an entire week in a house full of Fox Fae, trying to figure out how to confess to him that I was Water Fae. I'd be safe here and able to spend every moment fantasizing about my study abroad adventure.

When I saw the emotion embedded in Rune's gaze, I knew my mind was made up.

I squeezed the envelope to my chest. "Thank you. I can't tell you how much this means to me. But I still want to go with you."

His eyes brightened. "You do?"

"Italy means a lot to me. This trip to your hometown means a lot to *you*. I'm not backing out. I want to be there for you."

Deal or no deal, going along with this wasn't about the money anymore. It hadn't been for some time now. Sure, it had started that way. But somewhere along the way, things had changed. *We'd* changed. There was more between us now than just a business deal. There were real feelings, and it was my love for him that now fueled my desire to go through with this, despite my newfound Water Fae situation.

"I'm glad you still want to go," Rune said. "You're a pretty great girlfriend." He winked on the last word.

Laughing, I went back to painting, and he rolled over onto his back and closed his eyes. His words from the moment we'd sat down here played on repeat in my head. One message lingered now. If I wanted something, I couldn't sit idly. I had to reach for it myself.

"Rune."

"Hmm?" He opened an eye to look at me.

I swallowed hard. "I knew what I was saying."

"What?" he asked, sitting up on his elbows and quirking a confused brow at me.

I set my painting aside and faced him. "That night when we … well, you know. You said I was saying things I didn't mean. I did mean it. I *do* mean it."

His chest stilled as he stopped breathing. His gaze held mine for many unbearable seconds. Finally, he sat up all the way, but instead of saying he felt the same, he hung his head. My heart sank with it.

"Bria," he started. "I thought you understood this was all pretend."

A sharp pain pierced my chest. "I know. I just thought that—" I took a deep breath. "I thought you were starting to like me, too."

He closed his eyes and held his head in his hands. "How I feel doesn't matter."

"What do you mean how you feel doesn't matter? Of course it does!"

"No, it doesn't, because I won't act on it."

Biting back my hurt, I leaned toward him. "Why? I know you have an anti-dating code, but is that really the only reason?"

He met my eyes, his face pinched. "I won't let you in more than I already have. Saying it out loud, trying to make this into something more, would do just that."

"Why are you so against letting yourself love somebody? Not just me, but people in general? The guys all see it, too. You try so hard not to let yourself feel anything about me, girls in the past, and anyone else who may care about you."

"Loving people only sets you up to get hurt in the end."

He looked up, and when his eyes found mine, it was like the months we'd spent together vanished. His walls were up again, stronger than ever. His eyes were devoid of anything.

"How can you think like that?"

"Letting yourself grow to care about someone, letting people take root in your heart. It leaves you aching and broken when those people leave. I've lost enough people to know first-hand what kind of scars that leaves behind. The kind of wound you get from lost love never heals, so I refuse to let myself get attached to anyone now. That means you, too."

My heart ached for him. I knew what loss he meant. The pain he felt after losing his dad was surely unbearable, and after his mother separated him from his closest family, there was a void inside him that couldn't be filled. At least, he thought so. It felt like he thought nothing could make it better, and because of it, he refused to let it happen again. With time, I hoped that his friends and I could show him it was okay to let people in.

Meeting his eyes again, I was careful as I said, "You can't

live that way forever. It will hurt you more in the long run if you don't let yourself feel those things."

"Maybe." He shrugged and laid back again. "But that's my problem to deal with."

The mood turned somber after that, so I focused on my painting again to avoid thinking about our conversation. I mean, on one hand, it was kind of a confession on his part because he admitted I'd already wedged myself in his heart, but at the same time, it was a clear rejection because he refused to be with me. I had no idea how I was supposed to feel in this moment, but that didn't stop the hurt from taking hold in my chest.

"Sorry."

I looked up at the sound of his voice. He was still lying on his back, but he had his arm draped over his eyes.

I shrugged. "For what? If you don't like me, you don't like me. You can't help that."

"I never said that."

My heart betrayed me and fluttered at his words. It obviously didn't understand that we were supposed to be upset at the moment, not hopeful.

"I know it doesn't make sense to you, and I'm being a dick," he started. "I don't mean to hurt you. That's the last thing I want. I just don't know how to open myself up to those feelings anymore. I'm so used to acting like an ass to make people want to stay away. I don't know how to be anything else anymore. To be completely honest, I'm scared to try."

Carefully placing my painting in the grass, I flopped down next to him on the blanket. I laid out on my side, my head resting on my hand. He uncovered his eyes and turned his head to look at me.

"You're scared?" I laughed. "I'm scared. We're from two different worlds, Rune."

A little closer now that I knew I was Water Fae, but still different. That alone was a major worry of mine now. Because

I was his enemy, the thing he loathed most in the world. And to top it off, I was *the* Water Fae. The Princess. My gut twisted a little as I thought about how I'd tell him. It was such a huge confession, and the weight of it was already making my heart heavy.

We were just starting to really open up about our feelings, and if I made that kind of declaration now, it could ruin everything. I had to wait, especially since I was still learning what it meant to be Fae and the Princess of Water Fae. I'd have to tell him eventually, but I couldn't yet.

Finding my voice again, I said, "Even though it's scary, I want to try. I don't want to ignore my feelings, and you shouldn't, either."

He rolled onto his side to face me, propping his head on his hand. Our faces were inches apart, our bodies so close that when we breathed, our chests pressed together. My pulse quickened at the feel of his body so close to mine.

His amber eyes searched my face. "You have no idea how much I want to just give in. You're my weakness and strength all mixed together in one brilliant mess. It's just hard to let go of how I've lived for so long."

"I know it's hard. But you aren't alone. You have me, Akira, Bassel, everyone. We all care about you and want to see you happy, which starts with you opening up."

His features were strained as if his heart were being pulled in two directions. He wanted to give in, but he was still scared. It was going to take time for him to stop fighting against how he felt, but that was fine. I'd be there every step of the way.

Reaching out my hand, I wrapped it into his long, soft hair and tugged him forward. He happily leaned in, and his kiss sent electricity whizzing through my body. There was a hungry passion behind his kiss, and even if he couldn't say the words yet, I knew how he felt from that alone.

He rolled me onto my back and hovered above me to keep

his weight off me as he urged my mouth open to him, and I gladly obliged. We stayed that way for hours. Kissing with a burning intensity followed by a hot chocolate break, followed by me painting more, and then back to kissing. It was the perfect ending to a perfectly normal day.

CHAPTER

FORTY-FOUR

The next morning was hectic. It was the day of our departure, but before I could leave, I had one final thing to do. Before daylight was even up, I drove back to campus with my money and filled out paperwork for Italy. I wanted to turn it over to Professor Lichen in person, but seeing as how I was still supposed to be beat up from a car wreck, I knew I couldn't show my face. Instead, I dropped the folder and sealed envelope in her teacher's mailbox with a note saying my parents drove me in to deliver it.

As soon as the papers were in, a rush of something light and bubbly filled my chest. It danced in endless twirls and tasted of hope. With this, my future was set. I'd be going to Italy. I'd get to meet *the* Luca Romano, my idol, my hero. I'd get the chance to make my dream my reality.

I left the art building as the glow of the rising sun broke through the trees on the horizon. The pink hue kissed my cheeks, and I took a deep breath, inhaling the rich scent of fallen leaves caught on the wind. All of the pain, fear, and worry from the past two months left me on my exhale until I was left smiling into the sunrise.

It was a new day, and for better or worse, I was a new me. I'd grown a thicker skin and learned how to be a stronger version of myself. I'd taken chances that led to where I stood now, one step closer to being a painter. I'd fallen in love with a protective, hot-headed, and extremely caring Fox Fae. And I'd finally learned who I was.

I was Bria Ashmoore.

Future world-renowned artist.

Princess of the Water Fae.

Tears pooled in the corners of my eyes as I raised my face into the glow of the sky and whispered, "I hope you're proud of me, Mom and Dad."

My eyes searched the pink and orange clouds. I grinned through the emotion blurring my vision as I pictured the two of them smiling down on me from where they were now. We couldn't be together. I wouldn't get to hear them say it or see their faces as they watched me grow, but it was okay. I knew who they were now, and I knew that, even if they weren't here beside me, they'd always be with me.

In the sunshine.

In the wind.

In the water.

In my heart.

Everyone rushed around the house, getting ready and doing final checks of their stuff before we set off for the airport. That, paired with texting Dallas to coordinate the details of her secretly joining us, left me frazzled. My current predicament didn't help, either. Standing by my open suitcase on Rune's bed, I chewed on my nails. I wanted to look nice when I met Rune's family for the first time, so I was panicking over which dress to go with. I had no idea what they would like. Based on the photos, they preferred dated clothing, but obviously, I didn't have any of that.

With a groan, I settled on a black maxi dress. It wasn't anything like the Regency-era dresses they wore, but it was a dress, at least. Holding it up to double-check it was for sure the one I wanted, I nibbled on my lip. There was a chance they'd hate it, but I decided to go with my gut and stop second-guessing myself.

I tugged off my shirt and stepped out of my leggings. I was about to slip on the dress when two hands grabbed me by my hips. I gasped and went to turn around, but those warm hands pulled me back against his frame.

I looked over my shoulder, already knowing who I would see.

Rune, still in his Fae form after waking up this morning, beamed down at me as he moved his hands from where they were on my hips to wrap them around my waist.

Blushing, I quickly hugged the dress to myself, trying to hide my bra and panties.

"I'm surprised you got undressed with me in the room," he said. I could practically hear the smile in his voice.

Looking down at my feet, I tried not to get distracted by his strong arms around my bare stomach. "I didn't know you were in here."

"I came in while you were still mulling over that dress."

I glanced at him over my shoulder, my cheeks still flushed. "Why didn't you say anything?"

He shrugged. "You seemed to be in deep thought, so I didn't want to disrupt you. I'm glad I chose to keep quiet."

Grinning, he stepped away from me. I watched him over my shoulder as he walked to his closet. His tail trailed behind him and flicked casually while he dug through his clothes. He pulled out a black button-up shirt and a pair of black trousers.

Glancing over at me, his eyes traveled the length of my body in a slow, tantalizing sweep. With an amused smirk, he said, "If you don't put some clothes on soon, we're going to be late for our flight."

I realized then I was still standing there in my undies, watching him like a dog watches a ball. Flaming bright red, I hurried to throw on the black dress, pulling it all the way down to cover everything.

My eyes were glued to the far wall as I made attempts to calm my racing heart. There was no reason to freak out over this. After all, he'd seen me completely naked the other day. Not like my bra and panties were worse than that.

Trailing my hands down the front of the dress, I glanced at him. He was shirtless, his honeyed skin exposed in a beautiful display. He'd just taken off his sweats and was starting to pull on the black trousers. Heat curling low in my abdomen, I quickly looked away from him again. The sight of him in such a state never ceased to leave me hot and breathless.

"Um," I started, my eyes looking everywhere except at him. "Is this dress okay, or do you think your mom will hate it?"

"Well, turn toward me, and I'll tell you."

I hesitated. Surely he'd have his pants on by now. Slowly, I turned to face him, my hands clasped in front of me. My cheeks warmed when I saw him. He had his pants on, but he was buttoning up his shirt, which meant his beautiful body was still exposed. Despite my efforts, I couldn't tear my eyes away.

His eyes traced every inch of me, stoking the flame burning at my center. When his gaze finally met my own, he shrugged. "She'll hate it, but you look beautiful regardless."

I frowned, my heart stuttering for only a moment over him calling me beautiful. "Why will she hate it? I can change into something else."

He finished the last of his buttons as his lips lifted, his canines glistening. "It doesn't matter what you wear. She'll hate anything you put on because that's how she is. You aren't the girl she chose for me, so she'll judge everything you wear, do, and say."

My knees grew weak. I clutched my head and sat down on the edge of the bed. Panic was starting to take over all of my nerves. I was already anxious about meeting his mom, but now fear was clawing its way into my mind, too.

"I think I'm going to throw up," I mumbled.

"Don't worry about her or anyone for that matter. You'll have all of us there to protect you. Plus, you'll get to meet that fox you've been dying to see."

I wasn't too concerned with my safety, at least not in the way he thought. I was no longer a defenseless, naïve human. I was Water Fae now. The consequences of getting discovered had intensified with this realization. I hadn't controlled any more water since the night I fought Jonah, and I hadn't tried tapping into my powers, either. There was a very strong chance I didn't know how to actually control my abilities, which was a major concern.

Slipping up somehow was something I couldn't stop fretting over for multiple reasons. For starters, Rune could see my secret as a betrayal. I hoped I'd have time to come up with a good way to tell him in a setting that would allow him to freak out, then calm down and see that I was still the same Bria he'd fallen for, Water Fae or not. Not only that, but if I were found out by Rune's family, I'd be killed. Powers or no powers, I couldn't defeat a whole group of Land Fae on my own.

With a time crunch underway, Rune and I parted ways to finish getting ready. After curling my hair and applying a touch of makeup, I took one final look in the mirror. We were just going on a weeklong trip, but in that moment, with my reflection staring back at me, something inside me said everything was going to be different after today. I didn't know what, but things were rapidly changing, and I wondered what exactly was going to come from those changes.

Grabbing my suitcase, in which I'd finally hidden both of Rune's presents, I made my way into the living room. Everyone except for Akira was sitting around on the couches and chairs. We all had our bags ready to go. Everyone had on a dark dress shirt with black slacks. Even Avana, who was usually so lively, sported a black jumper. If people looked at all of us, they would assume we were going to a funeral—*hopefully not mine.*

"Damn, it feels depressing in here," Akira said as he came into the room.

I smiled when I saw him. He wore a black and white checkered shirt with a red scarf and red skinny jeans. His pop of color helped to take away some of the gloom, as did his ever-bright personality. I guessed no one was looking forward to this trip.

"Well, we *are* going to Myra's," Bassel said, confirming my suspicions. Everyone stood up. "Not much to be excited about."

"Your family scares me," Marlow whispered to Rune. His skin began to flash from normal to brown and gold patches, then back again.

"Calm down," Avana cooed to Marlow. "Go get some water, yeah?"

Marlow ignored her and instead trudged to the door, mumbling, "Scary fox. Scary fox. Scary fox."

I swallowed hard. It was no secret that Marlow was bizarre, but his behavior was making me even more apprehensive. Was Rune's family really that terrifying? I was sure I was going to pass out from how hard my heart was beating. I couldn't even bring myself to walk toward the door.

"Bria." Rune's gentle voice shattered my sporadic thoughts, grounding me again.

I looked up at him. Everyone was already walking out the front door except for me and Rune, who still stood by the couch, staring at me. "Are you coming?"

I gave a small, nervous laugh. "Do I have to?"

Rune moved closer and grabbed my hands. He squeezed gently and held my gaze with a confidence I didn't feel. "There's nothing to worry about. You're going to do great, and it's like you told me last night. You aren't alone."

Smiling, I squeezed his hands back. He was right. I wasn't alone.

Together, we made our way out the door. It was time to enter the foxes' den. I just hoped I wasn't their next meal.

ACKNOWLEDGMENTS

First and foremost, I want to thank every reader who picked up my book. From the bottom of my heart, I am so thankful to each and every one of you. This story has so much of myself in it, and it has been an incredible journey creating the story you read today. Because of you and your drive to read this story, you're making my dream that much more real. So thank you. Thank you for reading. Thank you for supporting me. Thank you for giving Bria and Rune's story a chance. I truly hope you loved it as much as I loved writing it.

A huge, huge, huge shoutout goes to my editors, Ariel and Nicole, with Ad Astra Editorial. Holy cow! You two ladies are absolutely amazing. Your feedback, your guidance, and your critiques really helped me to get this story to where it needed to be, and I will forever be so grateful to you. Ariel and Nicole, thank you both so much for pushing me to be better, to write better, and to think better. You have made my story the best version of itself, and I will never stop being in awe of you and the work you did. Thank you so much.

Thank you to my Beta Readers for your fantastic feedback and hype you made. Alexia, Anais, Ana-Maria, Danielle, Justine, Sabine, Samantha, and Taylor; thank you all so much. Your early feedback, comments, and excitement made this enjoyable and provided insight I needed to make a story readers would love. You all were amazing, and I can't thank you enough.

Thank you to my cover designer, Emily Wittig Designs. You made my vision a reality, and because of you, I have a book I am so proud to call mine. Thank you for making something so amazing.

Thank you to my formatter, Enchanted Ink Publishing. I've always admired authors with gorgeous interior formats in their books, and you made that possible for me. Thank you for making my beautiful book come to life.

Thank you to my mom and sister. You both believed in me without hesitation, and it's because of your endless encouragement that this story exists. Through every hard moment, every moment of doubt, you were there to tell me not to give up because I am worth it. My story is worth it. Rune and Bria are worth it. So thank you for being there and supporting me.

Lastly, thank you to my sweet husband. Writing and publishing a book isn't an easy or quick task, but you never stopped me. You pushed me to do what I love and to live the dream I've had for so long. You calmed me down in moments of doubt, washed away the stress of a writing sprint, and hyped me up when I needed it most. Thank you for being the greatest husband, friend, and supporter.

SYLVER MICHAELA

is an avid book reader, coffee drinker, true crime junkie, and animal lover. She is also a huge fan of K-Pop, Korean dramas, and East Asian culture. Nothing compares to a lazy day where she can relax on her couch with her pig, dog, and husband, binging Korean Period Romance dramas. When she isn't hard at work on her next romance, she can be found on her farm, reading amongst the donkeys, ponies, and goats.

HTTPS://SYLVERMICHAELA.WIXSITE. COM/MAGICALPRINCESS.COM

INSTAGRAM: @THE_SYLVER_MICHAELA

Made in the USA
Columbia, SC
01 August 2022